ILL MET
IN THE
ARENA

BOOKS BY DAVE DUNCAN

"THE DODEC BOOKS"
Children of Chaos
Mother of Lies

THE ALCHEMIST
The Alchemist's Apprentice
The Alchemist's Code

**CHRONICLES OF THE
KING'S BLADES**
Paragon Lost
Impossible Odds
The Jaguar Knights

**TALES OF THE
KING'S BLADES**
The Gilded Chain
Lord of Fire Lands
Sky of Swords

THE KING'S DAGGERS
Sir Stalwart
The Crooked House
Silvercloak

A MAN OF HIS WORD
Magic Casement
Faerie Land Forlorn
Perilous Seas
Emperor and Clown

A HANDFUL OF MEN
The Cutting Edge
Upland Outlaws
The Stricken Field
The Living God

THE GREAT GAME
Past Imperative
Present Tense
Future Indefinite

"THE OMAR BOOKS"
The Reaver Road
The Hunters' Haunt

THE SEVENTH SWORD
The Reluctant Swordsman
The Coming of Wisdom
The Destiny of the Sword

STAND-ALONE NOVELS
West of January
The Cursed
A Rose-Red City
Shadow
Strings
Hero!
Ill Met in the Arena

**WRITING AS
"SARAH B. FRANKLIN"**
Daughter of Troy

WRITING AS "KEN HOOD"
Demon Sword
Demon Rider
Demon Knight

Please see www.daveduncan.com for more information.

ILL MET
IN THE
ARENA

DAVE DUNCAN

A TOM DOHERTY ASSOCIATES BOOK
NEW YORK

ILL MET IN THE ARENA

Copyright © 2008 by Dave Duncan

Edited by Liz Gorinsky

Map by Jennifer Hanover

A Tor Book
Published by Tom Doherty Associates, LLC
175 Fifth Avenue
New York, NY 10010

www.tor-forge.com

Tor® is a registered trademark of Tom Doherty Associates, LLC.

Library of Congress Cataloging-in-Publication Data

Duncan, Dave, 1933—
    Ill met in the arena / Dave Duncan.—1st ed.
        p.   cm.
    ISBN-13: 978-0-7653-1687-5
    ISBN-10: 0-7653-1687-0
    "A Tom Doherty Associates book."
    PR9199.3.D847 I45   2008
    813'.54—dc22
                                    2008020386

First Edition: August 2008

Printed in the United States of America

0 9 8 7 6 5 4 3 2 1

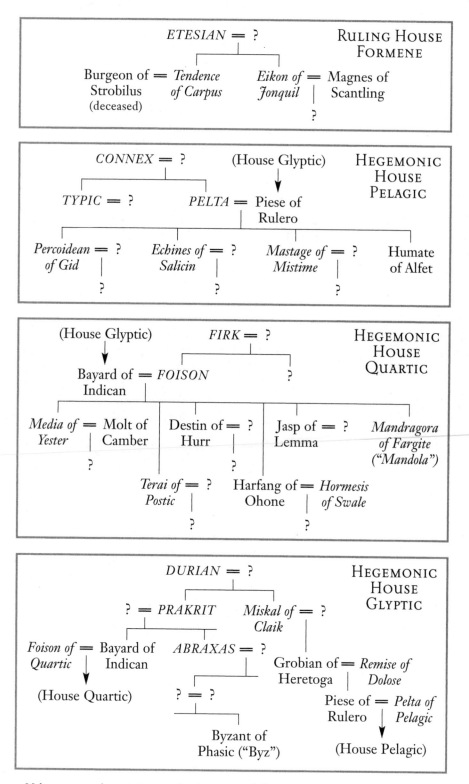

Male names are shown in Roman, female names in *Italics*, hegemons and rulers in *CAPITALS*.

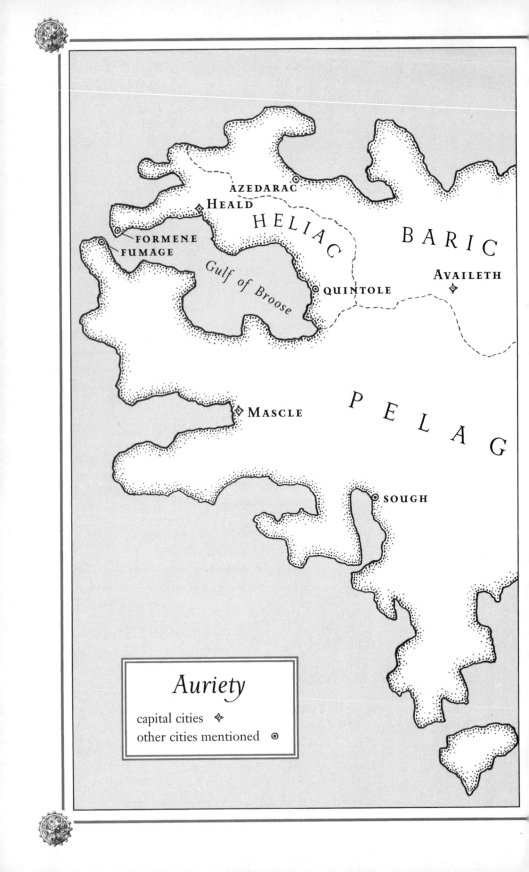

AZEDARAC

HEALD

HELIAC

BARIC

FORMENE
FUMAGE

Gulf of Broose

QUINTOLE

AVAILETH

PELAG

MASCLE

SOUGH

Auriety

capital cities ✧
other cities mentioned ◉

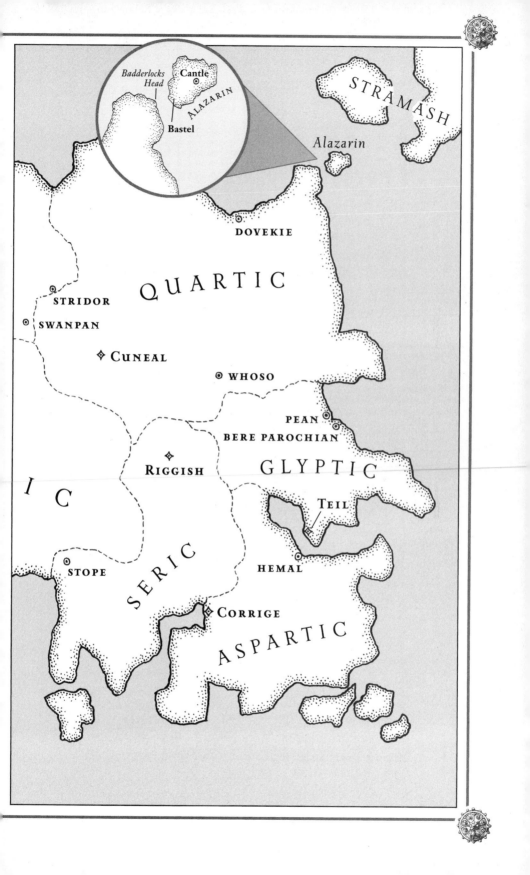

Badderlocks
Head
Cantle
ALAZARIN
Bastel

STRAMASH

Alazarin

DOVEKIE

QUARTIC

STRIDOR

SWANPAN

CUNEAL

WHOSO

PEAN
BERE PAROCHIAN

GLYPTIC

RIGGISH

TEIL

I C

STOPE

SERIC

HEMAL

CORRIGE

ASPARTIC

Notes on Aureity

Aureity is the major continent on a world that orbits a blue star every 1,886 days, for which the old word **pentad,** meaning a period of five years, seems appropriate.

The pentad is divided into twenty-nine **gnomons** of sixty-five days each. A gnomon is divided into **fifths,** whose days are named in the arbitrary sequence: bells, hands, blossoms, suns, dogs, triangles, women, pots, horns, swords, birds, boats, flails. A gnomon begins with bells-1, hands-1 . . . and ends with boats-5, flails-5.

The smaller white sun follows the planet in the same orbit, 60° behind. Thus the day begins with **bluerise,** is divided into four equal **watches** by **whiterise, doublenoon,** and **blueset,** and ends at **whiteset.** Night, known as the **Dark,** is a fifth watch, twice as long as the others.

Length and weight have been converted to familiar units on the assumption that the average male ordinary stands 5'9" and weighs 150 lbs. Nobles are larger.

Since ancient times the nobility of Aureity have bred their children for psychic strength. They measure nobility by **fourbears,** meaning great-great-grandparents (four generations back) who were themselves noble. A person with 16 fourbears has **royal** caste and wears a white caste mark. Twelve to 15 fourbears denote **princely** caste (red mark); 8 to 11 **highborn** (orange); 4 to 7 **knightly** (yellow); 2 or 3 **honored** (green). A single fourbear does not qualify a person for noble rank.

Magical power is closely related to caste, and is most strongly developed in the families of the seven **hegemons.** A few related lines, known as the **significant families,** are almost as gifted.

ILL MET
IN THE
ARENA

TOURNEY AT BERE PAROCHIAN

1

With both suns blazing overhead, birds are silent and even the trees seem to droop. From the balcony of my room I look down on a bay that shines like molten silver, fly-specked with fishing boats whose sails hang limp in the breathless air. No doubt their crews feel they are being steamed, just as I know I am about to be roasted. The heat in the arena will be intense.

Landward lie rolling hills and a mosaic of terraced fields whose red soil must be hard put to support even the peasants who cultivate it, let alone provide an income for its owner. Alkin's prosperity has been earned by her wits, and that is rare indeed among the nobility of Aureity.

The house bell tolls to mark the start of the servants' midday rest. Lesser bells in the distance pass the message on to the paddy fields and orchards. It is time.

I go inside. My cloak lies on a table, cunningly folded into a tight packet that will balance on the palm of my hand. I summon it to me.

◆ ◆ ◆ **PORT** ◆ ◆ ◆

I come forth on the cliff terrace, a hundred feet below. This, too, is admirably designed, a private retreat shaded by heavy foliage and cooled by spray from a filmy cataract nearby. Waves lapping the rocky shore seem to murmur soothingly, as if today even the sea is soporific. Half a dozen bronze duelists stand eternal guard with swords or javelins amid the flowers. Again, I marvel at the art and skill that have gone into crafting such a residence of dreams.

Alkin herself is artfully posed against the sea view, kneeling on a cushion. She turns her head to regard me.

I bow. "At your bidding, royal Alkin of Cupule."

"Honored, noble Quirt of Mundil."

She looks me over. I, in turn, regard her—with admiration. I see a woman of beauty and grace, mature but still slender, clad in a sari of silk brocade patterned in her colors, two shades of green, over a matching *choli* bodice. Her only adornments are an emerald bracelet and a thin silver brooch in the shape of a sword. The sword is the badge of her profession as a duelists' manager and the bracelet was the fee she accepted to manage me. She is authoritative and also motherly. Her matronly dignity must serve her well in dealing with her usual clients, who are males barely out of adolescence. Her face is unlined; the raven hair glimpsed under the edge of her head cloth is just starting to be flecked with silver. Her forehead bears a white caste mark, denoting the full sixteen quarterings of nobility.

That is what any man or any noblewoman of lower caste would see. How she would appear without illusion I cannot tell. She must be at least a generation older than she chooses to appear.

And what does she see? Firstly, of course, a man wearing her colors, green on green; a man in his prime, two pentads older than the "cubs" she usually manages. If my face does not hint at past suffering, it certainly should. Secondly, she sees a lot of me. Standard dress for a nobleman in eastern lands is a knee-length tunic with baggy sleeves, but a fighting tabard is much skimpier. For the arena we wear thick-soled sandals. Although the nobility of Aureity breed their children for psychic strength, consciously or unconsciously they also favor height, so that size is now almost as good a guide to magical powers as caste is.

Alkin says, "Impressive. If appearance alone could win you admittance to the tourney, noble Quirt, you would have no problem."

I bow again. "You honor me, my lady."

"But princely Sudamina will not be moved by that. She will insist on more information than you have given me."

"But not as much as you could extract. I appreciate your forbearance."

A noblewoman of high or middle caste has only to lay a finger on a man to read his memory like a scroll. Alkin has promised not to do that with me, and is reputed to have high ethical standards. It was that reputation that led me to seek her out.

Amused, she gestures me to a cushion near her. "It is a long time since I harbored a dark horse in my stable. Anyone can tire of routine."

I glance around the terrace. "We seem to be one short. Would you have me go and discover what delays the noble lord?"

She smiles. "I can guess what delays him. We can wait a little while yet."

I sit where I am bidden and cross my legs with care, self-conscious in the tabard as I never recall being in my reckless youth. I note that she has placed me close, but not close enough that I need fear she will suddenly reach out and touch me.

She says, "Since we do have a moment, noble Quirt, perhaps you would assist me. That brawny lad there? I feel he would look better closer to the rocks." She points to one of the duelist statues, a cast-bronze youth wearing a tabard and clutching a sword. The effigy is life size, and attached to a plinth. Altogether it must weigh five or six times what I do.

"Glad to help, noble. A former client?"

"Princely Piese of Lactual. He did marvelously well—Hegemon Firk of Quartic took him to be one of her senior champions. She later assigned him as consort to one of her daughters."

That explains why he looks familiar; I must have seen him around the court at Cuneal, long ago. But Hegemon Firk died before I was born, which dates Alkin herself. "Where would you like the bonny boy?"

Alkin says, "About there." An identical statue takes shape at the other side of the terrace. It is illusion, of course, but very well done.

The effort is within my powers, but the real challenge is to do it from where I am sitting. I take a few deep breaths and then extend my psychic strength. I heft the original, float it across to where she wants it, and gently set it down.

"Much better!" she says. "You are kind, noble Quirt."

We exchange smiles. We both understand that we have just been flirting in a harmless sort of way—she showing off some of her powers and me showing off mine. Men's psychic skills are physical—porting, hefting, wrenching—and women's are mental. They can dissemble, project images, and read minds. At conversational range noblewomen can tell when a man is lying. That alone explains why women rule the world, as my grandfather often says.

"My pleasure, noble. Pray present me to the rest of your heroes."

Smiling, she names the other five bronzes, each representing a cub who did so well in the arena that he was sworn in by either a hegemon or the matriarch of one of the significant families. Clearly Alkin measures success by the commission she earns, and such women pay enormous fees for their champions. When I last competed in the arena, I thought all duelists were mature men of the world and certainly considered myself to be one. The statues all look like boys to me now.

"Your quarters are satisfactory?"

"Admirable, noble lady," I say. "I have never enjoyed finer. In all my travels I have seen no home designed and decorated with finer taste, and few with a better setting."

She knows that my praise is sincere, not empty flattery, and smiles acknowledgment. "The original building did not do justice to the location, but nothing remains of it now. Cupule has been my life's work. And my boys have been my family." She sighs wistfully.

I know more about Alkin of Cupule than she knows about me. Her mother was Gemma of Gravic, a younger daughter of the ruler of Pean, the city across the bay. Gemma is still remembered as a lyric poet. In adulthood, Gemma served as sworn companion of her sister Murena, the heir. When royal Alkin was born, the old ruler gave her the apanage of Cupule, whose revenues would support her in a style befitting her caste.

But by the time Alkin came of age, Murena's daughter had succeeded to the throne and Gemma, too, was dead. Alkin was a mere royal cousin, a commodity rarely in short supply around palaces. All rulers try to limit the size of their nobility and the resulting burden of providing every baby with a lifetime support. Inevitably, Alkin was offered a consort of lower caste, to start her descendants down the steep path out of the nobility.

Alkin declined the man she was offered, and any second or third offers as well. She was banished from court then, and any children she ever bore would rank as ordinaries. She became a duelist manager. That calling is acceptable for a noblewoman, although rarely adopted by one of full royal caste. Cupule, with its marble halls, art collection, and highly trained staff, is evidence that she has been very successful at her avocation. When she dies, it will all revert to her tightfisted cousin, the ruler of Pean.

A bleat of vapid oaths announces that Scuppaug has come forth too close to the shrubbery at the south side of the terrace and snagged his cloak. Scuppaug of Sagene is currently the only other client in Alkin's stable and a typical cub duelist, still suffering from a lingering case of adolescence and arrogant beyond endurance. He always maintains a studied surliness, but today he wears the tabard for the first time and is hiding his apprehension behind rank ill manners. The tabard makes him seem all arms and legs and he sports an unfortunate juicy red pimple on his nose.

Scuppaug is of the knightly class, as shown by his yellow caste mark and the mere six quarterings on his cloak. His tabard is the same green-on-green as mine and his face, excluding the pimple, has a faint greenish tinge to match; I can sympathize, remembering how my own stomach misbehaved the first time I dressed for the arena. There is a world of difference between cheering in the stands and being roasted down on the sand.

Scuppaug should not be wearing his cloak yet, nor a sword at all, but Alkin does not comment. He should bow to her, but doesn't. Because I wear no caste mark or signet ring, he is entitled to ignore me and does.

"We are ready?" Alkin inquires. She holds out a hand in my direction, an ancient gesture that must date back to the Blood Age, when a man could touch a woman without fear. I stand up and then raise her, but I do it with psychic heft, not contact.

"You know the way, knightly Scuppaug?" she inquires.

The boy flinches. "Er, only by a roundabout route."

That is my cue to say, "I will be honored to return and escort you, knightly Scuppaug of Sagene. Ready, noblewoman?"

To try to transport two people at the same time would be insanely dangerous, but a high-caste nobleman can easily take one companion with him when he ports. I recall the arena at Bere Parochian.

◆ ◆ ◆ PORT ◆ ◆ ◆

Alkin and I come forth on the arrival stage, a wooden deck in the center of the blazing hot sand of the arena. Without that empty space to aim for, I might have impacted bystanders or any changes made since I last visited the target, with undignified or even dangerous results. Bere Parochian, adjoining Pean to the south, sits directly on the equator, and I feel as if I have dropped into a potter's kiln. After one gasp of lung-scorching air I move us up into an unoccupied spot on the terrace, which is cooler only by comparison.

Although I have never competed there, I know the Bere Parochian arena well. It is quite typical. The circular expanse of white sand is about a hundred feet across, enclosed by a brick wall fifteen or so feet high, which is topped by a narrow terrace. Behind that rises the high grassy berm of the amphitheater. Covered stands for the nobility take up much of the favored west side, but ordinaries are free to bring their straw hats and water bottles and sit anywhere else on the slopes. A dozen or so managers' booths in gaudy colors are lined up along the eastern terrace, and it is to them that I have brought us.

Nobles and ordinaries scurry past like troubled ants. The slopes and stand are filling up with spectators and already the whole amphitheater rumbles with the surflike sound of an excited crowd. I feel an almost-forgotten thrill myself, an echo of youth. I did not come here to enjoy myself, but I know that I will. The arena can be addictive.

We hurry into Alkin's green-green booth. It is merely an open-fronted tent, furnished with a low table and some mats, but at least we are out of the sunlight.

She turns to me with shapely brows raised in appreciation. "It has been a very long time since one of my lads brought me from Cupule to Bere Parochian in one port, noble Quirt. Those who try it usually drop me in the sand. I will mention this to Sudamina."

"I hope I may continue to surprise you this afternoon."

If noble dignity allowed, she would wag a finger at me. "Do not be overconfident! You must not think of the Bere Parochian games as bush league. It is only a bronze tourney, I know, but it is the top of the bronze circuit. It attracts important scouts and serious talent. I have seen baby dragons hatch here."

"I would love to run into a baby dragon here!" I say, quite truthfully.

The arena has a jargon all its own. The competitors are supposed to be young noblemen, showing off their prowess in the hope of attracting offers from agents representing rulers or even, if they are truly gifted, one of the seven hegemons. Such contestants are known as "cubs" and those of high caste are "cubs-with-teeth"—it is rare for any man to defeat one of higher caste than himself. The prizes awarded in the games themselves are immaterial. What a cub is after is the chance to swear lifelong loyalty to a liege in return for some worthy position in her government and the promise that he will eventually be paired with a mistress of equal or higher caste. A man whose children are of lower caste than himself has failed both them and his ancestors. His whole life will depend on his youthful showing in the arena.

I will ask to compete as a "blank," meaning anonymously, without name, caste, or lineage. Meanwhile, my boast about baby dragons has produced a very skeptical expression on my manager's face. I have beaten hegemonics in the past and if I say so, she will know I speak the truth. She will also fear that I have a murky past and insist on reading my memory.

I explain, "Only first-class opposition will help me demonstrate my strength, royal."

I am here to qualify for the silver circuit. A single bronze crown will normally suffice, but an anonymous contender may need more than one, because games marshals have complete discretion to admit or refuse applicants. To defeat a cub-with-teeth will help my campaign. There is even a certain hegemonic lout I would love to smear all over the arena, but there are many bronze tourneys and for him to choose the same one I have would be a bizarre coincidence.

"With your permission, I will go and fetch the cub with pustules."

Alkin's eyelids droop slightly as she notes how I have changed the subject. She is a very perceptive woman. "Don't show off in front of him too much, please. He's suffering enough already."

"I will bring him by easy stages. What is his range, do you know?"

"He claims sixty miles." She smiles wickedly. "It might not hurt to drop him on the sand, though, just on principle."

She is enjoying the novelty of running a blank and I am confident she will get me accepted. Princely Sudamina of Monticle has an ominous reputation even among games marshals, who as a class eat poison-fang carnivores raw, but she and Alkin must have known each other and worked together for many pentads. Friends bend rules for friends.

Down on the arrival stage, people are coming forth and disappearing all the time. How much time do I have to coddle young Scuppaug?

I come forth on the top of the bank, alongside a crowd of ordinaries. The nearer ones jump in alarm and at least a dozen fall on their knees to me, which is an unwelcome reminder that some noblemen are dangerous. Like the Enemy, for instance, my Enemy, the destroyer I am doomed to destroy.

I laugh to reassure them. "Up, up, good people! I did not come here to spoil your holiday."

From up there I have a view of the whole amphitheater, but at the moment I am only interested in the view toward the city a mile away. Normally the river plain would be deserted in the scorching heat of doublenoon, but today crowds still stream along every path through the paddy fields, heading this way. More are scrambling up the outer slopes below me. I have ample time to fetch Scuppaug, bringing him by several small hops and not making him feel any more insecure than he does already.

Meanwhile the ordinaries are still gaping at me, the children whispering excitedly at being so close to a real duelist. They are all dressed in their best: white cotton breechclouts for the men, bright-colored saris for the women. These inhabitants of Bere Parochian appear to be a healthy and happy throng, although any of them would seem small alongside even Scuppaug of Sagene. They have come here to be entertained by their betters, to see them contest together and hopefully—though even the humblest street sweeper would never put the wicked thought into words—bleed. Accidents do happen in the arena. Men sometimes die and that is a double tragedy, for their opponents are vilified as killers, banned evermore from competition and in effect from the nobility, because only a champion will ever be awarded a noble mistress. But apart from gambling, the prospect of blood is what draws the crowds and gives the games their zest.

"Enjoy your afternoon, yeomen," I tell them. "We will do our best to entertain you. And if you want to cheer for me, so much the better."

"What name should we shout, noble one?" asks a white-haired elder.

"Shout 'Green!' for me. I am a good fighter and have won many crowns." That will send them scrambling to the bookmakers.

Nobles are still coming forth on the platform and vanishing again in a continuous flicker of shapes. The elite's stands are filling up. The lowest section is reserved for the scouts Alkin mentioned, all hoping to identify some talented youngster who can be recruited before anyone else gets to his manager with a better offer. In other words—but words they would never use—they are looking for good breeding stock going cheap.

I count ten managers' booths, each distinguished by its owner's colors. Alkin's two-tone green is near the center of the line, which confirms my suspicion that she is a personal friend of the games marshal. But a couple of others are being dismantled, and that is a bad sign. If some managers are leaving, the card must be filled; my chances of being admitted have just plummeted. I send a quick prayer to Our Father White and go in search of Scuppaug.

◆ ◆ ◆ **PORT** ◆ ◆ ◆

On the cliff terrace at Cupule, the master of Sagene is slumped on a cushion in a sulk. His clumsily folded cloak sits beside mine and his sword has disappeared. He scowls. "You took your time, yeoman."

"I was sightseeing. Ready to show off your beautiful thighs for the girls?"

He jumps up, coloring furiously. "That is an indecent remark!"

"Tabards are indecent garments. You know the real reason they're cut so short?"

The kid hesitates and then bites the hook. "Why?"

"So the buyers can see if our knees are knocking."

He clamps his knees together. I should not mock him. A man of the knightly caste is in danger of seeing his descendants drop out of the nobility altogether. This cub will never rise to the silver circuit, although no doubt an agent for the ruler of some minor realm will make him an offer eventually. As one of his liege's low-caste champions, he will be assigned to guard duty or customs collection or some other near-menial office—I cannot imagine even the tiniest realm ever wanting Scuppaug of Sagene as vizier, which is as high as a man can rise in government.

The arena is his only hope to escape this fate. If he can shine there, demonstrating strength above the level his six quarterings predict, his future ruler may assign him a higher-caste gentlewoman as his mistress, and his children will inherit higher status than he did. He is the sort of consort Alkin must have refused in her day. It is much harder to climb the nobility ladder than it is to fall off.

I heft my cloak to me and set it on the palm of my left hand. "You know the lookout at Turanian Hill, knightly?" I am guessing that the porter who brought him to Cupule will have come by that portage.

Scuppaug hefts his cloak to him and balances it on his left hand. "Yes."

"Go there."

♦ ♦ ♦ PORT ♦ ♦ ♦

I come forth on the windy hilltop, close to the grove of miche palms at the summit. But not too close! I never forget how, as an adolescent just developing psychic powers, I bounced off a tree and broke an arm. After a moment, when there is no sign of my companion, I walk into their shade to wait. Three champions and their mistresses come forth and at once port out again. Just when I start to worry, the lad appears a hundred yards down the slope. An instant later he is at my side looking pleased with himself. I wonder how many hops he needed to get here.

"You know Cromb Castle, knightly Scuppaug?"

"No."

I see that he is shaking. "What's the matter, for suns' sake? There's nothing to be scared of!"

"It's my first time, that's all." He looks anywhere except at me.

"But no one ever gets hurt."

"Yes they do!"

Ah! "Rarely. You've seen it happen?"

He suppresses a retch. "It went right *through* him." His face turns greener.

"Ugly! But you won't be fighting today—"

"She said I might be!"

"Or the suns may fall, or I may drop us into the middle of the ocean. Cromb Castle."

♦ ♦ ♦ PORT ♦ ♦ ♦

Cromb is a ruin of great antiquity, a relic of the Blood Age when wild, hairy men ruled the world by violence. Now it is merely some rocks scattered over a grassy mound on an island not far offshore. Although the suns' reflections off the water are painful, the sea wind is pleasantly cool. I point out some landmarks to help my companion fix the portage in his memory. He listens and nods.

"And you can recall Turanian Hill from here?"

"Er . . . Of course!"

Now that he seems calmer, I say, "Whether you compete or not today depends on the numbers. A games marshal will always jiggle the roster until she has exactly sixteen contestants. Eight is too short a card; thirty-two makes a very long day. If she has too many, she rejects some, or leans on managers to pull them. I saw some booths being taken down, so today's games must be over the limit and you need not worry. If she had come up short, the managers would have thrown in a few greenhorns, like you, but then they fiddle the draw to match you against a blank. A loss against a blank does not count as an egg on your record, but a win does count, and you can hardly expect better odds than that, can you? If you don't want to continue, you can make sure you lose in the first round, which is not the slightest bit dangerous. Understand?"

He nods doubtfully.

"There's no shame in being beaten in the first round. A breath of wind can do it. It needs concentration as much as strength and even top men will bollix it sometimes."

"Honest?"

"I swear by my ancestors' graves."

"I didn't think a yeoman had any ancestors!" Scuppaug cannot understand why Alkin agreed to manage a contestant who wears no caste mark. He assumes I am an ordinary trying to masquerade as nobility. If he knew the truth he wouldn't speak to me at all.

"I don't. I just happened. Gingall Ridge . . ."

* * * **PORT** * * *

Ears pop. I steady the kid as he staggers. The view from the ridge is sensational, land and sea forever, but a wind like a skinner's knife blows up there always. A grandly dressed couple come forth a couple of yards away, flinch at the near miss, and vanish again.

"I can't recall Cromb Castle!" Scuppaug says.

I suppress a groan. His range is pathetic. "I don't know any portages between here and there, but that hill must be about halfway, so we'll try a line-of-sight jump back to that. Meanwhile memorize this one, Gingall Ridge. Remember this white rock shaped like an ear. Those two stumps . . . Now listen. Today you are in absolutely no danger. Alkin earns a commission from every buyer who takes one of her boys and—"

"Don't call them *buyers*, yeoman! They're royal agents! I'm not meat on a slab." He clenches his lips like an angry child.

"No, you are a potential stud for a royal herd." At that I flatter him. A nobleman of low caste—honored or even knightly class—who fails to find a ruler willing to take his oaths may end up in worse state than Alkin, because the apanage he received at birth may not be adequate to support a family. For all I know, Scuppaug's Sagene is no more than a row of rental cottages. The double standard shows—Alkin can accept money, or emerald bracelets, for her managing, but a nobleman who takes wages or engages in trade is disgraced and may even be unnamed by his hegemon. He can end up as an ordinary porter, married to an ordinary woman, and delivering letters around a city to feed his slightly oversized ordinary children. I don't remind my young friend of that dread fate, of course.

"Alkin takes your tuition fees, doesn't she? The old vulture will keep milking you as long as she possibly can. She won't let you get hurt."

"You insult your betters! You are a disgusting cynic!"

"I have much to be cynical about." My own terms with Alkin are different. I have told her that I need to make a name for myself as Quirt of Mundil, but I will not be accepting offers. I have other plans. She has been careful not to ask me what those are.

2

We come forth on the arrival stage and Scuppaug yelps in outrage at the blast of heat. I port us up to the managers' booths, but the row has changed since I left. Two more tents have gone, leaving a mere eight, and a red-on-purple one at the far end has sprouted armed guards, four large men with quivers of darts slung on their backs. The sword a nobleman usually wears is just for show, but steel darts are serious weaponry. A good champion can heft one clear through a tree trunk at a hundred yards. Who are these toughs guarding, and why? They have the look of a ruler's sworn champions, but their tunics are plain brown, not the usual highly decorated and distinctive livery. Scuppaug and I step into Alkin's booth. I lay my cloak on a mat. Scuppaug sets his cloak beside mine.

On the far side of the amphitheater, near the royal box, a band is playing with more enthusiasm than good judgment. The arena is packed, alive with excitement and anticipation. The notorious Marshal Sudamina puts on good entertainment.

Alkin is alone, posed on a mat with her legs tucked under her, looking fretful. "There has been a development," she snaps. "You will compete in the first round, knightly Scuppaug, but the marshal has promised to pair you with a blank and inform him that you do not wish to progress to the second round, so he will not throw you the match. The question is whether you wish to withdraw altogether, noble Quirt."

"Why should I?"

She stares at me suspiciously. "I did warn you! We have a baby dragon out there."

Scuppaug wails. "A *what*?"

"An extreme case of a cub-with-teeth," she tells him, "a scion of one of the great psychic houses—the hegemonics or the significant families."

Even these wonders must prove their skills on the bronze circuit before being allowed to compete in the silver. Obviously that is whom the big apes outside are guarding.

"Baby dragons are expected to compete as blanks," I explain.

Men may compete anonymously for several reasons. The marshal may enlist sworn champions when she has too few cubs to fill the card. Or blanks may be what an ordinary would call bastards, but the gentry refer to discreetly as love children: conceived outside a legal pairing. They may find employment as guards or champions if they show real talent, but they cannot hope to win a noble mistress. There are also addicts, men who have become so obsessed with the sport that they cannot leave it and settle down to serve a ruler.

A baby dragon is expected to compete anonymously because his name will scare all the genuine cubs away. Although a loss against a blank is not counted, it can still damage a youngster's morale, so serious managers often pull their clients out rather than let them be trounced. That is why the booths are being dismantled, but I do not understand why this dragon is already exposed. May he even be the opponent I did not dare hope for?

"The kid isn't very sure of himself if he proclaims his lineage ahead of time."

"The story is that he did enter as a blank," my manager says with a sneer of disdain. "His name was leaked 'by mistake.' He escaped from his handlers long enough to cozy up to a group of girls. Just ordinaries, of course—he cannot possibly be stupid enough to try to keep a secret near noblewomen—but one of them had enough noble blood in her veins to read him." She is disgusted by the notion of a man of the royal caste consorting with ordinaries. That can lead to fornication and miscegenation, which was probably the boy's intent, of course. "Now everyone knows."

"Not quite everyone."

Alkin sighs. "Humate of Alfet, son of Pelta of Pelagic."

"*Suns save us!*" Scuppaug cries. "The *hegemon*? The hegemon of *Pelagic*?"

I choke down a bellow of laughter. *Praise Our Father White!* The suns are favoring my cause at last. "Good! I enjoy a challenge." I grin back at two incredulous stares. Now that I think about it, I realize that this meeting is no extraordinary coincidence after all and I should not be so surprised. The Humate boy and I are both in a hurry; we both chose the Bere Parochian tourney because of its timeliness, as well as its prestige.

"Are you mad?" Scuppaug demands, wide-eyed, for only a hegemonic would dare take on another in the games. "Who are you?"

"Just Quirt of Mundil. Is anyone else staying around for the tourney?"

"Princely Sudamina is padding out the numbers," Alkin says. If the ruler's champions are being coerced into competing, they will be furious at having to face the humiliation of certain defeat at the hands of the baby dragon. This will be a strange tourney.

"I foresee an interesting afternoon."

Scuppaug stares at me as if my brains are running out of my ears, and even Alkin is eyeing me oddly.

She says, "You had better go and take the oath, nobles."

I shake out my cloak and tie the band around my neck. Scuppaug shakes out his cloak and ties the band around his neck. I slide my forearms through the corner loops. Scuppaug slides his forearms through the corner loops. Tourney cloaks are squares of the finest linen bearing "quarterings" to represent one's fourbears. Scuppaug's cloak is blue, and proclaims his precious six—two royal white circles, three princely red, and one orange highborn. My cloak is plain green.

"Ready, royal Alkin?"

◆ ◆ ◆ **PORT** ◆ ◆ ◆

Alkin and I come forth in the games marshal's box, a permanent roofed structure, open at the front and richly carpeted. A dozen referees in blue saris kneel at low tables, most of them writing or thumbing through papers. They all wear marks of either royal or princely caste and signet rings that mark them as sworn companions of the ruler. Bere Parochian is a rich realm, able to support a large court. Ten big men in the white robes of linesmen sit or stand around the walls, muttering to one another and looking bored. They, too, wear signets and marks of high caste, so they are some of the ruler's champions out of their usual livery. Usually linesmen and referees are paired couples, consort and mistress. I wonder if the two missing men have been coopted to compete.

Scuppaug comes forth at my side.

The games marshal sits in splendor on a throne and I get my first glimpse of the famous Sudamina of Monticle, whose frowns reputedly intimidate duelists who could wring her neck from ten feet away. She seems large, middle-aged, and ferocious, with stab-wound eyes and a sarcophagus mouth, but I shall never know if she is anything like that in reality. Sudamina is a cousin of the ruler of Bere Parochian and has been running the blossoms-1 bronze tourney here forever. It is thanks to her skills that these games are so highly regarded.

A youth in a blue and yellow tabard kneels on a cushion at her feet, speaking the oath in a steady voice. The elderly man in matching tunic nearby will be his manager-trainer. The boy ends and is dismissed. He rises. He and his trainer bow and port out.

Sudamina turns her carnivore gaze on us and there is a momentary pause.

Then she smites us with a smile like a lightning bolt. "I know you! No, it would be your father, of course . . . Don't tell me . . . Sky-something . . . ? No, Skayles! Skayles of . . . ?"

"Skayles of Boniform!" Scuppaug cries, glowing like a sun.

"Ah, of course! He won the bracelet."

Alkin insists on formalities. "May I have the honor, princely Sudamina, of presenting knightly Scuppaug of Sagene, come to hazard his fortune in your tourney?"

The marshal continues to enthuse. "Welcome, knightly. It must be four pentads since your father honored our games, but I still remember the wonderful demonstration of skill he gave us in the sword fight. You are so like him I would have known you anywhere."

This incredible feat of memory convinces our cub, who blushes so red I'm surprised he does not faint from lack of blood in vital organs. Speechless, he stumbles forward to kneel on the cushion before the throne. I glance at the spectators and detect a few smirks being exchanged. Of course Sudamina had received the information about the boy's father from one of the women working at the records or directly from Alkin herself, and Alkin must have added a plea for a pick-me-up for a very nervous greenhorn.

"Is your noble sire here to watch you follow his footsteps to glory?" the marshal asks.

"Er, no, princely. Mother wouldn't let . . . I mean he couldn't get away just now."

The old harridan has done her duty and now can get back to business. "Well, let us hope you can visit them tonight with some exciting news. It is an honor and pleasure to have you in our games. The oath, please."

Predictably he gets stage fright and forgets the words. I remember doing that myself in my first tourney. Then he begins to repeat them in jerks, as Alkin silently prompts him. He swears that his heraldry is genuine, his intentions are honorable, he knows the rules, and he will abide by them. Given leave to withdraw, he vanishes like a bubble.

No smiles for me. If the games marshal's glare represents her true feelings, she is in a homicidal fury at the mess young Humate of Alfet has made of her program. Although Pelagic is half a continent away, she will not dare refuse the son of its hegemon. There is another pause, during which Alkin is probably explaining to her that I have demonstrated exceptional strength in both hefting and porting.

The cushion is set a little too close to the lady for my comfort. Were she to lean forward, she would be able to reach out and touch the candidate kneeling there. Without waiting to be invited, I walk forward and kneel on the rug a yard back from the cushion. Even at that distance I cannot expect to deceive Sudamina, but she should not be tempted to try reading my memory. Or so I hope—we feeble males have only women's word for the limits of their powers.

Idiot! Alkin says in my head. *Do not provoke her!*

My defiance will certainly not improve the marshal's attitude toward yet another blank, but she will be reluctant to take her anger out on me when she is already so short of duelists.

"On the cushion!"

I elevate myself a foot vertically, heft the cushion in under me, and descend again, at the same distance from her as before. For a moment I think I have overdone it and she will order me out of her cousin's realm forthwith and forever.

"Your name?"

"Quirt of Mundil."

She must know that this is not strict truth, although I have used that name for a long time, so it is not a prominent lie. "Have you ever been vilified or expelled from a tourney for any reason?"

"No, princely."

"How long since you last competed?"

"About two pentads."

She raises her eyebrows at that, but she has now established that I am neither a killer nor an addict. "You have won crowns in the past?"

"Two bronze, several silver."

"You are entitled to display how many quarterings?"

"Several."

Back to glaring. "Has your mistress given you permission to enter these games?"

"I have no mistress."

"Your ruler, then."

"I cannot answer that question."

Scowl again. "You do *have* a ruler?"

How can I not? If a champion's liege dies, his loyalty automatically transfers to her successor. I squirm. "Not really."

"How can you have an unreal ruler? You are sworn to a hegemon, then? Are you or aren't you sworn? Yes or no?"

"I cannot answer that question."

She glares at me in shock. *"You were unnamed?"*

That is the question I have been dreading, the one Alkin did not ask. If I admit to being an unnamed, other contestants will refuse to compete against me, a man without rank, name, land, or honor. Sudamina will not admit an unnamed. Fortunately I have a riposte available, one I had hoped not to need, one so rare that she has probably never met it before.

I heft the cushion with me on it and float it back to its original place at her feet. I grit my teeth. "Read me, then."

She touches my forehead with one finger and gasps in outrage. "I cannot. You are blocked!"

"Yes."

She tries harder, sending jabs of agony through my skull. I wince and jerk away.

"Please, noble! You cannot break a hegemon's curse. You will hurt both of us." Perhaps any high-caste noblewoman can set a doom upon a man and even block him from being read, but only hegemons may do so legally.

Sudamina stares at me in horror. "You are doomed?"

"I am doomed. I ask to enter your tourney to further my efforts to escape from that doom."

She can tell I am not lying; that much is not blocked. To help a man work off a doom is a sacred duty—but then, so is almsgiving, and the poor still go hungry.

"What is this doom?"

That is about the only question she is *not* entitled to ask.

"I will not say." But I had better say something more positive or she will turf me out in anger and order another of the ruler's champions to go and dress for the arena. "Princely Sudamina, I swear to you that I am not daunted by the Pelagic boy. If this is his virgin outing, he knows only what he has been told and he probably did not bother with any serious coaching. If he is not a brash, overconfident brat, I will eat my sandals before your very eyes."

She curls a lip at my vainglorious boasting. "He would consider that you are the overconfident one."

I hate to beg, but my doom forces me. "And that makes him vulnerable. With respect, princely, I have competed in about a dozen tourneys, but I have witnessed hundreds. I know every trick ever tried, legal and illegal. Royal Alkin can testify that I have much strength. Put me at one end of your card and Humate of Alfet at the other, set me against the best you've got, and I swear I'll give you a tourney to remember."

She glares again. "In five pentads, yeoman Green, no contestant has ever presumed to tell me how to run my games!"

"In five pentads, have you ever had a baby dragon try to scare away all the serious opposition by revealing his identity beforehand? I may not have cute little Humate's strength or range, but I know the ways of the arena as he never will. I can beat him!"

"You would dare? House Pelagic has a reputation for spite."

Certainly I would dare. I would give my toes to humiliate Humate, but I feel the leaden weight of my doom descend on my hopes and realize that it will not let me do so. Befriending the kid will serve my dread purpose much better than antagonizing him; indeed, it will advance my quest considerably. "I suppose not. I'll have to settle for the bracelet. But I swear that I will frighten the rest of his milk teeth out of him first."

There is a long pause. Surely Sudamina would like nothing better than to see someone rub the young hegemonic's nose in a heap of warm pig droppings. The crowd outside sounds impatient, but the games marshal's box is very quiet as the linesmen and referees eavesdrop in astonishment. Probably no one has ever talked back to the marshal like that before, but they will be more impressed by meeting a doomed man.

A sword-girded champion in a highly emblazoned tunic comes forth beside the throne. His voice is as arrogant as his face. "The noblest wishes to know why she is being kept waiting."

The games marshal shrugs her big shoulders. "Tell her she must fret a song or two yet. I have to rearrange the lineup again." As the champion disappears she turns back to me. "Swear the oath, then."

I remember the words perfectly, but now they resonate with bitter nostalgia. How long ago! I was greener back then than my tabard is now. I rise, bow. I rise, retreat three paces, bow . . .

◆ ◆ ◆ PORT ◆ ◆ ◆

Scuppaug is waiting for us at the booth, looking more cheerful now.

Alkin conveys, *I want a private word with you, Quirt!*

With a nod, I head for the water bucket and proceed to drain the dipper four times. Well, that is what it would look like to Scuppaug, because I have my back to him, but the last three were empty. Alkin catches on.

"Have you drunk enough?" she asks him. "The heat down there will be intense. You must drink as much as you possibly can."

Scuppaug takes my place at the bucket. I encourage him. I encourage him again. So does Alkin. He does very well, until I expect to see water leaking out of his ears.

The crowd outside rumbles with impatience, and there is no doubt now that the white sun is higher than the blue. The band continues to bang and blow manfully.

Scuppaug empties the dipper for the fourth time and gives us a worried look, too embarrassed to put his problem into words.

I tell him. "Usual place." The men's pits are always outside the arena on the east, the Father's side, and visible from the top of the bank.

He ports out.

"If his psyche were as strong as his bladder, he would be hegemonic material," Alkin says with surprising vulgarity. She points to a mat close to her. "Sit there. Why did you not tell me you are doomed?"

I kneel. "It is not something I discuss unless I must."

"What is there between you and Humate of Alfet?"

"I have seen him at a distance but never met him, noble."

"That was not what I asked." Her glare is worthy of Marshal Sudamina herself.

"I mean the boy no harm, except that I have a perfectly normal desire to take a hegemonic down a peg if I can."

"A suicidal ambition. You know more of him than you are saying."

"I did not know he would be here today." I cannot lie to a noblewoman of Alkin's caste, but how much truth can I hold back? If I prattle about the lifelong cat fight between Pelta and Balata, I will frighten Alkin out of her wits. Nobody wants to get mixed up in hegemonic politics. She will withdraw both Scuppaug and me from the games and head straight home to Cupule. If I mention the possibility that the spitting may lead to open warfare, she will assume that the suns have boiled my brains. Most people believe that war was something that wild, hairy men did, back in the Blood Age. They are wrong, though. There have been wars between hegemons since those days and no doubt there will be again.

I say, "Listen, then. Humate must win a silver crown to prove his manhood. Normally he would not set foot in the arena for another pentad, but he is a hegemonic and already quite strong enough to beat most grown men. High royalty are paired by treaty, of course, and Humate is now betrothed to royal Tendence of Carpus, heir to Ruler Etesian of Formene, in far-western Heliac. This tourney is just a formality for him. As soon as he has demonstrated his psychic virility, here and at a silver tourney, the pairing will be solemnized."

"Why can't it wait until the boy is old enough?" Alkin asks, reasonably enough. A duelist manager is a sort of matchmaker, so I have caught her professional interest.

The main reason is that a ruler's heir needs permission from her hegemon to take a consort. Hegemon Balata of Heliac has not given her permission for the pairing and will certainly forbid it when she hears about it. Such a secret cannot be kept for very long, so the match must be rushed through.

"It is a sad story," I explain. "Royal Tendence was previously paired with a fine young nobleman, Burgeon of Strobilus. They were a perfect match, both politically and genetically. They fell deeply in love within days. Alas, about a gnomon after their union was consummated, but before Burgeon got his mistress with child, he died in a hunting accident. Tendence was desolate. She refused to consider a replacement. Etesian is a tolerant, rather muddled woman, and humored her with great patience, but now she has been offered the giddying prospect of a hegemonic consort for her daughter. Who can resist an infusion of hegemonic bloodlines into the family pedigree?"

Alkin is smoldering. "You still aren't telling me the whole truth, noble Quirt! How old is this Tendence widow?"

"Um, old enough to start tongues wagging about her duty to continue the royal line."

"Older than the boy, you mean?"

"About two pentads older."

"What!? That is disgusting! That is outrageous!" Alkin will find that arrangement as obscene as incest. A man is normally assigned to a mistress about a pentad younger than himself. "Men need much longer to mature than women!" She does not add that most of us never do. "How does the woman feel about this?"

"Miserable."

"The boy's mother must be crazy!"

Pelta of Pelagic may very well be mad, but the political stakes are sane enough. The realm of Formene, in Heliac, lies directly across the strait from Fumage, which is in Pelagic. If Ruler Etesian switches her loyalty from Heliac to Pelagic, Hegemon Pelta will have total control of trade in and out of the Gulf of Broose. This will give Pelta a huge financial windfall and be copious spit in the eye of her longtime rival, Hegemon Balata. Fortunately Alkin is no politician and does not see that yawning chasm.

"This *boy* is supposed to collect a token trophy so he can be tucked into an older woman's bed against her wishes?"

"That is the plan."

"It is disgusting!"

"I entirely agree."

"Well, if you think you can stop it, then go out there and do so!"

"My pleasure, noble."

Scuppaug comes forth, beaming. "They're starting!"

So they are. Alkin and I turn guiltily back to our business, the arena. The band is taking a break. The linesmen are down on the sand, dismantling the arrival stage and stacking the timbers. Those balks are a standard six feet long and a foot wide. Each one weighs more than I do and yet they flit through the air like a flock of birds, hefted by the combined psychic strength of the linesmen. In moments the cubical stack is complete and the champions port out simultaneously. I have never seen this operation conducted more smoothly, even in golden games.

A long fanfare echoes through the arena. The spectators rise as the royal procession enters, sweeping in over the bank with the ruler herself in the lead. She projects a majesty so intense that details of her age and dress are hidden in a blaze of grandeur. Close behind her floats her consort, who is clearly white-bearded and portly, but there is no way of telling whether he is hefting them both or the heavy psychic lifting is being applied by the two bodyguards at his back. Champions, gentlewomen, miscellaneous relatives, and guests follow, each noblewoman closely attended by a nobleman, just as Father

White forever follows Mother Blue through the heavens. Strains of the Bere Parochian anthem are drowned out by the ordinaries' cheering. Like a flock of rainbow birds the parade makes a dignified circuit of the arena before heading to the royal box. Tumult fades into blessed silence.

"Time to go, nobles," Alkin says. "May Our Father strengthen and Our Mother guide you both."

3

I port down to the scorching sand, into the furnace glare of the arena. Scuppaug arrives at my side. I push the corner loops of my cloak down to my wrists. Scuppaug does the same. Other contestants are coming forth on either side, sixteen of us in a line below our managers' booths. We bow to the ruler and games marshal opposite; the crowd cheers again.

I have never seen five blanks competing in one tourney before, although on one memorable occasion I saw four. Humate is not a blank. Just as his name so unfortunately leaked out earlier, a cloak with a stunning sixteen white quarterings must have conveniently leaked into his baggage before he left home, so the "accident" was deliberate. I have known trainers to use underhand tactics often enough, but never this one, because it can so easily backlash, and in this case it has done so—since Humate has scared away many of the legitimate cubs, Sudamina has replaced them with proven champions. He has made the contest harder, not easier. Tendence told me that he was the sort of arrogant juvenile hegemonic who would not listen to advice, and she is an excellent judge of character.

He is a lanky adolescent, already taller than most of the other contenders, although easily the youngest man present and about half my age. His face still has a boyish softness, exaggerated by an excited grin, glowing with all the confidence and good cheer that Scuppaug lacks, showing that he is enjoying himself and expects to continue doing so. Despite his pedigree, he can't be into his full adult powers yet, so I can probably make a fool of him if I want to. My pleasure at the thought makes me feel guilty. He is not the Enemy. His only crime is to be the spawn of an evil house. He sees me watching him and winks, which is deliberate insolence to an older man. I should know, because I played such games in my own youth. I wink back.

A woman in a blue sari comes forth in front of us with her attendant linesman. Now we get to learn the seeding order. "Royal Humate of Alfet, you will lead."

The boy frowns. Traditionally the number-two seed leads the flyby and number one ends it, so he had expected to go last. To be ranked second is an unwelcome surprise for the Pelagic wonder but it tells me that Sudamina has accepted my challenge. He glances around the rest of us, wondering who can possibly be seeded ahead of him. There is no heraldry to compare with his, not even close.

Most beginners would find going first an ordeal—Scuppaug certainly would—but Humate just shrugs, spreads his arms, and soars upward like a spark from a campfire. The kid has hegemonic confidence. And style, admittedly. As he begins to circle the arena, heralds posted along the terrace call out his caste, name, apanage, and ancestry: "Royal Humate of Alfet, son of noblest Hegemon Pelta of Pelagic."

The crowd *Oooos!* at hearing a hegemonic proclaimed in a mere bronze tourney.

The referee scans the line. "Knightly Scuppaug of Sagene."

"*Me?*" The kid's cry in my ear is halfway between a squeak and a croak.

"Great!" I whisper. "No shame in losing to him!"

"Oh! S'pose not!" Scuppaug grins and launches. Humate is already a quarter of the way around the arena and all Scuppaug has to do is follow. Self-hefting is easy. Doing it gracefully is not—head high, arms outstretched to extend the cloak as perfectly as possible, so the spectators below can view the heraldry. Humate's performance is perfection and the spectators are applauding even before he swings past the ducal box, performing the roll without a quiver. Poor Scuppaug! Heralds proclaim knightly Scuppaug of Sagene, great-great-great-grandson of the late Ruler Pomeys of Thrasonical, wherever that is. His cloak flaps like laundry on a line, he lurches up and down, tossed on rough seas. Watching those two in the air together is a perfect lesson in the right and wrong way to do a flyby.

And their cloaks could hardly be more different. Humate's is the most impressive I have ever seen in a tourney. All sixteen quarterings are white, four of them are crowns, indicating a ruler of one of the thousand or so realms in Aureity, and no less than three are stars, meaning that three of his fourbears were reigning hegemons. Scuppaug has only colored disks.

Porters move among us offering waterskins. I accept a drink eagerly and drench my head. I sweat an ocean with every breath but it dries at once.

Tourney seeding can never be exact, but the top four contenders can usually be foreseen and the marshal will display them last, first, ninth, and fifth respectively. If she has judged well, the final round will be between the number-one seed and either the second or third. After that, her first priority is normally to dispose of the blanks quickly and her second is to give the spectators an entertaining afternoon. That accomplished, a good marshal tries to deal gently with first-timers. A promising newcomer will get an easy first round to give him confidence. The unpromising, like Scuppaug, are set up with impossible opponents so they will not feel disgraced by losing, and Sudamina has certainly followed that rule by matching Scuppaug with Humate. All his life he will be able to joke about his first bout in the arena.

"Royal Implex of Adusk . . ." Another youngster soars into the air. He is a true cub, with sixteen quarterings, three of them royal. He performs slickly.

The fifth flier, normally fourth seed, is a mere knight, and the arena buzzes in bewilderment. The ninth cloak to fly displays about a dozen white quarterings, including crowns, and is worn by Despumate of Hurter, son of Ruler Nuchal of Skelder.

Now the spectators are agog to see who gets the honor of ending the parade. One by one the contestants are called, display, and return, lining up in seeded order behind the rest of us.

I am left on the burning sands with the one who will be my first opponent, a heavyset and exceedingly hairy man of about my age, wearing a blank blue cloak. He is too far away for conversation, just eyeing me with obvious contempt, grimly unhappy to be stuck down here in the fire pit entertaining the rabble. He is even sporting his champion's ring, so that everyone will understand that he is only obeying orders. When noble Blue is called, he reacts with shock and there is a noticeable pause before he takes off on his flight. Noble Blue had been certain that he would be number-one seed.

Finally the referee nods to me and noble Green can launch. Heralds posted at intervals along the terrace call out my alias for the crowd but the spectators are making too much noise to hear. A blank has been seeded above a hegemonic! The bookmakers will be going crazy. As I pass the royal box, someone hefts my feet. The nudge is not a serious effort to make me lose control and crash, just a twist to throw me off-balance and make me veer awkwardly. I am able to counter because it is a common prank and I was half expecting it. Humate is too far away to be personally responsible. Likely one of his guards was sent across to learn how strong the unknown challenger is. Now they know. I don't care. They will find out soon enough anyway.

How long can I remain anonymous? The reputation I won in my youth must catch up with me eventually. Even today, here in this rustic bronze tourney some roaming games afficionado may remember. *Why, he looks just like Mudar of Quoin! How old would he be now?*

I float around and set down at the end of the line. We bow again to the royal box and the crowd's applause.

The first round is the hefting contest—a trivial test of psychic strength, so simple it soon becomes boring, but a harmless and inoffensive way to weed out the hopeless. Linesmen and referees come forth in the center. Humate and Scuppaug heft over to join them and take up position on either side of the cubical stack of timbers. It is shoulder high, so each can see no more of his opponent than his face.

First man to win two consecutive rounds wins the match. As the lower seed, Scuppaug is granted the advantage of playing first. He hefts one of the top balks, floats it across, and lays it on the sand roughly midway between Humate and the stack. Any nobleman would find that easy. About the only way he could have failed would be to drop the timber on his opponent's toes. Humate lays a second balk on top of the first and hefts the load over to Scuppaug's side, and this is where skill starts to count, because he cannot see exactly where he is laying it down.

On his second play, Scuppaug sends back three with barely a wobble. He has not disgraced himself and can breathe easier. So can I, and certainly Alkin will, up in her booth.

The suns know how many timbers our baby dragon can juggle. There are legends of fireballs able to move fifteen, but not all timbers are the same size. He counters with four. Now Scuppaug must lift five. He manages to do so and even gets them across to Humate's side of the stack, but they topple as he is setting them down. The crowd offers a patter of applause, which must ring sweet in his ears.

Linesmen replace the balks on the stack again and Humate begins the second round. This time Scuppaug manages to lift a wall of six timbers, but drops it before he can raise it high enough to clear the stack. Although that loss means he has lost the match, I am impressed and raise my estimate of his future. His hefting is much stronger than his porting. With that power and some training, he will make a good guardsman. Even now he could wade into a mob of rioting ordinaries and throw them around like chaff.

Humate ports through to Scuppaug's side of the stack to shake hands, which is a courtesy not always observed. They fly back together. I can see Scuppaug's grin coming all the way—today's torment is over and he has acquitted himself well on his first outing. He soars up to Alkin's booth. Humate rejoins our lineup.

"How many tourneys a gnomon do you manage to wriggle into?" inquires my sour-faced neighbor, Blue. "On average, I mean." He's on the plump side, is noble Blue, sweating a lot more than I am. Caste marks are optional in the arena. It is customary to remove them, on the principle that a man is there to prove himself, not to brag about his ancestors. Blue has removed his, leaving only a faint smear of princely red.

I smile innocently. "I'm no addict. I do enjoy a bit of killing, though. It's the smell of the blood, you know."

He scowls and walks away to talk with someone civilized.

The second and third hefting contests drag by. The third pair are so evenly matched that they have to play seven rounds to produce a winner. The crowd frets and boos. The next pair are both strong and one of them wins by successfully passing over a pile of nine balks, which is remarkable. The spectators roar. The game is childish, but its very slowness means that the losers are weeded out gently, without the instant humiliation of the more violent events.

"Is there any real reason, grandfather," inquires a drawl at my shoulder, "why they make us stand out here in the sun?" Humate of Alfet offers me a drink from a waterskin.

I take a long one. I am of two minds about the boy. Oh, how I would like to squelch him, to make such a fool of him in the arena that thoughts of a pairing in the near future will be impossible and my beloved Tendence will be spared the humiliation of a child consort! But the core of my being is the doom that drives me to be avenged upon the Enemy. For that I must be nice to this brat, regardless of my personal feelings.

"Because of these tabards," I explain seriously.

"What about them?

"They separate the smart from the stupid."

"And how do they do that?" the boy murmurs. His eyes are level with mine and he must have some growing to do yet. He is lanky, but not gawky like Scuppaug. His shoulders are already wide, his chest broad, his hair dark and worn long like his eyelashes.

"The smart are those who have remembered to spread grease on it so it won't get sunburned and fall off."

Dark eyes twinkle. "I walked into that one, didn't I?" His voice still carries traces of boyish huskiness.

"You learn in time. The dread Sudamina expects us to meet in the final."

The boy shrugs. "I wish you luck." Is it arrogance to feel superior to everyone else when you have slept on silk all your life and eaten off gold? When puberty has brought you a psychic ability to tie steel bars in knots, or port two hundred miles in a blink? "Why does an old man like you bother competing?"

"For the pleasure of giving you a nasty surprise, royal Humate."

"Haven't had one of those since I learned to walk. Your name and apanage?"

"Green of nowhere."

His eyes narrow. "Don't push your luck, gramps."

If I accept that impudence I will be acting wildly out of character, so I smile sweetly. "If you threaten me, you juvenile turd, I will pull your guts out through your throat and strangle you with them." *You and the rest of your carrion brood.*

"Do try." The boy smiles contemptuously and strolls away, satisfied.

Time is passing. Father White will soon be overhead. Mother Blue is sinking lower in the sky, casting a reddish shadow of the royal box on the sand at the far side of the arena and frying us against the wall. In games jargon, the contestants' side is known as the broiler.

After a long age, we reach the eighth and final bout. Green and Blue port to the center. He sends over one. I return two. Three. Four. He is good, moving them fast to try and rattle me. I take my time, because I have seen too many surprises in this deceptively childish sport. Soon the load is high enough that it blocks our view of each other and the supply stack between us.

Blue is *very* good, as good as I would expect of a man of full royal caste. I dared Games Marshal Sudamina to send me her best and she has thrown a haymaker. He manages nine, but when he sets them down on my side, the pile shivers and the top two pivot out of line—the sand may have been uneven, the wood may have warped.

The applause stops. For a moment nobody in the arena breathes. But nothing falls. A referee calls, "Accepted!"

I am forbidden to straighten the pile until I have added to it, so this is going to be very tricky. I know I can lift ten, because I have done so on the silver circuit where the balks are larger, but I have never managed to set that many down safely, and the twist will make the task close to impossible.

I reach out blind to find a new timber and realize from the effort required that I have picked up two. I set them down again, still blind, knowing that even that move will lose me the round if one falls on the sand. I try again and this time a single balk rises into my view. I set it very gingerly on top, straighten all ten, breathe a silent prayer, and raise them.

By the Dark, this is some load! I can even imagine that my feet are sinking deeper into the sand, although if I were carrying it physically instead of psychically, it would crush me to soup. Very slowly, I lift it until I can see the remains of the stack below it—I could see Blue, too, if I wanted, but I must keep my eyes on my burden. Moving it horizontally is even trickier. The top three balks shiver and twist some more, but they do not fall and when I set it down on Blue's side, I know from the crowd's screams that I have broken or equaled a local record.

This round is over. Blue will never manage to move eleven. He tries, but the pile collapses when he adds to it, and he has to port out to avoid being mashed by falling timber. He returns at once but the heart has gone out of him and in the second round he drops a mere five.

I port through to shake his hand. He gives me a murderous glare and disappears, so I fly back alone with cheers ringing in my ears. I had forgotten how much I enjoy the zest of the arena.

There are eight of us left in the lineup and now the tourney will start to liven up.

Linesmen clear away the timbers, spreading them out as a platform under the ruler's box, where they will not interfere with the second event, the wrestling. Wrestling involves a best of three throws, defined as touching the sand with anything except the feet, and it is a fine test of speed, skill, and strength.

I detest it, because men who can heft eight or nine times their own weight are capable of inflicting gruesome injuries on one another by accident—I once saw a man crush his best friend's chest as flat as a shingle during training. The ordinaries love it because cloth is weaker than flesh and psychic holds sometimes slip and strip a contender naked. This instant loss of noble dignity holds great audience appeal. As a test of psychic strength, wrestling can degenerate into two men locked in a static glare-and-grunt session. More often it becomes a game of tag, for porting within the arena is allowed and the competitors flash in and out of view, rarely coming within arm's length of each other.

The first round pits Humate of Alfet against Implex of Adusk. They shed their cloaks and fly out to take position about twenty feet apart. A referee shouts "Go!" and Implex is hefted into the air and spun head over heels. He falls heavily, flat on his back—or is thrown down, more likely, because a noble should be able to break a fall. Instantly referees and linesmen gather around him and help him rise. I expect him to lodge a complaint, but he shakes his head when they ask him.

Humate has displayed not only an impressive juvenile speed, but an incredible range—I cannot heft a feather at that distance. He is awarded the point. The crowd murmurs like sea surf.

The referees order the two men farther apart to start the second fall. It doesn't help. Right on the signal Humate ports close; Implex performs a back somersault, thumping down on his shoulder blades with his legs up in the air. He squirms there helplessly for a moment. His tabard slides down around his chest and a huge explosion of laughter greets the sight of a nobleman in such a predicament. The noise is so great that it drowns out his cries of pain, for that sand is hot enough to scorch.

The referees shout at Humate, the linesmen heft Implex back on his feet. Both sets of officials gather around to inspect his burns. Expecting Humate to be expelled, I start calculating how that will affect my plans, but apparently Implex again refuses to lodge a complaint—it is unwise to antagonize a man who has a squad of bodyguards available to revenge slights to their ward. A linesman transports the loser away, and Humate heads back to the lineup.

The crowd disapproves and the arena reverberates with thunderous booing. It is still going on when Humate reaches us. As he takes his cloak, he glares around furiously. "What's goosing the rabble?"

At first no one speaks. Normally old hands pass the time by educating the cubs—it is part of the culture of the arena—but Humate broke the code by trying to scare away the opposition before the games began and now he is playing rough. He is not one of the boys.

Eventually one of the others says it. "Do you pull wings off flies, too? They came to see sport, not execution. This is bronze circuit, boy, not gold."

That is that. The hegemon's son can do nothing but stand and glower back at the crowd's scorn. He came to Bere Parochian to learn, didn't he?

The next pair are more evenly matched and put on a better show, winking in and out all over the arena, spinning around to find each other, stumbling, recovering, and generally playing to the crowd. The spectators' exaggerated cheers at the end are probably still meant to indicate more disapproval of Humate's brutal technique than approval of the second winner's finesse.

Again the last bout is the best of the event, although only very experienced spectators can judge wrestling. The marshal has pitted me against another of the ruler's champions, Purple, who is younger than Blue and a worthy opponent. At the signal, he instantly drops a hold like a wagonload of sand on me. I port free with an effort and yank his legs from under him. He recovers and clasps me in a whole-body grip that feels like the hands of an invisible giant, but I root myself to the spot like a monolith so he cannot raise me. I already know I am the stronger, but Purple was only a child the last time I competed, and I am badly out of practice. No words can adequately describe psychic wrestling. It can certainly hurt. A sandbag slams me in the chest, my right arm is yanked almost out of its socket, an iron band closes around my throat, and all the time I am maltreating him as vigorously—and as carefully. We must rough each other up without breaking backs or snapping thighs or doing any of the hundred horrible things that can happen to living bodies.

I lose the first throw and win the next two. By then I feel as if I have been hammered all over with stone mallets. I help him up; we exchange rueful and exhausted smiles. We give each other a real-muscle hug.

"How long since you were sworn, sonny?" I ask between gasps.

He grins widely. "Last birds-1." Only half a gnomon!

"Don't try this when you get to my age."

"I was holding back in case you broke," he says, winning the last word.

We fly back to the lineup together as the crowd applauds. He ports away, probably to a long soak and a rest. I am still gulping down water when the baby dragon accosts me, red-faced and spluttering with fury.

"What's going on here?"

I finish my drink and lower the skin. "It's called a tourney. Sixteen noblemen contest to see which of them is the best man at—"

"You know what I mean!" he yells. "Why are you getting all the good opponents and I get trash?"

"That's about to end."

He beams and puffs out his chest. "It is?"

"They've promised me a walkover in the finals."

The flash of fury in his eyes tenses all my muscles, but he just turns on his heel and stalks away, head high, fists clenched. His hegemonic mother could haul down the suns in fury if her precious boy had been turned away from the games; she can hardly object if he is given pushovers. But in fact, even Scuppaug was not a pushover by bronze standards, and Implex is probably a worthy opponent even by silver. Humate just lacks enough experience to realize how few men can come close to him. It's a man's world here and he is on his own; the rules prohibit him from going up to his manager's booth for advice or comfort. I do hope Marshal Sudamina is enjoying her afternoon as much as contestant Humate is not.

Now we have come to the fencing, the semifinals, which normally produce at least eight deaths—dramatic, bloody, and totally faked. Even so, the crowds love them. Arena fencing is like no other. There is little engaging of blades, almost no parrying, and certainly no cunning footwork in the sand. Instead there is an almighty amount of porting and wild slashing that encounters nothing, swords whistling through space where their targets were located instants earlier. Most of those swipes would cut a man in half if they connected—and if the blades were real. The hilts are real, solid metal wrapped with rough leather grips. The blades will clang and clash realistically enough, but when they touch flesh they vanish in a spurt of symbolic blood, giving the victim just enough of a jolt to knock him down. In fact they are illusions projected by the referees.

Rules vary, but at Bere Parochian the contests are best-of-three and the swords are two-handed scimitars of shining crystal. I've met such brutes before and know how they flash flames of blue and white sunlight all over the arena, especially in the fencers' eyes. It is as easy to dazzle yourself as your opponent.

Humate has taken his lesson in the wrestling too much to heart. Anxious not to finish his opponent too quickly this time, he starts off by leaping and slashing and porting around like a madman.

"That is quite a dance," remarks my opponent. He is the ruler's son, a genuine cub-with-teeth.

"He's going to regret it," I say. "Sword fighting is not like wrestling. It's too tricky to fake. If you get overly fancy your opponent can get in your blind spot. Then the lightning strikes your ass."

He raises eyebrows. "Thanks for the warning. Should you be telling me that, though?" He offers a hand. "Despumate of Hurter."

"Just Green today, I'm afraid. My real name here would provoke a funeral—mine. But at least you've nailed down a ring."

He shrugs glumly. "At whiterise I was odds-on favorite for the crown."

That is why addicts and other interlopers are unwelcome. Games are for the youngsters who must find themselves a future. Prizes matter to them.

The crowd shrieks. Humate stands in the center looking very foolish with illusory blood all over his face.

"What's your score so far?" I ask Despumate.

"One bracelet, one crown, no eggs. Now one ring. Unless you feel like bursting into tears and withdrawing?" He grins.

"Oh, I do, I do! But I won't. That's a great record. Should be enough to get you into the silvers."

"My manager suggests the pots-1 games at Azedarac."

I like this Despumate of Hurter. He has honor, because he stayed with his Bere Parochian entry even when a baby dragon hatched in the roster. Humate has stolen his crown and I will steal the bracelet.

Fencing has resumed out in the arena and this time Humate is obviously going for the jugular—no more nice-guy-playing-to-the-gallery nonsense. I watch him, trying to judge his physical speed. He is as nimble as a flea.

I say, "Good advice, except you may run into Humate of Alfet there, unless he gets kept in after school."

Despumate chuckles at that. "There's a silver on triangles-1 in Quintole, in Heliac."

"The Quintole games are very hard to get into. I think it's because they throw such great parties afterwards."

"Never been that far west."

I have been everywhere. "I'd be happy to show you the way, but nobody gets to compete in Quintole nowadays who doesn't sport at least two bronze crowns."

The crowd is booing. Humate has dispatched his opponent in two of the fastest fencing bouts I have ever seen. He has also confirmed his status as the boy they love to hate. But I am impressed. In spite of his youth, the master of Alfet is a psychic thunderstorm. Fully grown, he will be a worldbeater.

Despumate and I fly out together. The crowd cheers us. Referees hand us our scimitars, which are as impressive as everything else in this tourney—heavy and so convincing that I must resist the temptation to try the edge with my thumb. Officials spread out over the arena, because there must be a referee within range to maintain the illusion, plus an attendant linesman to move her out if the fight comes too close.

I warned Despumate about the blind spot that comes after porting, yet that is how I win my first point on him. After we have lunged and riposted a few times and I have learned a little about his reactions, I swing a mad slash and simultaneously port behind him, turning completely around. If I have fallen short, I am vulnerable and may even take a penalty for fouling . . . no, I have guessed his backward port exactly and he leaps on to my sword, scoring an illusory impalement of his own kidneys. Blood flashes brilliant red and the shock throws him down. The referee makes the call even before the crowd reacts.

Despumate hefts himself upright and looks at me ruefully. "You *told* me you were going to do that!"

"You expected me to put it in writing?"

He laughs. My sword grows heavier again as the blade reappears; we face off for the second of our best-of-three.

The second pass needs a lot more porting, in and out and round about. Despumate is good and now he knows all the tricks I do. I am marginally faster, but it takes time for that advantage to deliver a victory. By then thirst and hyperthermia have both of us reeling on our feet. I offer him my hand again, and we return to the broiler with cheers ringing about us.

Now it is time to start losing.

4

Humate is waiting for me with his arms folded and a defiant sneer masking his nervousness. A man who does not feel nervous before his first real javelin bout is simply not human. The crowd murmurs like some great sea beast, for this is when the games grow truly dangerous.

Water boys are waiting for me, and so are a couple of linesmen. Even they look weary and desiccated after so long in the arena; their white robes are dirty, their hair hangs limp. They watch understandingly as I gulp water. Then I catch their inquiring glances and nod agreement.

◆ ◆ ◆ **PORT** ◆ ◆ ◆

The three of us come forth on top of the bank almost simultaneously and then down at the pits together. Dried out as I am, I still need to relieve myself. Officially my escort is there to make sure I am not hassled by the crowds of fans who have taken the same advantage of the break in play. In reality my guards are more concerned about bribery and illegal restoratives.

The fresh air alone is restorative. Even at blueset, no equatorial paddy field is cool, but this one feels so after the furnace of the arena. I need to clear my head and think through my strategy for the showdown with Humate. I must lose, but not too obviously.

I have spent a third of my life working out the doom set upon me, hunting the Enemy. Less than a gnomon ago the suns rewarded my quest at last and I learned his name and station. But finding and punishing are very different things, and he seems invulnerable. Like any mortal, he might be struck down by a knife out of the Dark, but justice requires that a criminal be exposed and told his sentence. The Enemy stands above such proceedings, far out of my reach.

Fortunately, that same day I also learned of Humate of Alfet, only son of Hegemon Pelta of Pelagic and newly designated consort for royal Tendence of Carpus. Any pairing involving hegemonics is cause for lavish celebration, and House Pelagic is the richest in all Aureity. Festivities will last for days. The hundreds of guests will include the other six hegemons, matriarchs of the significant families, many lesser rulers, plus consorts and children and worthy relations. The entertainment will certainly include a golden tourney.

Golden games are invitational. The very best of the current contenders on the silver circuit are brought in, high-caste youngsters eager to compete for rich prizes and a chance to display their powers before senior royalty. The bidding can become ferocious, and it is normal for every contestant in a golden tourney to depart a sworn champion, holder of a much richer apanage than before, and betrothed or even already paired. Many a golden-games contender has begun by heaving balks of timber around and ended rollicking in a royal bed.

For me, this is a suns-given chance to catch the Enemy in a public gathering outside his own territory, an opportunity to denounce him before his peers. Dangerous, but possible, provided I can get myself invited. Mudar of Quoin was once the greatest but is now forgotten. Besides, an unnamed will not be hired as a gardener, let alone invited to compete. I must quickly build a new reputation as Quirt of Mundil, winning crowns unobtrusively, one here, one there, at tourneys spread over all Aureity. First a couple of bronzes to win entry to the silver circuit, and then two more crowns should do it. I believed I had enough time.

I also knew that the bride's family was insisting that Humate prove himself by winning a silver crown, for which he must first win a bronze. In retrospect, Bere Parochian was a logical choice for him, being the next of the regularly scheduled bronze tourneys. Befriending the boy can only boost my chances of being invited to his games. I had not expected Fuzzy-lip to let slip his true name, by deliberate accident, for his own warped adolescent reasons.

It is time to return to the arena, but the momentary pause has let me clear my head and confirm my new plan. For dear Tendence's sake, I long to make the boy the laughingstock of all Aureity, but then he will make sure there are no golden games to remind anyone of his degradation. The entire pairing may be called off, or at least postponed, and my campaign against the Enemy will be blocked.

Alas, my doom insists. Whatever my own feelings, I must throw the match.

"Ready, nobles."

◆ ◆ ◆ **PORT** ◆ ◆ ◆

From the top of the bank I see linesmen moving over the arena, psychically smoothing the sand as they float above it. The crowd is settling in, ready for the sport to renew. Down in the broiler, Humate is swilling water, attended by a water boy.

◆ ◆ ◆ **PORT** ◆ ◆ ◆

Tourney javelins are simple wooden poles with squared-off ends, but they move so fast that they can injure or kill contestants and even spectators. Every now and again some tourney will try to substitute illusory javelins, like the illusory swords, but the referees cannot project an illusion across the width of an arena, nor can they pass it from one to another fast enough. So we fighting nobles tough it out to prove our worth and the survivors win the most gifted women.

There is only one round in the finals. Hefting is allowed, porting is not. The loser is the first man to decide that he cannot dodge or deflect the six-foot wooden staff streaking at him and he'd better port away and live to play another day. Timing is very important.

Humate hands the waterskin back to the boy and scowls at my friendly smile. I am happy to see that he looks haggard.

"What's in this for you, noble Green?" he asks grumpily.

"That's a long story. What's in it for you, Humate of Alfet?"

He spears me with an even sulkier look. "Everything a man can ever hope for. A beautiful royal heir with the bloodlines to give me spectacular children. Her throne to share."

"She has promised you all this?"

"My mother has. And her mother has. My seed will raise her line to be a significant family. And *you* are getting in my way!" Now he tries to seem dangerous and manages to look like a spoiled child turning nasty. Yet he truly is dangerous. His guards must be some of his mother's champions. Even without orders from him, they may decide I have insulted House Pelagic. They are capable of breaking my neck from ten feet away and transporting my body miles out to sea.

A strident fanfare proclaims the start of the final round, our cue to proceed to the center.

We do not move.

"Are you threatening me or about to bribe me?" I ask.

The boy pouts. "Which will work better?"

"Bribery. We've got to give the crowd a show. Are you going to have golden games at your pairing?"

His eyes narrow. "Why?" he asks shiftily.

"Promise to invite me and I will let you win today."

"Go stuff your skin with dung."

"I swear I mean it."

"So do I."

I port out to the center, facing the royal box. Mother Blue blazes atop the bank, shining straight in my eyes, and sand stretches off in all directions as smooth as a calm pond. The air ripples in waves above it. Humate comes forth on my left—his choice, but it makes no difference. We bow to the ruler and her court.

I turn to my right, Humate to the left, so we are back-to-back. We have a few seconds yet.

"Promise to invite me and I'll throw the bout. I swear it. Last chance."

He whispers, "I promise."

"I'll aim high. When I shout, throw yourself flat."

Two javelins appear ahead of me, leaning against the wall, and I take off at a sprint. Humate will be doing the same in the opposite direction. He is faster than I am, but I know tricks he does not. Pounding through soft sand in cumbersome sandals, neither of us can make any real speed, and I do not go as fast as I could. I listen carefully to the crowd, an old-timers' trick. I can tell by the surging roar when Humate has reached his weapons, and I am still a long way short of mine. I do not even have to look around to know what he is doing. Armed, he turns and sees an old man floundering.

Porting is not allowed. I am physically stronger than Humate, so I could probably have beaten him to the edge of the arena had I tried. It would be over a longer distance that my wind would fail and show my age, but he may not realize that. The code of the arena is that neither player will throw until both are armed. A sudden bellow from the crowd warns me that he has started chasing after me, trying to get close enough for a fast shot.

The center of my back itches as if it can sense a spear coming straight for it. I fight the urge to look around or start zigzagging. When I am almost there, I dare to slow down even more—playing tricks again, dangerous tricks.

A sudden explosion of boos from the crowd warns me that he is about to throw before I am ready. It is loud enough to raise a flock of day bats from the roof of the royal box. Fortunately I am now within hefting range. I snatch the two poles into my hands and jump aside, turning as I do so. I have cut it very fine. Humate's javelin streaks in along my tracks and cracks into the wall at chest height, spattering me with chips. My gamble has paid off.

He did try to kill me, though. That's worth remembering.

If you don't believe a blunt wooden pole can penetrate baked bricks, you should remember that a man with a hefting range of twelve feet is effectively throwing with a twelve-foot arm. We can move those javelins almost too fast to see and we don't miss.

The booing has turned to cheers that I have survived.

The pole stops thrumming and I back toward it, carefully watching Humate, who has started to run forward again. I have two javelins, he has one. It takes most of my hefting strength to get his first throw out of the wall, but I do so, and now I have three spears. He stops, realizing that, if he throws again, his second javelin will also hit the wall and be within my reach. He starts to back away. Javelins are dangerous even in training, and Humate may never have practiced enough to learn the finer points of play.

I begin walking forward, herding him. He angles to my left. I turn enough to keep heading straight for him. In a restricted space I must eventually close with him, and the crowd can watch our progress by the tracks we leave in the smoothed sand. He twists and veers, but the distance between us closes relentlessly. He has two options. He can risk everything on a throw, or he can wait until I am within hefting range and try to snatch one or more of my javelins out of my grip.

Suddenly he runs forward, raising his javelin for a throw. I must decide if he is serious or if this is a feint to get close enough to snatch one of mine. As his arm goes back, I heft my three javelins ten feet behind me and sprint forward unarmed—and also barefoot. The sand is scorching, but my unexpected speed throws him off balance. When we are ten feet apart he tries to throw and I snatch his weapon out of his hand. Before he thinks to trip me up or snatch it back, I spin around and sprint back to my sandals. I scoop up my other three spears and turn around to meet his charge, but he is not charging, which was his best move after being caught by that old trick. He is sucking his throwing hand as if I blistered it or he took a sliver.

Now I have all four and Humate is disarmed. He looks close to tears, perhaps trying to imagine slinking home to Mascle to confess to Mommy that he has lost in a *bronze* tourney. To a hegemonic, Bere Parochian is slumming.

The crowd is screaming, "Green! Green! Green! . . ."

I resume my advance with two javelins in each hand. Humate backs up. His only hope now is to dodge my throws and retrieve the javelins, so he needs to be near the wall. I give him room, staying out of hefting range.

Eventually he stops at bay, folds his arms, and glares at me. This is the most horrible moment in any tourney, because I cannot miss at that range and if he blunders I will kill him. An experienced duelist would be preparing to concede by porting out the instant I throw, but Humate may not realize that he is beaten.

I raise both arms overhead to warn him what I am about to do. The arena is hushed. Then I heft all four javelins in a single spread and at the same time yell *"Ayee!"* as a man may when he makes a great physical effort. Humate cannot dodge four javelins, but I do not throw them nearly as hard as I could, and I already told him how to respond. If he hurls himself flat so they all pass over him and strike the wall, he will be able to recover at least one before I can get there, and with even one he can keep me away from the other three.

Instead, he panics. The poles hit the wall: *crack! crack! crack! crack!*

I am alone in the arena. I have won in spite of myself.

It is over. The cheering shakes the suns, as they say in Baric, but I have failed and my reaction is a desperate weariness and sadness. Mother Blue is setting, ending third watch. The world is taking on the gentler, subtler colors of Our Father White. I turn and trudge toward the royal box, while the arena roars for me, the audience on its feet, delirious. I don't suppose Humate cares what mere ordinaries think of him, but if he had not let slip his name he would have been the favorite, the boy wonder, and the mob would be booing me, the old spoiler. Crowds are strange beasts.

I step up on the edge of the platform below the box. A porter appears and offers me a waterskin, which I accept gratefully. Despumate and the other semifinalist come forth alongside me, and finally a grim-faced Humate. I offer him a hand, which he spurns.

We bow to the royal box above us.

We wait. There is some delay, but that is normal. I am cooked through.

"*Psst!* Noble Green?"

I turn to find Scuppaug standing on the sand at my back. He should not be there and his look of fright shows that he knows it. I step down beside him.

"Here!" He offers me something unseen. "Royal Alkin sends this."

I turn his hand over and see the gleam of emeralds between his fingers. It is the bracelet I gave her. I am enraged. "Have they been threatening her?"

The boy looks startled. "Oh, no . . . They just came to ask her what your real name is."

But Alkin has understood better than Scuppaug that she is being warned off by the enraged Pelagians. "Tell her to keep it with my thanks. I shall not trouble her further."

"But . . ." He does not understand. I doubt he ever will.

"You will see the gracious lady safely home?"

"Of course."

There is a glint in his eye. His chin is higher than before.

"And your own affairs prosper?"

He almost nods his head off. "Quite well, thank you for asking, noble Green."

"An offer *already?*"

"Two! Well, so far they just want to look over my pedigree, but royal Alkin says that there will certainly be offers." Under the circumstances, it is a fair attempt at modesty.

"That is incredible! On your first outing? Wonderful news! I am enormously impressed, knightly Scuppaug." I give him a courtly bow. He deserves it. Someone in the crowd has an eye for bargains.

They noted his hefting and they don't know he can't port pee into a bucket. I cannot resist adding, because I know who is listening, "And against a hegemonic, too!"

Scuppaug shoots a nervous glance past me, suddenly grins, and disappears. I step up on the platform and beam at Humate's glower.

"Just think what they would be offering if he'd won!" I remark.

"Not very likely!" He speaks through clenched teeth. "Or wise."

A herald comes forth before me. "Do you wish to reveal your name now, noble Green?"

I shake my head. I have no name.

The herald steps aside. Ruler Scrim of Bere Parochian comes forth in majesty at the wall side of the platform with her portly, silver-bearded consort. We four bow again.

The consort advances to the center, the herald proclaims the name of the semifinalist who lost to Humate, and he goes forward to be awarded a bronze ring and a few gracious words from the noblest. When he returns, Despumate of Hurter is summoned and repeats the process. Then royal Humate receives the bronze bracelet. He seems to reply civilly to the old man's remarks, although I cannot hear what is said.

I have been through this ceremony many times and can take no joy from it anymore. I will feel better after I have eaten and rested, but at the moment the Dark grips my soul. I have deprived young men of honors that would mean far more to them than to me. I cannot even take pride in defeating a hegemonic, because he is only a boy and I tried not to. And I have not hurt the Enemy at all yet, not directly. Instead I may have warned him that I have tracked him down at last.

"Noble Green."

I approach and kneel so the consort can set the bronze circlet on my brow. I rise, he shakes my hand. His face is spotted and pouched, cheeks sunken where he has lost teeth, eyes framed in wrinkles and clouded by age, but his smile seems warm and genuine.

"A very memorable day, noble Green. Or should I say . . ." he drops his voice to a whisper, *"Highborn Mudar of Quoin?"*

The efficient Sudamina of Monticle has been at work.

"Do so in public, noblest, and you seal my death warrant."

He nods without outrage or argument. "Are you already in danger?"

"I may be." I am sure of it. The moment I leave the arena.

"The dragon's guards are being watched." He smiles again, but grimly. "We disapprove of bully-boys at our games. Of course we cannot hold them here if they decide to leave, so you should avoid places you normally frequent. We shall understand if you prefer to skip the reception. Highborn Mudar, we thank you heartily for making our tourney so memorable today; you have our leave to withdraw at any time."

"You are most gracious, noblest." I bow to him and then to his splendid mistress in the background.

◆ ◆ ◆ **PORT** ◆ ◆ ◆

TRICKERY AT QUINTOLE

1

I come forth in the entrance hall at Cupule, a cavern of white and green marble overlooking the park. The door ward inspects arrivals from behind a stone trellis, but the sight of my bronze coronet brings her hurrying out with shining eyes.

She bows. "Noble Quirt of Mundil!"

Alkin's staff will be happy that their employer's stable has another winner. I consider that the lady herself owes me a meal.

"Royal Alkin and knightly Scuppaug will follow before whiteset. I must go, but I need a snack to take with me. I could eat a herd on the hoof! Ask Fortilage to bring it right to my room."

She frowns at that, convinced that a noble should never eat without the aid of at least five servants. I leave before she can speak.

◆ ◆ ◆ **PORT** ◆ ◆ ◆

Up in my room, I toss the crown on the bed, drop my tabard,

◆ ◆ ◆ **PORT** ◆ ◆ ◆

and come forth miles out to sea, thirty feet above the swell. I plunge very deep into sensually warm water, down to near-darkness. Normally I would linger and enjoy a long swim, but this evening I may have dragons on my trail. House Pelagic is not known for scruples and Cupule is the logical place to start looking for me.

✦ ✦ ✦ PORT ✦ ✦ ✦

I can't leave all the ocean behind. I come forth wet. As I towel myself, I reflect that my promising second career in the arena has ended already. After today, Quirt of Mundil is not going to be included on royal Humate's invitation list to anything except his own funeral. Hegemon Pelta of Pelagic may throw a royal tantrum and send a squad of assassins after me. Humate may. The Enemy himself may.

The only brightness in this murky scene is that I may have so shamed the brat that the pairing may be called off and Tendence assigned a worthier consort—not that I can imagine any man ever being worthy of her.

I throw away the towel and reach for the tunic laid out on the bed. Fortilage comes forth holding a hamper, gasps with dismay, and disappears. I pull on the tunic. With perfect timing he taps on the door. I tell him to enter.

"I should not have presumed so, noble Quirt of Mundil." Fortilage is elderly and wears the simple loincloth of an ordinary, but he is tall and an exceptionally talented porter. Even if he is not concealing a fourbear or two of his own, there is certainly some noble blood in his veins. Is that a wistful look in his eye as he glances at the crown lying on my bed?

"Why not? You did as I asked. I didn't scream!"

"Will there be anything else, noble?"

"Yes. Scuppaug will be bringing the lady back. Perhaps she might require . . . a parasol, maybe? You could, um, intercept them?"

He releases a hint of a smile. "In such circumstances she has often appreciated being advised of messages left here during her absence. Do you know by what route they will be coming, noble?"

I tell him how I led Scuppaug to Bere Parochian. He ports out and I am confident that Alkin will be returned safely, not marooned somewhere en route.

My tunic is simple brown. I add ankle boots and bronze crown, but no sword, no signet, no caste mark. From under the mat, where I hid it before dressing for the arena, I retrieve the plaque that has been my companion and guide for so much of my life. I look yet again at the face of the Enemy. I felt close to him this morning, but since then he has gained on me. No matter; I hang his likeness around my neck. The hunt will continue until one of us dies.

A dozen or so small islands adorn the mouth of the bay like teeth. Ranging from mere rocks to meadow-size, they must lack water, because no one seems to live on them. Nevertheless, some are wooded and offer private hollows or sandy beaches. I explored them yesterday, having nothing better to do, and discovered enough ugly litter to know that they do not lack for visitors. Who comes there? Smugglers? Pirates? Children in boats? Young noblemen and their lovers?

◆ ◆ ◆ **PORT** ◆ ◆ ◆

I choose a tiny beach so sheltered by bushes that I can sit on the sand and look at nothing except ocean and a few sails far away. The evening is calm and perfect, the silken sea moving in a long, soothing swell, slapping the rocks like the tail of some great, contented dog. My hamper contains enough food to satisfy half of Glyptic. I pour myself a glass of wine. I am weary and battered, but there is still ample time before whiteset for me to eat and then travel to Osseter. My shadow stretches out on the sand before me and raises a glass in response to my own offer of a toast. But then another, longer, shadow appears beside it.

"Don't let me disturb your celebration, noble Quirt."

Humate has changed into Pelagian costume of baggy trousers and ornate slippers. In his case both are jeweled and heavily embroidered with gold thread. His hair hangs loose to his shoulders and his chest is bare. Glittering with wealth, he stands over me, smirking. I tip my wine into one of his slippers. He jumps back with an angry shout and almost entangles his sword in a bush.

My emotions must be flaming in every shade of fury, amazement, and even fear. "I don't recall inviting you to join me. How did you get here?"

I mean, how has he managed to gatecrash my party? My manager's name was no secret, so any noble or porter who has visited Cupule in the past could have been bribed or forced to bring him to the apanage. Or has Alkin betrayed me? I never mentioned House Pelagic to her before this afternoon. I never told her the name of the Enemy.

"Called at the house. You weren't there. Asked where you'd gone. They pointed, and I came line-of-sight." Humate sits down between me and the scenery and crosses his legs; he smirks, his favorite mode of communication.

He's lying. Nobody in the world knew where I went when I left my room, not even the servants.

I spit out a *bycocket* pit, very close to his knee.

He switches his face from Smirk to Earnest Merit. "I came to warn you, noble, that some of my watchdogs are seriously annoyed by what you did today. Now they've learned your name, they're talking about coming to teach you a lesson."

They have not learned my real name, though.

"I cannot possibly be in more danger from them than I am right now, royal Humate. Nobody knows I am here with you. You can twist my head off like a cork if you wish to. If you want me dead, then kill me." I am recalling my room at Cupule, ready to port out instantly if he makes a threatening move, although I know I may not react in time. "I tried to give you the crown and you turned it down. How much are you offering for it now?"

Hope flashes in his big dark eyes. "How much do you want? See this sword hilt? These are real rubies and—" He realizes I am mocking him.

"And you would take it home and tell your mommy you won it

fair and square? Tut, tut, tut! Of course you'd have to bribe your guards to keep their mouths shut, and the whole games circuit of Aureity is still holding its sides, laughing about the hegemon's son beaten in a bronze tourney."

"You were using trickery! In an honest test of strength you would not do so well." His eyes narrow as he puts the threat into words.

"You will do better when you're older. You should have listened when I offered to let you win."

"And trusted you? For all I knew, you were an assassin sent to kill me. I am the son of the most powerful woman in Aureity, re- member. I have enemies."

"Not surprising."

He ignores that. He is trying to be nice to me, as well as he knows how. "You really want to compete at my golden games?"

I cannot possibly trust any promise he makes now.

"No."

"Then what? Who are you, really? And what do you want?"

"I'm an admirer of the fair Tendence of Carpus." Sometimes the truth is so unlikely it will deceive better than any lie. "I hate to see her being shackled to an immature brat. It's immoral and ob- scene."

Incredulous, Humate says, "And you think you can stop us?"

"I can stop you, boy. I can enter every tourney you do and keep you from winning anything at all. You'll never even get to the silver circuit. Next time I'll ask the marshal to pair us up in the first round and then I'll trick you out of the hefting contest."

"That's impossible!" His voice is growing squeaky.

I hold firm to my image of Cupule. "Watch me."

"You are a brave man to defy House Pelagic."

"It is time somebody taught you manners." I bite into a juicy *by-cocket*, certain that Humate must be as hungry as I am. Why has he come in person? Is he trying to buy me off or scare me off, or just waste time until his goons get here to dispose of the pest? Whoever brought him to Cupule may have gone back to fetch another man, and so on—two, four, eight. . . . Or he may bring a woman, and then Humate will pin me so she can impair me, turning me into a slavering imbecile, unable to speak, or feed, or clean myself. But why bother involving a woman when he can just kill me himself and take the bronze crown? Here, where there are no witnesses! I ought to leave.

I want to know how he found me.

"Why fight us when you can join us?" he asks. "My mother is always willing to swear in good champions. There could be good opportunities for advancement in Mascle these days. I have a cousin who is bored with her current consort. She's a royal, of course."

"Pimping? That's good. You're trash in the arena, but pimping suits you."

Humate has probably never been spoken to like that in his entire life. He pales, but keeps control. "I was joking! What takes your fancy? Courtier? Commissioner of Taxes? Warrior? Superintendent of Customs? I am offering you status and enormous wealth."

I throw the *bycocket* pit at him. It bounces off midair halfway between us and I swat it away.

He tries again. "Not wealth? Women, then? Of course the breeders will be anxious to use your remarkable bloodlines, but that can be arranged on the side. I can get you free choice—approval for any pairing you fancy."

"Suns! You're disgusting!" Fury is a dangerous luxury that I rarely permit myself. "Have you no shame? No honor at all, that you come here to bribe and threaten me?"

"What does a common porter know about honor?"

"More than you do, obviously."

He gasps a few times and tries again. "How much just to stay out of my way until after women-5?"

"Why women-5? What is special about that day?"

He bites his lip. "Or thereabouts. There's nothing special about that day. Let's say dogs-3, then. It's just that I have better things to do than strut around in a fire pit waving my pecker like a rutting ungulate. You may enjoy that; I find it childish. I just want to get it over with, see? Most men have more sense than to cross a man of my standing. You evidently don't. You are stupid, old man, stupid! If I ever set eyes on you again, I'll see to it that you disappear and never return."

"Oh, do grow up, sonny!" The farthest portage I can recall at the moment is Two Peak Hill. I take a firm grip on my hamper . . .

* * * PORT * * *

2

Osseter is a small settlement in the hill country of northern Seric, near the capital city of Riggish. The ordinaries grow rice and yams on the flats, their children herd cattle on higher ground, and most of them will never leave the valley in their lifetimes, any more than their parents ever have. The palace by the river is old but well built, a fading but still gracious matron.

When I was unnamed, I was rendered landless as well as nameless. Princely Emodin of Osseter and I had become friends when we were fire-eating youngsters on the silver circuit. He was talented enough to hold off accepting offers until he got the chance to compete in a hegemonic tourney, where the really big money is, but in the meantime he went home to visit his parents and caught the eye of his own ruler's younger sister. As her consort he has little chance to visit his original apanage and no need for the income. When we fled from Alazarin, he let us move in and live there as if it were our own. However long the Enemy may have looked for us, he never found us at Osseter.

Long-distance porting requires extreme concentration. My journey from Cupule takes longer than I expected, probably because I have too many things on my mind and can't recall all the best portages. Just before nightfall, when the shadows are long, I come forth in the Court of Birds. The aviaries have fallen silent, there is no breeze to stir the silver bells on the trees, but a boy in a corner plays softly on a lyre. He does not notice me.

Neither does Izard of Inmew, who sits cross-legged on the edge of a fishpond, seemingly intent on studying the play of twilight on golden scales, although he sees very little now. Age rests heavy on him—hair silver, back bowed, teeth failing, and the once-thick muscles are wasted. The sorrows he has known would fill many lifetimes. Very soon now he will go off to bed, for he lives in the ways of his ancestors, and for them whiteset was always bedtime.

My steps on gravel warn of my approach. I kneel beside him, doubling over until my head touches his thigh. "Your blessing, noblest Grandfather."

"Highborn Mudar! I was not informed that you had come. . . . Why were you not properly proclaimed? Ah! And what is this, mm?" His fingers have found the bronze crown. "Is it blossoms-1 already? I had lost track. . . . Well done!" He chuckles. "Did you have any trouble, mm?"

The lyre player rises and tactfully slips away.

"Indeed I did have trouble! I ran into a hegemonic—guess who?" I summarize the events of the day, needing few words, for the old man's wits are as sharp as ever.

"Was this wise?" he murmurs at the end. "Few men defeat hegemonics. You will have started tongues flapping." He has gone right to the heart of the matter, as always.

"Grandfather, it was stupid. The court had learned my true name by the end of the tourney. I did try to throw the match to that accursed boy."

"What is the boy guilty of that he should be accursed?"

"Nothing except youth itself. Forgive me."

He sighs. "We thought we had more time."

"We did have more time! Obviously things have been brought forward. It sounds as if the festivities will begin on women-5, less than sixty days from now."

"Is that the Enemy's doing, do you think? Has he learned of

you?" Izard's way of providing wisdom has always been to ask the questions and make me work out the answers for myself.

"I don't think so. His reaction would be a fast assassination."

"Then why was the date changed?"

"Most likely Hegemon Pelta is impatient to stamp on Hegemon Balata's toes. Or else royal Tendence herself ran out of delaying tactics and gave in. She is reputed to be against the match." I know she is, but a man without name, land, or honor must not insult a noblewoman by even thinking about her, let alone mentioning love.

"Women-5 does not give you much time to prepare."

"I doubt if I have even that long."

I should not have said that. Izard picks up on it instantly.

"What do you mean, dear one? Even if you do not get invited, the pairing celebrations are still your best chance to strike at the Enemy, aren't they?"

"Of course, noblest." But I was thinking of Tendence, not my doom. Royal pairings are arranged by treaty, and the Formene treaty must be signed before Hegemon Balata finds out about it. The moment Humate has proved his manhood by winning a silver crown, Tendence will have run out of excuses; then signatures and seals will be applied to fine paper. Then the happy couple may be bundled into bed; that is not the present plan, but plans can be changed. Many families prefer to delay public celebration until the woman is visibly with child.

"Grandfather, the plan is dead. The Enemy will learn of me long before then. Humate would rather just forget me, but his guards will report what happened today at Bere Parochian. The whole games circuit will have the news within days. I need a whole new plan."

Silence. A night singer makes a few preliminary cheeps in one of the cages.

"Describe this Pelagic stripling."

"Immature, brash, immensely powerful already, arrogant, arrogant, and also arrogant. He has older sisters but no brothers."

"Honorable?"

"He would say so, but when crossed, he sees his wishes as his rights."

The old man sighs. "Always a fault of the powerful. I must sleep on this, dear one. Sometimes even the Dark can provide enlightenment."

Stars are emerging. It is an honorable man's bedtime.

"Of course. I am remiss. How is noblest Hyla?"

"Good," he mutters. "Quite good these last few days. Content."

Content is good, but quite good means not good.

"I will pay my respects if she is awake and see her tomorrow if she is not. Meanwhile, here is something else to sleep on, noblest Grandfather. I met another client of royal Alkin, a cub of six quarterings. He ports at that level, but his hefting is up around nine or ten. Have you ever heard of that?"

"Of course psychic powers vary; you know that! I once met a man who could project illusions, like a woman. The breeders fought over him."

"Who won?" I sense from his tone that there is another verse to this song.

Izard chuckles. "House Seric, I think. But he turned out to be sterile."

I laugh as expected. "Have you ever heard of a man able to port to a *person*, instead of a *place?*"

He turns his milky eyes on me. "My dear boy! You are serious?"

"The boy Humate came to me on an island I had picked at random. He could not have seen me from anywhere. He found *me*, not the place."

Izard looks away. He looks at nothing, or looks at the Dark that cursed his life. "This is impossible. Are you *sure?*"

"Quite certain. I didn't think it was possible, either. He lied about it, so I thought it must be a trick. But it is possible, because I just did it myself! I ported here to *you*, noblest Grandfather, not to the house. My range for this is very short, about a mile. I could not recall you clearly until I reached the bridge, but then I came right to you. I expect that's why I never noticed before that I had this ability—and also because everyone always told me it was useless to try. Now I know better, so I can do it."

There is a pause. "I cannot. I am trying. No, I cannot recall a person."

"The light is very poor, but I assure you that Humate can and I can!"

Izard sighs deeply. There is just enough light in the courtyard to show the glint of tears on his cheeks. "And the Enemy can too!" he whispers, speaking to shadows and memories, not to me. "The suns be thanked! After so long! I never doubted, never. That this boy has this ability makes sense of it all!"

Humate has unwittingly solved an ancient mystery for us.

Spawn of an evil house I called him and so he is.

And I am another.

It is time for the household to gather and pray for safe passage through the coming Dark, but an unnamed man may not participate. I go to my room to meditate on the events of the day.

Eager to try out my newfound skill of porting to persons, as soon as the singing ends I make an effort to recall princely Vert of Ramist, the only champion my mother ever acquired. I can visualize him only very vaguely, because there is so little light wherever he is. All I can tell is that it is indeed him, and he is standing still, oddly off-balance and hunched over. Porting when you cannot see the target area is obviously dangerous, but I can guess from his posture where he is. I aim to come forth behind him, not in front.

As I expected, he is on the west terrace, leaning on the balustrade to admire the fading twilight. Vert wears a larger tunic than once he did; his scalp is pink and ringed with silver. Always cautious and meticulous, he is gradually becoming fussy and indecisive, but he is still a pillar of integrity and wisdom. For her own reasons Mother Blue never blessed his mistress with children, so he has been the father I never had.

His only weakness, if it can be called that, is a love of extremely large and shaggy hounds. His kennels never contain less than a dozen of them, and he goes nowhere without at least one in attendance. In this case his escort is Fidel, sprawled sleepily at his feet. I port in so close that I tread on Fidel's tail. He responds with predictable loud outrage and a fair attempt to take my leg off. I pin his jaws before they can close and heft myself out of range until he can recognize my scent and voice. I kneel and offer a hug in return for forgiveness and a slobbery face wash.

Then I rise and hug Vert, wiping off the last of Fidel's saliva in the process. Fidel rears up and licks the other side of my neck. Vert and I share the embrace with him. We hear laughter approaching.

"What under the suns do you three think you are doing?" demands Clamant, as she hurries out to join us. "I thought wild beasts had attacked."

I hug her also, although less boisterously. Princely Clamant of Coniine is Vert's mistress, and if he was a stand-in for the father I never knew, Clamant was much more my mother than my real mother ever managed to be. She is stooped now and her eyes are fringed with wrinkles, although none of that shows in public.

Together they offer me welcome and congratulations on my win at Bere Parochian, news which Izard has passed on. I lean against the balustrade and repeat the story of my disastrous day, telling how Humate of Alfet was delivered into my hands and I wasted the opportunity to befriend him.

"Did you truly want to do that, Mudar?" Clamant asks softly. "I know you hoped to win a place in his golden games, but when you left here you were talking about earning a reputation as a top duelist. In that case, some flunky would have drawn up a list of qualified contestants and included you. Now you say you were going to befriend the boy. If you mean that he would then have invited you personally, and you would have ruined his celebration by attacking the Enemy, wouldn't that be a betrayal of trust and hospitality?"

"Put that way, I suppose the answer is yes."

"Put what way is the answer no?" Vert asks dryly.

"I am doomed to destroy a man, royal. I cannot do it nicely. It doesn't matter anymore. Now that he knows my interest, never in a million pentads will Humate of Alfet let me near his golden games. Very likely he will cancel them altogether."

Clamant, typically feminine, asks, "So now that you've met Humate, what sort of person is he?"

"Spoiled rotten."

"Not a suitable consort for royal Tendence of Carpus?"

I have never mentioned my feelings for Tendence to anyone, but I do not try to keep my thoughts from Clamant—I just finished embracing her, after all. And she is still so close that I barely need to put my reply into words. Perhaps she can even view lurid images of my hands crushing Humate's neck to paste.

"He is also reckless," I say. "He let slip a very surprising secret."

I tell them how Humate can port to a person and how I find I can do it too. They marvel. Vert tries to perform this miracle but without success. Being the man he is, he is instantly worried about its implications for Hyla's security.

"You say your limit is about one mile. How far did the boy port to you?"

"More than that. Distances are hard to estimate over water, but I was at least twice that far from the house. For all I know, he came directly from Bere Parochian, more than two hundred miles."

Clamant is nodding. "He may be naturally stronger, or practice may have increased his range."

"Does practice really increase our ranges?" I ask. "We all assume so, but as soon as a boy finds he can move himself even a few feet, he is porting all day long. He grows stronger, but he is also maturing. Practice may not make any difference."

"Practice turns fluff into beards," Vert reminds me. "Keep trying anyway. Someday you may find this new skill very useful."

Clamant says, "The Enemy will kill Hyla if he ever finds her. We've always known that. That's why we left Alazarin. If he can port directly to her without knowing her exact location, then her danger is greater than we ever realized."

"Can I see Hyla?"

"She has been restless of late," Clamant warns. "But she will certainly be awake, so let us go in and see." The Dark rules the world and decent people should be indoors.

We find candles and go upstairs. Vert remains behind, because Hyla is a problem for women to handle and sometimes, although not always, her son. Hyla sleeps during the day, never in the Dark. She has good times, bad times, and very bad times.

One of her attendant ordinaries is sorting laundry in the anteroom. I smile at her, ashamed that I cannot recall her name although I have met her before. She smiles back in the way many ordinary girls return the smiles of noblemen. I cannot claim that I have never succumbed to temptation, but I believe I do better than most.

Even before we reach the door to my mother's chamber, I feel her thoughts. I have never heard her voice. She has not spoken a word since the Enemy came, but she constantly conveys her thoughts like a sower scattering seed.

I told you not to climb so high, dear. It was your knee last week. Now it's your elbow. I don't know how we're ever going to rear you, my fierce little cub.

Clamant puts a finger to her lips and peers inside. She beckons me to look also. My mother is kneeling on her favorite cushion, addressing the child playing with blocks on the floor, who is me, less than a pentad old. I step aside with a shrug, unwilling to intrude on her fantasies as long as she seems happy. But Clamant goes in.

"Noblest, I have brought a visitor to see you."

You are growing so fast, Quirt. You will be looking down at me soon.

When I was born, my grandfather named me Mudar, which was his right as regent, and he deeded me the apanage of Quoin. When I was stripped of my birth name, I chose the name of Hyla's twin brother, who died in the coughing fever, but somehow my poor deranged mother knows now who Quirt is.

"Quirt is here to see you, noblest Hyla."

I don't like those frescoes. I want them painted over at once.

My child self has disappeared. My mother is studying a wall that should not be in her room at all, but her attention is away from the door. I tiptoe in and kneel down. She seems absurdly small to have produced a hulk like me, but partly that is because most noblewomen project themselves as taller than they really are. Hyla lives in a world of visible fantasies, but is quite unaware of her own appearance. Her hair is white, although she has not completed her tenth pentad, yet her face is completely unlined. Her attendants dress her in ordinaries' cotton saris.

"Quirt won another crown in the games today," Clamant says hopefully. "He brought it to show you."

It is a cozy enough room, lit by many lamps, yet strangely impersonal. No, it is not "impersonal." It is "patchwork." Too many people live in it. One day Hyla is a child and wants bright colors and pictures on the walls. Next day she prowls the house collecting figurines or dark draperies or cut flowers. And the day after that she may be projecting another room altogether.

"The suns bless you, noblest Mother." I take off the detestable bronze crown. "See what I won today? I brought it as a present for you."

She turns her face to the window. *They say the new fruits are plumping up nicely. I blame all that rain we had.*

"Your blessing on your son, Mother?"

The blossoms are quite rotted. She is shedding age and her dress is becoming richer and more elaborate. This is a bad sign. *Quite rotted. Quite. Quite? Quick?*

Clamant takes her hand and pats it. "Quirt! Quirt is here. See, Quirt brought a crown to show you. He's over here, noblest."

Hyla glances in my direction but not at me. She looks away quickly. *We must go home. The noblest's palace is very fine, but I have been away too long. How graceful the swans are!*

Now she is barely more than a child—and I have been repeatedly assured that she really was as beautiful as that when she visited

Cuneal—but it will be at least a day before I can even hope to be recognized. Thinking her attention is entirely on her fantasies, I rise to my feet. It is a mistake. I am too big. Hyla looks around and utters a choking, gurgling noise, an attempt to scream.

The room darkens. The Enemy comes forth in the shadows. He is smiling, unsheathing his sword. He is tall, he is indistinct, rippling like a reflection in water, but he is smiling. Lethargy melts every muscle in my body. A sickly odor fills my nostrils. Very few women can project an illusion in more than vision. Even sound is rare, but Hyla's nightmare comes with sensation and pain and always that smell. He strides forward, pointing the sword at her face. She struggles to cry out and produces only the gurgles and whimpers of an animal dying in a trap.

Clamant is trying to comfort her and two of her attendants have come to help, but once the nightmare has begun it has to run its course. Anything I do or say will only make it worse.

♦ ♦ ♦ PORT ♦ ♦ ♦

In my room, I throw myself on my bed. I weep and pound the mattress with my fists. I never needed the hegemon's doom. I had already laid the same doom upon myself.

For two pentads I have hunted him, the man who wears the face of Hyla's nightmare. Half a gnomon ago I learned his name and house. Last triangles-5 I saw him in the flesh for the first time. He is older and dissipated now, his grossly florid complexion suggesting that he may not have very long to live, but I know him.

I must not let him escape me by dying first.

We break our fast at bluerise, four people cross-legged in a hall that would hold many dozens, while a dozen servants come and go, silently placing dishes and baskets within our reach. Izard chooses to discuss predators that have been seen on the upper slopes, presenting a danger to herders. Vert promises to organize a hunt. Clamant looks weary, as if she has been awake all night dealing with

Hyla. When the meal is finished we withdraw to a secluded terrace overlooking the mill dam, and only then is it proper to talk business.

Izard presides. As usual he asks questions. "Last night you said you need a new plan. Have you found one?"

I say, "No, noblest, I have not." I have, of course, but it will be certain suicide for me and I would prefer to live on and enjoy my success if there is a better way.

Clamant says nothing, although she undoubtedly detects my lie.

"But now," I continue, "now that we know about the Enemy's power to port to a person instead of a place, our first concern must be to safeguard Hyla. She is the only witness capable of testifying against him." In a sense, Hyla has been testifying against him all my life. A court would view her illusions and accept them as evidence. "He only needs to get near and he will be able to recall her."

"He has had long enough to try!" Izard says.

"But if he hears that I have reappeared on the tourney circuit, he will begin looking again."

From the way he bares his long, old-man's teeth, the sly rogue has clearly thought of something I have not. "And you have that same ability. He may use it to strike at Hyla, but you can use it against him! Suppose, dear one, that he learns you have identified him and plan to denounce him? What then?"

"He will come . . . He will go looking for me? For her? To Alazarin? He will have to start there."

Izard nods. "Have you ever seen a better ambush site than Cape Bastel?"

I glance at the others. Clamant is being noncommittal. She will never engage in such plotting, insisting that her duty is simply to serve her liege, noblest Hyla. She swore allegiance long ago, expecting to sparkle as first gentlewoman in a glittering court, receiving instead a lifetime's drudgery as nursemaid to a lunatic. Vert never liked the idea of my sneaking into the pairing celebration as Quirt of Mundil. His stony expression suggests that he likes the new plan no better. For once he speaks up to oppose Izard.

"Come, noblest! You think the Enemy will be deceived? If he looked for her on Alazarin before, then he knows she was removed to safety. If he didn't, why should he start now? The man is vile, but he is not a fool."

Izard does not like opposition. His craggy jaw snaps shut. "That will depend how well we set our trap. Bait must both smell tasty and hide the hook. Has anyone a better plan?"

None of us has. We start planning an ambush at Cape Bastel.

3

The long porting westward to Heliac is a sentimental journey for me. A cub launching his career traditionally begins at games far from home, so his friends will not hear about it and turn up to watch. Long ago I made my silver debut in the triangles-1 tourney at Quintole. But today, dogs-1, my first destination must be Formene. I do not leave Osseter until whiterise, for otherwise I will overtake the suns and run out of light to recall by. It is not long after bluerise when I arrive at Formene.

The entrance to the palace is the Court of Joyful Blossom—Heliacs are so fond of fancy names that they often seem to be speaking in code. They also like flowers, movable architecture, and bizarrely contorted thorny trees in pots, so that nowhere stays the same for long and even residents can have trouble porting around the complex. Joyful Blossom is divided into a maze of small cells. The one I know is seven-sided, floored with green sand, enclosed by walls of purple wicker, and about the size of a modest bedroom. In a gnomon or so it will no longer exist, and I shall have to enter by applying at a public gateway. Even now, I know I am being observed and inspected.

Here in the Court of Joyful Blossom, twelve days ago, I set eyes on the Enemy for the first and only time in my life. He came forth with armed champions all around him and was soon ported out again, but I saw him. He did not see me.

Lacking caste mark or sword, I am taken for a porter and made to wait awhile. It would probably be much longer, were this not a high-rated entrance that mere porters are not supposed to know. Eventually a slim young champion comes and looks down his nose at me as an invitation to grovel. His silken gown is thickly encrusted with heraldic embroidery and the naked sword at his thigh flashes blue and white in the sunlight. His hair is a lacquered sculpture ornamented with combs, ribbons, and bright paper decorations. Heliac nobles take great offense if you laugh at their coiffeurs and I find it almost impossible not to.

Without as much as a nod, I unroll and display a scroll bearing a single line of verse, incomprehensible words in a beautiful hand. My good friend royal Magnes of Scantling gave me this artistic passport and it works miracles. The flunky drops to his knees and touches his forehead to the ground at my toes—without getting sand in his hair. I bid him rise, we exchange fatuous compliments, and he transports me to a small, secluded court. On five out of six sides it is enclosed by dense hedge, but the sixth is the wall of a pavilion. The ground is patterned in many-colored sand to form a landscape picture of water and boats, which I know will be swept away the moment I leave, to be redone in another image, a labor of days. Heliacs are obsessively secretive.

My guide slides open the oiled-silk doors of the pavilion and bows me in. Then he vanishes, leaving me in a single room furnished with mats, a low table, and several angular, sharp sculptures. Only the garden side is open, the other three being translucent, without doors or windows. The refreshments on the table must have been delivered only instants before I arrived, because the wine flagon is still cool to the touch and the pastries are steaming.

Two people come forth outside. One is Magnes, a tourney crony from my youth, a bland, easygoing man of deceptively menacing eye and fiercely hooked nose. He is as large as I am, if you count the spreading belly imposed upon him by too much palace food. Although he is only my age, Magnes is losing his hair, so the absurd creation atop his head is somewhat skimpy. His first mistress died in childbirth and now he is consort of royal Eikon, Ruler Etesian's second daughter. It was he who found the Enemy for me.

At his side is royal Tendence of Carpus. For an instant she is tall and girlishly young, but for me she drops the pretense, becoming smaller and a mature woman. Heliac women wear simple robes and hairstyles, leaving the fancy dressing-up to their menfolk. I note vaguely that she wears a silken robe of peach and pale blue, but the world fades away as we stare wordlessly at each other. Tendence is delicate and exquisite, so I feel like a walking house beside her. I sink to my knees.

"I *said*," Magnes says, "do you need me, noble Quirt?"

"What? Oh, no. I mean . . ." I am still locked in adoration of Tendence. I behaved like this with one other woman, when I was a lovesick boy fresh off the circuit, but that was two pentads ago. Why can't I act like a grown man? Why am I trembling?

Magnes, I realize, has gone. If Ruler Etesian ever learns that her beloved heir has been left alone with a male stranger, she will keel over in a dead faint. I remember and cherish every meeting I have had with Tendence. The first one was enough to drive us both insane.

Totally insane! I rise as she approaches and dare to hold out my arms in a gesture of submission. She slides into my embrace and we kiss. Our first kiss, our first touch. She is so tiny that my monstrous great arms could crush her all by themselves, with no hefting assistance at all, and yet she could destroy me utterly. I wish she would, so I need not endure the agony longer.

"Why are you such a fool," I say when we draw breath, "as to fall in love with a doomed man?"

Her smiles are rare, but any one of them dims the suns. "Because," she says, "there is an integrity burning in you like Our Father shining through a thin mist. You make all other men look shifty,

Mudar of Quoin. I cannot linger more than a few moments, beloved. Sit here and tell me how your tourney went at Bere Parochian."

She kneels, a dainty porcelain figurine. I sit like a barrel between the great ugly mountains of my knees. But she has called me *beloved*! My mouth tells her my news while my soul tastes and savors and drools over that word. This is the woman who is to be delivered to Humate of Alfet like a lamb to a butcher.

I tell her, "A miracle happened at Bere Parochian. I had your betrothed lined up at the end of a javelin and I resisted the urge to cure his acne with it."

Tendence winces at my humor. Her eyes grow larger when I describe the meeting on the island at Cupule.

"Yes," she says at the end. "Women-5 is the date now. But Hegemon Balata will surely find out if they wait that long. The treaty will be signed the moment my betrothed wins a silver crown." She pulls a face. "My mother is a stubborn woman. She had them move a larger bed into my chamber yesterday, just so I won't forget the joy awaiting me."

"I hope you burn his brain out the instant he touches you."

Although Tendence almost never smiles, she has a wicked, razor wit. She has dimples that signal amusement and eyes that sparkle a lot. They sparkle now. "I know women who took their consorts in hand with the very best intentions, planning to make them just a tiny bit more civilized. But each improvement soon led to another. Improvement cannot add, only subtract, and now they are left with lumps of meat that can do nothing except what they are told to do. I want a companion who will entertain me, amuse me, talk to me, even talk me into things once in a while."

She takes one of my great monster hands in both of hers. "What madness we talk, my beloved! Pairing is not a brute thing to be left to chance. Think of all the care and work the genealogists have put into shaping us and our like over untold generations. Think how soon it would all be lost if we let caprice rule us."

"Yes, how can we be so crazy?" I cannot take my eyes off her face. "We are not unruly adolescents. We know that pairing must lead to love, not the other way around."

"Perhaps it is because we have been along this road before, you and I. We recognized it as soon as we saw it." No dimples. "Mortals cannot mourn forever. The road of life has many forks and, like it or not, we can only walk one path. The others wander away over the hills; we cannot guess where they would have taken us."

If her consort and my mistress had not both died. If I were not doomed . . . But that is useless flagellation. I sigh.

My beloved says, "You are holding something back."

"Yes. Thanks to Magnes I know who the Enemy is. Thanks to your betrothed's folly, yesterday I learned that I can port to people. Today I could recall you when I was in the Court of Joyful Blossom. I could have come straight to you."

Tendence gasps. "Then no woman in the world is safe anymore."

"Fortunately the skill seems to be rare, still." We both know it will not remain so. Old Izard rants about the number of ordinary porters there are around nowadays because so many promiscuous young noblemen spread psychic powers indiscriminately. "Take care never to be alone in a lighted space."

Silence. We dream in silence.

I rouse myself. "But the news is not all bad. I can kill the Enemy now. Whenever he is in Mascle I can port to him and kill him."

"Suicide? You came here to say goodbye?"

"I will leave before his guards have time to react."

"Then go and do it! Rid yourself of the curse and hurry back to me." She reads me. "But that is not enough, is it? Your doom requires *justice*. He must be denounced and exposed before he dies, and that means that his guards will have time to kill you first. Oh, dearest, you mustn't!"

In theory a hegemonic council could judge the Enemy. Tendence has already concluded that political complications deny us help from that quarter.

"At the very least," I say, "he must confess in front of witnesses.

I think my doom will accept that. I am on my way now to bait a hook. If he bites it, then he will be admitting his guilt."

Companion Magnes comes forth on the sand picture with Eikon, his mistress and Tendence's sister. Our time alone is up.

Tendence rises. "Can you find good enough bait, dear one?"

"I have an excellent worm in mind," I assure her.

4

My problem now is to find the worm, meaning Humate. He may have slunk home to confess his shame. More likely, Vert and Izard and I agreed, he will dismiss his Bere Parochian disaster as beginner's nerves and try again. A second failure on the bronze circuit would make him the laughingstock of all Aureity, so he will try to bully his way directly into a silver tourney. One bronze bracelet would not normally be enough to qualify, but I know he wields his mother's name like a club, whether she knows what he is up to or not. The next silver games after Bere Parochian are at Quintole on triangles-1—tomorrow—and then Azedarac on pots-1. Quintole is in Heliac and I doubt that he will dare show his face there, but I must make certain. So back I must go to the site of my first silver tourney.

First, though, I return to the hill where I left my pack. I change into a modest tunic of blue silk embroidered in pearls and silver thread. With the aid of a hand mirror, I paint an orange dot on my brow, the mark of the highborn caste—at least eight quarterings, less than twelve. I belt on a silver-hilted sword and slip a plain gold band on my ring finger. Now I look like a middle-rank champion of a minor ruler on personal, not official, business.

As boy-turning-man on the circuit, I was much impressed by my first sight of Quintole, with its busy harbor, bustling streets, great merchant houses, and especially its rambling palace complex. The palace's size and luxury proclaim the wealth of Quintole's trade and the family that controls it. I have seen the city many times since, but have never been back inside the palace. Will it impress me as much now? Youthful memories are as fragile as dried flowers.

Quintole's games marshal back then was, and still is now, royal Agynary of Duskish, a sister of the ruler. Agynary is almost as crazy as my poor mother, but also one of the most memorable women I ever met. Although I cannot hope that she will remember the boy I was as well as I remember her, I do need her help. With the games tomorrow, she will certainly be in the city somewhere, and the palace is the best place to start looking for her.

The public entrance is a spacious wooden platform on high ground overlooking the bay, surrounded by some of the largest trees I have ever seen, whose vast boughs overshadow and shelter it. I can admire the bay and the city between their monumental trunks in one direction, while others show formal gardens and more stick-and-paper buildings. Quintolians are not as secretive as Formenians, for I am allowed to witness other people coming and going. Many visitors are sitting around on mats, patiently contemplating the view while they wait.

When I have been sufficiently instructed in my insignificance, a youngster comes forth to greet me. He flaunts the same orange caste mark I do, but his hair is styled in a gilded lobster and he must have trouble sitting down in his elaborate draperies. We exchange bows and names—Quirt of Mundil in my case, not worth remembering in his.

I explain my need. "Would you honor my unworthy person by asking some page to lay this scroll on her doorstep?"

The letter I offer this time is a note signed by me, not a cryptic poetic passport. I do not doubt that it will be ported to Agynary immediately, wherever she may be, but will she receive me? Young Glorious deigns to sully his fingers with it. He offers me refreshment and entertainment, which I politely decline. He ports out.

I sit on the nearest mat, but I have not tired of admiring the view before the answer to my question appears in the form of a champion of princely caste in regalia even grander. He glitters all over, from the ribbons in his hair to the sparkly upturned toes of his buskins. It must take a team of valets half a watch to dress him. He wears a look of disdainful outrage, but I cannot tell whether he is offended by being sent to a beetle like me or by the message he brings.

"Highborn Quirt of Mundil?"

I heft myself until my eyes are at eye level, then put my feet down. "I am."

"You are invited to attend royal Agynary in the Grotto of Champions."

I laugh in his face, which turns even redder.

"Is that a subtle way of establishing my credentials? I thank you, noble."

Subtle Agynary is not. Her Grotto of Champions is a cave some miles along the coast, whose only physical access is an underwater arch. On sunny days it glows with an eerie blue light and on hot days it is wonderfully cool. It is dim compared with where I am standing, though, and I have to close my eyes for a few moments until I can recall it clearly.

◆ ◆ ◆ **PORT** ◆ ◆ ◆

In my youth Agynary was a notorious flirt, cultivating a reputation as a wanton who awarded highly unconventional prizes to winners of her games. Although she never went that far with me, it was she who made that decision, not I. I knew that a man making physical contact with a noblewoman risked being taken in hand, but that night long ago I was very young and had just pulled off a notable upset by winning my first silver crown against some stellar opponents. My future was assured; I was immortal; I would dare anything. I accepted her invitation with alacrity. In my case, at least, the result was a kiss that turned into a mocking laugh the moment it became really interesting. To be honest, she made up for it by offering me the company of some striking ordinaries. As this was before I met Mandola, I sinned badly, but that is irrelevant.

The Grotto has not changed. It is a strangely unsettling place, never at rest, for the pool rises and falls as waves wash the cliffs outside, and the air chews at you. The walls and roof are sculpted into fantastic icicles and draperies of white stone, constantly rippling with bluish lights from the pool below. The shadows hide secrets, because Agynary cannot port in and out by herself, so she must have some way of summoning help—either a bell cord or a concealed chamber where aides wait on her call. Most of the floor is too rugged to be of any use, but two flat terraces overlook the pool. The lower one is left empty, a portage for arriving noblemen, and the higher was furnished in my youth with a side table of refreshments and a sumptuous bed.

It still is. The games marshal is kneeling on the bed. Her skin glows oddly in the pallid underlighting, with more of it visible than a noblewoman should display to any man other than her consort. I am half as old again as I was when I first saw her, and she seems completely unchanged—young and innocent, arch and voluptuous, all at the same time. Izard claims that her sister has reigned for almost eleven pentads, so she must be as old as he is. My letter lies beside her.

I bow. "Our Mother bless you, royal Agynary of Duskish."

Her smile is a glory of white teeth and plump red lips. "I remember you. You did not know how to kiss."

"I learned quickly, as I recall."

"Come here."

I mount the two artificial steps to the second platform.

"Closer."

I advance until my shins are against the bed. It is a low bed, so I am looking down at her—the smooth shoulders, the sleek thighs and arms, the shadowed valley between her breasts. Now I am close enough for her to touch if she wishes. She is still a tease, perhaps crazy, certainly dangerous.

After a moment's staring up at me she says, "Did you come here for another lesson?"

"No, royal. I came to ask for help."

"Highborn Mudar of Quoin was shamed and unnamed, so I heard."

"Unjustly so."

"A consort whose mistress is slain? There is no excuse for that. What is a consort for if not to protect? Is breeding the only thing you are good for?"

She is trying to provoke me. I refuse to be baited. "I agree a nobleman should stand ready to transport his mistress out of danger if necessary, but he cannot be with her every moment of every day. Both champions and gentlewomen have paramount duties to their liege. Noblest Hegemon Foison unnamed me, but did not improve me, as she would have done had she considered me a felon. And I have spent every moment since then hunting for my mistress's killer."

Agynary looks skeptical. "Have you found him?"

"I have."

Pause. She seems a little more interested. "You expect me to take him in hand for you?"

"No. But you can help me bring him to justice."

Technically that is her duty, but Agynary cares nothing for legalisms unless she wants to. "Why me? You won the crown here, so I cannot let you enter the tourney tomorrow. That is a strict law."

"Mudar of Quoin won the crown and I am Quirt of Mundil."

"You were unnamed and that is another reason. I thought you might have come here to ask for sanctuary." She leans back on her elbows, being even more provocative. "Two days ago you competed as a blank and won a bronze crown by beating the Pelagic pup, an excessively foolhardy thing to do."

"I tried to throw the match to him, as any sane man would. He lost his nerve and ported out."

"His father will beat him yellow and purple when he goes home, which is nothing compared to what his mother's thugs will do to you when they catch you."

"You are well informed, royal."

She smirks. "We marshals tattle to one another. Bere Parochian reports to me, and I write to that awful woman in Azedarac. I wish

I knew where dear Sudamina finds the cute champions who deliver her letters. . . . So what are you up to? Be brief. You are very nice to look at, but I have better things to do than lie around here and entertain you."

"Has Humate of Alfet applied to compete here tomorrow?"

She gives me a slantwise look, calculating. "Why is that your business?"

"He would not normally be eligible yet, either by age or by achievement. Did he pressure you?"

Agynary straightens up with a startling change of mood. "Pressure me? That skinny maggot? What could he do to me?"

"Try turning him down and he will tell you."

"I don't want to turn him down—a hegemonic who can be beaten? He wanted to compete as a blank. I told his manager he must wear his stars; I never admit blanks. The studs will be climbing all over one another like roaches to try their luck at doing what you did." The lady is cautious, though, and cleverer than she likes to portray. She gives me another slanted glance. "Suppose I did turn him down?"

"He would threaten you."

"How?"

"With his mother. For example, he might tell you she will forbid Pelagic cubs to compete here in future, which would cut the tripes out of your games. But I warn you, royal, if you do let him enter, then your own hegemon, noblest Batala, will eat you raw."

This is not rustic Bere Parochian, where neither Alkin or Sudamina care about politics. Agynary wallows in them. I have her complete attention. Her eyes shine like steel buttons. "Don't tease, Mudar darling. Explain."

I explain. "The boy is to be consort of the Formene heir. It is a succulent arrangement. Ruler Etesian gains half-hegemonic pedigrees for her grandchildren. Hegemon Pelta spites her old rival, Balata, and wins control of the strait. She will be able to tax ships entering or leaving the Gulf of Broose. She will be able to shut out much more than just cubs coming to Quintole."

"*Death and the Dark!* And they call me crazy?" Agynary has aged a lifetime. I am looking at a tiny, withered crone in a sober, almost dowdy, brown sari. Her arms are shriveled sticks and loss of teeth has collapsed her face until her nose and chin almost meet. "Where did you dig up this madness?"

"I have it on excellent authority, royal Agynary. I think you and I can help each other."

"Sit down!" She pats the bed beside her with a twisted claw.

I sit where she indicates and when I cross my legs my left knee almost touches her—but not quite. I say, "I may be able to persuade the boy to withdraw his application. Then you will not need to offend either hegemon."

She cackles. "And what's in it for you, eh?"

"I must talk with Pimple. I must get him to listen to what I have to say instead of just breaking my neck. And for that I need you or your gentlewomen to convince him that I mean him no harm."

Her wrinkles writhe into a smile. "Don't you?"

"No. I may hurt his feelings, but nothing physical. There's very little wrong with the kid that a few years' growing up won't cure."

She knows that I do not lie. She is growing larger and younger again and her sari is shrinking. "You know his betrothed, royal Tendence of Carpus?"

I say cautiously, "I have met the noblewoman."

Another cackle. "You still remind me of celery, Mudar of Quoin!"

"Celery?"

"Long, green, and toothsome."

"Thank you."

"And still as obvious. But since Tendence isn't here, I have some very pretty girls who dream of bearing gifted children to support them in their dotage."

"No thank you." Her leer makes my hair stand on end. "How many entrants do you have for tomorrow?"

"Too many, as usual. My girls are working on the ticket right now."

"Do you ever hold elimination bouts?"

She pulls a gruesome gargoyle face. "Only if I have to."

"You should hold one tomorrow, but Humate need not know it is the only one. He won't care as long as you keep it to straight hefting. After his disaster two days ago, you can reasonably insist that he demonstrate some of the legendary Pelagic strength. He'll jump at the chance to show it off—I swear the kid could juggle four oxen if he had to. I need to borrow a tabard."

"And some crooked referees, I suppose?"

"Just brave ones, who won't be intimidated. A few unscrupulous linesmen will help though."

I cannot deny that Agynary is insane by some standards, but she is extremely efficient. Very soon after bluerise the next morning, she has arranged for at least two dozen people to be standing around in the arena, and most of them must have been dragged unwillingly from beds or breakfasts or lovers' arms. She herself is not present, just white-clad linesmen and blue referees, three of us contestants, plus miscellaneous linesmen and referees, all looking particularly grumpy. We are loosely gathered around the arrival platform, the linesmen waiting to start stacking its timbers as they do at the start of a proper tourney. The air is cool, the sand still warm underfoot from yesterday's heat.

Quintole's amphitheater is larger than Bere Parochian's, with grander boxes for the nobility and fixed stone benches for the ordinaries. None of those are occupied at this time of day. Mother Blue has not cleared the top of the walls yet and I need to shiver, although nobody else seems to be inclined to. My problem may not be temperature but fear. If the Enemy has learned that I am to be present here this morning, he will have arranged for me to die.

I am feeling ridiculous again in a saffron yellow tabard, uncomfortably tight around my chest. I have spent the night as Agynary's guest in the palace—alone and incognito, having declined her repeated offers of winsome company.

The other two competitors, Red-on-Lavender and Tan-on-Green, are not wearing caste marks, but are obviously genuine cubs-with-teeth. They chat like old friends, seeming quite relaxed, so they have probably been warned that this procedure is a sham, mere fakery intended to weed out either a boy too young or a man too old. That was the story I suggested, because it is close to the truth.

Then Humate ports in with two steely-eyed, quiver-bearing attendants. I go tense, ready to vanish the moment either of those goons draws a dart or ports within hefting range of me. They sport the purple and white livery of House Pelagic, but the boy is in a tabard of green and black, so he has changed his manager. On seeing me he first glares, then smirks and makes some smart-alecky remark to his goons. I have no doubt that the kid's handlers have been exercising him to exhaustion since Bere Parochian, thumping him through all the exercises and practice he neglected earlier. Now he thinks he knows all the tricks and the Pelagic strength that is his birthright can beat me or anyone else he is likely to meet. The latter assumption is probably right. We shall see about the former.

Everyone summoned is present; the linesmen begin stacking the timbers.

Humate ports to my side, blocking my view of his mother's champions. I take a step sideways so I can continue to watch them. They stare icily at me but make no threatening moves.

"What's your name today, old man?"

"Still Quirt of Mundil, sonny. What's yours?"

"Humate of Alfet, consort designate of royal Tendence of Carpus."

His boasting does not interest me; his ignorance does. Unless he has been kept in the dark, the Pelagic organization has not yet learned my real name. He cannot yet scream that he will not compete against an unnamed.

"Ready to do some heavy lifting?" He beams and flexes bony shoulders.

Anything he can flex I can flex better. "Yes."

"How many balks can you move?"

"Depends how big they are."

"Sixteen? No sneaky tricks today. Just honest strength." Smirk.

I smile. "You are very trusting, but I suppose that comes from inexperience."

"What do you mean?"

"Those timbers are parkwood."

He frowns and stares at the stack. "So?"

"Its density varies. One end is often heavier than the other and you can't tell which is which just by looking."

The senior referee beckons us. Humate ports to her, but I heft myself there, which takes longer and lets me take up position on his right, the south side. She looks like a competent, no-nonsense noblewoman of about my age, but referees always do. I have not met her beforehand. I trust Agynary has briefed her well.

"Usual rules," she says. "To win the match you must win two consecutive rounds. Winner dresses for the noon tourney, loser can try again next gnomon. I drew lots and you will play first, royal Humate."

"And may Our Father White give victory to the strongest!" Humate ports.

"Or Mother Blue to the smartest," I mutter, and stroll over to my place.

The linesmen have been primed to put the most off-center parkwood at the north side of the stack, but that cheat turns out to be unnecessary. To show his contempt for me and the elimination bout, Humate hefts the first balk off the top, moves it over to my side and just drops it.

I cry, "Objection!"

"What'yu mean 'objection'?" Humate ports through the stack to see where his play has landed.

The senior referee comes running with two others close behind.

"Objection sustained," she says.

Humate plants fists on hips and bellows in outrage. "What in the Dark am I supposed to have done wrong?"

"The rules say you must lay the load down, not drop it."

"It's only one timber, stupid!"

Hegemonic or not, no boy like him is ever going to browbeat a tourney referee. "But we were not close enough to know that you intended to drop it. Also it has landed in a tilted position, so that noble Quirt would have trouble balancing another balk on top of it."

"*He can straighten it!*" Humate does so with a glance.

Now her glare is lethal. "The rules forbid him to move the load until he has balanced another timber on top of it. Noble Quirt is awarded this round. Play on."

Scarlet with rage, Humate yells "*Cheat!*" at me and ports back to his place.

A linesman replaces the balk on the stack. I choose another, heft it over to the far side, and lay it down very gently.

Humate is doing breathing exercises to calm down. After a moment, the senior referee shouts at him to play or withdraw. That can't soothe his feelings much. He plays, laying a second balk on the first and successfully hefting the pair of them over to my side.

I take my time, too, for what I am about to try is very tricky indeed, especially with Heliac parkwood. I lift a fresh balk, lower it until the stack hides it from Humate, and then turn it. Very carefully, I balance it across the load, forming an X. It rocks and steadies. Now for it . . . I lift the threesome. When it comes into his sight, of course, Humate shrieks with fury. I ignore him. I know I have set it down successfully when he yells out an objection.

This time the conference is held on his side of the stack.

"On what grounds are you objecting?" the senior referee asks. *Ah, women!* I cannot believe any man in all Aureity could keep a straight face as she does.

The boy's confidence falters. "That's not allowed!"

"There is nothing in the rules to say that the contestant must align his timber with those underneath."

"But I'm not allowed to straighten it first, am I? You can't expect me to put another on top of it now and move. . . . It's impossible!" With biased parkwood it certainly is.

I intervene before the woman has to perjure herself. "I believe so. I have practiced this many times and I have never managed to add another balk successfully, whether I align it with the last one or with the rest of the load. Moving such a pile is out of the question. You have two choices, royal Humate."

"Killing you is one of them." He looks ready to start, white as chalk, fists knotted.

"No. That gets you vilified. You can continue the contest, but you will certainly fail. That means you are eliminated from the tourney. The alternative is this. Listen carefully. If you will withdraw your application to enter, then so will I. I will solemnly swear never to compete against you again in games anywhere. In fact I will coach you, if you wish. But I need you to come with me today, quite a long way. I have something to show you, a place I want to take you to, and a story to tell you. It concerns you, and it may concern very many people. I swear that I will do you no harm."

He blusters. "*You* couldn't hurt *me!*"

"With enough friends I could. But I won't. Tomorrow at whiterise you can return you to your bodyguards, safe and sound."

Humate's lip curls in contempt. "Where I go, they go!"

The muscle are staying out of earshot, but watching the discussion intently. As former duelists, they must see that I am stealing the match from their ward. How long will they tolerate my insolence?

"So you are afraid of me, royal?"

Humate almost shouts, "Afraid? I could twist you like a rope!"

That is the truth. He can kill me with a single wrench if he wishes, and his hegemonic mother will certainly see he escapes punishment.

"I promise I will play no tricks on the way," I tell him. "I will give you time to memorize the marks and never carry you beyond your range. You will always be able to come back here. Noblewomen, have I told him any lies? Have I shaded the truth? Do I have mental reservations?"

"You have done none of those things," the senior referee says, as the other two nod. "He speaks in good faith, royal Humate. I believe

96

he is trying to help you, although I refuse to pry into him to discover how or why."

"You have nothing to fear from me," I insist.

"I know that, ape-face!" The boy scowls down at the insoluble timber problem. Then at me. Then at his bodyguards. *Arrogant, arrogant, and arrogant.* His goons will refuse to let him go without them, but I suspect it will take more than two of them to stop him. I am certain now that he has not been home to Mascle to report to his parents. It was his own idea to enter the Quintole tourney and he can withdraw without having to explain to them or anyone.

He turns to the women. "Keep your pissy games, then. After I've gone, tell my men I'll meet them back here tomorrow at whiterise. What are you waiting for, Quirt?"

III

TRAGEDY AT CANTLE

1

In my room Humate sees a pile of clothes and two swords on the bed, an assortment of boots on the floor. He does not even need to look out the window to know we are in the palace.

"So it was a put-up job! The hags were in on it."

"Of course it was. Consider your embarrassment as growing pains." I squirm out of my overtight tabard and take up my tunic.

"You were cheating when you crossed the timbers, and the women lied to cheat me out of a victory."

"None of us lied. The first round you gave me as a gift. You have only yourself to blame for that. The rules are silent on the crossing trick. I've only seen it tried once—in an amateur tourney in Aspartic. The referees disagreed; the games marshal disallowed it under the 'spirit of fair play' rule. Yesterday I went to an empty arena and spent a long time trying it. I never managed to add a log when the one under it was crossed like that one was. Even without parkwood it would be close to impossible."

I belt on a sword. Then I go to the mirror and award myself a royal caste mark. Humate's face turns scarlet.

"Are you entitled to wear that?"

"Yes and no. Long story. Hurry up. We've got a long way to go."

He selects Pelagian trousers in purple and gold. "If I had played properly in the first round, did you have another sleazy trick up your sleeve?"

"Just the parkwood. It takes a lot of practice. The crossed-balk trick only works once, of course, because you can block it by laying down very close to the stack. I'll admit I was cheating, if that makes you feel better. I'm sure you're a lot stronger than I am."

That admission mollifies him.

"I told you this was serious," I say. "You don't realize how dangerous politics can be, royal Humate. Everyone knows that female rulers don't make war, that rape and murder were common back in the Blood Age when wild hairy men ruled Aureity but never happen now. That's not quite true, lad. Even wars do happen sometimes, and psychic violence is extremely horrible. If your mother tries to use her new influence over Formene to close the strait or tax shipping using it, then Heliac may make war on Pelagic."

He does not scoff at my argument, so he has probably heard it before. "Feces! Pelagic would slaughter Heliac!"

I think I can guess where he got that response, too.

"But not before Heliac has wasted Formene and slaughtered its traitorous ruling family, especially you. Answer me two questions. Whose idea was it that you should enter the Quintole tourney, here in Heliac?"

"Mine." He sits on the bed to inspect the boot collection. "Since you tricked me out of the crown at Parochian."

"And whose idea was it to pair you with Tendence of Carpus— your mother's or your father's?" His mother is an excessively stupid woman and his father is clever, grasping, and unscrupulous. I don't say so. The war threat is unlikely but not impossible. I would be more concerned about it were I not doomed. Nothing can take precedence over that compulsion, not even my feelings for Tendence.

"Mine." He does not meet my eye. "She's old, but a great body."

Not likely. Noblemen of his age are still trying to escape from their mothers' rule and have no desire to be tied down in formal pairings so soon. Ordinaries are their prey, because no man can share a noblewoman's bed and also keep secrets from her. No, his parents have forced him into this for their own political ends.

Tendence's betrothed stamps his oversized feet to test his buskins, takes up the sword. "Go on, then. Move us."

* * * **PORT** * * *

I go easy to start with. At each portage we discuss the landmarks, and presumably he checks that he can recall the one before. Then he nods and I move us again.

After the fourth or fifth he says, "Why the child's play? Is this the best you can do?"

I increase the hops, taking the longest whenever I have a choice. He does not object, so his recall must have at least as great a range as mine.

Halfway across Baric we encounter territory he knows.

"Availeth next?"

I say, "Convent of Light next. Availeth will be the one after. I can't recall it clearly enough yet."

His smile is somewhere between a smirk and a leer. "Want me to do it?"

"If you can."

* * * **PORT** * * *

We come forth at one side of the main square, narrowly avoiding a curry vendor's barrow and spooking a team of horses, which tries to bolt and is barely held back by the teamster. This is market day and Availeth seethes with people and livestock. Humate is pleased because he thinks he has shown his range is greater than mine, but he was just reckless. He could have killed or injured both us and other people. I was going to make two short hops so I could aim at a smaller, safer portage.

He does the next two ports also. After that I want a more northerly route than any he knows, so I take over again.

On a sunny mountain meadow, I demand a rest and sit down.

Father White is rising. Bird specks circle in the sky. Repeated porting is tiring. It gives me a headache, although other men report
chest pains or blurred vision. If I persist in spite of that warning, I
start recalling landmarks poorly and then porting becomes truly
dangerous.

Humate smirks at my weakness and sprawls out on the grass. He
has his confidence back now. By shedding his guards and going adventuring with a stranger, he is indulging in adolescent rebellion,
but he knows he can pin me and wrench my ribs out one by one if
he takes a fancy to. A day that started badly has improved. He tucks
his hands under his head and admires the clouds.

"Start talking, then, old man. Where are we going and what's
there that I have to see?"

"We're going to an island called Alazarin, just off the Stramash
coast. It's part of Quartic, though, not Stramash."

"Wild hairy men in caves?"

"Used to be. The Blood Age lasted longer there than on the
mainland, but Aureity civilized it as soon as its noblemen could
port across the strait. A few of the Stramash Islands still have male
rulers, but they have learned not to bother us."

"You live on this Alazarin?"

"I used to."

"So what's the story?"

"Long and sad."

Even today the strait between Badderlocks Head on the mainland
and Cape Bastel on Alazarin is a long hop, feasible only for men of
high caste. Alazarin is also a long way from Cuneal, the Quartic
capital. Consequently, as long as nothing goes wrong, the world
usually ignores Alazarin. Things rarely do go wrong. The soil is
fertile, the climate mild. The ordinaries earn their living by farm-
ing, fishing, or mining rubies. The ruler collects her taxes, remits
the usual tenth to the hegemon in Cuneal, and life goes on.

In the fifth pentad of the reign of Hegemon Firk, the epidemic
of coughing fever that raged across Aureity hit Quartic especially

hard. In Alazarin it took Ruler Aglare and three of her four children, but spared her consort, Izard of Inmew, and Hyla, their youngest daughter. Izard had always been a trusted and competent vizier for his mistress. He took charge of the government, simply because there was no one else to do so. He maintained order, organized relief, and saw that his baby ruler was well cared for.

Hegemon Firk herself went to join her foremothers in the Everlit Realm. A third of her court died, and the new hegemon, noblest Foison, was so occupied with more immediate problems that she did not even answer Izard's letters for almost three gnomons. No woman of competence and adequate rank could be spared to take over the regency of a minor, faraway island. Eventually Firk sent a companion and champion, who arrived by boat, stayed a few days, and ported home to report that Izard was doing as well as anyone could.

Stramash influence made male rule seems less bizarre in Alazarin than it would in most of Aureity, and the islanders knew and trusted Consort Izard. Prosperity returned, Alazarin remitted its taxes on time, and life went on. Once in a while the hegemon would dispatch a commission to inspect the island. The worthy ladies would fuss around for a few days and then go home to report that noblest Izard, although admittedly male, was neither brutalizing his daughter's subjects nor waging wars on others'. In fact he was performing very well and there was absolutely no need to appoint a female regent in his place.

Izard was never surprised by their glowing commendations. Had the distinguished noblewomen reported otherwise, he knew, one of them might have been appointed his replacement, and none of them wanted to risk being marooned on a remote island for pentads.

Ruler Presumptive Hyla grew up self-willed—spoiled, according to some—but undoubtedly a dark-eyed charmer, vivacious and witty. She was nimble and graceful, intelligent and well-liked, and her psychic powers began developing early, a sign that usually indicates unusual strength at maturity. By the end of her third pentad she was eager to proclaim her majority, take control of her government, and start appointing companions, champions—and a consort. In his first venture off the island since his own youth, her father took her west to Cuneal, the capital of Quartic. Most girls from her rustic background would have been overwhelmed by the splendor of a hegemonic court. Hyla took it in her stride.

Hegemon Foison was bewitched by this sparkling sea nymph and no one disagreed with her judgment, even in private. In short order she formally confirmed Hyla as ruler of Alazarin, successor to her long-dead mother.

The court had already plunged into an orgy of theoretical matchmaking, a favorite pastime of the nobly born. The hegemon's breeders, poring over Hyla's pedigree, finally agreed that her blood-lines were superbly balanced and of commendable quality. The young ruler herself pointed out that only the best studs could jump the ditch to Alazarin. If they were forced to make recommendations, the worthy scholars would add cautiously, then the lineage of House Baric might be the match that came first to mind. Their diffidence was no doubt prompted by the knowledge that hegemons do not always want their dependent rulers to be too highly bred and psychically gifted.

The hegemon's consort, noblest Bayard of Indican, was himself of House Glyptic and could rattle off the names of several nephews and cousins well qualified for the post of consort of Alazarin. Alas, even hegemonic family ties can become tangled, and his mistress turned two deaf ears to all his suggestions—her relations with her dear sister-in-law, Abraxas of Glyptic, were frigid at that time. She dropped a few hints to favored young bloods who hung around the palace and received surprisingly limp responses. Hyla herself was a dream, but a lifetime on a remote island held little appeal.

A reigning ruler could not be offered a consort of less than royal caste. One night, in a mood of extreme frustration, noblest Foison went so far as to ask noblest Hyla herself if any unattached young male around the court had caught her eye.

Hyla flashed her most charming smile and said that almost all of them had been trying to. "But since the noblest seeks my

opinion—which, I appreciate, is a tremendous honor—then I must
humbly reply that my choice is always to have faith in the holy suns
and trust them to do what is most fitting to confound the Dark. I
do believe that they will send a worthy champion to win my golden
games. I am most grateful to Your Serenity for this favor and concession."

Humate hoots. He rolls over on one elbow to stare at me. "You're
joking! She meant that?"

I continue to study the fluffy white clouds. It all happened so
long ago, and no one ever told me the whole story in one piece, as
I am telling Humate. I assembled it from fragments collected in my
childhood and adolescence.

"Hyla meant it. Hegemon Foison had probably not intended
anything of the sort, but somehow found herself agreeing that this
was what she had offered. She soon added conditions—Hyla was to
be ruled by her father, and he would be guided by a team of court
genealogists sent along to evaluate the applicants. Suns alone know
what sort of baboon a young maiden might fall for if her pairing
were left to her own discretion!"

"Hard to imagine," Humate agrees. "She really wanted *open*
games?"

There are golden games and there are open golden games. Bards
would have us believe that games began as competitions open to all
comers, with fights to the death and a king's daughter as prize. I
suppose such a system might have made sense in olden times, before
bloodlines and lineages and pedigrees became established. Standard
bardic ballads always end with the surprise winner revealed as the
handsome fisherman-woodcutter-blacksmith ordinary she reluctantly
spurned in the first verse. That no longer happens, if it ever did.

Most golden games nowadays are just lavish entertainments to
celebrate royal or hegemonic pairings. The festivities being planned
for Tendence and Humate may include such a tourney, with the best
of the best performing for the richest of the rich. By unwritten
agreement, though, the winners must be prepared to lose on the final

day, when mighty Humate enters the arena in his star-studded cloak. No matter how bad he is, he will overpower them all and claim Tendence as his prize. The guests will applaud. That is the traditional charade and if he were prepared to practice a bit and wait until he has grown into his full strength, then he really would trash them all. I have met adult hegemonics in the arena and I would rather wrestle earthquakes.

What Hyla was plotting was something in between, an arrangement not rare among the bourgeois, but almost unknown in noble circles. A rich merchant who has managed to acquire a wife with enough fourbears to give his daughters a minimum claim to caste may stage what are known as "open" golden games. Basically he is using his wealth to buy a better pedigree for his grandchildren, but there is never a shortage of impoverished young noblemen willing to accept such an arrangement, honor be damned. Even if the maiden's father is a dealer in fish, instead of a royal consort like noblest Izard of Inmew, the terms are still more subtle than the bards would have you believe. Any unattached nobleman may apply to compete, but his lineage and personality and the state of his fingernails will be examined in detail before he is admitted. Even then, while the overall winner will undoubtedly carry away a worthy purse, he will not necessarily be the one who ports the maiden off to bed. Her parents are not bound to accept him, or any of the contestants.

"Her idea did have merit," I say. "How else could she find an attractive and competent consort willing to spend the rest of his life on a seagirt rock? How else except by asking for volunteers? My headache's better. Let's move on."

Humate hefts himself vertical and scans the landscape. "Your head may be better. My stomach is not. Let's prey on the local peasantry."

◆ ◆ ◆ **PORT** ◆ ◆ ◆

He brings us forth in what is obviously the entry hall of a palace, and not a minor one, either. We both bear swords and white caste marks, so instantly a liveried flunky is bowing to us.

Humate names himself and demands to be taken to royal Arrand. Alas, the ruler and her consort are not at home, but any noble is welcome in the house of any other, even if they have never met, and her staff rush to serve us. Soporific doublenoon finds us digesting an excellent meal on a shady terrace overlooking flowers and a gurgling stream. That is, I am digesting; opposite me, Humate is packing away thirds. A harper plays discreetly in the background. I continue my story while wondering where Humate is putting it all.

Izard of Inmew took his daughter home to Alazarin and set the date for the games that were to prove so ill-fated. One event that happened just before they left Cuneal was to bring good fortune, though. Hyla had made several friends at court. Few of them were willing to face exile on her island, and those few all had mothers who refused permission. The sole exception was a young noble-woman, princely Clamant of Coniine, who was deeply enamored of a princely champion, Vert of Ramist, in one of those spontaneous mutual infatuations so detested by mothers, rulers, and genealogists. The lovebirds were willing to go anywhere at all as long as they could pair and go together. Despairing, their families agreed, and Hyla swore in her first companion and champion. After some teasing, she then appointed Vert to be Clamant's consort. Throughout all the troubles to come, they were to remain true to each other and the most faithful retainers any ruler could ever wish for.

Island or not, news of an open royal tourney illuminated the silver circuit like a flash of lightning. Cubs began arriving at Badderlocks Head within days, many coming by ship or horseback or line-of-sight porting, for few nobles knew the area well enough to bring them. Izard himself interviewed the hopefuls at the portage. Some he turned down right away, most for personal reasons, but a few because their pedigrees had one or more fourbears in common with Hyla's—a line can spread amazingly wide in a mere four generations. The main test was the crossing, though. He would port the applicants over to Cape Bastel and invite them to return him to Badderlocks. Those who could not do so were rejected.

Cantle, the only town of any size on Alazarin, filled up with duelist cubs and then overflowed. Talent scouts followed them like carrion birds, as did nosy nobility from all over Aureity. Likewise bookmakers and worse. Soon royal youths were paying silver for the right to sleep in barns. There were feasts in the palace after Mother Blue set and fights in the streets after Father White did. Hyla carefully gleaned all the gossip, so that by the time the actual contest began, she knew more about most of the contenders than they would have wanted. In the end thirty-one were accepted. To make the numbers work, she ordered Vert to dress, telling him he must prove himself worthy of her and his mistress. Izard acted as games marshal, a disused quarry as an arena, and even royalty had to sit on the grass.

The contests were more varied and the scoring more complex than in silver games, but after some days it became clear that three competitors stood out from all the rest. All three were royals, naturally, and two of them were named Piese—Piese of Enthetic and Piese of Greaten—which is not unusual when every noble pedigree worth its vellum traces descent from the legendary Piese of Draff, supposedly the first psychically gifted ruler to repent of his wild hairy ways and relinquish his throne to his sister as better fit to rule. Enthetic was big even by noble standards, a dark, saturnine, humorless man with incredible psychic and physical strength. Greaten was his opposite—smallish, fair-complexioned, and perpetually smiling. In the hefting, Enthetic could raise an incredible fourteen balks of timber, but he never played such a load successfully and often dropped loads much smaller. Greaten's limit was a still remarkable eleven, but he reached it very consistently. He was physically faster than Enthetic, perhaps mentally faster, and much better company.

The third man who came to the fore was royal Tarn of Gyre. He was a very good duelist, but in that constellation of stars he shone no brighter than sixth or seventh. He was pleasant, but spoke little. He was handsome enough, but the servant girls dreamed of others. He smiled, he kept his own counsel, and he won the heart of Hyla of Alazarin. Every night Tarn was among the select few appointed to dine at her table. It was rumored that the breeders had asked to review his pedigree a second time and become quite excited over the potential fit.

By the final day the field had been reduced to eight, and in the last bout the smiling Piese of Greaten defeated scowling Piese of Enthetic. When the eight bags of gold were handed out, Piese of Greaten's was the heaviest. Izard announced that Ruler Hyla would accept any or all of the eight as her champions, naming generous terms. Her choice of one of the eight to be her consort would be proclaimed that evening.

At the banquet Hyla sat between Tarn and Greaten, with Enthetic opposite. After the feast came the dancing and she was a superb dancer. She danced opposite each in turn, playing no favorite. But then, when the usual parade of dances was over and the company was eagerly awaiting the announcement, she asked royal Tarn of Gyre to dance the *lilacin* with her.

"What's that?" Humate demands. "For that matter, why are we sitting here? What are we waiting for?"

We are sitting, in the lee of a huge moss-covered slab, because if we stand up the wind tries to throw us over a precipice. We are waiting because I am having trouble recalling the next portage. It may have changed since I last crossed the strait, or the long trek may have just left me muddleheaded. My skull throbs like a drum, but I have a childish reluctance to admit such human frailty to my companion.

"I am giving you time to make sure of the landmarks. Next hop is a long one and there is no other way across."

We are on Badderlocks Head, chilled by the gale that never ceases there. Behind us the cliffs run back for miles on either hand. Our shelter is part of distinctive ruins that must date from the Blood Age, but otherwise the landscape is empty pasture. Enormous waves pound the rocks below us; gray-green sea fades off into misty, blue-gray sky. Somewhere out there, invisible even on the finest days, lies Alazarin. The storm makes my eyes water.

Shadows stretch long on the grass. Here, a world away from our start at Quintole, we are less than a third of a watch from whiteset already.

"The *lilacin* is a Stramash dance, but the ordinaries on Alazarin dance it. Even among them, for anyone except married or handfast couples to dance the *lilacin* is highly improper." I have regained Humate's interest. "I'm sure that the dancing at Hyla's golden games had been quite conventional until then. The male guests would dance to impress the ladies, then the ladies would dance for the men. There would be some combined dancing, but never any touching."

"I should think not!"

"Except when the Alazarin ordinaries demonstrated their local dances. By this time, at the end of the tourney, some male guests would have joined in with them, I don't doubt. But the *lilacin* is a dance for one man and one woman. It starts slowly, with them far apart, and it gradually builds in pace and excitement until they join hands and—"

"Holy farts!" Humate mutters.

"And it ends with an embrace and a kiss, usually a long kiss."

His eyes are wide. "In *public*? You're serious?"

"And so were they. I told you only lovers dance it. I am sure that Tarn had seen it done and knew what was involved. She would have asked him beforehand. Very likely they had practiced the kiss. Anyway, they danced the *lilacin* and everyone knew Tarn was to be her consort."

"He let her *kiss* him? Even before they . . ."

"Royal Humate, surely you do not expect the fair Tendence to admit you to her bed without finding out if you are keeping deep, dark secrets from her?"

He squirms, possibly because he has not yet had time to amass any deep dark secrets outside his own imagination. "I suppose not. Did Hyla drag him off to bed there and then?"

"No. Ready to try the crossing now?"

I have not set foot on Alazarin since the day I was unnamed. At first I worried that the Enemy might post spies on the island to watch for me, in the hope I would lead them to Hyla. They could not have followed me when I ported, but they certainly could have harmed anyone I was seen associating with. They may never have existed, those watchers. Even if they did, they will not still be watching now, after all this time.

Now I can recall Cape Bastel. It is low and wooded and its only practical portage is a sandy beach flanked by a line of grotesquely shaped sea stacks, which make excellent landmarks. As Izard pointed out, the site could also provide an excellent ambush. Normally this would not be true, because the beach is too large for the watchers to be sure of recognizing their proposed victim. They would have to port out of hiding to make a close inspection of every arrival, and precision porting on a flat stretch of sand is tricky. By the time they could get within hefting range, the victim might be anywhere on the island. Besides, a man with reason to fear an ambush will send helpers ahead of him to spring the trap.

But my freakish new power to target people makes an ambush feasible. Concealed behind the central rocks, I can recall anyone I know anywhere on the beach—I confirmed this with Vert yesterday. If the Enemy comes looking for me or Hyla, I can port right to him. By tomorrow Vert will have rounded up some loyal helpers for me, in case the Enemy brings bodyguards. An ambush is possible—and now I know I am not going to attempt it.

Humate jumps up and shouts into the wind, "Ready!"

♦ ♦ ♦ PORT ♦ ♦ ♦

2

 Oh, blasphemy! We are plunged into an icy, needling downpour. It is only the tail end of a roaring cloudburst that still conceals the far end of the beach, which explains why I have been having trouble recalling the scenery.

"Idiot! Get us out of—

—here!"

We are forty miles away, at Nuddle. By force of habit, I have brought us forth at the top of the watchtower, a structure far more ancient than the rest of the buildings. Rain is falling here, too, if only a drizzle, but any roof the tower may once have had rotted away ages ago. The floor creaks alarmingly under our combined weight.

"Sorry!"

We are outside the front door of the main house. Soaked and shivering, Humate and I trot up the steps together.

When Vert of Ramist and Clamant of Coniine swore allegiance to Hyla, and journeyed with her to their new home, they had moved very far away from their birth apanages, and Hyla granted them the apanage of Nuddle. Its lush orchards provide a steady revenue and a permanent fragrance of blossom. I spent most of my childhood there, playing in its woods, swimming in its pools. Vert and Clamant were father and mother to me while my true mother was a terrifying stranger locked away upstairs and Grandfather Izard ran the government for her, far off in Cantle.

The Alazarine nobility tend to build in stone, a tradition dating from the days of castles and Stramash raiders. Nuddle is neither fortress nor palace, but it is an overbearing rock pile, and the entrance hall is especially oppressive. Great pilasters flank all the windows, making the already thick walls seem even thicker. The ceiling is very high overhead, the staircase looks like a mountain spur, and the fireplace could burn a fishing boat whole.

There is no one here to greet us. Humate looks around the gaunt vastness with disapproval, no doubt seeing it as cold and impersonal. Caretaker servants have kept Nuddle clean in the owners' absence, yet it has a neglected air to it. It smells of dust.

"Where's this?"

"Nuddle. The apanage of companion Clamant of Coniine."

The boy pushes wet hair out of his eyes and knots his stringy arms to indicate displeasure. "Is this sty what you have dragged me all across the world to see? You said you had something to tell me. Start by telling me why you didn't outfit us with cloaks."

"A little rain won't hurt you. The climate here is very pleasant, neither too hot nor too cold. A little damp, sometimes."

"So why am I here?" He seems uneasy, all of a sudden. Perhaps he failed to take note of the Bastel portage well enough. If he cannot recall that, he is trapped on Alazarin.

"I brought you here to meet Ruler Hyla."

Humate keeps his feet planted in the puddles he has shed around them. "A ruler living in this cave?"

"Technically she is only royal Hyla of Sice. Hegemon Foison deposed her and gave the realm to another, but she will always be noblest Hyla of Alazarin to me. She is my mother."

Humate frowns at my caste mark. "So the Tarn of Gyre you mentioned is your father?"

"No." I had not planned to tell him this while standing in a desolate hall dripping rainwater on the flags, but he must be warned what to expect. In any case, Hyla will be asleep, assuming she managed the journey from Osseter without ill effects.

"The morning after they danced the *lilacin*, royal Tarn was nowhere to be found. Several other contestants had disappeared also. They should have said goodbye and thank-you, but not everyone is as polite as you and I are, nobleman. Despite repeated calls, Ruler Hyla did not open her door. Noblest Izard was informed and ported in to see. He found her lying on the floor, naked and catatonic. He summoned doctors. It was quite clear that she had been brutally beaten and raped."

Humate shrugs. "And?"

"What is that meant to mean?" I demand.

He shrugs again. "She asked for it. She *kissed* a man. You told me what the dance meant."

"My *mother*, boy!" I let him feel a touch at his throat. The threat makes his eyes narrow, but I know I cannot frighten a hegemonic.

He sneers. "Then tell me how the rapist got in unless she let him in? Or had he been in her chamber before and she left the lights on for him? And tell me how any man, no matter how strong, can rape a noblewoman? The moment he touches her she will control him. She could *impair* him! Tarn should have been the catatonic one."

I say, "Hyla's pillow was lying in a far corner. It stank of *hamulose*."

"What's that?"

"*Hamulose* is a poison extracted from some nasty jellyfish that live off the coast of Glyptic. It is absorbed through the skin, causing mental confusion, paralysis, and finally death. The rapist threw the pillow away before he assaulted her, but by that time she was paralyzed, incapable of resisting or crying out." I hear a clatter of claws on hardwood and know we are about to have company.

"Almost incapable," I add. "When he kissed her, she bit his tongue hard enough to draw blood. So then he beat her."

Fidel comes hurtling down the stairs and bounds across the floor to hurl himself at me. I heft him into my arms. He smells wet, is wet, and slobbers all over my neck. I set him down and tell him to sit, which he does, panting.

Humate is silent, staring. At last he licks his lips and says, "How did the man get into the room the first time, to poison the pillow?"

This has always been the problem. A nobleman who manages to see inside a private chamber can return there at will whenever it is illuminated. Women's quarters everywhere are guarded day and night for just that reason.

"It was assumed, naturally, that the guards had been negligent. They all denied the charge and Clamant found no evidence that any of them was lying. The only logical explanation was that somehow the rapist had picked the lock on an earlier visit, somehow evading the guards. I learned the truth only a few days ago."

"And what's that?"

I stand ready to port out if he turns violent. "The same way you came to me on the island in Pean Bay, royal Humate of Alfet. The rapist ported to a person, instead of to a place. It's a nice trick, one I had never even heard a whisper of before."

"I didn't!" he says hoarsely. "That's impossible!"

"No it isn't. The funny thing is, now I find I can do it too. And I didn't inherit that ability from my mother's family."

For a moment we stare at each other, neither willing to put the logical conclusion into words.

Suddenly I am alone with Fidel.

Waving his shaggy tail, Fidel jumps up and trots over to meet Vert, who comes walking down the stairs with a heavy tread.

"That was a very brief visit."

Disgusted that I have again mishandled the master of Alfet, I say, "He just realized that he gave away the family secret. Hyla?"

"Asleep. She took the journey in her stride. She recognized Bastel and Nuddle right away." Vert is pleased, but after two very busy days he looks his age. "I feel guilty that we don't take her out more often."

"Guilty?" I stalk across to the window to stare out at the drizzle. It matches my mood perfectly. "If you feel guilty, what of a man who uses his mother as bait for a killer? If you thought the first plan was unethical, what do you think of this one?"

Loyally Vert says, "It was Izard who suggested it, not you. Since he's willing to hazard his daughter, he obviously thinks there's no risk. We'll have her back on the mainland long before Humate gets home to report. Will the boy report? Does he even know she's here?"

"I told him. He may not pass on the information." I feel unclean. Ants of guilt crawl over my skin. "He probably won't. He'd have to confess that he exposed the family secret about porting." It doesn't matter. I have changed my mind and now I must explain to Vert that all his work has been for nothing. "Royal, the only reason I went along with Izard's plan was because I could think of none better. And the only reason Izard suggested it was because he knew

I was contemplating a direct assassination attempt, and he thinks that will be suicide."

Vert walks across to me and lays a fatherly hand on my shoulder. "Izard is resting. Come upstairs and put on a dry tunic. You don't think Baby Dragon is hightailing homeward?"

We cross to the stairs and start climbing. I go slowly, thinking hard. "I'm sure he is, but he can't possibly get there much before the Dark, so we can wait until morning to move Hyla." Alazarin is too small to hide in, although it is big enough to keep the Enemy occupied for a long time if he tries to search it. "I don't believe the kid will tell his father one word about me or Hyla. He would have to explain how I twice made a fool of him in the arena." When Games Marshal Agynary predicted that Humate would get beaten yellow and purple, she was not entirely joking, because Piese of Rulero, consort of Pelta of Pelagic, is known as a violent man whose mistress ought to keep him under better control.

Vert speaks softly, short of breath. "Four of the old guard are still functional. I spoke with Volet of Demy. He rounded up Wirra, Labba, and Kish. Here he comes now."

The men he mentions are survivors of the dozen or so champions who served my grandmother Aglare before the coughing fever came. They are Izard contemporaries, long ago retired to their apanages. I am amazed and humbled that they will even consider aiding my cause. They no longer owe even token allegiance to Hyla, since she was deposed and another ruler sits on the throne of Alazarin. They certainly owe nothing to me, the bastard offshoot of rape.

Yet that is obviously old Volet standing at the top of the stairs, waiting for us with a yellow-toothed smile of welcome. In the two pentads since I was last on Alazarin, he has aged greatly and grown enormously. He was always a big man, stout in my childhood and now so obese that walking must be hard for him. Bald, red-faced, and swathed in a fur robe, he holds out both arms to me, dangling a cane in one hand.

I port up to him. Fat or not, he is still capable of a rib-creaking hug.

"Mudar! Mudar, my dear boy! It has been too long." He releases me to look me over. His shaggy silver eyebrows twitch when he notices the white caste mark on my forehead, but I know he will not comment on it.

"Much too long, princely Volet. I cannot say how much your willingness to help moves me."

He chuckles, his lungs rattling. "I have no ambition to die of boredom, lad. Mustn't call you that. Royal Mudar! A little excitement is welcome. Besides, now you have tracked down that monster at last, we all want to help bring him to justice. A few days camping out at Cape Bastel with you won't kill us. I hope it will kill him, though!"

"You put me to shame. This is my struggle, no one else's. You and the others are all very kind, very brave. But the plan has changed yet again." I glance at Vert to include him. "I decided I cannot do what noblest Izard suggests. I can't *do* it! It's not just that I would be staking out my mother as bait. It's young Humate, too. I would be implicating an innocent boy in a plot against his father. So I will *not* lurk out at Cape Bastel waiting for Piese of Rulero to come hunting me, and I certainly do not want to impose on anyone else to do it for me."

Old Volet looks bleak. "This quest has consumed your life, Mudar. Why quit now?"

"I am not quitting! Call me crazy if you like, but what Izard proposed was not honorable!"

"You are crazy," Vert says, but his smile approves. "That was Humate who arrived with you, though? Why did you bring him here at all, then?"

"I was going to use him to send a message, a different message— Plan Three, if you like. But even that won't work now, because he's gone." It has been a deplorable day. I am not sure how much of our discussion the old man has been following—Plans One, Two, and now Three. Or is it Four? "Princely Volet, you can help in another way, you and your brave companions."

He beams. "You have only to ask, dear boy, you know that."

"It's just that I may have roused a sleeping snake and put all of us in danger. As long as you and your three comrades know the Enemy's name and know that Humate of Alfet was here today, then you will be able to testify if anything nasty should happen to . . . *Suns bless me!*"

Vert says, "What's wrong?"

I laugh. "He's back! Humate's back!"

♦ ♦ ♦ PORT ♦ ♦ ♦

Looking utterly miserable, he is sheltering from the drizzle under some trees about fifty yards from the front door. He could have marked the spot when he was with me on the tower earlier, but he is behind a massive trunk, and not currently visible from the house. He scowls when I come forth beside him.

"You saw me come in here!"

"I did not. If you can't find your way back to Badderlocks I'll take you there."

"Of course I can! I'm not a child! I was four portages beyond that." He thrusts out his jaw defiantly. "Then I . . . I just . . . I decided I wanted to hear the rest of the story. But you're not to keep hinting that my father is a rapist!"

In other words, he decided he was running away from trouble and came back to face it. Good for him! I am starting to think there may be something to my young half-brother after all.

"I recalled you and ported to you. It does look as if we must be related, doesn't it?"

"No it doesn't! I admit it's a rare talent, but there must be lots of men who have it by now."

"How long has it been in your family, then?"

He avoids my eye. "I don't know. And if you hint once more

that my father is a rapist, I will rip your tongue out. I swear it! I really will!"

"Then I won't. Let's go indoors, friend."

♦ ♦ ♦ PORT ♦ ♦ ♦

We come forth in the hall. Vert is there, holding Fidel's collar. Fidel growls softly until told to stop. Vert has only princely caste and Humate must take precedence, so I present the older man to the boy. They bow and speak formalities.

Fidel edges forward to sniff at Humate, who ignores him.

"A couple of dry tunics would be nice," I say. "And our guest may appreciate some refreshment." That feels like a safe bet, because I do.

"The Lake Room," Vert says.

♦ ♦ ♦ PORT ♦ ♦ ♦

Nuddle's living quarters are less forbidding than the ground floor. There are fresh clothes available in the Lake Room. In the next-door River Room four mats are set out around a low table bearing food and flagons of wine. I still have seen no servants, but Izard and Vert will have brought few, if any, with them. Clamant is absent, attending Hyla. Rain clouds are burying whatever remains of daylight, yet Humate shows no signs of impatience to leave. He seems content to stay overnight. So be it.

Perhaps he will murder us all in our beds.

Or perhaps he just fancies the delicacies before us, most of which must have been transported from Osseter—skewers loaded with meat and vegetables, pastries, pickled fish, candied fruits.

We have just banished Fidel, whose table manners need work, and sat down, when old Izard comes limping in and we all port upright again. I present the noble to the noblest. Humate acts the perfect gracious young courtier, bowing low enough to put his nose

119

between his knees. Formalities over, the meal can begin. He accepts the first cup of wine from Izard's shaky hand. His own hand does not shake at all—a boy in a life-and-death confrontation with three much older men and his hand is steady as a mountain. Wonderful thing, arrogance.

Only twice or three times in my life have I ever seen old Izard eat without servants hovering around him, but he unabashedly does his share of passing baskets and dishes around as we sample the fare. He even dries his own fingers after rinsing them in his finger bowl, all the while making polite conversation. He poses a few banal questions about our journey; he compliments Humate on his proposed pairing. And then he asks me, "How much of the story have you told to the royal master of Alfet?"

Wonder of wonders! I have *never* known Izard to permit serious conversation at a meal, let alone initiate it. "Noblest Grandfather, I told him about the golden games and how you found noblest Hyla unconscious the next morning."

Izard sighs. "It was a terrible sight for a father, as you can imagine."

Humate swallows an overlarge mouthful. "Noblest, there is no need to distress yourself recounting dire memories on my account."

"No, you must know. The evils that seeded that night are still bearing their rancid fruit. You are involved and must be warned. We called for doctors and, by the suns' blessing, one of them was familiar with the odor of *hamulose*. They brought my daughter back from the gates of the Everlit Realm by a timely administration of antidote. You cannot imagine the confusion in the palace that morning! Many guests were ready to depart and anxious to make formal farewells. I had to explain that Hyla had taken ill. And I sent for the eight winners of our games. Two were found. Three others were known to have left. Three remained unaccounted for, and none of them had removed his effects—Piese of Greaten, Piese of Enthetic, and Tarn of Gyre."

Humate seems to have lost his appetite. Holding a forgotten

fish in his fingers he stares at Izard in horrified silence. The old man has always been a good storyteller.

"To shorten a long, sad tale, royal master of Alfet, Tarn's body was found in an alley, gruesomely mangled, hardly a bone unbroken. A corpse washed up on the shore a few days later was identified from scraps of tunic still clinging to it as Piese of Greaten. We did not know all this then, of course, so when I reported to the hegemon's representatives, I listed all three missing duelists as suspects. We had their pedigrees, which would make it easy to locate their families."

He sips his wine. "Foison's champions rushed back to Cuneal to tell her of the tragedy. Tarn's family was devastated by the news. So, likewise, was the family of the master of Greaten. In due course their worst fears were confirmed. Piese of Enthetic, on the other hand, was very happy to have the original of his pedigree returned to him. It had been stolen at a tourney a gnomon or so earlier."

Humate says, "It was a different Piese of Enthetic?"

"It was the genuine Piese of Enthetic."

We all wait, and finally Humate clears his throat and asks the necessary question. "So who was the fake one, noblest?"

Izard spreads his long and bony hands. "We had no way of finding out. We have always just referred to him as the Enemy. But I see we are distressing you, noble. Let us enjoy our meal and continue the tale later."

"No, I can eat. Please continue." Humate puts the sardine in his mouth and chews it with no sign of enjoyment.

Izard sips his wine. "My daughter, as I said, did not die, but she was critically ill for a long time. She has never properly recovered from the poison. To spare our name from scandal, Hegemon Foison ordered the affair kept secret. She sent her consort, noblest Bayard of Indican, here to investigate, but all his efforts to identify the villain were in vain. I continued my unorthodox regency in the hope that time would effect a cure."

He does not need to say that he has lived under a shadow of doubt ever since, suppressing the terrible thought that perhaps his daughter did, indeed, admit a man into her chamber. For a noble of his standards, such shame is unbearable. Humate glances at me appraisingly. Izard is apparently staring into his wine cup, but he notices.

"Yes, Mudar is my grandson. The Enemy got her with child."

"Or—" Humate draws a deep breath and cautiously says, "*Some* man got her with child."

The old man nods. "Anything is possible. No doubt she let every contestant in the games have a try. But three days ago, royal Humate of Alfet, you demonstrated a highly unusual ability in front of my grandson. You are able to port to a person!" Izard skewers the boy with a steely stare.

To his credit, he no longer tries to deny it. "If the person is well lit and not too far away."

"How far?"

He hesitates. "I prefer not to say."

"Understandably so. Pardon my temerity in asking. But Mudar, or Quirt, here. The son of Hyla of Sice and the unknown Enemy. Why, he can do it also! That is very strange. Do you know of anyone else with this ability?"

Humate shrinks like a snail into its shell. "I know my father can. I have no brothers, and my father does not know whether my grandfather could, for he died when my father was very young. I betrayed my father's confidence when I let you find out about it. *But other families may well be keeping the same secret!* And just because yeoman Quirt can do this and I can do it does not prove that either of us goes around raping and murdering!"

Vert remains silent. Izard passes the conversation to me with a glance.

I say, "We know what the Enemy looks like, royal Humate."

Three days ago I wanted to crush this boy in the arena. Now I detest myself for putting him through this torment. He is not guilty of anything, so why must he suffer? He is displaying true courage under our assault, the stag beset by hounds.

He winces as if that news hurts. "How?" he asks.

"Vert, you have lived with this longer than I have."

Vert turns to Humate with obvious reluctance. He, too, must feel guilty at tormenting a boy over a crime committed long before he was born.

"Noblest Hyla has never recovered her wits and the medics say that this is because of the *hamulose* poison. Her nightmare has never ended. She has not spoken since it happened. She cannot sleep during the Dark. Tall men terrify her. A few days after the assault, she projected a muddled image of it. She has continued to do so every few days since, endlessly reliving her torment. The man she depicts has never changed. Always she shows us the one we knew as Piese of Enthetic. Of course, he must be much older now than he seems in her imagings. Then he was not much more than your age, noble, but that was more than six pentads ago."

"Any high—" Humate's voice wavers. He stops and starts over. "Any noblewoman can do tricks with dragons and dancing bones and swords of fire. You are accusing my father, a hegemon's consort, on the basis of a madwoman's delusions."

"That and a few other matters." I reach for the plaque I carry next to my heart. "Long ago, Izard paid an artist to view the illusions my mother projected and draw this portrait. He will have changed, of course. Do you recognize him?"

I hold it out. Humate leans forward to peer at it but does not take it. "A drawing of an illusion is still only an illusion." His face has set like frozen lava. "No, I don't know him."

Nobles of very high caste seldom tell lies convincingly, because they have never had reason to learn how. Perhaps having Piese of Rulero for a father has made Humate an exception, because he is a good liar when he wants to be.

And I am a scorpion in a bedroll. "For a third of my life, for more gnomons that you can remember, I have hunted the man who wears this face. I first saw you, royal Humate of Alfet, thirteen days ago, last triangles-5. It happened by purest chance." That is not quite a lie, for although my friend Magnes of Scantling had put me behind the spyhole for exactly this purpose, it was chance that

Magnes had recognized the Enemy earlier as the man his friend Mudar was looking for.

Humate looks sick and says nothing.

"You were in the Court of Joyful Blossom in Formene. Your parents had brought you there to meet your future mistress, royal Tendence of Carpus."

He holds out a hand, which is not quite as steady as before. "Let me see it again."

I give him the plaque. He studies it and returns it.

"There is a resemblance. The nose . . . I can understand your error. But no court would convict on such evidence." He holds my gaze defiantly.

I must admire such confidence in one so young. "Believe me, my purpose in bringing you here was not to convince you of your father's guilt. Your opinion does not matter. What does matter is that I am convinced. I brought you here to tell you that I have a doom set upon me that requires me to wreak justice upon the man we call the Enemy, whom I now know to be Piese of Rulero, your father and consort of Hegemon Pelta of Pelagic. I charge you to go home tomorrow and warn him that I am coming. However long it takes, I will find him. I will kill him. This may well lead to my own death, but I have no option in the matter. Warn him!"

Humate casually pops another fish in his mouth, chews it, and swallows ostentatiously to show he is not scared of us. "Why should I?"

"Will you leave him in ignorance, so he is grass to my scythe?"

This is a watershed. If Humate is half the fiend his father is, he will now break my neck, then Izard's, and Vert's. He will seek out Hyla and kill her, probably Clamant also, plus any servants he may happen to find when he searches the house. And when Mother Blue rises tomorrow he will head for home without a care. He can do it. Will he?

He shrugs. "I know noblest Piese of Rulero very well. I have known him all my life. Guilty or innocent, he will port straight here. And you will be waiting for him at Cape Bastel, won't you? You are trying to use me to lead my father into a trap! *My father!* You expect me to lead my father into a trap?"

The sprig is smarter than he looks.

And I hate myself. I am tired of trickery and deceit.

"No. No, I don't. I expect you to warn him about that danger. I admit we did consider an ambush, but I abandoned the idea. If I wanted to use you as bait, lad, I would not have told you that I can do your porting-to-people trick. An ambush on an open beach would be just about impossible without that."

The boy eats an *antsigne* to give himself time to think. He nods. "So why did you tell me?"

"Because it seemed dishonorable to use you as bait. Because I am doomed to find him and bring him to justice, not just to kill him. I have found him, but a mere bushwhacking will not satisfy my doom. He must suffer, he must worry. That is as near as I can get to justice. Go and tell him I am on my way. I can strike at him at any time, anywhere, and I do not care if I lose my own life."

After a moment, Humate says sulkily, "You are still using me!"

"Yes, I am. But you cannot refuse to pass on the warning, can you?"

"Suppose he just runs away and disappears?"

I shrug. That is certainly a possibility and perhaps the most logical response to my threat. I am gambling that a man who satisfies his desires by callously trashing other people's lives will never abandon his powers and palaces and exalted status to bury himself in some cave or peasant's cottage for the rest of his life. I say, "He won't."

Humate does not argue the point.

Yet he does not look as worried as I should like him to. What is he planning? I start nervously as he leaps to his feet, but all he does is stalk over to the darkening window. Izard rises because his guest has. Vert and I perforce do the same.

The boy turns. "Justice, you said, Man Who Claims to Be My Brother? Killing isn't justice! If my father is the monster you claim, my mother must know about it—you think they do not share a bed? A noblewoman is responsible for controlling her consort. If you have a charge to bring against a hegemon, you take it to a hegemonic council."

I smile, because that had been my own reaction when I learned the Enemy's name. "That's a nice theory, but it won't work in real life." The person who explained this to me was Tendence, later that same night in Formene. As her mother's heir, she has been taught far more political theory than any man ever has. She instructed me, and I parrot her lesson: "Any two of the seven houses can impeach and it takes four votes to convict. Look at the numbers and you will see that I cannot even get a hearing. Balata of Heliac would want to support me to spite your father for arranging your pairing with Tendence without her permission. But your father is sprung of House Glyptic and paired into House Pelagic, so he has two votes right there. Our own hegemon, noblest Foison of Quartic, laid my doom upon me and should therefore support me, but she is obsessively opposed to scandal and her consort, noblest Bayard of Indican, is another Glyptic, so Quartic will make three for acquittal. That's three to one so far. Baric and Seric are both neighbors of Pelagic and would certainly support Pelagic against little Heliac, if only for economic reasons. Aspartic could only make trouble for itself by voting against the majority. Its hegemon is almost senile anyway. So we finish up with six to one for acquittal. Balata of Heliac will look at the numbers and either abstain or vote with the majority, making it unanimous."

Humate does not reply. Standing in the window embrasure, he has turned at bay and is watching the wolf pack closing in.

"And all six smaller hegemonies could not force justice on Pelagic," Vert says. "Your mother is the most powerful ruler in Aureity."

Humate nods. "You are actually talking sense!"

Izard says. "We must adjourn. It is time for prayers. We shall be honored to have the scion of House Pelagic join us."

I excuse myself to go and attend my mother.

3

Two doors along the corridor I hear a child laughing. Peering in, I find Clamant kneeling under a lantern, embroidering, which is her way of spending happy time. She smiles and nods for me to enter. A young Izard, no older than I am now, is playing with his daughter, tossing her up in the air and swinging her around. There is no background and no sound except the child's laughter. Hyla herself is kneeling on a sleeping rug, raptly watching her own memories. Clamant has dressed her in a sari of deep blue and gold brocade and concealed her white hair under a mantilla. She is ready to receive company. I cannot recall the last time I saw her wearing her caste mark.

I find a mat to kneel on. "I can stay awhile, if you would like to join the prayers."

Clamant nods her thanks, gathers up her bag of threads, and departs. My mother continues her play. This is very typical of her good times. Visions of anything that happened after the Enemy's attack are rare, and almost always depict me as a child. She never responded to me as a mother should, never spoke to me or played with me, but at some deep level she must have known who I was, and her fantasies of those times show us engaged in normal mother-child interactions that never happened—that I certainly wanted and she must have wanted also, somehow, and been unable to provide. It is as if the poison locked her in a cell and only her fingertips can reach out through the bars to the real world.

Izard fades and is replaced by a bouncing white dog—Fierce, the companion of her childhood. Laughing child and barking animal race over parklands of memory. After a hard day, I am content to relax and soak in my mother's dreams, relegating the problem of Humate and the Enemy to other times. But then the dog becomes brown-and-black, so he is now Warrior, who was *my* dog, when *I* was young. That means Hyla has detected my presence, although she has never once looked in my direction. It is time for me to intervene.

"Did you have a good journey here today, Mother?"

She scrambles up from the rug and hurries into a corner, keeping her back to me. I make myself as small as I can, in case she looks around.

"Come and sit down. You came back to Nuddle today. Did you enjoy the trip?"

She remains in the corner, like a child thinking it has disappeared when it covers its eyes, but she is aware of my question, because one of the great rock pillars at Cape Bastel fades into view and then out again. I could not recall it any more clearly myself. The sun was shining when she came by there, obviously. Now the front door of Nuddle. Then back, a portage close to Osseter. This is very good, for her. She is communicating, at least with herself. Her palace at Cantle, with a youthful Vert and Clamant dancing the *lilacin* together—an erotic memory I have seen only rarely. Faint music also. My mother is reliving the happy times before the Enemy . . . Ah! Now the music changes and a line of men is dancing a fearsome *cenacle*, with wild stamping and leaping—aided by no small amount of hefting. How else can a man perform six consecutive backflips without touching the ground? We are back in the time of the golden games, for I recognize men who have been identified to me by Vert or Clamant: Tarn of Gyre, Piese of Greaten, and the Enemy, wild youths all, showing off for the ladies and one special lady. Hyla must have paid close attention, for I can practically smell the boys' sweat as they display their agility.

"That's very good, Mother! Do you remember when I was learning to dance and one day—"

Footsteps and voices in the corridor . . .

The projection vanishes. I shout a warning, but I am too late. Vert has thrown open the door and Humate marches in, speaking over his shoulder.

". . . but after her death in childbirth, the ruler could not bear to look at him, so she traded him to House Heliac in return for . . ."

He is tall. Until now I have not realized that his voice is very like the voice of the Enemy as I have heard it in Hyla's projections.

She spins around and makes the first real sound I have ever heard from her, a knife-edge scream of rage or terror. She hurls herself across the room as if to tear out his eyes. Humate falls back in bewilderment, literally into Vert's arms. I catch Hyla in a psychic web before she can reach her victim. She struggles, screeching her vile animal noise, and then Clamant comes rushing in to embrace her. I am able to release her.

I am on my feet by then and we are all talking at once, trying to assure Humate that we had not planned this, that she has never re-acted like this before, and so on. Understandably, he looks both disbelieving and shaken. He could have batted Hyla back against the far wall of the room, and it is amazing that he did not do so just by reflex. He has just had a very narrow escape from physical con-tact with a madwoman.

Izard has joined us. "Royal master of Alfet, I am shamed that you should be so treated in this house." No one could disbelieve Izard.

Humate starts to reassure the old man, then breaks off and sniffs. "What's that smell?"

"*Hamulose*," I tell him.

The room has dimmed and now there are two Hylas present. The one in the sari still shivers in Clamant's embrace, but Humate is staring in amazement at the girl on the rug, no older than him-self, very lovely, wearing only a silken nightdress in the summer night. The room darkens even more.

"We had better leave," Vert says.

"Let him be!" I say as Humate angrily shakes off Vert's hand. "It is too late to stop this. Watch, boy! Watch as much as you can stand."

But Humate has already seen the Enemy appear in the shadows, drawing his sword, moving forward to stare down at the girl squirm-ing helplessly on the sleeping rug.

"I came to show you that you made a mistake," the intruder

says, in Humate's voice. He pokes his sword into the pillow and flips it away. "We don't need that now. It has done its work."

Now it is Humate who makes animal sounds. He must know that voice, that face.

"And we don't need this either." The Enemy kneels to rip open the girl's nightgown.

Humate wails and turns away, as his father starts removing his own clothes.

"Watch!" I shout. "It gets worse."

He screams "No!" and covers his face with his hands.

He has lasted longer than I usually do. I take his arm and guide him out of the room.

Lamps glimmer on the table and the meal stands as we left it. I take up a flagon of wine and hand it to him. He drinks half of it at a gulp. Neither of us sits down.

"I swear that we did not plan that," I say again. "She reacts badly to tall men, but in this case I think it was your voice. We did not plan to expose you to that nightmare. She has never been violent before. I am truly sorry."

His eyes are knots of pain. He starts to speak, stops, tries again, and finally says, "I can see that you have a case. There is a resemblance. But the charge is absurd."

Vert has appeared in the doorway; I gesture for him to wait.

"The resemblance convinces me, royal Humate. Suppose I went to your mother and denounced your father as rapist and murderer—what would she do?"

It is an idiotic question. He just shakes his head and bends to replace the flagon on the table.

"We can discuss it in the morning," I say.

Vert bows to our guest. "I will show you to your room, royal. You will pardon my mentioning this," he gives a twisted little smile, rubbing his hands in his fussy way, "but your arrival this evening was reported to four distinguished noblemen, former champions of Hyla's mother."

Humate rounds on him. "That is just the sort of crude insult I would expect from a rural bumpkin. Go away."

Vert recoils and then stalks out, rigid with anger.

"My manners are no better than his, you know," I say. But I would not have warned a man of higher rank not to plot mass murder in the night.

Humate scowls at me, too. "You are a bastard, not born of a legal pairing. You are not entitled to wear any caste mark at all."

"It is more complicated than that. My case is unusual. Male rape is a crime of ordinaries. Among nobility, it is the woman who forces the man and the crime is extremely rare. I was certainly no love child, for my mother did not consent to the act that resulted in my conception. When I was a child, Izard petitioned Hegemon Foison to grant me the eight quarterings I inherited from Hyla, and the noblest consented."

"I never heard of that happening," he says suspiciously. "That's not proper!"

"A hegemon can dictate heraldry in her realm. She liked Hyla and probably felt guilty about having allowed open games instead of just appointing some personable young royal to be her consort."

"So eight. I still see white, not orange." His sneer makes him seem very young, very vulnerable. He would sneer a lot more if he knew I was unnamed later, so that what I have told him is irrelevant.

"But you forget that I am a doomed man. My doom forces me to do anything that seems likely to help me fulfill my destiny, legal or illegal. Complaints about my behavior must go to the hegemon who imposed the doom. I find that a royal mark helps me in my search for justice. At Quintole I needed help from Marshal Agynary and her staff, and she had known me as a highborn." I smile at his scowl. "May I show you to your room?" I usher him out. "This has been a terrible shock to you, I am sure, and you will need to—"

"Not really." The corridor is too dark for me to see his face, and perhaps that is why he can speak a virtual surrender. "I don't mean I believe you. I don't admit Father was the man who assaulted your mother, just that I've heard serious charges made against him before. He does have a temper. He broke my wrist once. . . . I know some people think that Mother ought to take him in hand. There have been reports of . . . of unwelcome attentions. Just from ordinaries, of course, not noblewomen. All noblemen get accused of that sometimes. The women want psychic babies and then think they can blackmail some money to support them. What's a fellow supposed to do when they beg?"

Refuse, and if his mistress discovers that he has conducted himself dishonorably, she should improve him so he can never do so again.

I open the door to the main guest room. It is as good as Nubble has to offer, large and well appointed, but the scent of perfumed oil from the lamps does not quite banish a faint smell of rot, and the wall hangings look faded and fragile. They have hung there as long as I can remember. Its windows face east and stars are in attendance out there. The rain has ended.

"Sit," Humate says, and flops down cross-legged on the sleeping rug.

Sensing that we are in for a lengthy chat, I close the door and take a mat near him. He waits for me to speak first, not looking at me. Does he want prompting? More convincing? Or comforting?

I say, "Temper? You say our father has a temper? The attack on my mother was no sudden pique. It was not a casual flirtation getting out of hand. I do not say those can be excused in any way, but every man has sensed the beast within himself and fears it. What was done to Hyla was deliberate, calculated rape and attempted murder. The Enemy came to Alazarin with the stolen pedigree in his baggage. Instead of competing as a blank, he stole another man's name, yet he performed at hegemonic or significant-family level. That suggested to us that he was a love child."

"A bastard, you mean."

"Yes. Ineligible to compete, anyway. He might have been vilified or unnamed, but nobody recognized him during the Alazarin games. Nobody recognized him at any later games, so far as we ever heard.

The tourney circuit is a small world and the open golden games had brought in all the real enthusiasts from all over Aureity; yet the brute who had claimed to be Piese of Enthetic was never seen before or since. Curiously, though, the pedigree had been stolen at a tourney."

"Doesn't mean anything. He could have taken it out of a manager's lodgings." Humate stares miserably at the floor for a while as if it might hold the answer to his problem. "My father despises games. He never competed in the arena. Games are beneath rulers' dignity, he says."

Or else he is afraid of being recognized as the fake Piese of Enthetic.

Humate says, "His own pairing was negotiated between hegemons. Why should we royals have to jump through hoops for the rabble? I wouldn't have, except the Tendence woman insisted I wasn't old enough. I offered to lift my tunic and show her, but Father said I'd better prove it the conventional way." He sighs. "You showed me that she was right."

"Not at all. You swatted flies with the first three men you met."

He chuckles. "I did, didn't I?"

"I beat you because I had more experience. Anyway, I have hegemonic blood on my mother's side, because Izard's mother was hegemon of Seric, and his father was one of the Lampas, a significant family. I'm at least half a dragon myself."

"Suns' asses, you are! Then I don't feel quite so bad."

Another charge against noblest Piese of Rulero is that he has raised his son to be a prodigious snob.

"Your . . . *Our* . . . father did compete once, Humate. Possibly he chanced to visit Cuneal and saw Hyla there and took a fancy to her, or perhaps he just heard about the open games and thought he would have some fun by winning and then refusing the pairing. He could not enter as a blank, not golden games, so he stole another man's name and lineage. With his bloodlines he must have expected to win the games quite easily, and probably the girl also. When he didn't, he flew into a maniacal rage. I've often wondered whether he made a fast trip back to Glyptic for the *hamulose*, or had brought it with him. He killed the men who had bested him—Piese of Greaten went to the sharks and Tarn of Gyre was battered against a wall until he was seven times dead. My mother was beaten and raped and left to die. I'm not sorry he was not around in my childhood. He might have broken my wrists, too."

For a moment neither of us speaks.

The whites of Humate's eyes shine in the lamplight. "You're saying my mother is guilty also, you know. Or do you suppose my father can keep secrets from her?"

"That is your problem, not mine." Tendence has told me that Pelta is mean-spirited and thin-witted, completely dominated by her consort and afraid of him. Tendence is convinced that her proposed pairing to Humate was Piese's idea, not his mistress's, and he has pushed it for political reasons, to gain control of Formene Strait. I believe Tendence in all things.

After a long pause, Humate says, "I do not for a moment agree that the rapist was my father, but I'll give you the benefit of the doubt."

"The benefit of what doubt, sonny?"

"I thought you were trying to use me in some sort of elaborate blackmail scheme, but it's gotten too complicated to be that. So I will accept that you truly believe you are the son of that unfortunate madwoman and the man whose picture you carry. Back in Mascle we have a portrait of my parents, painted at the time of their pairing, and he didn't look at all like that. But you genuinely seem convinced otherwise. You are not dishonest, just mistaken."

After a day of almost unbroken porting, I am deathly weary and must sleep. "You cannot imagine how comforted I am to hear that."

"You have convinced yourself that my father sired you. How can you condemn a man to death for bringing you into the world?"

"I can't," I admit. "But I neither love nor respect him. I was not doomed to avenge that crime. No hegemon would lay such a doom on a man."

I am eager to go to my room, the room that was my bedchamber all through my childhood. Tomorrow may be even worse than today. We must send Humate home to report, and move Hyla back to safety at Osseter, and find some other safe houses for her while I rattle the Enemy's chains.

"Mm. Then who put you on my father's trail, and why?"

I heave myself to my feet. "That's another story. I'll tell you tomorrow."

"No, old man. I want to hear it tonight!" Humate does not sound in the least tired. "You can't lay half this load on me and then just stop. You're telling me we're brothers."

I nod. "Half-brothers. It takes some getting used to, doesn't it?"

"And your mother-half wants me to help you kill our father. I need some brotherly advice from the father-half. Talk!"

"Tomorrow." I try to turn and discover that my feet will not move. The kid has pinned them. I pull as hard as I can and make no impression on his psychic grip. It is beautifully done, too—most pinning feels like iron bands or cement, but I can feel nothing until I try to break free. He just sits there, nonchalant, seemingly able to resist my efforts with no difficulty at all. I can retaliate—by threatening to pull his ears off, say—but wrestling Humate would be a very dangerous exercise. I cannot port out in the Dark, and if I could I would probably leave my feet behind.

I admit defeat. "All right, then, tonight. May I sit down?"

With a leer of satisfaction, he releases his grip. I heft a mat over and then a hassock to lean on. To tell him Hyla's tragic story was not easy. To recount my own will be much harder, but I suppose I owe it to him.

"I was born unwanted. Vert and Clamant and Izard made me welcome, although I wasn't. My mother was unable to react to me."

Where to begin? The day I met Egma?

"Like all young noblemen, I grew up dreaming of fame in the arena. . . ."

IV

Triumph at Cuneal

1

"The crowns and stars may be indiscreet," Eviternal of Patas announced firmly. "Contenders with only eight quarterings do sometimes win admittance to the silver circuit, but a cloak proclaiming that your fourbears include hegemons and rulers will make people assume that your royal parent married an ordinary."

"As soon as I set foot into the arena I will disabuse them of that misapprehension."

I was young and very brash. Izard and Vert had trained me and for the last few gnomons had taken turns conducting me to almost every tourney in Aureity, sitting with me in what is vulgarly known as the kibitzer cage, the box reserved for champions and their sons or other protégés, the next generation. A man who keeps his eyes and ears open there can learn everything he will ever need to know about the arena. Whoever the Enemy had been, he had demonstrated enormous strength in the arena and I had inherited at least some of it, so I would be competing well above the level associated with my caste. For a dozen gnomons I had been twitching to get started. I knew I was good. I thought I was stupendous. Looking back, I realize that I was barely ready, even then.

Eviternal seemed scarcely middle-aged, but she had been Izard's manager two generations ago and her movements were slow and cautious. She was retired now; he had brought me here to draw on her wisdom.

The two of them sat in a gazebo in a forest at Patas, which is just outside Stridor, in Baric. They were sipping perfumed tea while I held up my tourney cloak for Eviternal's inspection. Looking back, I understand that Patas was an idyllic spot, full of birdsong and drowsy blossom fragrance, sunlight dripping through greenery. I did not notice.

"I was thinking of the offers you will get," she said primly. "You may put the cloak away and my advice with it."

I apologized and hastily returned to my mat. "I certainly do appreciate the chance to learn from your experience, highborn Eviternal."

She sniffed.

Izard was shrunken and silent. Hyla's shame lay a generation in the past—my lifetime and about four gnomons more—but it tortured him still. To discuss it with an outsider was intensely painful for him, and I was not mature enough to make allowances for that. I just wanted my shackles struck off so I could leap forth and amaze the world.

"No matter how good you are, young man," Eviternal said, "the games are not mere sport. Their purpose is to find you a place in the world and the best possible breeding partner. Noblest Izard assures me that you have exceptional strength. Fair enough! But in all my days on the circuit, and they were many, I never heard of a noblewoman claiming that she was taken against her will. Eight fourbears combined with unusual strength are most easily explained by a massive scandal—such as adultery, or your father having being unnamed, perhaps."

That shocked me. Izard hid his face in his hands.

"Your strength may well win you an honorable office, but your pairing is another matter. No high-rank noblewoman wants her children to have fewer fourbears than she has." She thought for a while. "But perhaps the stars and crowns are not a bad idea after all. Rulers and hegemons cannot be dismissed lightly. Without them you will seem sprung from low in the nobility. With them, you attract attention. If you are as strong as you think you are, which I seriously doubt, we may be able to negotiate a longer-than-usual probation and a promise of a mistress with a minimum of, say, twelve quarterings. I know of precedents. There is a bronze tourney at Stridor the day after tomorrow."

"A good one, I hear."

The old lady smiled for the first time. "And my granddaughter is a good manager."

Her granddaughter, Egma of Strift, was a rank newcomer. I was her first client likely to rise out of the bronze circuit, but orphans cannot be choosy and she had Eviternal to advise her. She was a lanky girl with an angular, birdlike face and a harsh voice, but Egma and I got along very well.

Stridor is a good place to launch a tourney career, because its games are the first of a run of three bronzes in quick succession, so agents find it worthwhile to follow the young hopefuls around the circuit. I took the crown at Stridor so decisively that several agents asked to view my pedigree. Egma declined. After my second crown, at Swanpan, she had to refuse many more such requests and I became insufferable.

Old Eviternal was not as impressed as I had expected, but she agreed I could now try the silver circuit. "Quintole triangles-1 is building a good reputation," she said. "Start there."

"That's a long way!"

"So if you fall flat on your face, you can come back here and hope the news does not."

I had underestimated the old harridan. She knew I was worrying about the cost of hiring a porter to get me to Quintole. Although I was of age and now had income from my apanage, it was hard put to support me on the games circuit, and I was determined not to sponge off Izard. Eviternal arranged for me to meet Emodin of Osseter, who had just entered the silver circuit. He took me there, then I brought him back so we could transport our respective managers. That was my introduction to the fellowship of the games and the start of my long friendship with Emodin.

The next day I returned his kindness by beating him in the wrestling, but that is part of the code also.

I won handily at Quintole. Agents from larger realms began wooing the cryptic highborn newcomer, even accosting me in the halls and at the postgame reception for which the Quintole tourney was famous. I stayed just sober enough to refer all queries to my manager. That was the evening I met the unforgettable Agynary in her sea-cave bordello; also her girls.

After Quintole I went back to Cantle, on Alazarin, to tell Izard my news and flaunt my three crowns. He embraced me with tears in his eyes.

"I never doubted you," he said. "Beast though he was, the Enemy bequeathed you great strength. Use it better than he did. When will you pay your respects to the hegemon?"

This was a sore point between us. Uniquely, the Old Man was still running Alazarin as vizier for his "indisposed" daughter. Hegemon Foison had ordered the scandal hushed up at the time and hushed up it had remained throughout my entire life, as if the world had forgotten that Alazarin even existed. No companions made tours of inspection now. Change must come soon, though, because Izard was growing old and tired, Hyla remained incapable, and I could not succeed her. A male ruler was unthinkable, even in remote Alazarin.

"Foison is saving it for you, lad," he insisted. "She loved Hyla. Win another silver and then go straight to Cuneal. The noblest will swear you in as champion, find you a worthy mistress, and appoint her ruler of Alazarin, you'll see."

Intoxicated with youth, I spurned advice as a roof sheds rain. I wanted to make my own success in the world, not be banished to live with some unpopular palace discard. Being given my mother's realm back as some sort of compensation for her suffering did not appeal.

"When I've collected more silvers we can talk about it again," I promised.

Izard sighed. "Enjoy yourself, lad. These are the best days of your life."

I won my second silver crown at Stope, in Seric. Having made a lecherous fool of myself at Quintole, I had resolved to stay reasonably sober afterward, a decision that was to have very tragic consequences.

The reception in Stope Palace was small as those things go— perhaps a hundred noblemen in all, including sixteen boisterous young men in barely decent fighting tabards, a score of beardless youths lingering as close to us as they dared and eavesdropping in the hope of picking up valuable hints, landowners muttering about weather and crops, plus ancient toothless champions grousing in corners at how the standard had fallen since the games of their youth. There were many more women, all seemingly young and breathtakingly gorgeous, plus several hundred ordinaries: waiters, musicians, and entertainers.

We men danced for the women. They danced for us. We had a few joint dances, where we circled daringly close. The contestants were expected to perform for the company—singing, or dancing, or performing acrobatics. Emodin was a skilled juggler, with a fine line of patter. My party piece was to sing and play the zither. My voice was more nimble than my fingers, but as crowned winner I was given two encores. We played games—word games, mostly, but some childish hide-and-seek variants.

The merrymaking went on long after whiteset, which the country boy from Alazarin found very daring. Izard firmly believes that we are children of light and sleep is a blessing the suns send to comfort us during the dangerous watch of the Dark. To be awake in the Dark is not only folly but sin, he thinks. I found it a thrill. In Seric they claim that looking too long at the stars will drive people insane. Thirsty from a hectic dance, I wandered out on a balcony to stare up at them and sip a long drink.

You are very annoying, you know?

I was not aware of anyone near me, certainly not close enough to convey thought unless she had an extraordinary range. I turned to scan the terrace, but it was deserted. Was I insane already?

"On the contrary," I said, "I am quite extraordinarily lovable."

That is what I mean. You sing like a sunlark.

"I sang only for you, noble." I decided that she must be behind the butterfly shrubs, but even they were a very long way away. Unobtrusively, I elbowed my tankard off the parapet into the flower beds below.

And you lie convincingly. Why do you claim only eight quarterings? You are much, much stronger than that. I saw you at Quintole, too.

My interest shattered into shards of annoyance—another agent!

"Ask my manager."

I did. She said she was forbidden to tell me.

"Well, come here and I will tell you, if you are as lovable as you seem."

And she was!

Yes, she was. She came drifting across the paving like an impossible dream—young and tall and graceful as gossamer in the wind. Her sari was silver and pale blue, her hair was a cloud of blackest curls speckled with pearls like raindrops, she was starlight made woman. I had seen her around earlier and wondered what sort of ghastly frump would stoop to making herself so infinitely desirable. I stopped caring as she approached. I was young, remember, and Quintole had whetted my baser appetites.

She did not wear the silver knot badge of an agent, so all my excitement returned. She came uncomfortably, dangerously close. So close that she must smell the beer on my breath. I stopped breathing.

"If you had sixteen quarterings I would buy you," she said.

I could smell wine on her. My conscience screamed warnings.

"My price might be too high."

"I could pay it."

"You probably could," I admitted hoarsely. "If it includes pairing, then I am available for two apples and a sprig of lemon blossom. I will waive the apples, if pressed."

She laughed. "Why only eight quarterings?"

"It is all I am entitled to."

"Rubbish," she said, slurring the word. "Who was your father?"

"I don't know. If I did I would kill him."

"That is not very funny."

I was young. She was lovely beyond words and we were both a little drunk on a warm, fragrant, starry night. I said, "Look, then," and moved even closer. By the time I remembered that she would also learn what I had been up to at Quintole, only a few days before, it was too late to back off.

She laid cool fingertips on my forehead. I had never guessed that a reading could be done so fast—she whipped her hand away as if I were red hot.

"Oh! That's horrible!"

"Very."

She put her arms around me but I had nothing left to lose, so I did not protest. (*Me* protest? Nothing was less likely.) I swiftly made the embrace mutual and tighter. She was both soft and firm, both warm and cool, and her scent was intoxicating. I would willingly stand there and hold her forever.

"His caste must have been very high."

"But his morals were not."

"Mudar? That is your name?"

"Yes. And yours?"

She hesitated. "Call me Mandola."

"Mandola. Mandola? Mandola! Mand—"

"Mudar, dear, will you promise me something?"

"Mandola, darling, in return for what?"

"A kiss?"

"Just one?"

"Just one, and a very brief one."

"Then ask anything in the entire universe. That is all I have on me at the moment."

"Will you promise not to let anyone buy you yet? I want you, but your caste is a problem. I must take advice."

"Will half a gnomon be long enough? I am planning to win another five or six crowns before I started taking offers."

I felt her chuckle. "That would help. Where will you compete next?"

"Whoso, on boats-1."

"I will be there."

Then she kissed me. I cooperated with great enthusiasm. We held that kiss long enough for her to reduce my mind to the size of a housefly's, had she wanted to, but she did not seem to be working very fast, because I was aware of nothing except our mouths and bodies pressed together. Then my arms sprang open of their own accord.

"That is definitely enough!" Mandola said.

Even in the starlight I could see the blush suffusing her face. Mine felt a thousand times hotter.

"I beg to differ."

"Beg all you want. I will see you at Whoso. Don't follow me in."

I went instead in search of Egma and found her chattering business within a group of managers. She took one look at me and excused herself quickly. I retreated around a corner and she came after me.

"What is wrong?" she demanded.

"Absolutely nothing. Nothing whatsoever. Wrong, you say? Have you seen a girl . . . woman . . . a royal in a silver and blue sari, pearls in her hair?"

My manager's eyes stretched very wide. "Yes."

"Is she as young as she looks?"

"I would say younger."

"Younger?"

"But nubile."

I did think she was nubile. Oh, definitely that! "Do you know anything more about her?"

Now my manager was wearing a definitely odd expression. "I know she's here under a false name. I have heard rumors. You are not suggesting—"

"No, she is."

"Mother give me light!" Egma said. "That's utterly impossible! Whatever you're drinking, princely Mudar, you'd best sober up quickly."

"Never. The hangover would kill me."

Her full name was Mandragora of Fargite. Mandola was just what the family called her, back home in the palace in Cuneal.

At Whoso I was number-one seed and winning my third silver crown seemed almost easy. Two bronze and three silvers in five tourneys was a spectacular career, and would have been remarkable for a man of sixteen quarterings. It was the sort of score that a boy from a hegemonic or significant family might run up, except that he would normally stop as soon as he had shown his mettle. The other cubs began threatening to sit out any games I entered, but they all assumed I would be bought up soon.

At Whoso, with my latest crown still cool on my brow, I ported up to Egma's booth. A heavyset, middle-aged champion came forth outside it and strode in, resplendent in Quartic heraldry and a royal caste mark. He glowered at me as if I were filthy and stank like a goat pen. I was both, and also ragged, because my tabard had been shredded in the wrestling.

"I am sent to fetch you, highborn Mudar of Quoin."

"I am in no state to go calling on anyone."

He raised shaggy brows. "You would keep her waiting?"

Before I could answer I was in her bedchamber. My porter disappeared at once, leaving me alone with the hegemon's daughter. She was clad in scarlet this time, with rubies in her hair.

She said "Darling!" and hurled herself into my arms. Dirt, sweat, and rags did not matter at all, apparently. The kiss lasted about half a watch. This was our second meeting, after all, and Mandragora of Fargite was nothing if not decisive.

When we backed off an inch, I said, "Please can I go and make myself respectable?"

"No." She had a gamin grin that shrieked warnings. "I like you all sweaty and bestial and aroused. It's very flattering. But, darling, you will have to wait a little while longer." She marched over to the window, feet tapping on the tiles. I hefted a sheet from the bed and hid my shame in a silken wrapping.

"How did your mother take your news?"

"Much as expected. Screamed like a hunting horn. Threatened that if I ever see you again she will chain me in a dungeon and brick up the door."

This was Foison of Quartic we were discussing, the hegemon, *my* hegemon. When a hegemon puts someone's head on her shopping list, it is delivered by bluenoon. "And what did you say?"

"I told her to go scrub out the stables. Oh, this is so stupid!" Mandola stamped her foot. She *was* younger than she had pretended at Stope. Now she was not bothering to deceive me—I could tell that because her hair was cut short and she had a sprinkling of freckles on her nose—yet I found her reality every bit as gorgeous as her public illusion. "I mean, really! I'm a political nonentity. I have two older sisters with a million daughters between them. Why shouldn't I buy you and go off and live on your romantic little island with you forevermore? What do stupid quarterings matter? You would make stupendous babies. And if Mother ever wants me to brush her hair or paint her toenails, you could have me back in Cuneal in half a watch, couldn't you?"

"Less." That would be after a porter had brought the summons, though.

"Well then!" She stalked over and twined herself around me again. Sharp teeth nibbled my collarbone. "I will keep working on her. And you *must* keep winning! You were wonderful today, my hero. Where's the next tourney?"

"I've been invited to compete in golden games at Brach. Invitational!" I added hastily, guessing a misunderstanding might provoke dangerous reactions from my would-be mistress. "Not open games."

"Of course not, or I would kill you." She judiciously put a bite mark on my neck and then licked it. "Ruler Mottle imposing her daughter on some poor stud! I cannot stand the woman, but I'll tell her I'm coming and make it the social triumph of her life."

"It's just one day." I could use the purse of gold, but what would a hegemon's daughter know of that?

"One day will be plenty for me. I will see you there. But you *must* keep winning!"

"I'll try, beloved. But no one can guarantee success in the arena. I may run up against hegemonic opposition soon."

"I am certain you will," Mandola murmured. "Your skin tastes salty and sandy, both. You want to take me to bed?"

"Isn't that a capital offense?"

"So? Don't you want to show me how much you love me? Am I not worth dying for?"

"Will you let me?"

"No. I was just asking. You do love me, don't you?"

I kissed her as if I never intended to stop. At first she squirmed seductively against me, but I broke off when she began to go limp. Needless to say, I had a contrary problem. She buried her face against my shoulder.

I found my voice with difficulty. "My darling Mandola, I cannot imagine anything in the world I would rather be than your consort. You are the sexiest woman I have ever met. I lust after you ferociously. Life with you will be everlasting astonishment and joy. Have I told any lies yet?"

After a moment she looked up and managed her wicked gamin grin. "Am I really sexier than the girl at Quintole, the fat one?"

"I can't tell without trying you out."

"Monster!" She punched me. I kissed her again and she bit my lip. Then she kissed it better.

I won the golden crown at Brach but saw no sign of Mandola there. I was not surprised. A girl of her rank is a political asset to be traded off for her ruler or hegemon's advantage. She is lucky even to be told her future consort's name before the contract is signed, let alone meet him, and allowing her to choose her own man on a whim would be an unthinkable waste of a state resource. I tucked my mad dreams away in my vault of experiences. I could only hope that Hegemon Foison had not been serious about the dungeon.

But I kept on competing and would not listen to offers.

"You are insane!" Egma cried. "Three *hegemons* have asked for your terms and I've lost count of the significant families. Foison herself has offered an apanage with a revenue of a thousand saros a gnomon and a mistress of *royal* caste. What more can you possibly want?"

"Her daughter."

"Impossible! She would be a laughingstock. You have only eight quarterings."

"She can change that."

"And insult every major family with an unpaired son on its hands?"

My colleagues, too, grew impatient. Why risk adding failure to such a string of successes? I had six . . . seven . . . eight . . . crowns and counting. They called me the Grand Dragon and said I was being greedy, I was spoiling every other man's career. That wasn't really true. The agents had learned to compensate for me. If I had competed, then a bracelet was worth a crown and a ring worth a bracelet. And I was approaching the practical limit. No tourney admits a previous winner and there are only a dozen silver tourneys each gnomon, although a few others are held less often. The hegemonic games are the richest of all, celebrated each bells-1 in a different capital. Cuneal was next. I eventually promised Egma that if I saw no trace of Mandola there, then I would trim my dreams to the width of my bed, as Izard would say.

Porting back and forth across Aureity, I often wondered if the Enemy followed the sport and knew me for his own. Then I would remember that he had left Hyla dying and only wild good fortune had brought her a doctor who both recognized the smell of *hamulose* and happened to have the antidote in his bag. The Enemy could not know that I existed. He had not been heard from since, so most likely he had tried his vile tricks on some other high-caste lady and she had boiled his brain to idiocy. If he still lived, he was probably a slobbering, shuffling swineherd somewhere.

2

Cuneal is a fair city in a wide valley between spectacular snowcapped ranges. Scores of fine buildings of pure white marble flank the widest boulevards in all Aureity, and the hegemonic palace alone is a miracle of spires and domes larger than many of the world's cities. The amphitheater is said to hold thirty-seven thousand people, with even the ordinaries seated in covered stands. Mountains hold off the wind, marble reflects sunlight, and the heat down on the sand is sadistic. I have also seen it in winter with snow knee-deep.

Just to make matters worse, hegemonic games start at whiterise with a card of thirty-two contestants, so we have twice as long to shrivel up, or freeze, as the case may be. The nobility of Aureity breed their children for psychic strength, but the way they go about it puts a premium on sheer physical toughness also. No ordinary could endure what we do in the arena.

I arrived early, delivered Egma to her booth, and ported over to the marshal's box to swear the oath. When I returned, Egma was alone, but she must have been speaking with someone, because she was wearing a dangerous I-told-you-so expression.

"Let me guess," I said. "They can't field a complete ticket? No one wants to compete against Mudar the Spoiler?"

"On the contrary, master of Quoin. The list is oversubscribed. There are four blanks entered."

I sat down rather hard on the floor. Blanks never get close to hegemonic games. Even with the double ticket, there are always cubs enough.

"Noblest Foison has four sons?" My string of victories had just run out. "Do you know anything about them?"

Egma shrugged grimly. She had taken to sharing my dream, a little. Her commission on a hegemon's daughter's consort would be mind-boggling. "Three sons: Destin, Harfang, and Jasp. There isn't much else to know. Grandmother warned me this might happen. The family is going to stop you, Mudar! If they can't do it by fair means, they will use foul. Do you want to drop out now?"

Crazy kid, I just said, "No. They may beat me but they'll never scare me."

The news spread quickly. Emodin and several other friends drifted by to commiserate and drop broad hints that I ought to pull out. Trophies in hegemonic games are worth having just for the value of the silver in them and this time I was not stealing just one honest man's prize; the dragons on my tail would win them all and leave nothing for the true cubs.

"There is only one person who can make me withdraw," I insisted. If my answer was conveyed back to the authorities, it did no good.

When we assembled down on the sand, the four blanks were conspicuous in plain cloaks and tabards of gold and green, the hegemon's own colors—a nice touch, that, I thought. Three of them were too old to be cubs. The youngest, who wore a white cloak, ported over to me. He was a slim youth with dark curly hair. I recognized his grin.

"The unbeatable Mudar of Quoin?"

I bowed. "The very same. And I assume royal Jasp of Lemma?" Jasp was the fifth child, nearest in age to Mandola, but more than a full pentad older, she having been an unexpected afterthought. Jasp was the one to watch, according to Egma's information. He had enjoyed competing and had entered—and won, of course—more tourneys than were seemly for a hegemonic. He had recently been appointed consort to the heir of a sizable realm in Seric. What was he doing back home again instead of attending his mistress?

Enjoying himself, obviously.

"You have caused quite a stir in my family, friend Mudar."

"How is your royal sister?"

He shrugged, dark eyes gleaming with amusement—they always gleamed with amusement. Jasp saw life as one enormous joke. "Eating, I expect. She just ended a two-day hunger strike, her third. Threatens suicide right after dessert."

"I would do anything to save her life."

Jasp sighed. "No, it is hopeless. Mother offered to buy you and appoint you Mandola's majordomo or chief bodyguard or anything else she wanted, short of consort. The child is adamant. She wants your body."

That was both flattering and exciting. "The desire is certainly mutual. Your noblest mother disagrees?"

He chuckled and lowered his voice, although no one was daring to approach us. "I have never seen the old goose cackle so! No offense to your noble person, Mudar. It is your quarterings she cannot abide. She is adamant that you will not turn this into a golden games. She called us all in and made us swear that you shall not pass."

"Crushed lifeless, blood draining gently into the sand?"

"Too messy, too obvious. No," Jasp said sadly. "As a last resort, if you are not eliminated sooner, one of those horrible javelin accidents. We decided that would be simplest and comparatively painless. I was volunteered."

I have never known a death threat more beautifully delivered, nor more believable. His range and strength would certainly far exceed mine; even the lifetime ban on competing would mean nothing to him now he was paired. The supreme authority in Quartic, his mother, was hardly likely to press manslaughter charges.

"It is very brotherly of you," I admitted, "to go to such lengths to save the fair maiden from my baseborn lusts. But—you will forgive my wondering—suppose the victim and victor were somehow transposed? These things can happen, no matter how carefully we choreograph the catastrophe."

He shrugged. "Then your death would be considerably slower

and more painful than mine. But let us not dwell on such morbid thoughts. I never miss." Still he smiled, and so convincingly that I honestly could not tell if he was serious or joking. I was relieved when a referee and linesman arrived to start the flyby.

The three dark-horse brothers had not been seeded. Since I was, absurdly, seeded number one, I was the last to launch. As I soared past all the grandees in the hegemonic box, I braced for the usual hefting attack, but none came. What did come was a sending: *I love you! Win this and win me, darling.* I was getting messages like that quite often now, but I knew who was conveying that one, and it quelled any doubts I still had. Obviously Mandola had won the concession she wanted from her mother—pairing with me, conditional on my winning the crown that day. Then the old tyrant had called in her sons to make certain I would lose.

Hegemonic games require an extra event to cull the field. Cuneal uses a sport called rollerball, played by teams of four with a marble ball about five feet in diameter. First goal wins. Lifting such a monster is out of the question. It takes a good team even to roll it over the sand, especially when four equally good men are hefting in the opposite direction. Although the ball, forced in opposing directions, may sometimes squirt unexpectedly sideways, that day was the only time I ever heard of anyone being hurt in rollerball. A cub in the third match had an apoplexy brought on by the heat.

In theory, the rollerball teams are chosen by lot. No doubt the hegemon could have arranged for all three of her sons to be on one team and me on the other side, ready to be juiced, but—as Jasp had said—that would have been too crude and obvious. Mandola would have cried foul. Because no man can choose his teammates and no one ever has an opportunity to practice rollerball, it contains a large element of chance. That is another reason why hegemonic games attract so many contestants—sheer luck can often weed out the favorites before the real contest even begins.

My team won. So did the team with Jasp and his brother Harfang on it. Also the team with Destin, eldest of the three brothers. The suns shone and all four of us were through into the second round. The hegemon had gotten what she wanted. Was that surprising?

I fully expected to be eliminated in the hefting contest. I already knew I was going to be matched up with Blue, alias the hegemon's second son, Harfang of Ohone. A balk of wood is a balk of wood, and to try and match strength *mano a mano* with a hegemonic was insanity. He could probably lift thirteen or fourteen of them, many more than I could. There was no wind to topple a tall pile, as often happens.

The fact that Harfang was broad, brutish, and unusually hairy was quite irrelevant to his psychic strength, but I would have felt irrationally happier had he looked effete and poetic. He definitely did not belong on display in a fighting tabard. Egma knew little about him. He had competed only twice, the minimum needed to acquire a silver crown, and his only known interest was hunting, so I could be thankful I was not meeting him in the javelin event. He was rumored to be unhappy with his pairing and his new home, somewhere in farthest Pelagic, but men often whine about the unfairness of life.

As we waited for our turn, I bowed. "Royal Harfang of Ohone?"

He gave me a surly nod. "Why are you doing this?"

"I am in heat." I thought that remark reasonably witty when the marble wall at our backs was hotter than a forge.

"You are insane. You'd better lose to me, sonny. You don't want to go up against Destin."

"I swore to give my best and I will." What a fool kid I must have seemed to him!

"So did Destin. He's going to break your legs in the wrestling."

I believed him and my insides lurched. "Nice of him to resist my neck."

Harfang shrugged. "And if he doesn't, Jasp will put a spear through you. Women like our mother do *not* tolerate defiance from smart-alecky young bastards, Mudar! She has given us specific orders. This is your last chance to walk away a whole man."

I spat in the sand. "That for your mother and her orders. Do your worst, killers."

He ported twenty feet away, leaving me to brood.

When our time came Harfang and I flew over separately and set down on opposite sides of the stack. Being unseeded, he played first, floating a balk across to me. I capped it and returned it: *two*. Was I going to bow to their threats and throw the match to him? *Four.* I could win one round before I had to decide. *Six.* I didn't have a hope anyway. Harfang could play this game with me sitting on the stack and never notice the difference. *Eight.* I had never managed ten, not all the way.

Royal Harfang of Ohone lifted a wall of nine, which gracefully leaned forward and clattered down on the stack.

The crowd said, *Oooooo!*

I bowed to offer sympathy. Harfang's scowl almost boiled my eyeballs.

Of course we all have unfortunate accidents sometimes, and it must be a long time since he dressed for the arena, but . . .

I began the second round. Some atavistic, hairy competitive instinct kept me going. We both played flawlessly until he sent me back eight. That was when I had to decide whether to chicken out with all my bones intact or preserve my honor. Common sense said I should not risk making him attempt ten. Even for a hegemon, that is tricky. Honor won. I decided to do my best. After all, only very rarely did I successfully send over nine.

That time I did.

Harfang lost control of his response before he began to move it horizontally, so he had to make a hasty exit or be crushed to death in a rain of timber. For a moment I stood with my jaw hanging open while the crowd's roar echoed and reechoed in the great amphitheater. I had beaten the son of a hegemon!

No, the son of a hegemon had lost. That was not quite the same thing.

I ported over and offered a hand. For a moment I thought he was going to bite it with his great apish teeth. He shook it instead, not mangling my fingers too seriously. We flew back with applause ringing in our ears. I had won!

I said, "Thanks."

"Remember what I said about Destin."

"Do you know when he'll do it?"

"Right away, likely. He hates the arena. Shy, he is."

That sounded very much like a hint. I was encouraged to think that royal Harfang was a true gentleman.

Destin and I would be the final pair in the wrestling. Jasp of Lemma won his bout easily. He ported to my side and had me recount the entire story of Hyla while I waited. He never lost his smile, but his questions were shrewd and penetrating. I found that encouraging, too. Perhaps he had been sent to form an independent appraisal of the upstart? Perhaps he was actually on Mandola's side? Perhaps I was deluding myself. A touch of madness would not be unlikely, for sunlight reflecting off the sand and the marble walls was stripping the flesh from us. Cuneal Amphitheater is the worst oven I know, even hotter than Bere Parochian, which stands right on the equator.

"But your honored mother must know all these facts better than I do."

Keeping his eyes on the play, he said, "My batty mother will never discuss the Alazarin tragedy."

I looked along the line of patiently melting contestants. "Is royal Destin a good wrestler?" I could hardly expect all three sons to defy their dam as Harfang had done.

Jasp snorted. "Strong enough to maim you, which he has promised Mother he will. He's always been a good momma's boy."

"He sounds like it," I said.

The laughing eyes lost their twinkle. "And he doesn't have mistress problems like Harfang does. Those can really throw a man off his game, highborn Mudar. Name any price you want short of my sister, and it's yours. You have my word on it. I do beg you not to be a fool. This time you are in real danger."

Destin was as weedy as Harfang was burly, but lack of muscle did not mean he could not snap my bones if he wished. He was also fair of skin, which that afternoon meant that he was extremely red of face. According to the gossip Egma had picked up, Destin of Hurr was a patron of the arts and a great dandy. He did not look it that day. His hair hung in rat-tails, his tabard was sweat-stained and dirty. I was in no better state, but I was used to it.

I ported to him and bowed.

He curled a lip at me and ported away.

Seeing that the preceding pair were into their third fall, I called for a waterskin and took a long drink. Then royal Destin and I were ordered out and the crowd applauded.

"Isn't that wonderful!" I exclaimed. "Oh, I do love the little people! They make us seem so effete! We nobles are so overmannered, don't you think, so foppishly *clean*? Every one of the smelly darlings knows that you have to stop me at all costs or your mommy will spank you. Just look—thirty-seven thousand of them, all waiting to hear my bones crackle, my ligaments snap, my screams for mercy."

Destin shuddered and did not reply.

The senior referee rattled off the rules in a bored voice. "Turn and start walking. When I shout 'Go!' you may begin."

The first half of the word had barely reached me when I ported. I bounced twice—once into hefting range of Destin, and out again before he could get a psychic grip on me. I came forth forty feet away, and I swear I heard his yell and the ripping sound for a second time. I waved the remains of his tabard in the air like a flag. Destin was so appalled that the tug of the tearing cloth and his own efforts to cover his privates threw him off balance. He teetered wildly, but managed to port himself upright before he hit the sand.

"Hold on the play!" quoth the referee.

Destin did not hear her. Destin had not stayed around to wait for a replacement tabard. Arty dandies do not belong in the arena at the best of times, certainly not when stripped naked before thirty-seven thousand shrieking, guffawing, practically hysterical witnesses. A man who leaves the arena forfeits the match.

The noise rolled on and on. By now everyone knew that the real game today was the unbeatable Mudar against the hegemon's sons.

Two down, one to go.

Bubbling like a dye maker's cauldron, I returned to the remaining three contestants. Jasp still wore his smile—I was starting to wonder if it was a tattoo—but the other men were scowling. One was my friend Emodin of Osseter, who was now due to face Jasp in the fencing.

"Don't worry about these hegemonics," I said breezily. "They're only amateurs."

Emodin grinned nervously.

"True, true," Jasp said. "Mere dilettantes. But may I present a solid professional?" He turned to the other man, the fourth blank. "Mudar, meet champion Bradawl of Cenacle. Cousin, this is highborn Mudar of Quoin."

Bradawl was older than the rest of us, with eyes colder than icicles. I bowed to his royal caste mark.

"Cousin?" I repeated unhappily. Three sons, four blanks.

Bradawl flexed ogreish shoulders. "Noblest Foison is my mother's sister."

"And his father is a brother of Hegemon Balata of Heliacs," Jasp said. "His cloak has *seven* stars and one crown—absolutely incredible heraldry! Bradawl is captain of the palace guard, and an absolute *demon* with a sword! Let me tell you . . . No, it's too gruesome. Ah, it seems we have to go, princely Emodin."

Left alone with my monolithic companion, I sighed and said, "She doesn't miss a trick, does she?"

It took a moment for the ice to melt, and when his lips decided to smile, slightly, his eyes did not. "Actually I volunteered for this duty, highborn Mudar. An unpleasant duty is still a duty. As you say, her boys are amateurs and I knew the noblest would be *extremely* unhappy if you won today. Mortified, in fact. So I offered to make certainty inevitable."

"And dear Auntie was so overcome with gratitude at your giving up your afternoon that she promised you a little something on the side if you win?"

The smile fled. "Five myriad saros, since you ask."

I winced. "What are you going to do with it? Buy a palace?"

"Several. I laid it out in bets against your taking the crown. I haven't decided what I will do with my winnings."

"Good odds?"

"Varied." He shrugged. "About twenty to one on average." This time the smile was in his eyes, glittering like sunlight on steel. "So I do not intend to lose, you arrogant ditch-born bastard child of scum."

"I can see where your loyalty lies," I said. "Of course you will completely ruin all the bookmakers, so collecting from them may be a problem."

"Bookmakers?" His sneer ranked with the best I had ever seen. "Have you never heard of *honor*, sonny? Nobility do not descend to dealing with *bookmakers*."

"Ah, so you gamble with your friends? And you knew that noblest Foison had made my winning impossible but they didn't. Honor is too subtle for me."

Noble Bradawl replied with a proletarian suggestion that men of his caste should not even know.

Amateur or not, Jasp was incredibly fast and made short work of Emodin, the best arena swordsman I knew. Their match was still a worthy spectacle, because Cuneal uses swords of fire, red flames hot enough to hurt on near-misses. I had little experience with them, but Bradawl could have little more, and the novelty might throw him off form more than me . . . maybe.

There was only one way I could hope to take him. Watching him in the wrestling, I had judged him to be struggling a little at the end. He was at least two pentads older than me, perhaps even three, and my wind and stamina should outlast his. I did not doubt that he was fit, but he must have been away from the arena for a long time and I was at the peak of my youthful powers. I drank an ocean of water and braced myself for an ordeal.

I won't go into detail, because I have never known a fencing match to last even half as long. Harfang had thrown the hefting; Destin had almost given me a bye in the wrestling; Bradawl made me pay back double. I stayed in close, forcing him to use muscle and not mere psychic strength, thrusting, feinting, riposting, slashing, parrying. He won the first hit, which was a serious blow to my hopes. But as I stood there, waiting for the referees' signal, I could hear the crowd chanting my name. That gave me strength to go on.

I did go on. I did win the second point. The crowd's roar made the arena tremble. But I was trembling much harder. The pace was murderous, and I kept thinking of the boy who had died in first watch, in the rollerball event. The heat had grown more intense since then. But if I was feeling it, what of my much older opponent? As we faced off for the third and final round, I thought I saw a hint of panic in his eyes.

"Now we're both playing for keeps, aren't we?" I jeered.

The chief referee opened her mouth and Bradawl's sword slammed into my chest. Flames exploded and I was hurled flat on the burning sand by a violent psychic shock. I hefted myself upright like a scalded frog, screaming, *"Foul!"*

He had most certainly hefted to me before the signal was given. I yelled out more objections, he yelled back, the referees tried to speak, and none of us could hear anything over the massed booing of the spectators. A referee came almost nose-to-nose with me to hear me explain my protest, while another questioned Bradawl. Then they all gathered in a huddle to discuss it. I knew I was in the right, so what was there to discuss? He had cheated and the match should be awarded to me. Obviously—so I concluded—they had been given orders that on no account was Mudar of Quoin to be allowed the benefit of any doubt whatsoever.

The women were quickly joined by a linesman porting in

from . . . From where? Almost certainly from the royal box. Bringing instructions from the marshal or from the hegemon herself? There was more discussion. Finally the chief referee beckoned us both in close.

"The objection is not sustained," she announced, and Bradawl showed all his teeth in joy. "But the hit is not allowed. Prepare to fight again for the third and deciding point."

So he had neither cheated nor scored fairly. The women knew I was not lying and must know that the captain of the palace guard was, but they dared not rule against him, for fear of the hegemon's wrath. I had never heard of such a craven judgment and never have since. In retrospect, I have learned that truth is rarely absolute. Bradawl may have truly believed he was in the right, just as I knew I was, and the hegemon may have ordered that I be given the *benefit* of any doubt so that my beloved Mandola could not cry foul also. But at the time I was certain I was being cheated of a win and my blood boiled.

Many men find anger an impediment. Fortunately I have the gift of using it as an ally. I looked at the red-eyed, haggard chief of police before me and saw him as a foul old lickspittle, an unscrupulous toady, a human turd, and I vowed that I would fall dead on the sand rather than lose to such filth.

Give him his due, Bradawl of Cenacle was as tough as the Cuneal Ranges enclosing the valley. Our third round went on longer then the first two combined. I drove and drove and drove, and he fought to the absolute limit of human endurance. It was only when I seriously thought I was about to collapse in a heap of dust that he dropped his sword and fell on his knees, croaking for water.

I was so near my own limit that for a moment I just stared at him in bewilderment. How could I ever find the strength to face Jasp of Lemma? The mere thought was crippling.

Except that up there in the royal box, my love was watching.

We finalists had a few moments to talk while the linesman smoothed the sand. More than a few. I have never seen the task take so long, and I guessed that they were stretching it out to give me time to recover. Relays of porters brought me water. I drank it, ate salt, drenched myself, then went back to the beginning, and did it all over again.

The family was down to its last chance to stop me. Now Jasp had to make good on his boast but, despite all the stories of wild and hairy ancestors, very few of us men are natural killers. He kept asking me about Alazarin, but I suspected he was appraising me as much as the island. I knew I might be deluding myself.

"It can't be a hard realm to run if a man has done it for so long," I said. "And Izard needs to retire. He is too proud to ask, so if you are the survivor of our match, do please ask your mother to relieve him of his duties."

How big was it? About two hundred miles long. How many cities? Just Cantle, a smallish town. A sleepy little place.

Jasp sighed. "So what is there to *do* there? My sister would go into a permanent molt. She cannot sit still through an entire dinner."

"I can have her back here in thirteen hops. She can spend her days here and sleep in Cantle, or the reverse. Day in and day out."

For a moment the ebony eyes lost their sparkle and glinted like razors. "Thirteen? The gazetteer says forty. You really have that range?"

"I swear."

"That's hegemonic strength."

"Ask my father."

"He is the problem." For once Jasp lost his smile. "I like you, Mudar of Quoin, I really do. I can see why my little sister fell flat on her back at the sight of you and I wish you could stay and breed me dozens of noisy nieces and nephews. But a hegemon's daughter simply cannot bed down with a man of less than royal caste. It would be a worldwide scandal. I am truly sorry."

I put on my most implacable expression—I have sometimes been accused of stubbornness. "It does seem impossible, now you put it that way. Tragic, really. But I swore faithfully to your sister, royal master of Lemma, that I would keep on winning, and I shall do so until she tells me to stop. I will win today or die trying. Either you kill me or I kill you and then die on the rack. So let us agree that this shall be a match to the death, no quarter, no pretense. One of us will die now. Shake on it." I offered him my hand.

He shook it. His palm was drier than mine.

Side by side, we hefted out to the center.

I trotted over to the wall to collect my spears. When I looked around, Jasp was just collecting his.

It is common for two contestants who know and trust each other to indulge in a little showmanship at the start of the javelin contest. The crowd expects it. Emodin and I did it every time we met in the final round, which was quite often. We would throw spears straight up, for example, an impossible trick for an ordinary. I would lob Emodin a few easy ones, knowing that he would lob easy ones back. He could juggle javelins, and even catch a slow one out of midair, a feat I rarely pulled off.

That sort of foolery did not belong in mortal combat.

The Cuneal arena was far too wide to risk a throw until we could get closer, and porting is forbidden. I was on the north, so I turned to my left and began walking around the wall. Jasp turned east also. I had my throwing arm toward him, then, but that is a trivial advantage. Staying close to the wall matters, because there one can salvage one's opponent's misses. In this bout there would be no misses.

Our feet made no sound on the sand and the arena fell totally silent, the only time in my life that I ever experienced that. Something—perhaps the way we had dispensed with the usual preliminary clowning, or perhaps just gossip that for once happened to be true—had alerted the spectators to the fact that they were watching a genuine hunt. My fatigue had vanished. I will not admit to feeling bloodlust, but my mind was wonderfully concentrated. I was quite determined that I would not port out of harm's way, no matter what Jasp of Lemma chose to do. I would win my woman or die in the attempt.

The suns blazed off the marble blocks of the wall, once smooth and now all pitted where spears had struck them over scores of generations.

Step by step we approached the east side of the arena in mirror image. The royal box was on the west, as always. Up there a mother and daughter must be wondering why they had sent son and lover to perform cold-blooded murder in front of their eyes. If they weren't searching their souls they certainly ought to be.

As the curve of the wall brought us around, the distance between us began to shrink more rapidly, approaching the range where I knew I couldn't miss. How good was Jasp? Javelin throwing is not simply a matter of inherited strength; it needs practice, and unless he was an avid hunter, he could not be as adept as I was. I veered a little farther away from the wall.

He noticed and did the same.

He had a lot more to lose than I did.

I knew from watching his match with Emodin that his reflexes were incredibly fast. On that I gambled both our lives. As fast as I could, with as little warning as possible, I whipped back my arm and threw. I threw with all my strength and skill; I threw to kill, as I would never have dared throw at Emodin. In the same motion I hurled myself flat on the sand. It was like leaping into a bath of molten lead, but it might have saved my life had he thrown, which he did not.

The roar of the crowd filled the arena. I scrambled to my feet, ready to throw again, but there was no need. My first spear lay in clear view. Jasp had gone.

3

I dragged myself across to the winners' platform through an ocean of noise. The crowd was on its feet, jumping and shouting as if it would never stop. Trembling with release of tension,

I stepped up on the timbers and accepted a water flagon from a porter. When I returned it, Jasp was standing beside me. Smiling, of course, but there was a lot more in that smile than there had been earlier.

"You are the meanest whelp of a *gree* I ever met." He offered me a hand.

I took it with both of mine. "Noble, you are stark raving crazy!"

"I thought I was a dead man."

"So did I," I admitted. "I'm glad you're not."

"See you at the party." He vanished.

Emodin appeared and embraced me. "I thought you had killed him, you crazy man."

"It was the only way to win." I was too exhausted to say more.

We stood there and baked.

And baked.

Apparently Cousin Bradawl was not coming. As I guessed then and confirmed later, he had fled from his creditors, having lost a legendary fortune. The crowd had worn out its lungs shouting, and began to rumble impatiently. Porters brought us more water. Still we waited.

At last a herald came forth, looking flustered. And then the royal consort, noblest Bayard of Indican, arrived—alone. He was silver-haired but still handsome, craggy as an aging tree. His smile was a formality. He continued to smile while the heralds and trumpeters made their noises; he awarded Emodin his silver ring with royal grace. Formality ended when I walked forward and knelt to him. He looked down on me with bared teeth.

"You tried to kill our son!"

"Noblest, I warned him he had better kill me first."

"Why, for suns' sake? You must know what would have happened to you!"

"Because I do not care what happens to me if I cannot be your daughter's consort."

Still scowling, Bayard held out a hand to the herald, who gave him the silver crown. It was a massive hoop of silver, with no artistic merit because it was designed to be melted down, not worn. He slammed it down on my head. Fortunately, I have a thick skull.

"Rise," he said. "You have won more than that bauble, princely Mudar of Quoin." He scowled even harder. "Her Serenity has agreed to raise you to royal rank and appoint you consort to our youngest daughter. Welcome to the family." He vanished.

I doffed my crown in a wave to the crowd and was rewarded with one last, mighty cheer. It seemed a good way to be leaving the arena for the last time, as I thought. I had won more in it than I could ever have dreamed—royal status, palace life, and the woman I adored. I did not expect to return until I brought my royal sons to the kibitzer cage.

♦ ♦ ♦ PORT ♦ ♦ ♦

Up on the managers' row, Egma's booth was besieged by a roaring mob. All the agents and managers were there, attempting to make and receive offers, but every contender was there also, completely ignoring them. It was they, old friends now, who swooped on me to congratulate me. The news was out.

"Was that it?" they yelled . . . "You got her?" . . . "Are you satisfied now?"

I said, "More than satisfied. From now on I'll stay out of your way."

Their happiness at my success was genuine, for it meant that they could continue to dream of their own triumphs still to come. Earlier accusations of greed forgotten, they thumped my back and pumped my hands, and I had to take time to make my farewells, however impatient I was to reach Egma.

It was a wonderful relief to be in shadow again. I found her kneeling at the table, negotiating with a champion and a gentlewoman, both wearing Quartic heraldry of green and gold. They looked horrified, she was smiling blissfully. Mandola was standing in

back of them with a liveried champion at her side. I bowed low to
her. She grinned gleefully. She was clad in purple and lavender, with
constellations of amethysts twinkling in her hair—her projection skill
was so perfect that she could wear any color she wanted with equal
success. I was not at all sure that I was awake and not dreaming this.

I am buying you. Nod if you approve. If you don't I shall buy you anyway.
I nodded vigorously.

"Five myriad is the standard fee for supplying a consort for a
hegemonic other than the heir," Egma insisted, with the confidence
of a woman who has just become rich beyond her dreams.

"But," the old champion protested, "noble Mudar has only
eight quarterings and the normal commission—"

"Don't be stingy, princely Meacock," Mandola said impatiently.
"Whatever the price, he's cheap by the pound. Besides, Mother is
going to promote him to sixteen quarterings before blueset."

"Then ten myriad saros!" Egma proclaimed triumphantly.

"And appoint him my consort."

"Twenty-five myriad!"

Meacock and his companion howled in unison.

"Pay her!" Mandola snapped. "Ensoign, show the master of
Quoin the family entrance."

Her green and gold porter reacted with a look of doubt, as if
she was telling him to break rules. Persuaded by her glare, he nodded across at me and transported us both to the palace.

◆ ◆ ◆ **PORT** ◆ ◆ ◆

The hall was vast, below the largest dome I had ever seen. Over
the previous couple of gnomons I had become quite blasé about
palaces, but this was the abode of a hegemon, and on a scale all its
own. Light streamed in from windows so high that no others could
overlook them. Roof and walls were intricately carved, and every
surface, even the floor, blazed with color. There were freestanding
sculptures, tables, even a fountain. I gaped at so much luxury. Guards
stared coldly at me.

"The floor is easiest, noble Mudar," Ensoign said. "There are many halls like this in the palace, but the floors are distinctive. I find it easiest to recall the central medallions."

I thanked him and memorized the pattern.

◆ ◆ ◆ PORT ◆ ◆ ◆

Back at the manager's booth, Egma and the gentlewoman crouched over a document, arguing details. Champion Meacock had left.

"All agreed!" Mandola said gleefully, dancing across to me. "You're mine as soon as Mother signs the papers. Hurry! We mustn't be late for the party."

◆ ◆ ◆ PORT ◆ ◆ ◆

I expected her to kiss me the moment we came forth in the entrance, but she just grabbed my hand and ran, leading the way to one of the many doors, and through it into a labyrinth. "These are my quarters," she said. "Ours now, whenever we're in Cuneal. Servants along there and in there and there. Bathing room there, wardrobe department along here . . . our reception hall . . . but only the guards bring strangers in here . . . that leads to the nursery wing for when you've done your duty by me. And this is where we'll sleep. Or not." She spun around and held out her arms.

It was a very brief kiss by her standards, but as sweet as ever. "Mmm!" she said, breaking loose. "I wish we had time to finish that, but we mustn't give Mother time to change her mind. There's three tunics on the bed. One of them must fit you."

I had my doubts about that, but I took up the largest pile of brocade and was appalled at its weight. From now on I would be a glittering heraldic monument, a sworn champion, but these colors were the green and gold of Quartic.

"I thought it was you who bought me," I protested. "Why your mother's colors?"

Mandola rolled her eyes at my ignorance. "Because I'm not a ruler yet. I can't swear in champions! As soon as she appoints me, then she will transfer your oaths to me. What are Alazarin's colors, anyway?"

"Ruby and sea-green."

"Mm," she said doubtfully. "Garish! Well, I can always change that. Come along."

I followed my mistress designate through an arch to a bathroom as large as Alazarin. The pool was filled, ready for me.

"Be quick!" she said.

"Turn your back, then."

"Certainly not. I want to unwrap the present Mother just bought for me." Gamin grin in place, she brazenly watched as I stripped and plunged into the water. When I came up for air, she was waiting with towels, ready to dry me.

I had thought when she spoke of a party that she meant the reception for the contestants that always followed games, but no. There had to be a private family gathering first, to inspect the new boy. Porters took us to the Upper Court, a hexagonal garden atop a high tower. Marble trellis enclosed it from prying eyes in the rest of the palace complex below but let in a cooling breeze and a breathtaking view of valley and mountains.

There, among banked flowers and precious artwork, the rest of the family were sitting or kneeling on silk cushions and sipping snow-chilled drinks. Liveried ordinaries moved among them with refills and tasty snacks. This was to be my family from now on, and the realization of how I just changed my life left me almost speechless. I felt as dainty as a full-grown ox as Mandola began taking me around and presenting me, for I was terrified I would knock over some priceless vase or statue. Her introductions were accompanied by impudent psychic comments for my personal benefit.

"My honored sister and Mother's heir, Media." *And if she doesn't succeed soon she's going to die of boredom.* Media was majestic and dignified to the brink of petrification, but she said a few kind words about remembering my mother's visit to Cuneal.

"And her consort, royal Mort of Camber." *Not half the man you are, darling. Mother chose him for his brains; Media has never forgiven her.*

"Our sister Terai can't be here, unfortunately. I know she'll be devastated at missing you." *She loves seeing Mother mad.* "She's resting. She gave birth just this morning." *Another boy unfortunately— can't remember if that makes eighteen or twenty.*

Then to the brothers and their mistresses. Jasp smiled up at me, of course, and his welcome seemed genuine enough. His mistress had stayed home. *She's gravid. Spews a hundred times a day. Don't you dare give me any of those sick-making brats.*

Destin was the most elaborately dressed person present. He had decided to see the funny side of his abrupt departure from the arena and was smoothly gracious. His mistress mumbled something inaudible and avoided my eye. *Don't be upset. When you stripped Destin she almost exploded. She's desperately trying not to start laughing all over again.*

By that time I was having the same problem myself.

I saved my lowest bow for the anthropoid Harfang of Ohone, who had refused to promote his mother's foul schemes. He scowled at me, but winked at me later, when he thought no one else was watching. His ruler mistress, Hormesis, definitely disapproved of me and was curt. *Don't take offense, darling. It was to spite Mother for harnessing him to the horse that he let you win.*

Mandola and I had just found places to sit in the circle when Hegemon Foison herself came forth on the dais. I had a blinding impression of a woman about Mandola's age, twelve feet tall, clad in gold and royal blue, and exalted in a blaze of majesty and authority. I was hurled backward off my cushion and spilled my drink all over myself.

"Oh, Mother!" Mandola's yell was the loudest of several complaints. "Stop sulking! The deal has been made."

I sat up, my splendid tunic soaked with sweet wine and my head still ringing from psychic overload. Foison had now dropped all pretense and was revealed as a surprisingly short, almost dumpy, woman with silver hair and doughy features set in a pout. At her side, Bayard was just as he had seemed in the arena—massive, ponderous, sliding into esteemed old age. A couple of champions lurked nervously behind them.

The hegemon glowered across at me. "Mudar of Quoin!" She made my name sound like a Stramash expression for dung. "I have grave forebodings about you, Mudar of Quoin. I fear you will bring great unhappiness to all of us. Women of my family have always had precognitive powers."

She can foretell the weather fifteen minutes ahead.

Mandola rose and so did I. We went forward together and I knelt before the dais. I had to crane my neck to look up at a foreshortened view of the hegemon's cascade of chins and angry, piggy eyes.

"It will not be by my will, Your Serenity."

"I did not say it would be!" she snapped. "But the outcome will be dire! Child, you are still of a mind to go ahead with this? There is nothing I can do to dissuade you?"

"Nothing in the world," Mandola said firmly. "I hold you to your promise! He won me fair and square. Swear him in."

"Swear him in!" Hegemon Foison spoke as if through a mouthful of broken glass.

One of the flunkies came forward. Still on my knees, I repeated-after-him the oath of lifelong fidelity to the hegemon and her successors. He produced a signet ring and slipped it on my finger.

Pause. "Now the rest of it!" Mandola said menacingly.

Grumpily Foison nodded to the champion.

"An edict," he said, unrolling a scroll. " 'To our trusty and dearly beloved champion, Mudar of Quoin: Whereas . . . ' "

I think I am about to belch, my adored remarked inside my head. I almost choked.

The proclamation raised me to royal rank and awarded me my mother's sixteen quarterings entire, as if I had been born of her parents. The other flunky held out a portable writing desk, complete with vellum, ink block, and brush. With a poor grace, Foison signed, affixed her signet, and made it all legal.

"There! That's done. Congratulations to you both."

The rest of the family was wisely staying out of the squabble, but Mandola had won the day and would not be gainsaid.

"And the last part! Assign him his duties."

The hegemon of two hundred realms shuddered and pulled a face. "There is no hurry on that, my darling. We must arrange for a wonderful pairing celebration. It will take three or four gnomons to prepare. There is no need for unseemly haste!"

Lightning crackled. "But, Mother darling, there is need for seemly haste, or you will have all the aunts counting on their fingers. Arrange whatever you want. Invite the world. But you should assign him his duties now because he is going to start work tonight!" *You'd better get me drunk first, darling.*

Somebody had a coughing fit, probably Jasp.

Foison made a whimpering noise. "I know you will regret this! Very well. Noble Mudar of Quoin, we appoint you consort to our daughter. Swear him in, herald."

And so I swore to obey, defend, and—when so instructed—impregnate the specified lady, forsaking all others unless instructed otherwise.

Thus I became the consort of royal Mandragora of Fargite. Sporting my ring and a white caste mark, garbed in a tunic that fit me better and did not stink of wine, I escorted her to the tourney reception. If the royal family arrived even later than usual, nobody complained. My companions of the arena—the tabard-clad friends I was about to leave—were ecstatic, as I would have been had I not been so grossly exhausted. I succumbed to their entreaties and gave them one song, without my zither. The wine had gone to my head and I sang a risqué love song to my mistress. Mandola loved it, of course. The hall cheered.

I met a few dozen other new relatives, guided by her silent comments—witty, scurrilous, or both.

Surprisingly, noblest Foison made the best of it and became graciously maudlin. She had done her doggedest, she admitted, and I had beaten her, so it was really quite romantic. Her daughter had always been headstrong and I might find life hard at times in future, but I must appeal to her if Mandola ever became totally unreasonable. . . .

Mother rarely drinks this much. She'll be a bear tomorrow.

We were watching the women dance when a slurred voice behind me said, "You tried to kill my son!"

I turned in alarm to face Consort Bayard, red-faced and inflammable.

"Noblest!" I said. "I *couldn't* kill royal Jasp. I had watched him compete all afternoon and I knew he was much too fast for me. I knew he would be able to port out in time." That was about nineteen-twentieths true.

"Dung-eating liar!"

Mandola exploded. "Father! You're drunk!" *Darling, I have never known him like this before.*

"You shut up, hussy," he said. "Slattern!" He turned his blasts of wine fumes back on me. "Well, she got you. Why don't you dance the *lilacin* with her? 'S tradition, ishn't it?" Bayard went lumbering off.

Mandola stared after him in dismay. "I've never seen him like that before!"

"I did take a risk with Jasp," I admitted.

Silence. She looked around the hall. Pause. Then she smiled, faintly. "He says not. He says he was waiting to see if you would throw to miss or not. You didn't."

Now I could see her brother grinning at us from the far side of the buffet tables. "You can *hear* him?" I had not even suspected that a woman could convey at such a distance, or a man convey at all.

"Course not! I told him to nod or shake his head. What's a *lilacin*?"

"A scandalous dance." I was more hurt by Bayard's sneer than I liked to admit, but Mandola was close enough to me to know that. "Show me?"

I took her hand unobtrusively so she could read me.

What's the tune? Stop staring at that fat girl. Can you dance it to this? She could convey music, too! The beat was the same, so I nodded. *Show me the steps again. Take me up to the orchestra.*

I did not want us to make a spectacle of ourselves. I thought nothing could be in worse taste than dancing the *lilacin* that night, but Mandola knew her family and I would not disobey her. I was infatuated enough and just drunk enough that the thought of the finale had me aroused already. I ported us up to the musicians' gallery.

There were a few other preliminaries to attend to—I needed boots to stamp, she needed a whip to crack, and she had to order more lamps lit in the bedroom so I could recall it clearly—but the next time the floor was cleared, Mandola and I danced the *lilacin*. Leaping, stamping, whirling, we didn't dance it very well, but I don't suppose it had ever been seen in Cuneal before, perhaps never on the mainland. We were the sensation of the evening. When we joined hands there were gasps of outrage from the old and whoops of glee from the younger crowd. When I folded her into the final embrace, the hall roared like the arena.

Then we were gone to the sudden silence of her chamber, and no one saw us again until about bluenoon the next day.

4

It was decreed, by a notably grouchy Foison, that the pairing celebration would be a small, family affair.

That means about a thousand people, my inner voice said.

Five of us had gathered for a strategy conference in a openfronted hall that would have held hundreds—the hegemon and her consort, Mandola and hers, and heiress Media, who spoke barely a word and looked less interested than the faces sculpted on the marble pillars. Mandola's prophecy that her sister was likely to die of boredom soon seemed ever more credible. We principals sat or knelt at the front, where we had a spectacular view of the mountains, but the day was so still that boys wafted punkahs at us. In the background, but within conveying range, half a dozen low-caste secretaries knelt ready to advise Her Serenity. Consorts and porters waited patiently farther back.

"Family includes five hegemons," Bayard growled, "and seven significant matriarchs." The noblest's consort was even more sullen and bloodshot than she was. "You'd best include the rest or there will be bad feeling."

Two thousand, then. I do love you.

Foison sighed. "Pass me the citrus punch, if you please, er, Mudar."

I hefted the jug to her and refilled her goblet without spilling a drop, which was a deliberate display of precision.

I wish you'd just lifted it so I could admire the way your arm bulges.

I was finding it hard to concentrate. They could invite the world or nobody at all as far as I was concerned. Well, Izard, of course. And Vert and Clamant . . . And some of my friends from the arena? Mandola had suggested golden games and been brusquely told she'd already had those.

A couple of gentlewomen started busily consulting scrolls. Information was conveyed.

"Pots-1 next gnomon, then," the hegemon declared aloud. "Can we be ready by then?"

That was the day of the Azedarac games, so a lot of my friends would be busy. Most of them would not qualify for invitations, but if Mandola was to be ruler of Alazarin, she would need champions of her own. I must suggest she buy some of the good ones while they were still available. Emodin, for instance.

"I beg your pardon, noblest. My mind was wandering. . . ."

I know what you were thinking, you lecherous devil.

For once I wasn't thinking that, but it was an interesting suggestion.

Foison took another draft of nonintoxicating fluid. I had never imagined before yesterday that the ruler of my corner of the world was a grumpy, soggy-faced, rather stupid old woman. In my games career I had met almost a dozen rulers and their consorts. Some had been older than Izard and some as young as me, but none had disappointed as much as the hegemon of Quartic did. She was dull and dowdy. I could not imagine how she had produced human lightning bolts like Mandola and Jasp.

"I said, royal Mudar, if you have friends you want to invite, you must give their names to the chancellor."

Not more than three because we mustn't be extravagant.

If I caught my mistress's eye I would erupt in a deplorable attack of snigger. "That is most gracious of you, noblest."

"And you will *not* involve my daughter in primitive orgiastic dancing!"

I waited for noblest Bayard to confess that last night's *lilacin* had been his idea, but he didn't.

We'll organize a chorus line to do it for us, said the voice inside my head.

Later, Mandola showed me more of the palace. I would transport us to the Upper Court, she would point out where she wanted us to be, and I would take us there on line of sight. After a brief exploration, we would go back up and start again. In a complex covering several square miles, we would not soon run out of places to explore.

We took a cuddling break in a small garden where bright birds flitted and golden water snakes coiled ever-changing patterns in shady ponds. There were dozens of such grottoes, each one different.

She said, "You are mad at my parents."

"I am not. Why should I be mad when they gave me everything I want in the world?"

My mistress laughed and nibbled my ear. "Yes, you are. And you have cause. They are being very unfair. Mother turned the games into mortal combat, then Father blamed you for playing by her rules. He was horrible to mention the *lilacin* to you. It was my idea that we dance it, not yours."

"It doesn't matter."

Another nibble. "You must understand Mother, though. She cares only about appearances. Her daughter must pair with a man of royal caste and that's that."

"I am of royal caste now."

"But all her *friends*—I use the word loosely—they all know that she promoted you by edict."

And not once, but twice, two edicts. I had been love child, then highborn, and now royal. My career mocked the whole system.

Mandola sniggered into the neckband of my tunic. "She more or less told me I could have you as my gigolo as long as I promised to be discreet. It's the thought of scandal that appalls her. Scandal is worse than incest or murder! Now you won me in a tourney, so the gossip will be much worse. Serves her right."

"But she's the *hegemon*! She can do anything she wants. Why is she being petty?"

"Oh, that's typical of people, love, especially people with a lot of power. They always find someone else to blame for their own mistakes. You outwitted them or outfought them and they can't help resenting that a little. I admit I have never known them to be so unreasonable. I have never known them to drink like they did last night, but they'll come around when they get to know you better. I am *so* sorry. Would you like to take me somewhere where I can make it up to you?"

No sooner said than done.

About the fourth day of my servitude—my wonderfully enjoyable servitude—my mistress announced that she ought to visit Alazarin. I merely suggested that we should put on some clothes first, because we were in the bathtub at the time, but I had been dreading this. I knew that my backwoods homeland was going to shock her. It could not possibly live up to her romantic notions.

As I had bragged to Jasp, I took her to Alazarin in thirteen hops, or fourteen counting the one from Cape Bastel to the palace in Cantle. Can you imagine how I felt when we walked in on old Izard? The palace bugler doubled as a gardener, so there was a delay while he ran to find his livery, but I forbade anyone to warn the old man. He was working on accounts with his bursar and clerks in the great hall—which was a large closet by Mandola's standards—six old folk sitting in a circle clicking abacuses, completely surrounded by heaps of scrolls.

Izard looked up with a frown of anger when the fanfare rang out, for it is a serious breach of courtesy to make a formal visit without forewarning. His expression when the herald proclaimed royal Mandragora of Fargite, daughter of noblest Hegemon Foison of Quartic, was worth the journey all by itself. Not as frail as he is now, he hefted his old bones upright and hurried forward to greet her. I followed my consort in my proper place, two paces behind, and he ignored me.

Mandola bowed to him, and he to her. He welcomed her to Alazarin, and of course he must have known that he was addressing the new ruler. After so many years, his relief had finally arrived.

"My porter you have met already, noblest," Mandola said.

His faded old eyes turned to her oversized companion in the liveried tunic. Then he saw who was wearing it, glanced at the imposing signet on my hand, and beamed in joy. I had deliberately not put on a caste mark.

"I came, noblest," Mandola said, "to invite you to my pairing festivities. The scroll, please, Mudar."

Izard blinked uncertainly.

I handed him the roll. "Congratulations, noblest. Royal Mandragora has agreed to accept your son as her consort."

"Son?" He blinked several times.

"It says there that noblest Foison of Quartic has assigned to royal Mandragora, as her consort, a certain champion, royal Mudar of Quoin, son of the late Ruler Aglare of Alazarin and Consort Izard of Inmew."

"Royal?"

Legally, I was now my mother's brother and grandfather's son. Although that sounded like some sort of bizarre incest, Izard soon caught on and embraced me with tears trickling down his cheeks. Mandola laughed and hugged us both.

In three days I had seen only the highlights of the complex in Cuneal. I walked Mandola around the whole palace at Cantle in less time than it takes to dance the *lilacin*. She insisted it was wonderful and charming, exactly what she had expected, and she loved it. Women can dissemble; men cannot. Men cannot even tell when they are being lied to. I was fairly certain that her personal apanage of Fargite would turn out to be bigger than Alazarin, which was going to be no more than another apanage for her. She would delegate her duties as ruler and we would spend most of our time in Cuneal.

We went out into the town. Some long-ago ruler must have designed Cantle from scratch, because its roads are straight and wide, meeting at right angles. It has numerous shady squares, and there are laws against chopping down trees without royal permission. The gray stone houses are roofed with thatch, and the palace is only a group of them linked together, with a pompous gatehouse for show. I wanted only to stroll the streets with my mistress, but our courtly garb blazed there like the suns and people fell on their knees to us. The word spread. Soon cheering crowds were flocking in around us and I grew nervous.

"They mean no harm!" Mandola said, amused.

I was worried for her sake, not mine. Defending her was my purpose in life now. "But they may do harm regardless. Any mob is a beast. This one is an enormous puppy, wanting to be friendly, but still dangerous. Your mother will be very upset if I let you get trampled to a tortilla so soon, my love."

"Show me your apanage, then, Quoin. Wait! First lift me up on that sundial."

I did not bother with the sundial; I just hefted her shoulder-high so everyone could see her. She raised her arms for silence and then made a brief speech, confirming who she was and thanking them for their welcome. Someone started a three-cheers and on the third cheer we left.

* * * PORT * * *

Quoin is a fishing village with old and poky streets tangled like yarn a kitten has worked on. There we could walk the cobbles un-molested. People still knelt as we went by, but they did not mob us. They whispered excitedly and smiled at me. I presented many of them by name. Children appeared with flowers, which Mandola accepted with gracious thanks and kisses. She stole all their hearts.

I took her down to the harbor to look at the boats, the fishing nets drying on their racks, the lazy ripples plying the weed-draped stones of the breakwater and slapping against the pier. The smell of the sea was sharp enough to make my eyes water, but nostalgia was helping it. Boyhood had ended; I would not be frittering away long summer days at Quoin in future.

"This is very picturesque," she said bravely.

"'Quaint' is the word. 'Minuscule' is another. 'Smelly' likewise comes to mind."

"But you love it, I can tell. And the people all know you."

"I know them, yes. Most of them. As soon as I could port, I started coming here often. I love sailing, and helping pull in nets, and generally playing at being an ordinary."

One stormy day I had rescued two men from a foundering boat, but I would let other people tell her that story.

"Where's your house?"

"There isn't one," I admitted. "I could build one, but I'd have to increase taxes to pay for it. If I have to pay for all these fancy court tunics you just ordered for me, children in Quoin will go without their next pair of shoes."

Mandola turned away to stare out at the bay, sparkling in the sunshine. *You are quite the most extraordinary man I have ever met! I have never heard a noble speak like that.*

"Izard does. He taught Vert and Clamant to think like that too. I'm cheating, I admit, because Alazarin has a huge income from the ruby mines, and Izard would have built me a house here if I'd had any need for one. But Cantle and Nuddle are only a wish away for me, so why bother with another house? Can you stand to meet my mother?"

My mistress frowned. "Tomorrow. What I really want to do now, lover, is visit Cantle again, but this time anonymously."

"We can try."

✦ ✦ ✦ **PORT** ✦ ✦ ✦

Any palace keeps a stock of clothing in the guest quarters, because visiting nobles prefer not to act as porters, and after a search we found a gown and bonnet to fit her. Having wiped off Mandola's caste mark, we sallied forth to wander among the stalls of the market. I don't think we fooled many; she was taller than any man in sight and I was a head more—but we were not mobbed this time.

Izard had already organized a dinner for that evening, so we could meet Cantle's nobility, such as it was, and Mandola was gracious to all of them. I doubted her mother would have been. They all ported off home before dark and we were able, and expected, to retire also. The ancient custom seemed quaint by Cuneal's standards, but we newly-paireds did not complain. For the first and only time in my life, I slept in the state bedroom.

The next day harsh reality interrupted our lovers' idyll. Foison had designated Mandola to be her official representative at some deathly boring ceremonial function that evening, so that she would not be absent from Cuneal more than one night. Izard was dropping hints that the island's future ruler ought to review the institutions of government. Choosing the least of the available evils, Mandola announced that she would pay a courtesy call on noblest Hyla, officially still the ruler of the island, and living at Nuddle.

* * * PORT * * *

I took us to the top of the watchtower so she could admire the orchards, the village, and the river beyond, all nestled among the soft curves of the hills. Perhaps I am biased by childhood memories, but I truly believe Nuddle to be one of the most beautiful places in all Aureity. Mandola, I had already learned, was more interested in people and cities than landscapes, but even she was impressed.

"How gorgeous!" she said. "You must take me everywhere!"

The only person in sight was Fretty the kennelman, so I took us down to him. He was overcome to meet the next ruler and groveled in the mud, which was very unlike him, for he is usually a cynical old rogue. I told him to warn the house that we were coming. Then I escorted my mistress on a tour. We strolled under ripe fruit and fragrant blossoms, for all sorts of trees grow in the orchards at Nuddle and they flower at will. I showed off the swimming holes and favorite places of my childhood. When Mandola met Clamant and Vert the previous evening, I had stressed how like parents they had been to me, so I did not need to repeat that, but I warned her again about Hyla. Hegemons' daughters are normally sheltered from nasty things like crime and disability.

"She won't respond," I said. "She will give no sign that she's heard you or knows that you are there, and yet somehow she does know. It's as if there are two of her, and the real one is buried very deep, where it cannot get out. She never spoke to me when I was a child—she has never spoken to me ever, not once. But now she conveys pictures of herself talking to me as a boy, all the things she

181

wanted to say, I suppose, and couldn't. Her projections are the most vivid I have seen. They can be harrowing."

I should have arranged the visit for evening, I realized, because psychic projections are less distinct by candlelight. In daylight they seem much more real. That was to prove a tragic misjudgment.

We went in and were made welcome. Clamant and Vert presented the servants I had known all my life, all of whom were agog to find me of royal caste and consort of their next ruler, but were even more impressed by Mandola herself. Fretty had changed his clothes and sneaked indoors for a second look. She was charming to every one of them, unlike her mother, who rarely noticed servants, and never spoke to them unless they were out of range of psychic projection.

Eventually we all went out to sit on cushions on the flower terrace, where Mandola told stories of our courtship, my struggles in the arena, and the simultaneous civil war that she had waged to win me. We were served perfumed tea, and after a while Hyla was brought out to join us. She knelt on a cushion, smiled vaguely at Clamant, ignored everyone else. Given a cup of tea, she drank it at a gulp, instead of sipping it. We spoke to her, each of us in turn, and she never reacted—except when a yodel bird perched nearby and burst into polyphonic song. Then she smiled and clapped her hands like a child. This was what I had predicted, and yet now I saw her through Mandola's eyes and was embarrassed. I wished I had not brought them together, but at least this was one of my mother's good days and we were not being subjected to reenactments of the Enemy's attack.

Mandola started to reach out to her and paused, looking to Clamant for permission.

"Go ahead, royal lady. There is no one there."

Mandola laid a hand on Hyla's wrist and nodded sadly.

But Hyla turned and looked straight at Mandola, as if surprised. That itself was unexpected. For a moment it seemed as if she were about to awaken from her age-long dream and speak to us.

Puzzled, Mandola said, "Greetings, noblest. I am Mandragora of Fargite."

Hyla moved her lips slightly, but made no sound.

"Your son Mudar is my consort. He is a wonderful man. You must be very proud of him."

Hyla frowned, as if troubled, and even that was a striking response from her. I glanced at Clamant, who looked bewildered. Then my mother lifted her gaze to look above and beyond Mandola and her eyes widened.

Look at what? Mandola glanced around and cried out in alarm just as I leapt to my feet.

In full sunlight the figure standing there seemed as solid as the marble birdbath behind him. He was big and young; he wore a scarlet fighting tabard with an all-black cloak, and he was staring down at Mandola. It was the Enemy, and had I not known that he must be more than a generation older now, I could almost have believed he had returned to haunt his victim—except that it was not Hyla he was gloating over.

"Mudar!" Mandola cried.

I hefted her high over the table into my arms. "It's not real, love, but that's the Enemy."

This was not the usual reenactment, because there was no odor of *hamulose* and the monster had been conventionally clad when he entered Hyla's bedchamber. This was how he had dressed for the arena, but if it was a memory of some particular view of the fake Piese of Enthetic, it was one I could not remember ever seeing before. Disconcertingly, his eyes followed Mandola and seemed to look across at us as I held her. That was undoubtedly because he was a figment created by Hyla, and she was looking at us, but the impression that he was actually present was eerie. Vert and Clamant were on their feet, both muttering prayers or curses, and only Hyla, the generator of all this alarm, remained at ease on her cushion, watching with apparent interest.

The Enemy faded away, his sneer intact.

Hyla was blissfully unmoved by what she had done. I admit I was shaken and Mandola was quite distraught. I nodded my thanks to Vert and Clamant. . . .

Any man who ever loves must eventually experience the horror of first seeing his dear one grieve. I took Mandola to a shady grove by the lake half a mile away, and just stood there, hugging her while she sniveled onto my shoulder. I have never felt more helpless. Her reaction was quite unlike anything I had expected from her. I realized that I did not know her very well, despite our recent intimacy.

"We usually get more warning of her projections," I said. "That was very sudden."

Mumble, meaning *not that*.

I tried again. "Hyla's a tragic figure, but you must remember she has been like that all my life and most of the time she seems quite happy and—"

Mandola pushed me away angrily. "I feel such a fool! I *never* cry! Even when Jasp used to punch me, I never cried."

"I bet you punched him back."

"No, I kicked him. I put slugs in his bed, too." She forced a moist, red-eyed smile. "You never saw this!"

"Of course I didn't. It would have been a terrible shock to my innocent boyish disposition if I had witnessed my mistress weeping like a baby, sobbing and hiccoughing and—"

"Stop!"

"Turning purple . . ."

"I will improve you, I swear it!"

I kissed her and she didn't.

I turned serious. "It was very strange, though. I never remember Hyla ever projecting an image of the Enemy quite like that one."

Mandola shivered. "The way he looked at me . . . You know, darling, I am almost ready to believe in Mother's nonsense about precognition. I did *not* want to meet Hyla. I had bad feelings about it—and now this!"

"Then your instincts were right. Let me know if you ever have them again. Are you ready to head back to Cantle and say goodbye to Izard?"

"He wants to lecture me about governing Alazarin, doesn't he?"

"It does needs real governing," I said. "Hyla was only an infant when it last had a proper ruler. Izard can't swear in champions and gentlewomen, so he's been running everything practically on his own. Do you *want* to be ruler of a flyspeck realm like this? It doesn't matter to me. I should like to see Izard relieved of his duties, but I don't care if you take them on or someone else does."

Mandola smiled a little sadly. "Mother has decided it's a good idea. It sort of explains her peculiar choice of consort for me, and it will give me a ruler's honors without too much responsibility . . . won't it?"

"Eventually, yes. Right now there must be a thousand loose ends that needing tying up."

"Then I must start knotting. Take me there."

♦ ♦ ♦ PORT ♦ ♦ ♦

We found Izard in his study, and this time the old rascal had a trap ready to spring. From a tatty leather bag, he produced a wonder.

"The famous ruby coronet of Alazarin, royal. It has not been worn since the days of my dear mistress, Aglare."

Even so, it had obviously been very recently polished. I had never heard of it, let alone seen it, but it brought a gasp of amazement even from a hegemon's daughter. The coronet itself was of blue-green jade, almost invisible behind dozens of blood-red rubies, some of them as big as my thumb joints. She tried it on and pulled a face at the weight. Wily old Izard produced a hand mirror for her. As a bribe, this was hardly subtle, but I could see my mistress reappraising the advantages of governance.

She inspected her image from various angles. "When my . . . When your daughter visited Cuneal and met my parents, did she wear this?"

"No, noblest. When we left here, she had not yet been confirmed in her rule, she was only ruler presumptive."

The ruler designate removed the coronet and reluctantly returned it to its bag. She was obviously contemplating an appearance in Cuneal wearing it, and the sensation it would cause. My love would not have been the perfect woman if she had been totally lacking in vanity.

"You mentioned some reports you wished me to look at?"

"Whenever it would be convenient."

Mandola's smile chilled me. "I believe you have given Alazarin honest and capable government, noblest Izard, and it is my intent that it will continue to receive it. I am going to do what my dear mother does when presented with a problem—she tells Bayard to deal with it. Your grandson knows the island as I never can. I appoint him vizier. Tell him what needs to be done."

"*Mudar?*" Izard looked at me in horrified disbelief.

I shrugged. "And where are you going, ruler presumptive?"

Mandola projected innocence. "I thought I would visit the traders' stalls again . . . buy some of those bijou local handicrafts, you know . . . souvenirs?"

"Excellent. You'll need some money from the state treasury. Is Trindle around, Grandfather?"

Trindle was a couple of gnomons younger than I, boyhood playmate and grandson of one of my grandmother's champions, who had married an ordinary. Trindle only barely qualified for the knightly caste. He served Izard as a porter, but he was reliable and good company. I felt quite at ease sending him off to escort my mistress around Cantle. He could not cross the strait to Badderlocks but in case of trouble, he was quite capable of transporting her back to the palace in a single hop.

"And if she tries to send you away," I warned him, "you stay within porting distance and watch over her. She showed absolutely no interest in shopping yesterday. I think she just wants to be alone for a while."

"Hardly surprising," my erstwhile friend remarked sadly. I balled a fist at him and he leered.

When they had gone—Trindle self-consciously sporting a

sword—I sat down with Izard, crossed my legs, and grinned happily at him over the heap of scrolls on the mat. He eyed me doubtfully.

"I hope your ability to comprehend numbers has increased dramatically, royal Mudar."

"I know now that one and one make one, under certain circumstances."

He started to pout and then decided to humor my wit with a discreet smile. "Shall we begin with the annual revenues?"

"No," I said cheerfully. "I don't know a myriad saros from a heap and do not want to. I doubt if Bayard knows either. Noblest, I won't be here very often. I'm going to be porter extraordinary. Until I get my darling mistress well and truly gravid, she is going to have us buzzing around Aureity like horseflies in a stable. What Alazarin and Mandola need is a good team of champions and companions to take over from you. I know several excellent men on the circuit, and if my beloved cannot match them up with certain young ladies she knows and has mentioned, I am sure they can soon find their own mistresses."

"Mudar! How can you even suggest such a thing?"

"I'm serious. The best duelists see themselves becoming hegemons' champions and will scorn Alazarin as the far end of nowhere, but I know several hotshots who will take any terms under the suns just for the right to pair with a woman they already have their eye on and cannot presently hope to have—like Vert and Clamant. Let's draw up a list of the offices to be filled."

He sighed and shrugged. "A deputy vizier, of course, to do your work. She'll want to appoint one of her own friends for that and pair her with a good consort. Bursar, chief of the palace guard . . ."

It soon became obvious that Alazarin would need a dozen people to replace Izard himself. We had just reduced the most-urgent list to six couples when Mandola's screams exploded inside my head.

◆ ◆ ◆ PORT ◆ ◆ ◆

5

I came forth in the marketplace before I was even fully upright. People were screaming and fleeing, so I ported again to the center of the tumult and found her. She lay on the cobblestones at the base of a stone wall. Blood high above her showed where she had struck. She had been hefted into it headfirst—no mere physical strength could have impelled her with such violence. There was no doubt that she was dead. Trindle lay about ten feet away, half hidden behind a mountebank's stall, with his sword beside him and his head at an impossible angle. My first reaction was rage.

◆ ◆ ◆ **PORT** ◆ ◆ ◆

I stumbled in the soft sand at Cape Bastel and spun around to make certain that the rest of the beach was as empty as the part I had been facing.

◆ ◆ ◆ **PORT** ◆ ◆ ◆

There, on Badderlocks Head, maybe, just maybe—I caught a glimpse of him about thirty feet away. I blinked at the sudden buffet of wind in my face and by the time I could look properly he had gone.

That was the end. A myriad high-caste champions cannot catch a fleeing nobleman. He could have ported to any one of a handful of portages and as many beyond each of those, and be two portages farther again by now.

◆ ◆ ◆ **PORT** ◆ ◆ ◆

In the marketplace at Cantle, Izard had arrived with some men from the palace, and the corpses were being covered with blankets taken from a stall. The crowd had gone, leaving the square eerily empty. Awnings flapped in the wind; crows were landing to hunt for crumbs between the cobbles.

Even then reality could not reach me. I was still armored in a shell of denial. This could not be, must not be. I would force time to run backward and return my darling. Life could not possibly be so cruel, so unjust. It was a bad dream and soon I must awaken.

Haggard and distraught, Izard had aged two pentads. "The Enemy again?" he said hoarsely.

"Yes. She recognized him. She saw one of Hyla's projections at Nuddle not a quarter watch ago. When she saw him in the market, she recognized him! That was the trouble." I told him what she had cried out to me: *Mudar! He's here! He's back—the Enemy.* And then: *Mudar! Help!* "Perhaps she said something to him, or else he just saw the recognition in her eyes."

I had not been there when she needed me.

I hefted the body of my love, blanket and all, and transported her back to the palace. In a few moments Izard arrived with Trindle. We set them in the entrance hall, and he flopped down at a table and put his head in his hands, beyond speech.

Still I felt nothing. I knew insane rage would come soon and do no good. The emotional half of my mind had frozen; the rational part seemed to be working much harder than usual. I knew I was in considerable danger from the hegemon, who would surely blame me for neglecting her daughter. And at the end, when the pain hit, my problem would be to hunt down the monster and kill him. I could not demand justice for the beating and rape of my mother— those crimes had happened before my birth and were not my concern—but the Enemy had smashed my beautiful beloved, and for that I would rip out his heart. Even for my young friend Trindle I wanted vengeance. How much more I should want it for Mandola when I recovered enough to want anything!

"I must go and find some witnesses," I said.

"Why now?" Izard whispered into his hands. "Why come back now, after so long?"

That was obvious. "The pairing invitations, of course. All this time, the monster has believed that Hyla died. *Hamulose* is fatal. It was a miracle that she lived. He can have known nothing of me, or what happened at Alazarin after he left, and he wouldn't care to ask anyone. He wouldn't care, period. Foison ordered the matter hushed up, because the old biddy thinks it is wrong to talk about unpleasant things. Pentads go by, and then out of the blue comes an invitation, naming an apparent son of yours and Aglare's. The Enemy knew your sons had died of the coughing fever, and if one had survived, he would have been unacceptably old to pair with Hegemon Foison's baby. So we'll find that he was asking questions—about Hyla, and me, and you. I want to know what he was asking, and what Mandola—"

Izard's weepy eyes emerged to stare at me in horror. "You're suggesting that *the Enemy* was invited to your pairing celebration?"

"Of course not!" I said, although that misapprehension was to misdirect my life for the next two pentads. "If he was a nobleman he would have competed at Hyla's golden games under his own name. He must be of royal blood, but for some reason he cannot claim his parents' rank. No, he wasn't invited, but a dozen clerks have been scribbling for days in the palace. Invitations have been going out by the hundred, and they're not secret, they're talked about—'What am I doing next pots-1?' 'Where's Alazarin?' Thousands of porters and footmen and champions all over Aureity have read or overheard the details. The Enemy's strength must make him a valuable porter."

Suddenly I thought of another peril. "Hyla! Hyla can identify him. Hyla is a witness still. If he's just discovered that she's still alive, then he'll hunt her down. And you, Grandfather, and Vert, Clamant, anyone who remembers him from his first murders. You are all in danger. You must leave! I'll come back for you. . . ."

⋄ ⋄ ⋄ **PORT** ⋄ ⋄ ⋄

I cannot have been as calm as I remember, because Vert and Clamant insist that I burst into the house at Nuddle yelling my head off. I do not recall it that way.

I know I told them the terrible news about Mandola. I warned them that they must move Hyla to safety, somewhere off Alazarin, somewhere on the mainland.

"Eviternal of Patas!" I suggested. "Izard's old agent! You know the way to Patas, Vert. Eviternal knows the story and she will shelter you until we can find a safe house. I'll send Izard to help." I left without waiting for a reply.

◆ ◆ ◆ PORT ◆ ◆ ◆

I had been gone only moments, but Izard had rallied and sent women out to interview witnesses, who would do a much better job of getting the story than I would, for I loom over ordinaries like a sea bear. The palace was in turmoil, of course, with much hysterical weeping and shouting, so I ignored several voices shouting my name as I hurried across the hall. Then a woman lurched out of the crush and grabbed my arm.

"Noble Mudar, noble Mudar!"

I looked down and saw a face familiar to me from my childhood. "Goodwife Agonic!" Even for an ordinary Agonic was a short woman and now she was plump and careworn, and her face was shiny with tears. She had been my nursemaid when I was a child, and before that a lady's maid to Hyla.

"It was him! I saw him. That Piese of Enthetic! I knew him right away."

I gripped her shoulders and restrained an impulse to lift her to eye level. "Tell me! Tell me everything."

Agonic had always been as sharp as a fishhook and levelheaded as a paving stone, an ideal witness. She had attended Hyla all through the time of the games. I glimpsed a few scared childish faces around her, for she had raised a plentiful family since leaving palace service to marry a stonemason, but only her testimony interested me then.

"We were in the market," she said, "shopping . . . the whole place buzzing with the news that young Muddy . . . begging your pardon, noble . . . that noble Mudar had been bought for the hegemon's daughter and we were all so excited and glad for you and then I saw this man coming . . . so tall he had to be a noble, pushing through the crowd, heading for the gossips' bench where the old men sit and I just thought he was one of the new ruler's companions attending her, but then I thought, 'That's a face I ought to know.' He's older and fatter, but the same dark, squinty look in his eye. . . . And then a tall lady came around Young Kylin's stall . . . I mean almost right in front of each other . . . he turned away very quick and she . . . I think she tried to grab him, and shouting . . ."

"She knew his name?"

But Agonic was not sure of that and she was too good a witness to let my excitement warp her testimony. Mandola had recognized the intruder, yes, and had shouted something that *might* have been "Piese of Enthetic" but might not have been, either. The stonemason's brood began to weep at the memory of what happened next, and Agonic had to break off her tale to comfort them.

It took quite a while to get the rest of her story, but it carried a lot of conviction. The Enemy had been dressed as a noble, she said, with a sword and a ring and a royal caste mark, but not livery. Of course a man who could steal a pedigree could steal a silken tunic and the rest of noble regalia, but Agonic was certain he had been a real noble. Alas, Agonic was a good witness but she knew nothing of the world outside Alazarin and little outside Cantle town itself. Her evidence was good, her conclusions must be weighed with care. Any very tall man could paint a white spot on his forehead.

My beloved mistress had been slaughtered as I had guessed and Trindle, her guardian, a heartbeat later. The Enemy had vanished forthwith. A moment later I had appeared and disappeared . . . I thanked Agonic profusely and offered her a reward, which she angrily refused until I ordered her to accept it.

I found Izard and told him that Vert was going to move Hyla and Clamant to the mainland, and seek refuge with Eviternal of Patas, and he agreed that his long-ago manager would be willing to provide a refuge, at least for a while.

"You must go and help Vert," I said. "Save him some trips."

The old man bared his teeth in pain. "I have to break the news to Trindle's family and I cannot do that until the bodies have been made decent and prepared for burial. You go and help Vert."

That was how we fled from Alazarin. I transported Hyla; Vert brought Clamant, and we went into hiding. Izard followed later. And I went on to Cuneal, bearing the terrible news.

6

I had borne Mandola from Cuneal to Alazarin in thirteen hops, but it took me dozens to return her. I could not concentrate well enough to find the longer portages at all, so I was constantly forced to detour, and even the short hops took more effort than they should. Sometimes I just sat and sobbed. I remember nothing else about that journey—I thought nothing, felt nothing, met no one. Long afterward on my travels, I became familiar with a song about a weeping youth carrying a coffin. I often wondered if the poet had seen me go by that day.

Father White stood on the crest of the hills when I came to Cuneal and twilight was already filling the valley below me. I had brought my love's casket to the Altar of the Suns, which stands on a prominent ridge and is visited only at the blue solstice. It seemed a suitable resting place until her formal return to the home of her foremothers could be arranged. And now I must break the news.

I came forth in the family entrance. The guards saluted, for I was still family so far as they knew, but I beckoned and their leader was instantly at my side. He looked at me oddly, seeing my bedraggled and overwrought condition.

"I must see noblest Bayard at once."

"Royal Mudar, the noblest is hosting a banquet for viziers of the eastern realms and left orders . . ."

"Ignore those orders. It is *essential* that I speak with him now, and I mean *now*. Understand, champion?"

"Yes, royal!" He was gone.

He was back, and Bayard was with him, still chewing. He managed to bark at me anyway.

"You had better have a very good . . . Oh, suns! What's wrong?"

"The Enemy came back. Mandragora . . . she's dead."

He swayed. I thought he was going to faint, and the champion caught him, but then he snarled angrily and was released. "Foison foresaw this! How did he come back? Who saw him? Dead how? Where were you, for the suns' sakes?"

I started to explain, then he remembered that we had an audience.

"Not here. Come."

◆ ◆ ◆ PORT ◆ ◆ ◆

He took me to the Upper Court, where I had been introduced to the family after the tourney. Now there was no food or drink available and most of the furniture was missing, but he did not sit or tell me to sit. I told him what had happened. His face grew paler and paler, seeming to age in front of my eyes.

At the end he said, "Stay here," and vanished.

I flopped down on a marble bench to torment myself with memories of lost happiness. If only I hadn't taken Mandola to meet Hyla. If only I had not let her go alone to the market. If only I had guarded her myself, instead of trusting Trindle. If only I had not been so bloated with pride as to think I deserved a woman like her. Slowly the day died.

The stars were shining when ordinaries arrived, puffing from their long climb and bringing torches to provide more light. Once they had set those up and lighted them to make the courtyard bright, porters could take over, bringing in a throne. When they had gone to report that it was ready, two champion-companion pairs arrived. The only one of the four I recognized was royal Chiliarchy of Drayage, who was one of Foison's special cronies and about the least popular person at court, because she was chief revenue officer and had the job of questioning the nobility on whether they had paid their just taxes. She could detect a lie at a hundred paces, it was said.

Finally came Bayard and noblest Foison. At first she ignored me, not even bothering to mask her raw eyelids and the ditches that tears had eroded through the paint and powder on her cheeks. She settled on the throne and adjusted her draperies. The two companions stood close, their champion attendants farther back, and Bayard behind her. He beckoned to me.

I went forward, bowed, and knelt on the cushion directly before the hegemon's toes, dangerously close. I had guessed by then that I was going to be unnamed at the least, possibly impaired, and I truly did not care. Life was nothing but a huge, oozing wound of "might-have-been."

"Tell us," she said hoarsely.

I told the story again, in more detail.

"Where is she now?" asked Bayard, always practical.

I told him.

"You say Mandragora *recognized* him?" Foison demanded scornfully.

"She had just seen noblest Hyla's projection of him, a very clear projection. Of course he must be older now—the witnesses described a much older man than Hyla shows—but I found one very sensible, reliable ordinary who remembered him right away as Piese of Enthetic. *And* she thought she heard Mandola hail him by that name! So then he killed her."

"But who is he, this monster who haunts your island?"

I had wondered little else all day.

"Of royal blood, certainly, but he cannot use his own name, so a love child, or he has been unnamed for some earlier crime. He may be married to an ordinary; he cannot be paired with a noblewoman, or she would have improved him long ago. I think he is most likely a porter in some palace."

"Why do you think that?" Bayard demanded.

"Because I think he saw the pairing invitations you have been sending out, which described me as Aglare's son. Piese of Enthetic knew that there was no such person, so he came to see what was happening. And then a young noblewoman hailed him by name and he panicked."

"You will find this man!" Foison declared.

"Dearest!" Bayard protested.

"Be silent!" She leaned forward and clasped my head in both hands. "Mudar of Quoin, I unname you! Henceforth you have no name, no apanage, no caste, no rank, no office, and no kin. You shall be no one until you work off this doom that I do set upon you: that you must find the man who killed my daughter, Mandragora of Fargite, and bring him to justice for his crimes. Until you have done this, your doom be to wander the world searching, knowing no rest and no peace."

The words rang in my skull like blows of bronze hammers. When she released me, I toppled unconscious to the floor. I awoke halfway though the Dark, frozen and stiff. Everyone else had gone and the lights were out, but the load she had laid upon my shoulders remained, and lingers still.

Treachery at Teil

1

"You truly are crazy," Humate says.

Half the night watch has slipped away while I have been talking; the lamps have flickered out and I am hoarse. Yet all this time Humate has sat inhumanly still, a graven image staring at me, listening in silence. His face is a white mask in the starlight.

I say, "I'm surprised you're still awake."

"I'm astonished you're still alive. Old Auntie Foison might have killed you, or impaired you."

"There have been times I wished she had."

"But to break the news yourself? Crazy man!"

"Yesterday, just after I brought you here to Nuddle, you ported out. You headed for Cape Bastel and Badderlocks and home . . . but then you came back. Why?"

I expect him to say it was his duty.

He doesn't. He sneers. "It was a manhood thing, was it?"

"Very much so." I heft myself upright and straighten my stiffened legs. "I owed it to Mandola. You owed it to yourself."

Humate leans back on his elbows on his mat. "So what did you do next? If you think my father was the culprit, why did it take you so long to find him?"

"I'll tell you in the morning." I turn to the door, vowing to pull his teeth out if he tries to pin me again.

"If you get the chance."

I pause at the door and look back. "What does that mean?"

"You don't know Isatin," Humate tells the ceiling. He lies on his back, arms under his head.

"No, I don't."

"Champion royal Isatin of Ulnar. A second or third cousin. When I took off for Bere Parochian, Mother made him my nursemaid. He's a snarly old fart. Has a good memory, though."

Death and Dark! "I do know that name. I beat him at javelins once. He remembered me?" It helps not at all that my contemporaries seem old to Humate.

"Your face, he did. He had to ask some old-timers your name."

Sudamina had found out my original name, but he had not.

"And what did they say about me?"

"That you had been one of the best ever, but you were vilified or unnamed ages ago. That you are a felon, still hanging around games trying to get readmitted. Sudamina let you in at Bere Parochian because my name had scared away so many brave lads. Isatin told me this after the tourney was over, of course. By then you'd bea— tricked me out of the crown."

"Real men don't invent excuses, sonny. You didn't know my original name when you came to me on the island at Cupule."

"I did by the next morning."

"Then why didn't you expose me at Quintole, if you knew I was an unnamed?"

He chuckles as if he has been waiting for that question. "Because I knew I could slaughter you in the hefting. I can out-heft any man in Pelagic, now, except my father, and I can usually get him purple in the face. Hadn't counted on more of your sneaky tricks. . . . Besides, if I knew you had been unnamed, Agynary was sure to know, so there was more trickery going on and she must be in on it. I wanted to find out what it was."

"Isatin wasn't one of the goons you had with you yesterday morning in the arena. I'd have remembered him."

"Obviously. Or I wouldn't be here. *You* wouldn't be here. You don't frighten me, nameless man. You don't scare me one little bit.

Try anything fishy and I'll crack your skull. Those two goons, as you call them—Vagrom and Slype—are both long on pedigree and short on brains. Grith is cunning but only a princely and he wasn't there either. I wish I'd been around when the dummies got to tell Isatin that they'd let you kidnap me."

"You think Isatin went streaking back to Mascle and told your . . . told *our* father what was happening?"

"My father. Not yours. Possibly, but Isatin hates to admit he can't handle me, which he can't, of course. He tried to insist I go home after Bere Parochian but I refused—didn't want to face the raging parent until I'd won a crown. I promised I would do better at Quintole. Then you turned up again . . . The reason I agreed to leave with you yesterday was that I knew Isatin would be after us like a terrier after rats. And he is."

"Is he really?" I yawn to show how this juvenile bragging bores me.

"Yes, he is. When I left here yesterday, I got as far as the lily pond with the *miche* grove. Vagrom and Grith were sitting there. They didn't see me. I wasn't ten feet away, but I was behind them. They were obviously waiting for the others to catch up. You are no longer the hunter. You are the hunted."

I suppress a shiver. If he's lying, he lies very convincingly.

"The only reason I came back here," Humate adds sleepily, "was to hear the rest of the story before they wrench your neck until you stare up your own ass. You may go now, Mudar of Wherever-it-is. Sleep well, yeoman."

"Good night, Brother." I close the door.

Working my way by touch and memory back to my room, I consider Humate's parting threat. It is credible, although Isatin's timing would have been very tight. If I had been the boy's keeper and my charge had run off with the suspicious character who had once been Mudar of Quoin, what would I have done? First, I would have swallowed my pride and sent word back to Mascle, whatever the risk of punishment from his irate parents. But any good champion in Isatin's place would have already reported the catastrophe at Bere Parochian and very likely that is what Isatin did, no matter what Humate believes. Piese of Rulero may even have been skulking somewhere around Quintole, keeping an eye on things and ready to react.

I should have thought of that possibility sooner.

And, yesterday? Royal Isatin knew my original name and realm. When Humate left with me, he would certainly have given chase, probably beginning by ordering his men to rendezvous in Cuneal. Almost all champions are familiar with the seven hegemonic capitals, and those who did not know a good route from Quintole could be transported by others. In Cuneal he would have hired a long-hop public porter who knew the way to Alazarin; more than one if he could find them, but we get so few visitors that there is little demand. Piese of Rulero, if he was with them, would have had no need of a porter. In either case one guide is enough to start the relays: one takes one, those two come back to take two more, and so on. The numbers add up very quickly. It is unlikely that Isatin's whole force could have reached Alazarin before Dark, but he may well have been able to blockade the crossing.

I jump as a warm tongue washes my hand and I realize I have company, Fidel padding along at my side.

No one knows that Hyla is here in Nuddle, but a few hours' questioning in the town will uncover memories of Clamant and Vert and their apanage. If Ruler Chiliarchy cooperates with the strangers, she can certainly suggest the most likely places to look for her predecessor.

And what of the Enemy himself, Piese of Rulero, hegemonic consort of Pelagic, the brute who once was Piese of Enthetic? He knows the way to Alazarin and he can bring an army of his mistress's champions. Ruler Chiliarchy will certainly cooperate with a hegemonic consort if he comes in person and cares to reveal his identity. We allowed for the possibility that he would follow us, and we are prepared to move Hyla to safety at first light. Nevertheless, I do not dare lie down. Instead I settle in a comfortable chair to think and doze a little. Fidel curls up at my feet, thumps his tail a few times, and soon starts snoring.

Fitful dreams mingle with the memories I have been sharing with the boy who is, improbably, my father's son.

Why did it take you so long to find him? Because Aureity is a very big place, with seven hegemons and well over a thousand rulers, all of whom keep champions and porters. There are also uncountable nobles living quietly on their apanages, never visiting a court.

A monster like the Enemy should not survive in the golden land of Aureity. Hundreds of people saw him perform at Hyla's golden games. Although the Hegemon Foison managed to bury that scandal successfully from the eyes of the world, the brotherhood of the arena knew what had happened to Tarn of Gyre and Piese of Greaten. Had the imposter shown his face in any games anywhere after that, word should have gotten back to Cantle or Cuneal. Were he already paired, his mistress must have detected his crimes the moment they touched, so he had to be an ordinary, married to an ordinary. That is what we all assumed until he reappeared in Cantle and slew Mandola.

But Mandola's killer had been a nobleman, the witnesses said—big, swarthy, and sumptuously dressed, although only goodwife Agonic remembered him from the golden games four pentads earlier. The stranger had been asking in the market about the new ruler and the previous ruler and noblest Izard, which must have seemed odd, but no ordinary will question a noble's right to ask anything he wants.

Foison doomed me to find him, but all I had to go on was his face. I sought that face mostly among the ranks of porters, working my way around the major towns of Aureity and hiring on as one of them. Porters see more of the nobility and the insides of their palaces than most outsiders do. But I did not neglect the nobility, for I also attended as many games as I could, gnomon after gnomon—small wonder I learned all the tricks of the arena. In every tourney I looked for the face I wanted among the noble guests and the old hands coaching their sons in the kibitzer cage.

Whenever I saw an old friend or made a new one, I would produce the plaque. "Have you ever seen this man? He is older than this now."

Why did it take me so long to find him?

Because I was a nothing, without name or land or status, while the man I sought was in fact the consort of the most powerful woman in Aureity. Although I would never say why I wanted him, anyone who did recognize the face on my plaque was not about to tell me so. Conversely, if they knew Piese of Rulero well enough to tell him that someone was looking for him, they probably knew him well enough to know not to. He is malicious, quarrelsome, and easily provoked. And so we sailed our own courses, beyond each other's horizons, never sighting each other.

Two pentads, a third of my life.

How could I have guessed that the man I sought was consort of the richest, most powerful woman in Aureity? Of course I knew that Piese of Rulero was reputed to be a recluse and unsociable. I knew a distinguished guest was delegated to hand out the prizes when the hegemonic games were held in Mascle, whereas in other capitals this honor was claimed by the hegemon's consort. I assumed that this was merely a Pelagic custom, just as the Cuneal games began with rollerball and the Teil games with a porting race to some distant city and back.

The Dark never lasts forever. Half a gnomon ago, I was sitting on the grass near the kibitzer cage at the silver games in Sough, an obscure, third-rate bronze tourney in Pelagic, when a very large man sat down beside me, close enough to indicate he wanted to talk. That was enough to make my heart leap even before I turned to regard his waxed and sculpted coiffeur, resplendent with ribbons, beads, and flowers. A Heliac, obviously, I concluded, but then under the visual monstrosity, I recognized the gimlet eye and eagle nose of my old friend, royal Magnes of Scantling, just daring me to as much as smirk. Magnes, I recalled, was a champion of the ruler of Formene, and consort to one of her daughters.

The first thing he said was "Let me see that picture of yours again."

An unnamed is not supposed to pray, but I sent my joy winging to Father White as I passed the plaque over. Magnes studied it, nodded a couple of times, and returned it. "He's fatter than that now." So was Magnes, but he seemed prosperous and content. "Why do you want him?"

I had never answered that question before, but in our youth I had trusted Magnes enough to do javelin tricks with him in the arena, and he was the first who had ever asked for a second look at the plaque. "To bring him to justice, preferably a slow and excruciatingly painful justice."

"Won't be easy."

"His name?" Even in those two words I heard my voice tremble.

Magnes studied me with a wry smile. Exchanging information always requires trust, especially life-and-death information.

"I approve of your aims in principle, Mudar. I'll be happy to heat some of the irons for you. But I don't want to involve certain innocent people. You tell me your story and then I'll tell you my problem with this man. As the Mother is my witness, I will."

I told him about Hyla and Mandola. And Tarn of Gyre. And Piese of Greaten. And young Trindle. And finally Foison and my doom. Magnes's rubicund face grew pale and paler, his eyes more menacing. Normally he is a bluff, hearty, easygoing man, belying his fearsome looks, but by the time I had done, he was growling like a hunting cat.

He shook his big head. "Compared to that, friend Mudar, our complaint against him seems trivial." He explained how the widow Tendence, his mistress's sister and heir to the realm of Formene, was about to be forced into pairing with a skinny boy for reasons of political trickery and strong bloodlines.

I cared nothing for that, not then.

"Just tell me his name," I wheedled. "Whisper it in my ear and I will denounce him to his hegemon."

"I don't think that would be advisable, Mud. It's noblest Piese of Rulero."

"Mother of Light! Pelta's consort? He's hegemonic himself, then!" That explained his homicidal arrogance. "What house by birth?"

"Glyptic," Magnes said. "A distant cousin of Hegemon Abraxas." That blood would explain the Enemy's strength, although Magnes's information was wrong, as it turned out. "I think my mistress and royal Tendence would like to meet you and discuss strategy, see if we can make common cause."

Down on the sand a weedy cub dropped a mere two balks and the bored crowd booed. Incredulously, I realized that my long quest was over. I would never, never—so I assumed—*never* have to visit an arena again.

"Formene?" I asked, rising. "I'll take the first stretch."

✦ ✦ ✦ **PORT** ✦ ✦ ✦

2

Taking turns to do the porting, we headed north. Heliacs are so obsessively cautious and secretive that even a family member like Magnes is required to enter the palace through the Court of Joyful Blossom so that the guard will know he has returned. The response was instantaneous—a flunky appeared before him, already kneeling on the sand. The lad was glorious in a sequined robe, a bejeweled sword, and hair sculpted with ribbons into a pagoda shape, but he sported a red caste mark and I assumed he could summon impressive help if he ever required it. He touched his face to the ground.

"My companion will remain unnamed," Magnes decreed, exercising an authority that few people outside the royal family would possess. "Pray inform royal Eikon that I have returned and will await her pleasure among the Small Jade Horses."

We came forth in a large hall, apparently a freestanding building with a high roof of heavy timbers supported by thick wooden pillars. The walls were panels of oiled silk bearing images of flowers, but the floor mosaic design did include green horses among other improbable creatures. There was no furniture whatsoever and not a single door or window.

"Won't be long," Magnes said. "I wouldn't have come to the Horses unless I brought an important visitor."

"Don't you ever want to look *out*?" I asked.

He laughed. "This is the public part of the palace. We have windows elsewhere. See those columns? We get a lot of earthquakes in Heliac, but this whole building can move as a—"

A man appeared and disappeared at the far end. Then a whole gang of them, coming and going in a continuous flicker of shapes, all bringing things, so that in moments they had set out cushions, low tables, dishes of food, and flasks of tea. The servants vanished. A small orchestra began playing just outside the silken walls.

While we waited, I took out my plaque and studied the face of the Enemy. *Piese of Enthetic, Piese of Rulero, at last I have you!* "How long have you known?"

Magnes cleared his throat. A man so large and fierce-seeming rarely has cause to seem bashful and never does it well. "Well, I don't *know* yet, do I? It may be only a chance resemblance. And everyone knows he's a recluse. It wasn't until, oh, perhaps maybe a pentad ago that I ever set eyes on the man himself. I thought he reminded me of someone. . . ." Magnes was looking at jade horses, not at me. "After a while I remembered that plaque of yours. . . . But how long is it since our paths crossed, Mud? A pentad? I don't go to games often."

He had tracked me down easily enough when he wanted to, but I felt no anger. He had sworn troth to his ruler and his mistress. Making trouble for everyone by antagonizing a hegemonic consort would not have been true loyalty. Scores of men must have done the same, recognizing my quarry but declining to identify him to me. All this age I had been searching among the undergrowth, never looking up at the treetops.

Two more porters came and went, but these two brought Eikon and Tendence. I knelt. Magnes bowed and presented me. There was much formal speech and ceremony from all four of us before we could settle on the cushions around the food, and even then there could be no meaningful discussion until we had all eaten a few tiny pastries and sipped tea.

Like all noblewomen, Ruler Etesian's daughters seemed young, tall, and beautiful. Like all Heliac women they wore simple mono-chrome silk kimonos—Tendence's pale blue, Eikon's pink—but their hair was pinned up high and decorated with flowers. Tendence was soft-spoken and reticent, Eikon just the opposite. Once we got down to business, it was she who took charge, firing questions and com-ments at me in a harsh, almost masculine, voice.

I showed my plaque, and the sisters agreed that the face it showed was very probably a younger Piese of Rulero. I told my story, hesi-tating only once, to ask Magnes if I should give all the gruesome de-tails of the attack on Hyla and Mandola. He shuddered and said I had better do so. The royal ladies were understandably appalled. And when the conversation proceeded to their problems, I was pre-dictably disgusted to hear Eikon describe how a woman of more than five pentads was to be paired with a boy of three.

"Our noblest mother," Eikon said scornfully, "has sworn to dis-inherit and unname her if she refuses the match. She is adamant and will not listen to reason. Quite apart from the injustice of that threat, yeoman Quirt, I have no desire to replace my sister as Mother's heir. Tendence has been trained for the succession all her life and I have not. More important, though, the hegemon will be furious. She would be angry enough if Etesian assigned any man to Tendence without her permission, but she will see a match with the son of her lifelong rival as a deliberate insult."

Eikon was one of those women who believe that all the troubles of the world are caused by simple bad manners. If people behaved politely, we should have no problems at all, and the louder this dictum was stated, the truer it must become.

Tendence spoke little that day, but everything she ever does say always goes to the heart of the matter. Magnes was out of his depth and knew it. He was a bluff, straightforward man, too honorable to swim in such murky political waters.

As tactfully as I could, I asked the obvious question: "Why, then, do you not just inform noblest Balata of the conspiracy, so she can stop it before any harm is done?" A hegemon can overrule her rulers on anything, especially something as vital as an heir's pairing.

Eikon deferred to her sister.

Tendence said, "Understand, yeoman Quirt, that I love my mother dearly, although I don't deny that she is a stubborn woman. Hegemon Balata has a ferocious temper and utterly detests noblest Pelta. We are much afraid that Balata, if she catches wind of what is being planned, will rally every champion she possesses and come forth right here in the palace to depose Mother by force. She would be well within her rights. She can do it, and in such a case she well might."

"She may depose our entire house," Eikon said with an unladylike scowl.

"Will not noblest Balata be even more angry if she discovers the plot after the treaty is signed and the pairing is, er, completed?"

Tendence sighed. "But noblest Piese has promised that by then he will be here to defend us with a force of Pelagic champions at his back. Pelagic has far more noblemen to call on than Heliac does." She smiled very slightly, and for the first time in my sight. It was a beautiful, heartrending smile, showing dimples. "You must think me a very wicked woman, yeoman, defying my royal mother and rejecting her choice of consort when I am already old to be childless. I swear to you that there is more than personal whim behind my stubbornness. I have promised to accept any other noble she assigns me without complaint, even another as young as royal Humate of Alfet. The genealogists believe that the children Humate would sire on me would inherit enough strength to raise our house to the rank of a significant family. I share Mother's excitement at that prospect, but I dread that she will provoke noblest Balata to violence. Noblest Piese is reputed to have an evil temper also, and what you have told us today brings me no comfort."

"You are talking *war*, royal Tendence? *War* between Pelagic and Heliac?"

She nodded. I shivered.

Eikon said, "What you have told us of his history makes the possibility seem no less likely."

No, it did not. "Nobles, I agree with you that my detested father is capable of any crime. I swear to you, royal Tendence, that I shall do everything I can, everything my doom allows, that is, to help you defeat his evil schemes, for I do not doubt he is using you and exploiting his own son for squalid political advantage."

We were talking the day away. The orchestra played on, precluding any attempt to eavesdrop on our discussion. Blue had set, White cast forest shadows on the translucent walls, and I was so famished that I had to restrain myself from grabbing great handfuls of the tiny delicacies displayed on the table. I took one only when my hostess did, until I noticed that she was eating much more than she had earlier. In fact, Tendence had observed what I was doing and was making it easier for me. She was also, I realized, smaller than she had been at first. Her hair and eyes were a warm brown, instead of fashionable black, and she had a chipped tooth. Eikon had not changed, but Tendence had dropped her projected persona, which was a huge honor to offer a casual visitor.

Something was happening between us two, a sort of mutual madness. I had soon decided that Tendence of Carpus was a warm, admirable person, who should not be forced into such a shameful predicament. Undoubtedly the huge relief of finally knowing my Enemy and the sudden end to my long search were also playing tricks on my mind. Possibly Tendence felt a similar relief, seeing in me an unexpected ally in her struggle against Piese of Rulero and his hegemonic mistress. If so, she was grossly overestimating my power to help her. But it was almost two pentads since my mistress and Tendence's consort had died, and lack of a mate was something else we had in common.

No! I was still doomed, still unnamed, landless and penniless. I must *not* give way to such insane dreams. We must all concentrate on strategy.

But now that I knew the Enemy, I needed help to bring him to justice. Now that Tendence knew his history, she was even more reluctant to be paired with his son.

"Piese of Rulero," I said sadly, "is shielded by his mistress, Pelta of Pelagic, the most powerful woman in Aureity." How could we four defy her?

"Why doesn't Quirt just tell his story to noblest Etesian?" Magnes suggested. "She won't want a monster like that in the family."

The ruler's daughters shook their heads in unison. Their mother was too stubborn, too determined to win significant family status for unborn grandchildren.

" 'It is the son you are pairing with,' " Tendence said, in what I assumed was an imitation of her mother's voice, " 'not his father. And if he shows signs of violence, you can easily improve him.' "

"Can't you appeal to the hegemonic council?" I suggested. "I cannot drag 'noblest' Piese before an ordinary court. He must be tried by the council."

Tendence corrected me. Her own problem could not go to the council because her pairing was a local matter, within the prerogative of Hegemon Balata, and the other six would never meddle in her affairs. War, if it came, would be different, but by then the damage would be done.

My case was certainly a council matter, but Tendence, the trained ruler-in-waiting, quietly analyzed the politics for me. Any two hegemons could summon a meeting of the seven, but I would be unlikely even to win a hearing, let alone a verdict. Certainly Balata would support any charge against her enemy's consort, especially one as outrageous as murder and rape, but the other five, knowing of their ingrained feud, would dismiss her complaint as mere spite. Even old Foison, who had doomed me to find her daughter's killer, would likely refuse to convict a cousin, however distant, of Bayard, her own consort. Noble families always cover up scandal because it may injure the pairing prospects of their children. Pelta would be privately ordered to improve her consort, and that would be that. My doom might not accept such tepid justice.

"But we are not even ready to take action," Tendence said. "No offense, yeoman, but we must have a firm identification. Hegemon Pelta will be bringing her son to Formene for formal initialing of the terms. Of course her consort will accompany her. Can you round up some reliable witnesses to support your testimony?"

She meant noble witnesses, of course. Ordinaries' testimony would not be admissible in such a case. "There were none to the murder of Mandola and Trindle, noble. It happened too fast. But there are still men who remember Piese of Enthetic at my mother's golden games."

Magnes stirred his great bulk. "Light is failing. We must offer Quirt hospitality for the night."

For a moment Tendence's eye met mine. Then she looked away quickly.

"Of course," she said. "Noble Quirt is now our ally and is welcome to stay in our house."

We shared great troubles, the noble heir and the landless nobody, and we were soon to be compounding our sorrows with the worst tragedy of all, which is love.

3

I spent most of the next half-gnomon in the palace as Magnes's guest, without ever setting eyes on my hostess, Ruler Etesian. I saw royal Tendence rarely, and at first only in the company of her sister and usually Magnes. Near the end, though, when we could no longer hide our feelings for each other, Eikon arranged for us to have a few precious moments alone, whispering the bittersweet follies of the insane.

Hegemon Pelta's visit to Formene was repeatedly postponed as Tendence kept raising objections to the terms of the pairing contract. She insisted, quite rightly, that Humate of Alfet must follow the age-old tradition and prove his manhood in the arena. Magnes and I assured her that no normal youth of his age could hope to prevail against full-grown cubs of four pentads. Alas, as I was to discover at Bere Parochian, his hegemonic heritage won out and only lack of training betrayed him.

Both mothers wanted Humate and Tendence to begin their cohabitation right after the signing, it being customary to confirm the pair's fertility before going to all the expense of staging suitable festivities, with the risk of loss of face if no children appeared thereafter. Tendence refused, pointing out that Hegemon Balata could annul a betrothal by decree, but not a pairing, and Etesian reluctantly accepted that argument. In fact the Pelagic delegates did not argue very hard, either, because they would have much stronger justification to meddle in Formene's affairs once their hegemon's son was an official member of the ruling family. Foolish Etesian could not see that her defiance of her own Hegemon Balata was going to put her totally in the power of Hegemon Pelta and the gang of bullies that the ruthless Piese of Rulero would send along to "protect" Humate.

It was easily agreed that the celebrations would be held in Pelagic, so that Hegemon Balata need not be invited. The invitations would go out at very short notice and would not identify Tendence of Carpus as heir of Formene, so Balata might not even get wind of the plot until after the deed was done.

And finally, Tendence insisted that the festivities include golden games. They were traditional, but her real reason for wanting them was that they would let me spring the trap we had devised, where I would gain access to the assembled senior nobility of Aureity. As one of the winners, I would denounce the Enemy before his peers and throw the entire assembly into chaos. Or so we hoped.

Eventually the two sides reached agreement and the hegemonic visit to Formene was scheduled for triangles-5. It was time for me to leave. In the morning I headed east, to Osseter, near Riggish. Not long after blueset, I walked in on Izard, Vert, and Clamant, who were just starting their evening repast. Soon Hyla would waken and need attendance until morning.

Izard blinked a few times and then beamed. "Mudar, dear boy!" He is the only one who still calls me that, in defiance of Hegemon Foison's ancient decree. "It has been a long time. We were starting to get worried about you. Wine for the noble! And food."

The two servants hurried out. Vert nodded happily at me as I hefted a cushion over from the side of the room and sat down at their table.

But Clamant beamed. "You have found him!"

"Now, whatever makes you think that?" I asked, nettled that my epic news had been snatched away.

She smiled a mother's knowing smile. "Because I have not seen those stars in your eyes since before Mandola died. If you had brought him to justice already there would be suns shining there. Tell us!"

I suspected it was Tendence who had brought those stars back. I had loved Mandola with all my heart, but I had been little more than a boy in those days. Time does heal eventually. I waited until the servants had brought a wine flask and a plate for me. As soon as Izard dismissed them, I confirmed Clamant's insight.

"I need," I explained, "reliable witnesses to confirm the identity of the man who once called himself Piese of Enthetic. Do I have any volunteers?"

Vert was an obvious choice. Izard's eyes were failing, but hurricanes and earthquakes would not have kept him from joining our mission of vengeance. We added Kish of Homarine, one of my grandmother Aglare's champions. He was just as old, but his sight was good and he had been a linesmen in the ill-fated golden games, so he had known Piese of Enthetic very well—too well, he always said.

He had known right from the beginning that the man was rotten all the way through. The journey west would be a strain on the old champions, but Vert and I could do the porting, going at a gentle pace, taking a whole day.

And so it was.

At doublenoon on triangles-5, noblest Hegemon Pelta of Pelagic arrived in Joyful Blossom, brought forth in an eight-sided court floored with blue sand and enclosed by painted wicker walls. She was accompanied by her consort, noblest Piese of Rulero; her son, royal Humate of Alfet; and an escort of five champions, all wearing Pelagian voluminous trousers. The vizier and three of Ruler Etesian's most senior champions at once came forth to greet the visitors. There was much kneeling and bowing; gracious words were spoken. Then the visitors were transported out to more comfortable quarters to enjoy genteel social intercourse and the ceremonies of signing the treaty.

The court in question had been assigned to the Pelagic commissioners and their consorts prior to the start of negotiations. What none of the visitors knew—although they could have guessed—was that several of the wicker panels concealed narrow cubicles, backed by solid stone walls and roofed over so that they would be dark. Guards standing or sitting in those boxes could watch and not be seen. This was no more than standard security in Formene or any other realm of Heliac. The greeting party had been waiting in one of those dark, stuffy cubicles for what must have seemed like an eternity.

Unknown to noblest Etesian, one of the other observation cubicles contained four more witnesses, who had been placed there by some of her champions and companions, which strongly suggested that the ruler's senior aides must be on Tendence's side in the pairing dispute. Izard and Kish sat on stools, Vert and I just stood, and I wondered if the pounding of my heart would be audible out in the courtyard. A third of my life I had waited to set eyes on my quarry, my murderous, monstrous father.

And suddenly there he was. I ignored his mistress—she looked however she wanted to look; her appearance was irrelevant. But the Enemy, noblest Piese of Rulero, was unmistakable. I would have known him anywhere. Big, of course, because he was of House Glyptic. He was taller than any of the champions present, Pelagic or Heliac, taller even than the youth beside him, and also grossly fat. His face was puffy and inflamed, and someone had scribbled with purple ink all over his nose. He looked diseased, certainly physically and perhaps mentally, although I might be influenced by my knowledge of his history.

"*Yes!*" Izard whispered. Kish was nodding like a hungry woodpecker.

And the rest of us agreed: "Certainly." "Yes." "That's him."

I wanted to kill him there and then. Did not the ghosts of his victims cry out from the Everlit Realm? Piese of Greaten. Tarn of Gyre. Mandola. Trindle . . . Hyla, dead in fact if not in name. Those were all I knew of. How many more that I did not? And now Tendence was to be ground in the Enemy's mill?

That made me glance at the acne-spotted boy standing between his parents and smirking at the Heliacs' coiffures. Rawboned rather than lanky; very nearly as tall as his father and destined to be taller. This callow *child* was to be forced upon the woman I adored?

Then the three Pelagics were gone. More champions arrived to convey their escort to the ceremonies and the court emptied.

"So now we know," Izard muttered. "At last! After so long."

"What can you do about it?" Kish asked, peering at me in the dimness.

"I can give his son a very memorable pairing ceremony," I said.

4

The sky is brightening. I rise and stroll along to Vert's room, with Fidel hurrying ahead. Then all I need do is open the door and send in Vert's wake-up face-wash. When I hear his roar of fury, I port to Humate's room and confirm that he is fast asleep. I leave again as silently as I came, hoping to let him snore till doublenoon, long after the rest of us have left the island.

The kitchen, which I remember from my childhood as a warm, busy, cheerful place, is chill and shadow-haunted now, echoing creepily and smelling more of dust and neglect than of roasting meat. It is big enough that even the massive table in the center that can seat twenty laborers does not make it seem crowded. I am working my way through some cold meat and stale bread when Vert and Fidel join me. Vert looks grumpy and unshaven. Fidel sniffs at my hand, explaining that he would like to share.

"We mustn't waste any time," I explain. "Humate claims his father will invade Alazarin with an army at dawn."

"The little snot is lying."

"I'm not." Humate wanders in, yawning and stretching.

I pour him a beaker of juice, a product Nuddle never lacks. "When he left here last night he ran into two of his bodyguards at Jade Pond."

"And I suppose he swears by the holy suns that he didn't bring them back with him?" Vert disappears into the larder with Fidel on his heels.

"I do and I didn't." Humate sits on a bench and leans elbows on the table. He stares across at me with big, dark eyes, as if my own eyes were looking out of a mirror at me, except that mine would not wear that mocking, amused expression.

"Thanks," I say. "But, remember, it was evening when you and I arrived. If your nursemaid, this Isatin, sent word of your disappearance home to Mascle, neither your father nor any of his champions is going to get here in time to stop us leaving this house. He'll never find us after we do."

Vert emerges from the larder with a wheel of cheese, a flagon of ale, and a ring of sausage. A fist-sized chunk of cheese breaks loose and flies across the room to Humate. He is showing off his hefting range.

"I doubt very much," he says while chewing, "that my father will bother, old man. He'll leave it up to Isatin to decide whether you are a danger to me, or him, and if Isatin thinks you are, then you become a scattering of body parts. You are not important to Piese of Rulero."

"I will seem so when I bring him to justice."

"But you won't. You can't." Humate wipes his mouth on an arm. He is enjoying himself. "You are mistaken. My father is not the face on that miniature you carry."

Vert says, "Yes he is. I saw him, too. And so did Izard, and another witness. And we saw you with him. We recognized him as Piese of Enthetic, a vicious rapist and murderer."

Humate scowls at him with dislike. There is an ominous crash from the larder. Vert bellows "Fidel!" and dashes to investigate. The larder door shuts itself behind him and the bolt slides. I am not within range of it. Humate is. Fidel is under the table, at our feet.

"I told you," I say. "It doesn't matter whether you believe or not. What matters is that I believe. And I will have justice."

The larder door rattles and emits muffled shouts. It bounces on its hinges. I ignore it, concentrating on my insidious half-brother. Vert's ring of sausage rolls across the table to him.

"How? You think you can sneak up on a hegemonic consort? You ever been to Mascle?" He is very confident, very smug, very young.

Vert comes forth outside the larder and glares at both of us.

I nod. "Many times."

"It's not much of a palace for a hegemon, is it? Not like Cuneal or the others. That's because you only see a small part of it. Mascle's only our business address, really. We have hill palaces, shore palaces, lake palaces. Drop in and ask for Father and somebody will go and tell him he has a visitor, but he's rarely within five days' walk of Mascle itself. He and I can recall places from a far greater distance than we can recall people, and I doubt your talent is different. Your threats aren't going to scare him at all, Quirt-Mudar. His guards will get you long before you can get him." He smirks.

I say, "I see. Give him my message anyway. Tell him Mandola sent me."

Mockery morphs into menace. "I could kill you now, yeoman Quirt, all by myself."

"I know that," I say with as much calm as I can muster. If he chooses, he can take my head home in a bag to Daddy.

"Your sidekick there has all the mighty strength of fish soup. I don't want to chastise you, but you are slandering my father and implying that my mother failed in her duty to clip his claws." He licks his fingers, watching me carefully. He must be as worried about a sudden attack as Vert and I are. Violence crackles in the air. He is mighty, but together we would have a good chance against him if we had set up a plan beforehand. We had not.

"However," he concedes, "I do admire your cheek, thinking you can take on a hegemon's consort. I'm willing to humor you."

"I could be bribed by an offer of his head in a bucket."

"No," Humate says. "But I will help you bring the matter to the council."

"That is not a possibility. I told you: It takes two hegemons to convene a meeting. The only hegemony that might support us is Heliac. We wouldn't even get a hearing."

"I can get you a hearing." His snooty confidence is damnably convincing.

I notice that the sky is bright beyond the dusty windows. I wonder if my young half-brother is spinning out this conversation until the Pelagic troops can arrive. Then his words register.

"You can? How?"

Humate swallows his cud. "The council is summoned by the senior hegemon. It's only if she refuses that you need two of the others to overrule her. The senior hegemon is my dear aunt Abraxas of Glyptic. I have to let you into a dark family secret. Go away, princely."

Vert looks to me. "How far do you trust this oversized fetus?"

I say, "I'll trust him until I have reason not to." Apart from throwing javelins at my back, that is. "I want you and Izard to move Hyla and Clamant out of here, though. And don't try the crossing— if my half-brother says it may be booby-trapped, then it may be booby-trapped. You know lots of hiding places on Alazarin. Leave word with Groof."

Groof is one of Vert's prized dogs back at Osseter, on the mainland. She can't speak, but her kennelman can. Vert nods, understanding my hint. He ports out, back into the larder to listen. He has forgotten that both Humate and I have psychic recall of persons.

The boy ponders a moment, either wondering where to begin or planning a complex lie. "Family scandal. My dear Aunt Abraxas and your Hegemon Foison detest each other."

"Old news. Even before I was born, when Hyla went to Cuneal, those two were daggers drawn. Izard told me there were rumors Foison might dismiss her consort, because Bayard is Abraxas's brother."

Humate chuckles. "You don't see the connection? Well, then. When you told me about your pairing with Mandola of Wherever—Foison and Bayard's daughter—you said that noblest Bayard suggested you dance the *lilacin*."

"And?" Again I wonder if he is just wasting time until his friends arrive. I do wish Vert would go upstairs and organize Hyla's escape.

"How did Bayard know about the *lilacin*?"

"I told you. After Hyla was attacked, noblest Foison sent her consort to Alazarin to investigate the crimes. He does all her dirty chores. Undoubtedly he was told how Hyla had announced her choice by dancing with Tarn of Gyre."

Humate registers triumph around a mouthful of sausage. "Bayard was on the island right after the alleged rape? So he must have seen those muddled impressions Hyla conveys. Bayard's not notably swift, but you think he couldn't recognize his own cousin?"

I repeat "Cousin?" stupidly, while my mind whirls. "Distant cousin, I was told."

Humate sighs. "No. 'First cousin once removed,' in the breeders' jargon. Try again. Leaving out all the irrelevant sprigs, my little-lamented fourbear, Hegemon Durian of Glyptic, had two daughters. Prakrit became hegemon after her and begat Abraxas and Bayard. Bayard spawned a whole litter, including your sweetie

Mandola. Durian's other daughter, Miskal, dropped a son, Grobian of Heretoga, who was paired with royal Remise of Dolose. Because of something he did to her on a sleeping mat one night, she produced Piese of Rulero, my father. Mine, not yours. Have you got that: Durian, Prakrit, Bayard, Mandola on one line and Durian, Miskal, Grobian, Piese, Humate on the other? So Grobian was Bayard's first cousin. Piese was your Mandola's second cousin. Abraxas is my second cousin twice removed, but I call her Auntie for short. Got it now?"

My head nods but my mind rejects this. Nightmares darken the sky ahead.

Humate is triumphant. "We hegemonics hang out together like starlings. So if Bayard saw Hyla's projections, he must have recognized his naughty cousin Piese right away. This was six pentads ago, remember, while he still looked as he does on your plaque. That is why you are definitely mistaken, yeoman—why you are no relative of mine. Because, by law, decency, and all that's holy, Bayard should have arranged for the rapist-murderer to be promptly reported to his ruler or hegemon for drastic improvement. I'm sure that didn't happen, because my father still talks in sentences. He can feed himself and he doesn't wear diapers."

Humate spits out a piece of gristle in Fidel's direction. I cringe before all the horrible implications. Of course the great families are intricately interrelated. I had known Piese of Rulero was of House Glyptic, but I had not understood he was so close to the main line. Humate must have worked this all out last night, while I was telling my story.

"That isn't all," he says, leering. "Your Mandola was Piese's second cousin, as I said, so I was her second cousin, once removed, and if what you allege were true, so would you be. That was incest you were doing, old man. If you were a noble it would be, I mean. Ordinaries let even first cousins marry, but it puts blots on our pedigrees. It doubles up fourbears, so any brats you sired would not have been royals. None of them could have been confirmed as ruler of anywhere. Shocking! Doesn't that explain," he adds smugly, "why her mother fought so hard against letting you into the family? Hegemons don't like having grandchildren with more than two arms and less than sixteen quarterings."

Nobody had ever mentioned this problem to me, of course, because my father was supposedly unknown. If true it might explain the way Foison had granted me royal caste by moving me up a generation, making me in effect my mother's brother. On the other hand, she had had to fake something; to have acknowledged that I was conceived by rape would have made me ineligible for any caste at all.

"All very interesting," I tell him. "But if Bayard had recognized the Enemy as a cousin, then why did his mistress doom me to bring him to justice? You're saying she condemned me to identify a man she already knew?"

Humate shrugs and stretches his arms, glances at the window. "She's a batty old bird, Foison. That's why I'm offering to let you take your case to Abraxas instead. Auntie may be tough as boiled leather, but she's always fair. She and I get along well, although Father cannot abide her. I've watched them screaming at each other before a score of witnesses. She used to suggest all sorts of peppy stuff I could do to annoy him. Happens in the best of families. The old coot will give you a fair hearing if anyone can, I promise you. If she believes your story, then she will haul down the suns on him, cackling with glee."

He gnaws at the sausage. "Besides, I don't want to leave you running around trying to throw spears through my dad. You might hurt somebody else by mistake. So . . . What's the matter?"

Matter? I must be staring right through him, but I am staring at the past. "Mandola," I whisper. Why had I not seen this sooner? "I brought her to Alazarin. We were newly paired, dizzy with happiness. We owned the world to the end of time. But I took her to meet Hyla, and Hyla projected the Enemy, a very vivid likeness. . . ."

"Oh?" Humate says cautiously.

"Mandola was terribly upset. She knew him! Of course she knew him. You hegemonics band like starlings, you say? Mandola *recognized the Enemy* as her father's cousin, Piese of Rulero. This was two pentads ago, before he got all bloated, I expect. And not long after that she saw him in the market in Cantle—saw him in the flesh. And he saw her."

I stare back at those eyes that are my own eyes.

"So you're right and you're wrong, *Brother*! Foison did know who the Enemy was. That's why she didn't want me in the family. Not because of incest, but because sooner or later we were certain to come face-to-face. And when I won the crown against all odds and she had to accept me, she must have sent Bayard to Pelagic to warn Piese. No doubt it was pure accident that he ran into Mandola in Alazarin. He'd really come here to kill Hyla! Hadn't he, *Brother*? Doesn't that make sense? To kill Hyla so she could never be a witness . . . or to kill me!"

After a moment, Humate says, "Shit," very quietly. He has lost color.

"Is that the best you can do? Grownups need more than dirty words."

He sighs. "Maybe you do have a case. The best I can do is take you to Abraxas. Tell me again about that projection. You say Mandola tried to read Hyla? Made contact?"

"Yes. Mandola took hold of Hyla's wrist."

"And she reacted strangely? High-caste women can recognize people by touch, did you know that? So you might just wonder if your deranged mother somehow recognized a relative of the man who, um, attacked her? I'm not saying I believe that, you understand. . . ."

"That might explain the unusual projection of him. So I've convinced you, have I?"

Pause . . . Then he nods. "Almost."

"No tricks?"

He reaches across the table. "No tricks—Brother."

"Brothers," I say.

His hand is icy cold, but he shakes with a squeeze. I squeeze back. He manages to grin.

He stands up, slipping the rest of the sausage into his pouch. As

I push back my stool and rise, he walks around the table to put us eye-to-eye. "That beach at Cape Bastel and then the ruins at Badderlocks Head? That's the only way across?"

I nod. "Even that is a very long hop. Why?"

"Because if Isatin has either of them staked out, you're liable to get a few dart-holes in your tunic on the way. Don't forget that bloodstains should be washed out as soon as possible, or they'll mark."

It isn't quite that simple. Both sites present problems for bushwhackers, as I discovered when I inspected the area with Vert two days ago. But my half-brother seems to be trying to help.

"I appreciate the warning," I say, "and I'd hate to see you caught by the near-misses. Let me do the porting, and I'll try a fast run through."

He grins quite believably. "Do it. I know how fast you can be."

I want to trust him, however much my instincts for self-preservation are screaming that he tried to kill me in the Bere Parochian arena. His mother's champions will not shoot darts at me if he is with me, surely? But there must be a dozen other ways and places he can betray me between here and Teil. So the sooner the better.

"I won't linger. Bastel, Badderlocks, and two more. Then we'll talk some more, right?"

"Right." Humate glances across at the larder door. "Got that, Vert? We're leaving now. Go, big man."

PORT ◆ ◆ ◆ *PORT* ◆ ◆ ◆PORT

Humate yells "Wow!" and falls flat on his face.

I am thinking much the same. Fast porting is an arena skill I have always been good at, but I never tried it in on long-distance travel before, nor when transporting a companion. We have flashed from the kitchen at Nuddle to the base of a sea stack on Bastel to windswept Badderlocks head to Cataract Cliffs to Private Beach without drawing breath. Both of us pitch headlong into powdery sand, thirty feet apart. One more jump like that and I would have lost him and likely killed myself too.

My companion scrambles to his feet and grins all around. Mother Blue is just clearing the horizon, huge and blinding, turning the sea into an incandescent turquoise glare. Surf explodes in diamonds on a reef about a mile out to sea; baby ripples play on white sand that stretches north and south for miles. A great palace sprawls along the top of the cliffs of red rock overlooking this idyllic spot, but I have never seen as much as one footprint in the sand here.

Humate raises both arms in the air and bellows out the morning prayer to Our Mother at the top of his voice. I have twisted an ankle, so I stay where I am. He finishes his prayer with one of his knee-kissing bows and stalks over to me, still grinning.

"Where *is* this?"

"Don't know. I call it Private Beach. We're about five hundred miles south of Badderlocks. Did you see anyone there, or at Bastel?"

"Brother, I had my eyes shut!" He flops down, tears off a third of the sausage and offers it to me. "That was wild!"

I accept the sausage as a peace offering, not from hunger. Did he think that his calling me brother would put me off my guard?

"Feel like a swim?" he asks, ignoring the chill wind.

"We're in a hurry, remember?"

Humate peers around, like a dog sniffing. "I can't recall anywhere from here, so you'll have to lead. Take us as far as Pean, Big Brother, and I'll do the rest."

5

Teil is a pleasant town, capital of Glyptic. I have attended the hegemonic games there often enough, and as a porter I delivered many letters and people to the palace's public entrance.

Humate has ported us to a family entrance, a bright circular hall. Its floor and ceiling are unremarkable enough, and like all entrances it is left unfurnished. But any portage requires some memorable feature, and here it is stained glass. A dozen high windows blaze like a myriad suns of richest hue. We come forth facing Humate's favorite, a muscular hero in a crimson tunic thrusting a sky-blue sword into the throat of a purple dragon, spilling jets of emerald blood.

I prefer others, but I admire the overall effect of the room. There is no visible doorway, and I am still looking for the door wards' spyholes when a middle-aged champion of knightly caste comes forth to greet us. In contrast to the riotous colors of the windows, his livery is subdued and tasteful, the orange and black of House Glyptic. He bows to me as the elder, but my companion speaks up first.

"*Stars blossom in the forest of the night.* Humate of Alfet and a friend. We need to see the hegemon on a matter of urgency."

The star quote is clearly a family code, for door wards cannot be expected to remember every one of the hundreds of people who claim relationship to a hegemon. It must be a low-rank code, though, because even when quoted by a royal it does not make the flunky leap to obey.

"Her Serenity does not receive in this watch, royal. May I announce your arrival to her confidential secretary?"

"No. I'll see royal Byzant. I repeat: The matter is urgent!"

The champion bows and is gone.

"She's old," Humate grumbles. "I don't suppose she rises much before Father White does."

I survey the windows again and concentrate on one displaying a tangle of multicolored fish. I have barely memorized its design before a man appears beside Humate. He is slightly older, a powerfully built youth in a brown duelist tabard. His hair is matted with sweat, his tabard dusty, and he has sand rash on his knees and elbows. Without question, he has been summoned from practice in the arena.

"Who let you in, Runt?" he demands.

I join them. He notes my white caste mark and drops his flippant grin.

"Brother, this is royal Byzant of Phasic," Humate says. "The hegemon's youngest grandson, a notorious and lecherous bully. Byz, meet royal Quirt of Mundil."

The youth starts to bow . . . stops. *"Brother?"*

Humate is enjoying himself, of course. "My half-brother really. Whatever grade of cousin I am to you, he's the same. Byz, he really needs to see Abraxas. It's urgent!"

"Doublenoon, maybe. I can try then. She's pretty busy these days with the jubilee planning."

Humate jumps as another visitor comes forth nearby. "Byz, let's go somewhere private, this is serious."

"The arena, then. North side, front row."

◆ ◆ ◆ **PORT** ◆ ◆ ◆

Mornings are cool in Teil, but the amphitheater is pleasantly warm. In the center a dozen or so youths are being drilled in fencing, but no one interrupts a hegemon's grandson up in the stands having a private chat. Byzant and I complete the formalities of being introduced. Then we sit on the bench with Humate between us.

Byzant says, "Speak, Runt."

"Quirt has authority to wear that caste mark, but he is a love child."

The older boy flinches. Even the best families have bastards, but few are acknowledged. "Whose authority?"

"I'll get to that. Remember Mandola?"

"Mandragora of Fargite? Bayard's daughter. Only vaguely. Died in a boating accident. First funeral I ever had to go to."

"There is reason to believe that my father murdered her."

Byzant waits a beat, then says, "Oh. When you say serious, you mean *serious*?"

Even Humate cannot be flippant when telling such a story as

225

mine, and he tells it well and succinctly—the attack on Hyla, my birth and triumph in the arena, Mandola's murder, the doom laid upon me. He brings himself in when I appealed for his help at Quintole yesterday, omitting Bere Parochian. He does not mention his father until he describes how he recognized the Enemy in Hyla's visible nightmare.

Byzant takes it well, too—listening intently, twice putting in a perceptive question but not otherwise interrupting. He is clearly smarter than most. When it is time to comment he goes right to the heart of the problem.

"So Piese of Rulero may be a rapist and murderer, and Aunt Foison doomed a man to find a criminal when she already knew the man's identity?" He looks to me for confirmation.

I nod. "I accuse Consort Piese of being the monster I have hunted so long. I believe Consort Bayard has known of his crimes since before I was born and covered up for him. Foison would stop at nothing to prevent me from becoming her daughter's consort. When I outwitted her, she or Bayard tipped off Piese that he would have to kill me and probably my mother. She doomed me to find a man she already knew."

"Horrible!" Byzant grimaces as if he has bitten into something obscene. "Quirt, I am appalled at these accusations. Of course only my grandmother can judge the truth of the matter, and what happened a long time ago may well have been corrected since. I mean the criminal may have been repaired, so he cannot offend again. But if he was discovered, you should not have been left doomed, and if his identity was known beforehand, you should not have been doomed at all. The council has ruled on far less serious matters. Certainly the noblest must hear of this."

I am impressed and encouraged by his reaction. "Also, royal Byzant, the monster is now aware that I have learned his identity. In the past he has slain three men and one woman, raped and tried to murder my mother. If he has not been repaired, he will try to silence me and those close to me. I agree with Humate that this matter is urgent."

"So do I! Of course we must make certain that he is no longer dangerous." Byzant rises. "If you will excuse me for a few moments?" He is gone.

Humate grins with the pride of hero worship. "Byz's one of the best!"

I am inclined to agree. I soon suspect that the hegemon does also, because he reappears in an astonishingly brief time.

"I am to take you to the Rainbow Terrace, Cousin Quirt. I'll come back for you, Runt."

◆ ◆ ◆ **PORT** ◆ ◆ ◆

We come forth outdoors, in a small court enclosed by portable screens; we are facing a wall bearing a faded, ancient tapestry. Four armed champions stare at me with menace as Byzant gives them my name. He winks out. One of the guards orders me to follow and leads me into a maze.

I can smell and hear the sea, but the Rainbow Terrace is sheltered from chill breezes and prying eyes by innumerable stained-glass screens. Where the art in the family entrance was deliberately memorable, this is inchoate and random—many layers of glass splotched with colors that constantly change as the suns move. The result is a transient polychromatic haze that defies both eye and memory. I have no doubt that the tapestry I saw will be rolled up and stored away for years before it is used again, and the screens themselves will be rearranged after my visit. Hegemons guard their privacy and persons.

At the heart of the maze the guard stops, repeats my name, and disappears.

A tall, spare woman kneels on a cushion in rainbow glory, sipping perfumed tea and nibbling small cakes. Her eyes are a steely gray, her fingernails long and pointed, her gown a shimmering pearly silk spangled with color from the glass. I know Abraxas of Glyptic has reigned for a very long time. As Bayard of Indican's elder sister, she must be old, but I have no idea how old, and her appearance is little help in judging that. Her hair is silver and she has not banished all the cruelty of age from her face. The moment I have completed my bow, she gestures for me to sit on the mat on her right, close enough for her to judge my truthfulness. She looks me over disapprovingly.

"You claim to be related to us?"

"Noblest, had my parents been legally paired, I should have the honor of hailing Your Serenity as a distant cousin."

She purses her lips. "It is no sign of good breeding to mention yours. A seagull has besmirched your forehead."

I wipe my caste mark with my forearm, knowing I will simply turn the white dot into a smear. Her disapproval does not thaw.

Humate and Byzant enter. Humate folds himself double in a gymnastical bow.

"By the suns you have grown a yard!" Abraxas says, with a guarded hint of affection. "You sit there." A dagger fingernail directs him to the far side of the low table. "And you . . ." She sighs at Byzant. "You are not decently clad, but you had better stay. You have already learned too much; we shall do better trusting you with the rest, whatever it is, than having you running around asking questions. Try to be invisible when the servants are around. Yeoman Quirt?"

"Noblest?"

"Talk! The whole story. Speak clearly but do not treat me as an idiot."

I talk. We all sip tea. The hegemon nibbles her morning biscuits. Eerily silent servants float in, place more substantial fare within reach of Humate and Byzant, and depart.

I begin by talking quickly, and when my audience raises no objection, pick up the pace. Abraxas shows almost no reaction at all, but Byzant is much more readable. He gapes in astonishment at his cousin when I mention Humate's proposed pairing. Humate, of course, smirks. Abraxas merely purses her lips again. Yet her silence is more eloquent than most people's chatter. Her eyes never leave my face and by the end of my narrative, I have decided that I am in the presence of a remarkably quick-witted noblewoman. She is everything that Foison of Quartic is not.

"I see." She sets her cup down on the table and sighs. She makes no further sound for so long that I conclude she is conversing with some of her sworn companions. There could be many people within a few feet of us, behind the screens.

Byzant grows nervous. "Did I do wrong, Gramma?"

She shakes her head sadly. "You did very right. Yeoman Quirt has a viable charge against Hegemon Foison. He may even have one against me."

The rest of us exchange shocked glances. Mother Blue has moved, bathing Abraxas in green and pink.

"And I, Aunt?" Humate asks anxiously. "I couldn't just go away and leave Quirt hunting for Father to kill him, could I? And I didn't want to kill Quirt—although I could have done." He glances pugnaciously at me.

"Of course not. You did very well, boy. You had a very hard decision to make, and I believe your choice was absolutely correct. This is a matter for the Seven."

"And repairing . . . Does it *hurt*? I mean, if Father has to be repaired—"

"No, it does not hurt. He will not be quite the same person afterwards, though. You did very well. I will see that the council commends you. But haven't you heard enough of this . . ." She pauses to appraise him. "Never mind. Yeoman Quirt, you are entitled to an explanation. Royals Humate and Byzant, if you wish to stay and listen to a very distressing story, then you must agree to let me bind you to secrecy afterwards."

Humate nods. After a moment, so does Byzant.

"Very well," the hegemon says, in the manner of one beginning a long tale. "It is no secret that my mother began to behave very oddly in the latter part of her reign. She had suffered two dangerous miscarriages, which may have contributed, and her consort died. But no matter what the cause, an irrational hegemon cannot be tolerated. I had recently come of age, and the council agreed that Prakrit must be deposed. We moved her to Dolose, an isolated place but pleasant enough, the apanage of royal Remise, whom I appointed my mother's guardian. I judged that she would be a capable warden, but I was mistaken. My mother had not been in Dolose a gnomon before she became pregnant."

Byzant goes white. Then Humate does. I expect I do, too.

"Yes, at her age," the old lady said dryly. She takes a sip of tea. "I haven't told this story in pentads. It gets worse. Of course any woman of high caste can enslave any man she can get her hands on and no one could blame the baby's father. By the time his mistress detected what had been happening, the damage was done."

She smiles grimly. "You want to know who the lucky man was? Brace yourselves. It was Remise's consort, royal Grobian. Yes, my cousin and Prakrit's own nephew. Even by ordinaries' standards, that is incest."

Humate says, "But then . . ."

"Yes. Your father is my half-brother as well as being my cousin. Grobian had been a charming, witty, dazzlingly handsome young lad, but he was never the same after that. He died in a few gnomons—probably a suicide. His mistress, too, was brokenhearted at her failure, for the fault was certainly her lack of vigilance. She agreed to pass the baby off as hers, but she died within a pentad.

"When Piese was left an orphan, I brought him to court, officially my cousin, but however much we tried, he sensed that he was not quite one of the family. Of course we would not tell him why, and his questionable status cannot have made life easy for him. Even then he was inexcusably liable to lose his temper and become violent."

She pauses to reflect, biting her lip. Sunlight emblazons her face with strangely ominous gold and scarlet sigils.

Humate says, "Who knew?"

She frowns at the interruption. "Bayard, for one. He ported to Dolose to visit his mother and found her big with child. Your father is his half-brother. Indeed, your father is as much a product of rape as Quirt is. And I suppose if I allow one of them caste, I should allow the other. Royal Mudar, then."

I bow my head to acknowledge the concession.

She curls her lip in distaste for a moment, then continues. "The psychic powers Piese developed at maturity were remarkable even by hegemonic standards, but he reacted badly to the competitive environment of the arena. After the second incident, I was warned by the palace trainer that he should never be allowed to enter a real tourney. This presented me with a very difficult decision. It was up to me, as hegemon, to decide if he was a public danger. If I decided he was, then I was also the senior female relative who would have to repair him. I had never been fond of Piese. Curiously, that made my decision even harder. Had I loved him dearly, I think I would have found the horrible dilemma easier to resolve, because I would have trusted my own motives better. From what you have just told me—and you spoke no lies, I regret to say—I made the wrong call.

"I kept hoping I would find a suitable pairing for him, a woman who could take him off my hands. I delayed too long. For this you may well blame me.

"My brother Bayard was, of course, consort to Foison of Quartic and father of her children. Foison and I were not on speaking terms in those days, officially because she had caught me trying to subvert some loyalties along our common border. In reality it was because she had learned the family secret from her consort and was shocked to her narrow-minded core. She felt she should have been warned in advance what sort of perverted family she was joining.

"But one morning just like this one—unpleasantly like this one—Bayard came to see me in a state of great agitation. He had evidence, he said, that Piese had committed a very violent and horrible crime. He would not go into details and I confess I did not press him for them. I sent for our problem brother. He could not be found. No one could recall seeing him around the palace for half a gnomon. As I said, I had waited too long."

"He had been in Alazarin?" Humate says. "In the golden games."

"And other places, too." Sadistically, the old lady pauses to pour herself more tea and sip it.

"A gnomon or so later, he turned up here with a rather ugly and loud young woman, Pelta of Demersal, sister of the new Hegemon Typic of Pelagic. They brazenly informed me that they wanted to be paired! She was considerably more exalted than the mistress I had planned to find for my black sheep brother. They verged on the unseemly in consanguinity and Piese was certainly of much higher rank than Typic had been planning for . . . Are you all right, Nephew?"

Humate looks as if he had just been handed his own death warrant. "I didn't know that Mother's sister . . . I always thought my aunt Typic died *before* Grandmother Connex!"

"Can you answer his question, Byzant?" Abraxas inquires grimly.

Byzant shakes his head. We are discussing events that occurred before even I was born, and long before he was.

"Then you should pay more attention in your genealogy classes, even if they do teach garbage at times. Records can be faked, remember! Humate has been misled. Connex went first to the Everlit Realm. Typic inherited, although not for long. She was happy to see her sister settled without rancor and I confess I was relieved also. Just looking at the pair of them together, anyone could see that they had been intimate, so Pelta must be aware of whatever Piese had been up to. I assumed she had already made sure that he was incapable of similar behavior in future."

She lets the silence congeal. She is a very cunning old woman.

Byzant is the first to ask. "What happened to Hegemon Typic?"

"She died tragically just days after her sister's pairing celebration." Again the hegemon pauses, but none of us dare ask the obvious question this time. "She fell downstairs and went into premature labor. . . . Bad falls are a danger for those who are great with child. They are also a hazard for those with both wealth and unscrupulous relatives."

Her glance challenges each of us in turn to comment. Humate's pallor is almost a pale green, and Byzant looks little better. It seems to be up to me, but even I never expected this further revelation of horror.

"Is that possible, noblest? You are hinting that Piese, after his rampage at Alazarin, sought out Pelta and offered to make her hegemon if she promised not to improve him! I don't doubt that he was capable of thinking of it, but how could he ever trust Pelta not to improve him after Typic's death? Obviously she has kept her side of the bargain, or Mandola would not have died, but how could he know she would? Why did she?"

The old woman smiles sourly. "You seek to put limits on evil? Only a mind like Piese's could see the opportunity, but consider what choice Pelta had after her sister's death—if indeed it was a murder. All men resent being diminished by improvement. If she merely improved Piese so that he lost his capacity for violence, he would still be capable of denouncing her as his accomplice. So she would have to wipe his vindictiveness also, and that would make a noticeable difference in his character. With his now-diminished responsibility, he might blurt out the truth inadvertently, so she must go on and wipe his memory. People would certainly notice and start to wonder what could have provoked such a massive impairment. The council would have questioned her. No, she who rides the tiger can never dismount!

"It *may* have been an accident. Remember that. Of course I suspected, but there was nothing I could do. To have gone before the hegemonic council accusing the new hegemon of Pelagic of inciting her consort to murder her sister would have involved accusing myself of negligence, and Bayard and Foison also. I am not as dyspeptic about scandal as stupid Foison, but that mouthful was too big for even me to swallow."

Byzant looks almost as shaken as Humate. He has had no preparation for such tales of horror.

"And now you, kinsman," Abraxas tell me, "come to open the old wounds and add new ones that shame me in my old age. Mandola? Such a sweet child! Impetuous and headstrong, yes, but so full of joy! I was heartbroken when I heard she had 'drowned.' I never heard a whisper that her death was not what was reported. Even after so long, your news is a heartfelt blow."

I ask, "Do you believe that noblest Foison knew who murdered her?"

"How could she not have guessed? And how could she be so cruel, so hypocritical, as to doom you to hunt for a man whose name she already knew?"

"She was probably crazy with grief that day."

"And guilt?" Humate mutters.

Abraxas fixes him with a stony eye. "What are you hinting, boy?"

He looks around the faces and realizes that he may have stepped into serious trouble with that remark.

"From what you tell us, noblest, royal Mudar was Mandola's first cousin as well as her second cousin. But Foison hadn't told them that their pairing was incestuous. Do you suppose she sent my father to Alazarin? Or Bayard did? They could have told Piese that the mess was all his fault, so he must do something to make it right. Mandola's murder may have been an accident, but why was my father there at all? Alazarin isn't exactly on the way to anywhere. Could Foison or Bayard have sent Piese to Alazarin to kill Quirt?"

The hegemon shudders. "Is there no bottom to this cesspit? What do you think, royal Mudar? Is that possible?"

I say, "I do not know, noblest. If the pairing invitations had gone out, it might have been his own idea to go to Alazarin to find out who I was. But if Foison and Bayard knew that Piese of Rulero had been the fake Piese of Enthetic, they bore much guilt already."

"And I do too! And so, more than anyone, does Hegemon Pelta of Pelagic, for not repairing her murderous consort. You are right to be bitter. We women of Aureity like to think we have banished violence from the world, but we are wrong. Always it rises again and often women condone it or even start it. Humate, your proposed pairing with Tendence of Formene is outrageous political skulduggery. That alone justifies a meeting of the council. I have already ordered notices prepared and porters alerted. The council will meet here in Teil, tomorrow at whiterise."

Humate smiles quizzically at me. For a moment I am shocked that he can still smile at all after hearing both his parents condemned as murderers. Then I realize that he has done the impossible he promised—he has brought the whole affair before the hegemonic council.

"Will that satisfy your doom, Quirty?"

"I suppose so," I say. "But we have reason to believe that the Enemy is still at large, noblest. He may well be on Alazarin at this very moment, seeking out my mother to kill her—I cannot say to 'silence' her because he did that five pentads ago. She can still be dangerous to him. By your leave, I will hurry back there at once. And if royal Humate wishes to accompany me, then I will welcome my brother's help."

Abraxas closes her crepe eyelids for a moment. When she opens them, she does not look at me. She says, "*Now!*"

Instantly my arms are frozen, as if encased in solid rock. I cry out at the pain in my shoulders.

"Easy, easy!" Byzant tells Humate. "Pull like that and you're liable to tear him in half, lad."

TERROR ON ALAZARIN

1

"My sincerest apologies, noble Mudar," the hegemon says. "Just a gentle restraint, please, Peavy. Do not let him port out!"

Cool fingertips touch the back of my neck and all my muscles lock up. I am a rock perched on a cushion.

"You may release your holds now, nobles," Abraxas tells Humate and Byzant. The strain on my arms disappears, but I still cannot move them. I cannot move anything. "You will be allowed to speak, royal Mudar, as long as you promise to be discreet." She nods to the companion who stands behind me.

I find I have my lips and tongue back, but I restrain myself from cursing the treacherous old hag root and branch. My fury is tempered by fear, because I know that I am now in deadly peril. Abraxas did claim that she was not so obsessed by propriety as Hegemon Foison, but I have only her word for that. She may intend to bury the whole Piese of Rulero scandal by burying me, and I walked into this trap of my own free will. How could I have been such a fool as to trust the Enemy's son?

"Your hospitality is flawed, noblest."

She nods sadly. "It is indeed, and I am ashamed to treat a guest so shabbily. However, there has been far too much violence already. Were I to release you now, young man, you would go racing back to your savage little island, intent on vengeance. Either you would end up killing my errant kinsman, or he would start by killing you. Neither outcome is acceptable, for justice is not served by repeating the crime. He will be summoned before the Seven and questioned about his part in the sad events you have described. He cannot dissemble to us. If he is guilty he will be improved so that he cannot offend in future."

"You call that justice?"

"*I do!*" The words blaze with hegemonic authority. "It is the best we mortals can manage. Our medicine can neither cure your poor mother nor restore the dead to life—your mistress, the boy who tried to guard her, the murdered competitors in those ill-fated golden games. The evil is done and we shall not add more. If the man you accuse is indeed guilty of those atrocities, you and your hegemon will have to be satisfied with seeing his will erased, his powers stripped from him, and his name expunged. Then may he live long to enjoy his fate. Ah, royal Jarrah of Havener!"

The newcomer wears orange and black livery, but it is more elaborately decorated than most and he is a mature man of obvious authority. Just to look at him is to award him respect, but then, hegemons are not served by idiots or low-castes. He bows and answers some question she conveys to him in silence.

"I regret not, noblest. I have not had time to question all your champions, of course." He exchanges a smile with the hegemon. Her stable of champions must be numbered in hundreds, if not thousands. "Among those presently available, the closest any can reach without outside help seems to be a fishing village called Dovekie, on the northern ocean. Two of your men are confident they will recall the way there, and two more think they will."

Dovekie is in northern Quartic, and it is the closest town to Alazarin to hold games—a bronze tourney every third gnomon, poorly rated because it is so far out of the way, but a favorite for low caste locals. The hegemon turns her frown on Humate. "Come here, Cousin."

Humate rises with alarm and goes around the table to her.

"Closer! Kneel, where I can see you without straining my old neck. Now, royal master of Alfet, can I trust you?"

"Of course you can, Aunt," he says hoarsely. The kid looks much like a fox in a trap. In his situation, I should be very tempted to port out and go home.

Abraxas shows her teeth. "If I send you with Jarrah to this Dovekie, will you help relay him and his followers from there to Alazarin?"

She is asking him to betray his father. To his credit, he hesitates. He looks to me, as if seeking advice.

"Do it," I tell him. "You may help prevent more crimes."

Our elderly cousin glances at me for a moment and says, "Mm?" Then she turns back to him.

"Yes, noblest, you have my word." He nods without enthusiasm.

"And do you give me your solemn word that you will follow Jarrah's orders? That you will not take off on your own, or betray him in any way to the man he seeks?—and you know who I mean. You will not warn that man? You will, in fact, do all you can to help royal Jarrah deliver our summons to him and escort him back here to Teil?"

Humate straightens his shoulders and smiles. Obviously he has just seen that he is in a strong bargaining position, for without help from him or from me, Abraxas's posse will have to find local porters to lead them to Alazarin, which will not be easy. Very few public porters have the strength to cross the strait. Furthermore, even if Jarrah and his band can reach the island, they will have no idea where to start looking for their quarry. Humate is essential to their mission.

"I will help royal Jarrah deliver your warrant, noblest," he says, "but that's all! I won't use violence against my . . . against the man you want or any of the champions he must have with him—if he is there at all, I mean. I won't help them hurt him. They're not to hurt him!"

"Certainly not!" the old lady snaps. "I forbid violence. Do you understand that, champion? Violence only to block violence, the absolute minimum restraint?" What else is she telling him in private?

Jarrah salutes. "Understood, noblest."

"You'd better warn him," I said, "that he's hunting a remorseless multiple murderer who—"

"I did. How many will you take?"

"I'll start with a party of eight, noblest," Jarrah says confidently. He will say everything confidently, always. "Including royal Humate as our guide. When we get to Quartic, we may have to split up or start running relays. I can't know until we get there. My own experience will take me only as far as Whoso, which is just across the border."

Abraxas falls silent for a minute, thinking or perhaps conveying. Then she looks at Byzant and smiles. "I can hear you from here, Grandson. Will you be discreet?"

Hope flashes in Byzant's eyes. "Yes, noblest!"

"Very well, go and change. You know more about the background situation than royal Jarrah does, so you and Humate may advise him on the politics if he asks. But only if he asks! Get ready and report to him as soon as possible." She chuckles at the empty space from which Byzant has just departed, then looks back to Jarrah again. She is a very decisive and effective woman.

"Take him along as my representative," the hegemon says. "And send two . . . no, make it three . . . men here to take royal Mudar into custody. Warn them that they will be dealing with an exceptional arena duelist."

Her champion acknowledges me with a respectful nod. "He is that indeed, noblest. I watched him perform several times when I was preparing for my own entry into the games, and there never was a better. He displayed both strength and guile."

Neither guile nor strength can help me now. As long as those fiendish female fingers remain in contact with the back of my neck, I am a human meal sack.

"Go, then, and the suns be with you both."

Humate and Jarrah vanish, leaving me alone with the hegemon and the companion who holds me helpless.

"Royal Mudar of Quoin, we are deeply sorry to have to treat you like this." Abraxas certainly looks and sounds contrite, but she has had a dozen pentads or more to practice her dissembling. "I will merely have you moved to some pleasant country villa for a couple of days, if you will give me your parole to stay there until I send for you."

"No."

She smiles sadly. "I expected that reply. Then we must apply sterner measures, but you will not be harmed unless you try to break loose. Confine him."

I hear heavy male footsteps. The immobilizing touch on my neck remains as other hands blindfold me.

A man says "Noblest!" as if acknowledging an order. Then, "Royal Mudar, if we let you stand up, will you cooperate or resist?" He has a Pelagic accent.

"Rot in the Dark."

He says, "As you wish. Companion?"

My jailer transforms her touch to a gentle grip on my neck and another on my arm. I melt, sprawling out on the floor, half on and half off the cushion, a jellyfish stranded on a beach. My jailer must have moved with me, for her hold never loosens. Then other hands take my ankles and wrists. Porting more than one person at a time is very tricky, but champions specializing in security are trained to the job.

"Count of three," Pelagic says. "One. Two. Thr—"

* * * **PORT** * * *

I grunt with unexpected pain as my transporters twist me between them. I land facedown on cold and stony ground. Seabirds mock. I can hear surf and smell the sea. "Curse your—"

"One. Two. Thr—"

* * * **PORT** * * *

Grass. Hot sun on my back. Earth in my face and up my nose, and my legs are in a thistle patch. I am glad to hear cries from the man holding my ankles and protests from the woman. I have lost a sandal.

"One. Two. Thr—"

◆ ◆ ◆ **PORT** ◆ ◆ ◆

We land in a crunch of twigs and dead leaves. More stones, too, and sharp ones this time. I smell humus and mast. Indeed, I have beechnuts up my nose. This time I tell my captors what I think of them and their training in some detail.

"You had the chance," the Pelagian says. "Keep your hole shut or I'll have the companion muzzle you. All ready, Muntjac?"

There is no reply, except probably a nod or a gesture, which I cannot see. We must have reached the jail. The moment I realize that, I start trying to recall—recall anything or anywhere at all. There is perhaps a hint of a marble slab somewhere, upright, longer than it is high, curiously carved . . . No, it is too far away, too long ago. It has changed or my memory of it has faded.

"One. Two. Thr—"

◆ ◆ ◆ **PORT** ◆ ◆ ◆

Cold! This time I am lying half on and half off a blanket, which covers a very rough and sharp floor, probably bare rock. I can hear water trickling somewhere and smell a lamp with a badly trimmed wick. I am underground.

Confining a high-caste nobleman is not easy. Firstly you must move him far away from any landmarks you expect him to know, not letting him memorize any along the route. Then you must put him where he cannot travel by line-of-sight. A forest would make a good jail, except that he could heft himself above the treetops and port along line of sight to any hill or building. He can port out of any normal cell, or heft steel bars aside. Caves are the cells of choice.

"We're here," the leader says. "Royal Mudar, you have a few

242

minutes' worth of oil to get yourself organized. There's lots of water. We were told you'd be here for one day, so we've supplied three days' rations, two blankets. Any questions? No? Ready, team? Go!"

My paralysis disappears and I know I am alone. I sit up and pull off the blindfold. It leaves my eyes adjusted to the dark, so I can see as well as I ever shall by the wan gleam of the single smelly lantern. The cavern is about seven yards long and half that wide, but the walls are highly irregular, adorned in many places with shiny white pillars and draperies of rock, which may hide openings to other chambers. My blanket is laid out on the only flat spot I can see, for white spikes stand almost everywhere, reaching up toward long rocky icicles dangling overhead. The rest of the roof is out of sight. The sound I heard comes from a small waterfall that feeds a pool nearby. I shall not die of thirst, and no doubt the three days' rations are in the basket by my feet.

Obviously Abraxas's security champions have been well trained. At least one of them may have been left behind outside the cave to keep watch over my prison, but I cannot apply my newfound skill of porting to persons because I did not get a look at any of them. They went to a lot of trouble to keep themselves hidden from me. Is that standard practice in the palace of Teil, or did Abraxas order it specially in my case? She admitted that the Enemy is her half-brother, so if anyone other than Humate and I know of his secret ability, it is probably she. Perhaps her brother, Bayard of Indican, can do it also, or her grandson, Byzant. Piese of Rulero is a Glyptic on both his mother's and father's sides, so the trait may be common in her family.

Meanwhile, the Enemy is hunting for Hyla to kill her. That I cannot doubt. He is welcome to scour all Alazarin down to bedrock as long as Vert has managed to move her back to Osseter, but I have no assurance on that. They are all at risk—Hyla, Vert, Clamant, Volet, Wirra, Kish, and the rest. I *must* get out of this dungeon.

I have very little time before I run out of light. When that happens I shall have to stay close to my blanket and food. How did they port me in here? There is only one lamp and it sheds so little light that I doubt a man could port in here even if his eyes were adjusted to darkness beforehand. The blankets are dry, not damp and clammy as they will rapidly become in this moist air. The food, I assume, is fresh. So these things were brought here ahead of me. That was why the leader asked the person called Muntjac if all was ready.

There must be an entrance somewhere—hidden, of course, because I can rip down almost any door. I rise and start exploring with the lantern. Having only one sandal left, I do it by hefting, floating all around the cavern to inspect the walls. I find two or three gaps that probably continue a long way, and one that certainly does, for the stream disappears down a wide natural drain. The lamp has started to flicker. I shake it and hear no oil sloshing. Now it flickers even more, and I beat a hasty retreat to my blanket nest.

I dare not risk exploring side passages lest I be trapped there in darkness. Surely, for their own convenience, they would have put me close to the door? Or is this the only flat spot they could find? The flame flickers and jumps. I am going to be stranded in the Dark for five watches or longer, and the thought makes my skin crawl. Not even stars.

My jailers did not need a door! A window would serve them just as well, because all they needed was enough light to let them port in. I raise the lantern high and look all around me. Yes, there! Everywhere the floor is coated in smooth folds and draperies of white travertine, except at one end, about three yards from me, where there is heap of jagged, dark gray rock fragments and soil.

My light goes out and the Dark pours in. With a pathetic whimper of prayer to Mother Blue, I haul the other blanket around my shoulders, hunker down, and think hard. I cannot recall even that faint image of a marble slab that I saw earlier.

The heap of debris I saw must have fallen from the roof. It could be a natural fall; it could have been created by some desperate inmate trying to dig his way out at the risk of burying himself alive; but it just might have resulted from someone enlarging a narrow chimney when a cave was turned into a dungeon.

They did not take away my sword, because swords are only for show. Swords also make quite good hammers, especially mine, which has a steel ball as a pommel. I heft the sword over to where I believe the heap of rubble is, and then straight up until I hear it strike the roof. Back down a little, sideways a little, then up again. Tap. Tap, tap, tap . . .

Time drags by and I begin to lose hope. Sometimes the pommel gets wedged between two of the dangling rocky teeth and I have to heft it out. Sometimes I knock fragments off and they clatter noisily to the floor or splash into the pond. Tap, tap, tap . . . The Enemy will be on Alazarin by now. He will have learned about Nuddle. Or he may have caught Vert and the others at Cape Bastel or Badderlocks Head. Tap, tap, tap, tap . . .

I grow stiff with sitting in the same position, but fear to move lest I lose my sense of direction. Tap, tap, tap . . .

Clink!

2

I lower the sword to the floor and leave it there to mark the spot; then I reach upward for what it has found me. Just as porting requires visualization, hefting involves a sense of touch—that is how we can lift a balk in the arena when the stack is hidden behind the growing wall of timber. Sensing something other than rock, I grip and wrench. I force, applying all my strength, gritting my teeth as if I am hefting ten balks at a tourney. I fear I am going to tear down the entire roof. At last comes a burst of noise and a rattle of pebbles.

Light explodes into the cave like a flash of lightning that does not know how to stop, blinding me. A wooden trap about the size of a slice of bread falls into the pool, and my heart shrivels in despair, for the opening I have made is no larger than that. The chimney looks to be about ten or twelve feet high and lined with timber. It admits a narrow beam of light, true, and that reflects off the white travertine. There is enough light in the cell now for a champion familiar with it to port back in again, but that does nothing to help me to port out. I still have no portage to aim for. Blue sky and clouds will not do.

I return to my blanket to brood. Clever bastards! I wonder how many men have been imprisoned here over how many generations.

Then I wonder about the first one. . . . How did anyone find this cave, if that shaft is so narrow? Not by porting, because if you try to peer in from the surface, your own head will block the light. They must have started by climbing down a ladder, or being lowered on a rope . . . a very skinny young nobleman, perhaps; someone like Humate. Once he was in, he could port out and bring other men back. Only after that could they have lined the shaft with timber, narrowing it.

I start wrenching again, tearing the thick boards free and dropping them in a corner, out of the way. The original shaft is bigger, as I suspected, but the gap outside the casing has been filled with rubble. A steady stream of dirt and pebbles begins to fall, building a cone, splashing into the pool or rattling off across the floor. Then larger blocks start to come. I may make the shaft wider at the cost of blocking it completely at the bottom.

There may also be guards up there, and I do not wait for them to hear what I am doing. Covering my head with my arms, I heft myself up through the dust and the rain of pebbles, up into the shaft. It is narrow for my bulk, and I have to squeeze, losing half my tunic and some skin, but the cost is worth it. I emerge into the suns' magnificent day.

Free!

There are no guards in sight. A dry-stone wall encloses a compound containing an elaborate cairn of large boulders that must serve as a landmark for porting, and a shabby thatched shed with a pronounced lean to the west. Surveying it from above, I notice two wellheads, which presumably mark other dungeons, but both covers stand open, so there are no other prisoners to release.

The setting is a scabby valley, dry, steep-walled, and devoid of trees. Great rocks lie scattered around, and a line of sinkholes probably traces the flow of an underground stream. The only animal life in sight is a herd of goats, which have not noticed me. I soar higher, until I am above the uplands, and in all directions I see only more of the same sort of indigent grazing landscape. This is Aspartic landscape, not Glyptic.

The white is higher than the blue, so doublenoon has passed. I must go.

I recall the marble slab clearly now. It is the back of a garden bench; I cannot remember where, but that does not matter. Before I leave, I have a grudge to pay off. I descend back down to the compound and proceed to demolish the cairn, hefting the smaller boulder into the dungeon shafts, and rolling the others well apart. I push over the shed, which collapses willingly enough with a groan of relief and a cloud of dust. This is not mere spite, although there is some of that, too. If Abraxas sends her men to check on me, they will be unable to find their way back here without a long search. I have no wish to be followed back to Alazarin. Her intentions may be as noble as she claims, but why should I trust her a second time after the way she treated me this morning?

◆ ◆ ◆ **PORT** ◆ ◆ ◆

Yeoman Cantharidin was, and may still be, a wealthy rancher whose wife had given him a couple of quite passable daughters but no sons to inherit his estate. That was enough excuse for Cantharidin to organize golden games for them, and his wealth enticed a dozen or so low-caste noblemen to enter. No agents bothered to attend, because the venue was far off any beaten tracks. I did, for the same reasons. It was early in my quest, soon after my dooming, and I reasoned that the Enemy might be attracted by the anonymity he would find there. He did not show, and the games were a bore, but the daughters reeled in consorts able to supply some fourbears for their future children.

247

Cantharidin had been very proud of a certain elaborately carved and conspicuously expensive marble bench on the grounds of his mansion, which I used as a portage marker. It is still there. Fortunately, no one is sitting on it when a filthy, bloody, half-naked man comes forth in front of it. At once I know where I am and can recall the next portage, the quay at Hemal, a small port in Aspartic.

I port out at once and begin my long trip north. On the way south I had divided the work with Humate. Single-handed, it will be an ordeal. However, I must break my journey at Osseter, in northern Seris, which is about halfway to Alazarin. If I find Hyla, Clamant, and Vert all safe there, then my worries will be over. Or at least most of them will be, because a vengeful Piese of Rulero may manage to track down some of the old champions from Hyla's day—Volet, Kish, and the rest. None of them know where our secret refuge is, but that may not stop the Enemy from trying to make them tell him.

It takes me eight ports to reach Osseter in its sleepy valley. I come forth in the Court of Birds, as I did four days ago on my return from the Bere Parochian games. This time there is no boy playing music, no sleepy Izard of Inmew meditating on his day just past. The birds screech, squawk, and shriek at my appearance. During daylight hours they make good watchdogs.

I cannot recall Hyla, or Clamant, or Vert, or Izard. Fretty the kennelman I can, so I leave the birds before anyone comes to investigate their clamor.

◆ ◆ ◆ **PORT** ◆ ◆ ◆

Fretty is in the upper pasture, putting half a dozen dogs through their paces. My appearance provokes an explosion of startled barking, but dogs are no threat to noblemen, who can heft them aside if they try to attack.

Fretty looks as surprised to see me as they are, but stares in alarm at my battered, bloodstained condition. We have known each other all my life, for he was with Vert at Nuddle. He is scrawny now, but only his skin has changed; the core of the man is as solid as it always was.

"Have you heard from noble Vert?" I ask. "Noble Izard?"

Two head shakes.

"If they do come, will you tell them to come to Teil? There is to be an important meeting in the palace tomorrow."

"Teil, noble?"

"Teil. Remember the lady from Teil, who looked better in a veil. Got it?"

He laughs toothlessly.

"Don't tell anyone else I was here, and watch out for strangers. They may be very dangerous."

Ignoring my headache, I move on.

◆ ◆ ◆ **PORT** ◆ ◆ ◆

In the room that has been mine for two pentads, but rarely used, I clean up, put on a fresh tunic and sandals. Having no spare sword, I purloin Izard's, which he almost never wears. I still bear too many scrapes and scratches from the rock chimney to look respectable, but I am certainly improved. I add a royal caste mark. Now to work.

◆ ◆ ◆ **PORT** ◆ ◆ ◆

My fastest road to Alazarin takes me through Whoso, which champion Jarrah told Hegemon Abraxas he knew. He must be far beyond there by now, and it is a sizable town, so we are unlikely to use exactly the same portage. I enter and leave without incident. Beyond Whoso I can avoid Dovekie by heading due east until I reach the coast and then backtracking along the route I took Humate this morning. In my long search for the Enemy, I have been everywhere.

Humate and I did not visit Dovekie, but we went past it and I am sure that he will be able to recall one of the portages I did use. He can port Jarrah there; they can go back for two more and so on. Jarrah specified a party of eight because relays double each time, like generations on a pedigree. I've probably made up some of the Glyptians' lead time, but not much. I cannot hope to get ahead of them.

Private Beach is deserted as always, the sand still wet as doublenoon's high tide goes out. There is no shade except around the palace on the cliff top. I have never gone exploring up there and today would be a bad day to start. There are trees at Cataract Cliffs.

✦ ✦ ✦ PORT ✦ ✦ ✦

I come forth in the gorge there and a few steps put me under the cover of some wild *bycockets*, where I can sit on a fallen trunk and rest my aching head. Up on the bench, my usual choice of portage, the view of the sea and coast is spectacular. Down here is a secluded and peaceful spot, with the gentle, never-ending sound of the falls in the background and insects whining nearby. Just from where I sit, I can see at least three kinds of spoor in the sand beside a minor stream as it wanders aimlessly through the shrubbery and reeds.

What tracks can I follow on my own hunt? Hyla and my friends are obviously trapped on the island, or I would have found them at Osseter. They may still be at Nuddle, in which case they are probably already dead. They may have taken refuge with one of my grandmother Aglare's now ancient champions. If the Enemy has invaded Alazarin in force, he can probably compel the locals to lead him to those men's apanages, but not without committing acts of war. Is he really that desperate? Did he bring enough men, and even if he did, will they obey him when he orders barbarities? And how will Ruler Chiliarchy react to all this?

I may be imagining dragons that do not exist. Piese himself may still be home in Mascle, half a world away, quietly fishing or breeding parrots or plotting his takeover of Formene. At worst, surely, he was informed that his son had gone off with the reborn Mudar of Quoin, whose mistress died in an unfortunate collision with a wall two pentads ago. Humate can look after himself, so why should his father interfere? That would be a confession of guilt.

That is the reasonable view, but it does not explain why Hyla and Vert and Izard were not back in Osseter, and the Enemy is not reasonable.

I persuade myself that my head feels better. Time to go. If I can safely pass Badderlocks Head and Cape Bastel, then I have been worrying unnecessarily. If I can't, then I will have a much better idea how the battle goes. I recall the largest of the mossy walls at Badderlocks and crouch down small.

◆ ◆ ◆ PORT ◆ ◆ ◆

The resident gale promptly bowls me over but I roll on the wiry grass. I am still hidden by the masonry from all directions except the sea itself, and the only signs of life out there are two very distant sails. Birds swoop overhead; the air is moist and salt and very, very busy. Surf growls continuously far below. I rise, cautiously, bracing myself against the wind, while my eyes water. I count six dead men in Glyptian black and orange within about twenty feet of me.

Trying to run in that wind, I stagger from one to the other. I find no sign of Humate of Alfet or Jarrah of Havener, but one of the dead is the hegemon's grandson, Byzant of Phasic. That certainly raises the stakes. The council will make somebody pay dearly for him. I mourn for all of them, but Byzant was only a kid, and a good kid at that.

Two bodies show bloody puncture wounds where darts have gone through them, the others look more as if they have been wrenched. Not one of them has been laid out for burial or for easy transport home; they lie as they died. Why such contempt for the dead? The Enemy could not have done this by himself, and common decency dictates that a body should be taken home for burial. Even if you will not do the right thing by the fallen, why leave them tumbled like carrion, without even closing their eyes?

What has happened here? The bent-grass is too tough to take footprints. Having heard Abraxas's instructions, I cannot believe that Jarrah made the first aggressive move. Did the Pelagians suffer no casualties? Where is Humate?

Three days ago, before I headed west to Quintole, Vert and I argued long and hard over which side of the strait would make the better ambush site. He said here, at Badderlocks Head, because the ancient ruins are the only real landmark along many miles of coast. I countered that there is not enough decent cover and the wind makes the place uninhabitable for any extended stakeout. He maintained that the beach at Cape Bastel is too big a target to cover adequately, unless you have an army. Now I worry that Piese of Rulero may have brought an army.

One thing I did gain from that inspection trip with Vert—I scouted out a hidden portage at Bastel in some shrubbery on the landward side of one of the great sea stacks. I recall it.

◆ ◆ ◆ **P O R T** ◆ ◆ ◆

I come forth among ferns and dogwood, under trees and hidden from the beach by a mossy wall of rock about a hundred feet high. The air is warmer by far, and quite still. I heft myself to the top of the stack and from there I scan the beach, dazzling under both suns and a clear blue sky. I see no one. There is something odd near the water, perhaps just a log of driftwood. Anxious as I am to move on to Nuddle, and well aware that it may be bait in a trap, I do need a closer look at that.

I port along to the top of the next rock, and the next, and still the whole beach seems deserted, no one hiding in the bushes behind the rocks. Now I can see that the "driftwood" is a body. A flock of wading birds is working the sand close to it, so it must be dead.

◆ ◆ ◆ **P O R T** ◆ ◆ ◆

The birds take off in a panic at my sudden arrival. Jarrah of Havener is lying on his back with his livery torn and muddy, his dart quiver empty, and his torso twisted at a strange angle. He has his eyes closed against the glare, but his head is not lolling sideways as it would if he were unconscious. I kneel beside him so that my shadow falls across his face.

He opens his eyes.

"Royal Jarrah!" I say. "How are you injured?"

His eyes wobble and focus. "Mudar? How by the suns did *you* get here?"

"Never mind me. What happened to you?"

"That *toad*, that putrid *night bucket*! He broke my back. Told me to wait here for the tide." The man I admired as so competent is now quite helpless.

"Who did?" *Not Humate! Oh, suns, let it not be Humate who did this!*

"*Noblest* Piese himself. Water?"

"I'll do better than water," I say. "I'll move you to Cantle, the capital, to the ruler herself . . . Can you not port?"

He grimaces. "I don't think the lower half of me would arrive. It isn't even here now, so far as I can tell, nothing below my waist. Let me tell you while I can." His voice is so feeble that I can barely hear it over the steady murmur of the waves.

"No, we must get you to doctors."

"Doctors won't help. Moving me may kill me. Listen."

I glance anxiously along the beach. The Enemy and his men may arrive at any moment, going or coming. "Quickly, then."

He smiles faintly. "I have all the time in the world. There's no pain, just anger. Piese of Rulero murdered me. Remember that. The boy picked up your route at Dovekie. We relayed. He transported me to Badderlocks and we found two Pelagians there—Slype and Grith, he called them. He asked where his father was, and the Grith one said he had no idea, back in Mascle probably. He said Isatin had told the two of them to wait there and hold you if you tried to pass through, going or coming."

That is plausible, because Humate named Slype as one of those who had seen me "kidnap" him at Quintole. But were they there to catch fugitives or were they waiting for reinforcements?

"Go on."

"Humate told them you were in jail in Glyptic and wouldn't be coming. We had an important message for his father, he said. Grith said he would deliver it. The kid was too smart to fall for that. He ported out and I followed, back to the rest of my squad. He told me Grith was a smarty and probably lying. We picked up Guar and Mestizo and came back, and the Pelagians had gone. The four of us fetched the rest. . . ."

The wading birds have reassembled and resumed their foraging not far away. Still there are no people, but every nerve screams at me to leave before the Pelagians return. The biggest waves are sending frothy ripples close to Jarrah's heels.

"And then Humate transported you across the strait?"

Jarrah nods almost imperceptibly. He speaks with his eyes closed, forcing the words out in a whisper as dry as salt. "They were waiting for us—at least two dozen of them. They pinned us to the sand. Then the consort, Piese, he just said 'Go!' and they were all gone except for him and two others. They went to Badderlocks, didn't they?"

"I don't know," I tell him. "There's nobody there now, nobody at all. I expect your men went back to Dovekie to find a porter."

"Why would you lie to a dying man, Mudar of Quoin?" Jarrah has had time to work out what must have happened when that murder squad materialized on the headland, darts ready, catching the Glyptians unaware.

I shudder. "You're right. There are no living men over there. Six dead Glyptians. The council is going to tear Pelagic apart over this."

"Good. Oh, suns! That whoreson is strong! He hefted me down here, close to the waves. He pinned me and twisted me around to make me yell, and I couldn't do a thing. Then he got the hegemon's warrant off me and said he ought to make me eat it, and . . . and he broke me! Like a twig, he just broke me!" Jarrah's face screws up with shame.

It sounds as if Piese sent all his men off to Badderlocks before he murdered Jarrah, and committed the crime well away from Humate, so his son wouldn't see the details. He doesn't trust his followers.

"Did his men come back?" I ask. Had they finished their foul work at Nuddle and been on their way home when the Glyptians intruded? Or had they still been assembling, here at Bastel?

"Don't know."

Of course not. Jarrah had been lying helpless on the sand, staring at the sky, hearing only the waves, waiting for the tide. He wouldn't see or hear the Pelagians returning from Badderlocks and heading out to Nuddle, if that was what they did.

"Never mind," I say. "We'll get him. The council will condemn him. I don't know how badly you're injured, but there are good doctors and surgeons here on Alazarin. Let me take you to Cantle."

"Remember what I said," the dying man whispers. "It's all true. And I'll testify if I'm able."

I raise him as gently as I can, still lying flat. I recall the "great" hall in the little palace in Cantle. . . .

◆ ◆ ◆ **PORT** ◆ ◆ ◆

3

There is no one in the hall except a man mopping the floor. He has his back to me. I stretch my memory to its limits, back to the day I was doomed. Chiliarchy of Drayage was there. Later she was appointed ruler of Alazarin. I try to recall Chiliarchy of Drayage . . . tall, angular, acidic manner. I find her, or think I do. She is lying flat, so she may be asleep or sick. I may even have the wrong woman. So be it, murder can't wait.

◆ ◆ ◆ **PORT** ◆ ◆ ◆

Clad in a loose kimono of red silk, Ruler Chiliarchy is stretched out on what to me is still my grandfather's bed. He wouldn't know the room, with its filmy hangings, dense wool rugs, and overpowering flower scent. One maidservant is trimming the ruler's toenails, another her fingernails. Her hair is undressed. Since it is not far off blueset, I assume she is being readied for a party of some sort. She is a great deal older than I remember her, but that was two pentads ago and she is not at present dissembling.

Understandably, she cries out in alarm when two men come forth in her bedroom. The maids scream and flee to the door.

"Noblest Chiliarchy, excuse this intrusion. This man is gravely wounded and must testify against his killer while he still can."

I float Jarrah closer to the bed. Chilarchy leaps clear with surprising agility. I cannot slam the door while still supporting Jarrah, and I fear that the ruler will follow her servants, but she stops in the entrance. I set Jarrah down and heft a carafe of water to me from a table in the corner. I wad a corner of a sheet and wet it, put it to the dying man's lips.

"I know you!" the ruler says shrilly.

"Quirt of Mundil, formerly Mudar of Quoin. Hyla's son. And now nothing. You watched me being doomed." Then I bark *"Listen!"* when she tries to speak. "Alazarin has been invaded by at least two dozen armed men led by Piese of Rulero, consort of Hegemon Pelta of Pelagic. He broke this man's spine and left him on the beach at Cape Bastel to drown. He is searching for your predecessor, noblest Hyla, so he can kill her properly this time. There are six dead men on Badderlocks Head, and the suns alone know how many more people have died already. This man is royal Jarrah, champion of Hegemon Abraxas, who was trying to serve a summons on Piese. Read him!"

"This is madness! What is Hyla doing back here?" She has pulled herself together, shedding about three pentads, growing taller. Her hair is elaborately coiffured. She strides back to the bedside, glaring across at me.

I hear footsteps and excited voices out in the corridor.

"Madness! But true, every word." And she is close enough to know that.

Again I wet the cloth and moisten the dying man's lips. Chiliarchy leans across the bed to touch him and makes a sudden lunge, trying to grab my wrist instead. I have been expecting her to try that.

◆ ◆ ◆ **PORT** ◆ ◆ ◆

I come forth atop the watchtower at Nuddle, fully prepared to defend myself to the death if Piese has posted guards there, but there is no one. I crouch down behind the parapet, out of sight of the land around.

I cannot recall Hyla, or Izard, or Vert, or Clamant. Or Humate, for that matter. I do not know his father well enough to try recalling him. So am I too late? My loved ones may be lying dead below me. Or they may have escaped to the mainland and taken refuge somewhere other than at Osseter. Or they may have arrived at Osseter just after I left. Or they may be hiding somewhere else on Alazarin.

◆ ◆ ◆ **PORT** ◆ ◆ ◆

I go down to the same clump of trees that Humate used yesterday, from which I can watch the front door. I see no one. I creep closer, until I can make out a dead dog lying on the steps. Poor Fidel! Was he defending his master or was he simply left behind in the rush to evacuate? The Enemy has certainly been here.

◆ ◆ ◆ **PORT** ◆ ◆ ◆

The entrance hall has never seemed more like a mausoleum, but there are no more bodies. I inspect every room, even the cellar, and I find nothing. The remains of breakfast still lie on the kitchen table, buzzing with flies.

Chewing on some fruit, for I have not eaten since morning, I pace the floor, thinking hard. If I go looking for Hyla and the rest, I may simply lead the Enemy to them. He cannot recall me, any

more than I can him, but Humate knows me well enough to recall
me, and he has never told me what his range is.

Champion Jarrah said there were at least two dozen Pelagians
involved. High-caste males need no bodyguards and rarely bother
to take more than a single companion when they travel.

Isatin had been assigned to guard Humate, though, so when
I "abducted" his ward, he sent word back to Mascle, and Hegemon Pelta dispatched her consort with a major force of champions
to "rescue" their son. Traveling eastward, into the suns' path, they
would not have reached Badderlocks before the Dark. Today they
should have had plenty of time to do everything they wanted, even
if the main force did not set out from Mascle until this morning.

But this logic leads me nowhere. I still do not know if Vert and
Izard have managed to elude them.

As soon as Jarrah and Humate left Badderlocks to fetch their
companions, Grith and Slype ported across the strait and told Piese
to expect company. Piese wouldn't have had time to round up his
gang if they were scattered all over the island, so they must have
been already assembled there at Cape Bastel. Either they were staking out the beach to prevent the "kidnappers" fleeing to the mainland, or they had finished their deadly work and were preparing to
head home. Piese issued orders—to kill or arrest the "accomplices,"
probably—and then all he had to do was wait for his errant son to
come forth into his loving arms, trusting that his men would handle
the Glyptians.

But arresting champions is very nearly impossible, as I proved
this morning. One dart from either side and the fight would be on.
Even if most of the Pelagians just tried to take prisoners, four or
five men pinning one will almost certainly break him.

And now? Sworn champions are proud and honorable men, by
and large. They have high-caste mistresses, who will know right away
if they commit crimes. Once the boy had been rescued, what excuse
could Piese of Rulero offer his men to justify further violence?
None, obviously. Shocked at what they have done, the Pelagians
have fled home, taking their own dead and wounded, if any.

So I am not up against an army now, only the Enemy himself and maybe a few unscrupulous trusties. Or perhaps nobody! Humate will have told him that the game is up and he is ordered to submit to examination by the hegemonic council tomorrow. By any rational argument, Piese should have fled into hiding. But Piese is anything but rational. Now he is more dangerous than ever, for he has nothing left to lose and only revenge to achieve. I must find Hyla, Izard, Vert, and Clamant, alive or dead.

✦ ✦ ✦ PORT ✦ ✦ ✦

The fat, princely Volet of Demy, whom I met again yesterday at Nuddle, was my grandmother's senior champion and served Izard as chief of police. Demy is a dairy farm near Cantle. I come forth outside his house, which stands some distance back from the barns and cottages, but the entire population seems to be milling around there, a hundred or more men, women, and children.

An elderly man on the porch is shouting for order, and was probably close to obtaining it until my arrival threw everything into pandemonium again. I narrowly escape knocking over two youths. Several of the men are armed, and one hurls a pitchfork at me. I snatch it out of the air. Then I raise myself to head height and raise my arms for silence.

Several voices shout "Mudar!" and "It's old Izard's grandson!" and the noise dies away into faint cheers.

"Yes, I am Mudar of Quoin! I just got here and I don't know what's happening." I can tell already that none of the people I seek is within the apanage—although their bodies may be, for I do not know if I can recall a dead person. "You, there! Foreman Emption! Explain the trouble."

The man on the stoop is a memento of my boyhood, a solid, earthy ordinary with the stoic calm of an oak tree and the largest hands I have ever seen. He taught me how to milk cows.

"Murder, royal! Foul murder!"

I heft myself to the porch and barge inside, people scuttling out of my way. Emption follows me in. The fat old master of Demy is at home. He is in his living room and a young female ordinary lies beside him. They are both dead, both bloody and contorted. I turn away in revulsion at the mutilations. They were beaten and tortured before they died. The blood on the floor is still not dry.

Oh, suns have mercy! Last night Vert told Humate about the "four distinguished noblemen" who were helping us. So Humate has not been sent home, he is helping his father, whether willingly, or from filial obedience, or in fear of punishment. He must have led Piese to Nuddle first. Finding it deserted except for the dog, they started looking for those four noblemen's apanages. The Enemy may even have recalled some of them from the days of his youth, the days of the golden games, but it wouldn't matter if he didn't. It must be easy enough to learn whatever you want if you have the psychic strength of a hegemonic and are utterly ruthless.

"How many of them?"

"Four," Emption tells me. "Didn't see them myself. Three royals and a princely, I was told. And one of them was young, a twig as tall as a tree, they said."

"You must tell noblest Chiliarchy about this!"

◆ ◆ ◆ **PORT** ◆ ◆ ◆

Emption cries out in surprise as I set him down at the palace gate in Cantle.

"Tell the noblest!" I repeat. "I must go and catch these monsters."

◆ ◆ ◆ **PORT** ◆ ◆ ◆

Homarine, the apanage of royal Kish, is a fine old stone house on the rocky northern coast. It is very isolated.

I come forth on the doorstep, where I know I cannot easily be seen from the interior. Humate would detect me right away, of course, but I do not recall him or anyone else. The door is locked, so I port through it, into the kitchen, which is untidy but deserted.

In the dining room I find a scene of disorder—a table laid for five and a meal abandoned.

So Piese is now attending to the violence in person, aided by Humate and two champions. Humate was the twig as tall as a tree. Those two and a couple of henchmen—Emption mentioned one of princely caste, who is most likely Grith, the clever one. The fourth is likely either Slype or Isatin. They failed to find their quarry at Nuddle, failed at Demy, missed them again here at Homarine.

But now there is no blockade at Bastel. If I can find the fugitives, we can escape from Alazarin.

Where will they have gone this time? Izard will be very reluctant to drag danger into the lives of innocent ordinaries, but the number of former champions he can call on is dwindling rapidly. Ruler Chiliarchy has no force capable of opposing the Pelagians. I wish I knew the range at which Piese and his son can recall people. Alazarin is small enough that if the two of them split up and start a search along line-of-sight portages, they may find the fugitives just by luck. They would have to have a rendezvous point, of course. . . .

◆ ◆ ◆ **PORT** ◆ ◆ ◆

Nuddle is central and its watchtower gives a good all-round view of the hills. I come forth in the trees this time and instantly know that Humate is not there, but Hyla, Izard, Clamant, and Vert are. Found them! I port into the hall, hear voices from the kitchen. I pause when I reach the door, because one of those voices belongs to the Enemy.

I am still holding the pitchfork.

Then I smell *hamulose* and recognize what he is saying. He is one of Hyla's projections. I lift the latch and walk in.

"Good evening."

Clamant, just coming out of the larder, screams and drops a bowl, which shatters in a hail of pottery and vegetables. The two men are seated at the great table in the middle of the room, on which rests a bulky sack. Vert curses and jumps to his feet, knocking over a stool. Izard starts to rise and then smiles and sinks back again. Hyla has squeezed into a corner as if trying to walk through the walls; she has her hands over her ears, while her younger self stands close behind her, being systematically punched by the Enemy. Both of them are naked at this stage in the endlessly repeating nightmare.

"Oh, are we glad to see you!" Vert says. He looks much older than he should.

So does Izard. Clamant seems calm but she is dissembling.

"Likewise," I say. "Sorry to be so long, but I've had a busy day. I take it that you have been playing hopscotch with the Enemy? You are not planning to stay here long, I hope?"

"Not long, no," Clamant says in a rush. "Your mother can't take much more. She's been projecting that torment scene for hours. We came here to pick up some food. If we have to port out in a hurry we'll meet at Astacus Ford, but we haven't decided where to go next. We thought the White Caves would be safe, and he very nearly caught us there."

I appropriate a steaming dish of rice that no one else seems to want and begin gobbling. "I think the way out to Badderlocks Head may be open. I suspect that Piese and Humate are quartering the island between them. They can both recall persons, remember. I was told that there were four killers at Demy, so they probably have one companion each."

"Humate ratted!" Vert says. "Little turd! I saw him with them."

I am surprised to find myself defending him. "He probably had no choice. Hegemon Abraxas has called a council for tomorrow. She sent Humate along with a party bearing a summons to the Enemy. Humate was extracted and the rest of her champions murdered. His father would probably say that his son had been 'liberated,' but whatever you call it, you can't expect a boy like him to discard a lifetime's conditioning and turn against his own father, a father he has been taught to revere like a god. How many grown men, even, could defy a monster like Piese of Rulero?"

"So what do we do?" Izard asks wearily. All three of them are pathetically glad to have me there to take charge. They are too old for such adventuring, and I'm not sure that I am young enough.

"We could make another try at crossing the strait, but it's very close to whiteset. Let's go to Quoin and get some fishermen to take us out to sea. By morning we can be well beyond the Enemy's range for recalling people. And porting out to a small boat must be more difficult than, say, invading this kitchen."

But then the Enemy does exactly that.

4

Big though the Nuddle kitchen is, the sudden addition of four very large men creates havoc. Clamant is sent flying by Piese of Rulero himself. A Pelagic champion I recognize as Isatin hits the table hard enough to send it crashing into Izard. The old man goes down heavily, but Isatin collapses with a screech of pain. Vert leaps up and is hefted back against a wall with enough force to stun or maim him, probably by the princely Grith, because the Enemy fixes on me.

I feel his psychic grip on my throat, but before it can tighten enough to choke me, I heft the pitchfork at him, confident that I will kill him at that range. He shoots it straight back at me like a javelin, but I have already ported over to the corner where Hyla is just starting to turn around.

◆ ◆ ◆ **PORT** ◆ ◆ ◆

I bring the two of us forth among the fruit trees at the far end of the north orchard. I set her down on the grass in front of a substantial trunk, and she tries to burrow inside it. To be safe, I should have taken her to the far end of the island, outside Piese's recall range, but I cannot desert the others to his nonexistent mercy. I port twenty yards away. I am betting that Hyla is the only·one he knows well enough to recall, and that he will come for us himself. Only he and Humate can port to people and I have tied Humate in knots too often.

Sword in hand, for moments that feel like a lifetime, I stand in the gathering dusk under the pink and purple clouds of whiteset. In the distance I can just see Hyla, still hiding her face against the bark, her nightmare playing out beside her. My guess works. Suddenly there are two Enemies standing behind her, one young and naked, kicking a naked girl on the ground, the other old and ugly, momentarily distracted by the projection. He is dangerously close to her, but in a moment he will look around for me and the chance will be gone. I send my sword streaking along the narrow alley between the trees. I send it with every ounce of my psychic power, the same cast I used against Jasp of Lemma to win my lover in the Cuneal games so long ago. It heads straight for the Enemy's back and the battle is won—I think.

Jasp was much younger, was watching me, and the range was greater, yet he barely escaped. With none of those advantages, Piese of Rulero vanishes in time; the sword flashes by and impales a fruit tree. He really is the best, even now. How Piese of Greaten ever topped him to win the crown at Hyla's golden games I cannot imagine.

I can, however, imagine him coming right back. I recall Izard and Clamant and Humate still in the kitchen, but not Vert. He may be dead already.

◆ ◆ ◆ PORT ◆ ◆ ◆

I come forth up on the watchtower with Hyla at my side. My mother struggles feebly and I whisper soothing nonsense while repeatedly scanning the house and grounds for signs of the Enemy. He must know where I am, or at least where Hyla is, and I do not know where he is. I sit her on the parapet and then join her there, just out of her reach, planning to count to twenty and then leave.

I have progressed as far as ten when Piese comes forth in front of us.

"Not bad, *son*," he says with a leer. "Your bloodlines—"

The floor collapses beneath him, aided by a savage downward wrench from me. He has a long drop to the bottom. I don't truly expect it to kill him—he will port out before he hits the piled debris down there—but it may rattle him a little.

♦ ♦ ♦ PORT ♦ ♦ ♦

Back in the kitchen, Grith spins around when Hyla and I come forth. I give him what Vert got and what Mandola got, two pentads ago—he hits the wall with the top of his head and a sickening crunch. I return Hyla to her corner, where she evidently feels safest. Casualties are mounting on both sides. Vert is stretched out on the flagstones, unconscious and bleeding from his mouth and one ear. Clamant kneels beside him, anxiously checking his pulse and his eyes. Isatin is lying under the table, moaning and whimpering with every breath; there is blood at his mouth, so he has internal injuries. Izard is sitting on the floor, sagging back against a wall, wearing a dazed expression and a bruise on his face that is already swelling into a black eye. I can't count on more help from him.

That leaves Humate, staring at me, chalky white. He is appallingly dangerous, but he hasn't moved against me and I haven't the heart to strike him down as prudence says I should.

"Well, Brother?"

He croaks something unintelligible and shakes his head.

I push harder. "Jarrah is dying of a broken back. The Glyptians are all dead, including Byzant. Nice kid, he was. But what's another murder or two at this stage?"

"No, no!"

"Yes, yes! Whose side are you on?" I demand. *"Decide now!"*

With a screech, Hyla turns around and goes for him, just as she did last night.

Humate is gone, but so is Hyla. I roar with rage, but he has gone beyond the limits of my recall. I scream vain curses at my folly and at that treacherous whelp of a diseased breed. I must move the others to safety before Piese returns.

Too late.

He is dusty and rumpled, and there is blood on his arm, so perhaps the collapsing roof did him some good as they went down together. I slam a psychic noose around his throat to choke him.

He breaks my grip like a cobweb. The pitchfork leaps from the floor and comes against me, tines first this time. I manage to stop it, but the best I can do is keep it poised motionless in front of me, a foot away from my heart. Even that takes every ounce of my strength. I am relentlessly pushed back until I collide with the larder door. When I try to move aside, the pitchfork goes with me.

"You're really quite good, *son*," he says cheerfully. "Good blood will always tell, as I was about to say a few moments ago, before I was so badly let down. I've often worried about what would have happened if I'd found you in Cantle that day, instead of poor Mandola. I was so sorry to have to do that to the sweet child. But she recognized me, so she had to go. It was you I wanted, you understand? I worried about whether you might be a little too much for me to handle, what with your reputation in the arena and so on. Now I know that I had nothing to fear."

Clamant is the only mobile one left, other than us two, and I am immobilized by my psychic duel, which I am losing. The pitchfork is inexorably moving toward my chest. I cannot push any harder. I am certain that Piese is playing with me, and when he is ready he will nail me to the larder door.

Clamant picks up an iron skillet.

"Not a good idea, princely," he says, flashing her a slobbery smile. "If I have to stop what I am doing to deal with you, I'll just impale your friend first. I can, any time I want to. Am I right, Mudar-Quirt?"

"Yes. Don't interfere, Clamant. Humate did tell you that you are summoned to the hegemonic council, didn't he?"

He chuckles. "Yes. But I'm not going. And neither are you. You have been a confounded nuisance, by-blow. Ever since that bug-brained Foison doomed you I've been having people sidling up to me, whispering, 'There's a man going around looking for you, noblest; he has a painting of you and asks everyone if they know you.' You have no idea how *bored* I got hearing that over and over! Now, where did my other son go? Your brother?"

"He escaped, monster. He had the brains to get as far away from you as he possibly could, sensible lad."

Piese draws breath sharply.

"Then I may have to kill him, too. I will not tolerate insolence. But you're first. Where did you leave weirdo woman?"

"I won't tell you." I can't, because I have no idea where Humate has taken Hyla, or why.

"Don't talk to your father like that, sonny. You will tell me. I can stick these prongs in you anywhere I want and as often as I want. I can kill you instantly, or I can make you scream so loud they'll hear you in Teil. I'll ask you just once more: Where did you take Hyla?"

"I will not tell you, you ill-begotten, incestuous spawn of a mad-woman."

The fat man's face flushes an ugly puce. "So, you're just like all the rest of them, blaming me for having a crazy mother. Now you're in really *serious* trouble!" The pitchfork drops suddenly and lurches closer, despite my best efforts to deflect it. It hovers a finger-length away from my crotch.

"Daddy will start your lessons here, I think," he says.

Humate comes forth on the far side of the table. Piese glances quickly to see who it is, but that makes absolutely no difference to his control of the pitchfork.

"Where did you go?"

Humate stares in horror at me and the pitchfork. He looks seriously ill.

"Well?" his father demands, watching me again. "Forget to bring back your tongue?"

"No, noblest. I moved the woman to a safe place. She's the one you want, isn't she?"

"Yes, yes. Good boy! Where did you put her?"

Humate, by either good fortune or incredible psychic control, has put Hyla right behind his father. *But nothing is happening!* She is just standing there, staring at the back of Piese's head, listening to his voice, not projecting, not springing to the attack as she did when she met Humate yesterday. The Enemy is right there, within reach, but she doesn't seem to understand. And any moment he will detect her. . . .

"Er . . . Is it safe for me to tell you, noblest?" Humate mutters. "While they're all listening?"

"Oh, yes. None of this dog pack is going to leave here alive. So, where did you put her?"

"In those caves by the sea."

"I enjoy those pictures she was making," Piese said. "Did you see them? Your old dad was really something in those days—wasn't I just?"

Move, Hyla, move!

Humate says, "Yes, noblest."

Piese smirks. "Fine figure of a—"

Hyla takes his head in both hands. *No, I certainly will not pair with you, royal Piese of Enthetic, not if you were the last nobleman in Aureity.*

The pitchfork, released from his heft but not mine, streaks across the room and explodes against the wall in a shower of splinters and crushed metal. Piese squeals like a tortured dog, but that is all he does. He seems to be paralyzed, rooted to the spot, and moving only his eyes, which roll wildly.

I know you cheated in the sword juggling, and the fetching race, too, so first prize will go to Piese of Greaten. You tried to lie to me!

Piese of Rulero gurgles and squeals. He sags to his knees and Hyla bends over, not releasing her grip. Humate is staring in dismay at what he has done. He is still a danger, although I strongly suspect that it is already too late for him to save his father from whatever is happening.

"Brother!" I say. "You did it! You came through!" Giddy with relief, I port to his side of the table and try to hug him, but he pushes me away.

And I shall pair with royal Tarn of Gyre, who is a much better man than you will ever be. Hyla releases her victim and rises to her feet, grinning ferociously, all her teeth bare. Piese collapses to the floor, bloody drool running from his mouth where he has bitten his tongue.

"Thank you, thank you, Brother! You saved the day."

Humate moans. "But . . . he's my dad!"

"And mine. And he's a monster."

Humate looks at me in dismay.

"If you want to weep on a shoulder," I say, "that's what big brothers are for."

"Men don't weep!" His eyes are brimming over.

"Oh, yes they do. After the day you've had, you are entitled to curl up in a ball for a pentad. But you made a hard decision that was the right decision, and everyone will honor you for it. I'm very proud of my brother. You're a good man, Humate of Alfet! Right or left? Your choice. They're both available."

I clasp him again and this time he submits. Trembling violently, he chooses my left shoulder and weeps for a man without pity.

VII

TRYST AT FORMENE

1

My doom is gone. I am free of the dread weight of it and even the air feels lighter. Clamant leads Hyla to a chair. Never before have I seen my mother smiling, and she smiles like a cat full of cream.

Released, Piese has crumpled to the floor like a dropped quilt. His eyes are open. He is weeping. Indeed, he seems to be quite conscious, but unable to speak. Still red-eyed, Humate is staring down at him in disbelief, coming to terms with what he has done.

"We need you," I say. "We must be quick. It's almost too dark to port. Have you been to Cantle?"

He wipes his nose with his wrist. "No."

"I'll show you."

✦ ✦ ✦ PORT ✦ ✦ ✦

We come forth outside the palace gate, where there is good light. There are two guards on the gate, something I have never seen before. They are both of knightly caste and will not take action against two royals.

"I am Mudar of Quoin," I tell them. "We have injured men to deliver. Call for doctors right away. And notify the noblest."

The kitchen at Nuddle is too dark to recall.

I bring us forth at the front door, which fortunately faces west. We run up the stairs, heading for the kitchen.

"I'll take Vert. Can you take Izard, and we'll come back for your father?"

"I'll try," Humate says.

Izard is in a chair, smiling but still a little dazed. "Well done," he says. "Well done, both of you. Noble Humate of Alfet, that was a—"

"Shut up, old man," Humate says, and they both vanish, as does the chair.

Vert has his eyes open, and when I kneel down beside him he seems to recognize me. "I'm taking you to Nuddle," I tell him.

At the palace gate, I am just in time to glimpse Humate before he disappears again. Protesting loudly, Izard is being hefted away on a stretcher. I lay Vert on another. A crowd is starting to gather, while more men and stretchers are arriving from inside the palace. Ruler Chiliarchy herself is directing the action. She could have reacted to the emergency no faster had she been told to expect it, and my opinion of the lady soars.

She heads straight for me. "How many more?"

"One more wounded. The worst is over. Piese of Rulero has been impaired and seems to be no more threat. What of his men? Have you located them? What are they doing?"

My queries earn a regal glare, for rulers do not like being questioned. She takes a step closer and I back up two.

"We found the bodies on Badderlocks Head and at Demy. No one else."

I sigh with relief. "Then I think everything is going to be all right. Jarrah of Havener?"

"He died a few minutes ago. Where is noblest Hyla?"

"Humate and I will bring her. We have to bring Piese first. . . . Here he is now."

Humate and Piese come forth. Piese is limp, dangling in the air like a cloak on a peg, toes not touching the ground. Ruler Chiliarchy heads for them faster than anyone, but then she cries out and backs away.

"*Dark!* Who did that to him?"

"Royal Hyla," Humate says. "He needs washing."

♦ ♦ ♦ PORT ♦ ♦ ♦

Clamant has brought Hyla to the front door, but the wounded Pelagian must still be inside. Humate has remembered, for he arrives at my side.

"I'll bring Isatin," he says, and runs up the steps, past the women. I just stare.

Clamant is smiling—indeed, almost glowing, which is strange when her consort has been injured. But Hyla is frowning. She is frowning at me as if . . . as if she ought to know me.

"Mother?" I whisper.

"Quirt?" she says doubtfully.

"Yes, Mother! Yes, yes!"

"So big!"

Humate and I planned to be up before bluerise. We've both slept in. We shall be late for the council, but I insist on paying my respects to our patients.

Vert is mending. He is more alert now and the doctor is very hopeful. She says his mental processes seem quite normal.

Piese of Rulero is still bedridden and likely to remain so, she thinks. He cannot port or heft or move much except his eyes, which never stop. But—the doctor adds with a convulsive shudder—his mind is still alert. He recognizes people and knows where he is. He just cannot do anything about it.

"Of course," she admits, "I have not done more than a superficial probe yet." And probably never will, her manner suggests. What is going on inside there is best left well alone.

I cannot weep for him.

And Hyla of Sice has slept well, which is astonishing for her in the Dark. She recognizes me again and even says a few more words. Now that the emotional blockage has gone, the doctor suggests cautiously, she may continue to show progress. Never back to normal, of course, but in time . . . who knows?

"Are you coming or not?" Humate demands, peering around the door.

"I've been waiting for you," I say. "You think you're such a crackerjack at porting that—"

❖ ❖ ❖ PORT ❖ ❖ ❖

2

The hegemons meet under a canopy in the center of the arena at Teil. It is the smallest of the seven capital city arenas, but still very large. Their marble thrones are grouped in a broken circle, an almost-closed crescent small enough that they all can judge the honesty of the witness in the central hot seat. Behind them sit their respective heirs, so the seven are really fourteen. Half a watch or so ago Hegemon Pelta of Pelagic moved to the back row, yielding her seat to her eldest daughter, Percoidean of Gid. That probably means that Pelta is now being judged. A Pelagian champion I do not know is currently testifying.

This may seem a very public place to hold such an august meeting, but any palace teems with high-caste women who would simply love to eavesdrop on such a conference. Here they cannot draw near enough to listen without being seen and chased away. Liveried champions galore stand guard, while others come and go with messages.

Councils are rare events. The word is out and kibitzers have been arriving constantly from all over Aureity, in a madcap display of every dress style and fashion imaginable. The spectators mingle freely with the witnesses waiting in the stands, eagerly discussing the testimony that has been given or will be given. No one minds, because no one can deceive these judges or even withhold relevant information from them. Vendors stroll around selling food and drink.

I have been sitting there for two watches and am terminally bored. Humate and I were a watch late in arriving, so our welcome was cool to the edge of frostbite, and I was immediately summoned to testify and explain. Abraxas began by demanding to know how I escaped from what she called custody and I insisted on calling a dungeon. Several other hegemons took over the questioning when I mentioned that the Glyptian jail was a cave in Aspartic; Abraxas did not seem pleased to have that little secret revealed. The mood became much darker when I described finding the bodies on Badderlocks Head. I talked and talked.

Eventually I was dismissed but told not to leave the arena, and Humate was called right after me. Most of the following witnesses were unknown to me, although I recognized Pelagic, Quartic, and Glyptic dress. A few whom I did know surprised me, notably Magnes of Scantling, but he left as soon as he was dismissed and I had no chance to talk with him.

At times the noblests merely debate among themselves. Once Abraxas herself changed places with her heir. I guessed that she was being judged for having released the unstable Piese upon an innocent world, or perhaps she was merely answering for her folly in locking me up yesterday, for she was soon allowed to return and take charge of the meeting again.

Then it was Foison's turn to move to the back and I was called again to testify briefly about Mandola's death and my dooming. The shadows have lengthened since then and Foison has not resumed her place in the inner circle. I assume that her daughter Media has succeeded at last.

Suddenly I have a visitor as Foison's consort, Bayard of Indican, ports to the bench beside me. I have not seen him at close quarters since the day I was doomed, and his haggard face appalls me. His neck looks like tree bark. He stares at me as if my appearance has the same effect on him.

"It wasn't right," he says. "I protested at the time, you know."

I shrug.

"Always we thought . . . Always we were told the problem had been solved. After Hyla's games he paired with Pelta and she assured us that she had improved him, so he was safe now. And he seemed to be. Nothing happened until you and Mandola . . . You know now why Foison opposed the match."

"But you told him about me. You sent him to Alazarin!"

"No!" he says plaintively. "No, no! I went to see Pelta and warn her that he was going to be recognized. Foison could not bear the thought of having to tell you and Mandola about him. She wanted Pelta to come to Cuneal, break the news to you, and reassure you that he had been improved and bygones were bygones. We thought if he apologized and Mandola could tell that he was sincere . . . But then the next day you came and told us he had killed our daughter! We were . . . Foison wasn't herself that day."

"I wasn't exactly myself after she had finished with me."

He nods bitterly and stares at nothing for a while.

"But again," he mumbles, "again Pelta assured us that she had improved him. Properly, this time, she said. She had been a little light on him before, but now she had improved him properly. Suns, man! Of course we believed her. All those murders . . . Of course we thought she would have fixed him properly. I just wonder now if she ever fixed him at all."

"Well Hyla fixed him properly yesterday," I said. "And personally I think the council ought to fix Pelta, too. And probably you and Foison as well. Go away."

He goes away.

The white sun will be setting soon. I suppose the meeting will adjourn for the Dark and resume tomorrow. I wonder how Vert and Izard are faring. And Hyla, of course.

For the last watch or so Humate has been sitting several rows below me and seems to have recovered most of his customary gall. At least two dozen royals I do not know have visited him there, presumably members of his enormously extended family. The men all shake his hand or embrace him. The women do not touch him, of course, but most of them are very deferential to him and all are smiling. His actions seem to have met with universal approval, which is well earned but won't improve his personality much. Now he is alone and fidgeting. He looks around to make sure I am alone, then ports to my side.

"What in the name of blather are they talking about now?" he asks. "Gab! Gab! Gab!"

"How well do you get along with your sister? That one, down there?"

"Percoidean? Perky's all right. A bit uppity at times. Why?"

"I think she's your new hegemon."

He opens his eyes very wide and takes another look at the proceedings. The last witness has just ported out. Abraxas, sitting in the center of the inner row, beckons one of her own retainers, who ports to her for instructions.

"You mean they just deposed my mom? Just like that? They can do that?"

"She didn't control our father. They can do anything." Not wanting to add to his burden of guilt, I don't mention that his mother will be very lucky to escape improvement as well as deposition for conniving in the murder of her sister, Typic. "Foison is out now, too. She doomed me unfairly. You rattled the world yesterday, Brother."

He chuckles. "I'm just getting started."

The champion down by the council turns to scan the stands. Abraxas directs him. He ports to us.

"Royal Humate of Alfet, you are recalled."

"Me? Again?"

"Reward time," I say. "Go down there and wow 'em. Demand three mistresses and half a hegemony for an apanage."

Humate vanishes in mid-snigger. The champion grins briefly at me and then disappears also.

Izard should be here. Above all, so should Hyla. And Piese. I cannot hear what is being said, but Humate is leaning back in the witness chair with his legs crossed, an impertinence that should earn him a thorough tongue-lashing if not a real lashing. He must be in high favor even with the hegemons.

Suddenly he rises, bows, and is standing at my side.

"You're next." Surprisingly, he is scowling.

I rise. "How did it go?"

"I lost."

"Lost what?"

"You'll see. Don't keep the hags waiting."

◆ ◆ ◆ PORT ◆ ◆ ◆

I bow to the assembled hegemons. Abraxas nods and points to the witness chair.

"Once more, royal Mudar of Quoin."

My surprise must show, because most of the noblest ladies smile. I was yeoman Quirt this morning.

"Since your hegemon granted you royal caste," she says, "and then deprived you of it unfairly, the council has ordered it restored. Noblest Media has consented."

I glance at the new hegemon of Quartic and am awarded a reasonable imitation of a smile. "My sister's death was never your fault," she says, then shuts up like a mussel at low tide. Her mother, seated now behind her, remains a crab. Her lifelong struggle to keep up appearances at all costs has collapsed in ruins with her deposition.

Abraxas says, "Last night you killed a sworn champion of the hegemon of Pelagic, princely Grith of—"

"We were attacked. I hefted a man against a wall only after he had assaulted Vert, gravely injuring him."

Heads nod.

"A plea of self-defense? Shall that be accepted, ladies?" Abraxas smiles around the group and they all nod. "The hour grows late and some of us have far to go before the Dark. Sisters, do any of you have additional questions to put to this witness?"

Heads shake. They are probably all exhausted after a day of this—it may have been the busiest council in a score of pentads—but the only ones who actually show fatigue are Foison and Pelta, who are not bothering to project otherwise.

"We have one last item of business then, sisters. Royal Mudar, Hegemon Foison forfeited your loyalty by her unjust treatment of you. You may swear again to her successor, but Hegemon Balata has a suggestion to put to you."

I turn to face the hegemon of Heliac, who has the end seat on the left. She is a large, imposing, and stony-faced woman, definitely not the sort to take chances with. Her voice sounds like gravel in a bucket.

"Royal Mudar, I have agreed wholeheartedly with my sisters' opinion that Ruler Etesian of Formene should be deposed. Her conduct had been treasonous and unconscionable. We also disallow the obnoxious pairing she planned to impose on her heir, who is now her successor. The council has heard testimony that the new ruler may be willing to swear you in as one of her champions. Have you any comments on that?"

Humate lost! He told me. I stutter for a moment while my heart ports back and forth across Aureity, bouncing off the suns in passing. I have my good friend Magnes to thank for this.

"I should be happy to present my pedigree for consideration by noblest Tendence's breeders."

"The latest version," mutters someone behind me.

"On that understanding," Abraxas says, "we are prepared to dismiss you with our thanks—and our apologies. As a token of its appreciation, royal Mudar, the council has voted you the favor of audience, meaning that you may present any child of yours at any of our courts with noblest honors, and this right shall endure for four generations after you. Go with our blessings and may the suns smile on you and your line forever."

"Um . . . I, er . . . Thank you, noblests."

I rise, step back, and bow, but the women rise also. Abraxas must have signaled to someone that the council was adjourned, because trumpets blare into the sunset.

◆ ◆ ◆ **PORT** ◆ ◆ ◆

3

Humate is sitting where I left him and greets me with a leer even larger than his standard smirk. "And you won. I am heartbroken."

Personally I think the big winner has been royal Tendence, but I am biased. "All the world admires a good loser. I expect you'll be spending the evening with your family?" I offer a hand.

"You expect wrong," he says, rising but ignoring the hand. "I'll stay well clear of their nattering for a while. If you're going where I think you are, Big Brother, I'll keep you company on the way. Me first?"

"Go."

◆ ◆ ◆ **PORT** ◆ ◆ ◆

The light is poor for porting, but Humate has not yet learned that suicidal challenges can be refused. After two narrow misses with trees and one with the edge of a cliff, he overtakes the sunset, and Father White rises in the west for us. I feel guilty that I am not rushing back to Alazarin, although I can do nothing to help Hyla and Vert recover. I am also weary and drained by the last few days' turmoil. So I let my exuberant half-brother continue to do the porting, which he clearly enjoys, until we are almost across Seric. There he brings us forth in the portage entrance to a palace.

I have never heard of Ruler Chanterelle of Descry, and she clearly has no recollection of ever having met Humate of Alfet, but he had recalled her door and the code of the nobility allows no exceptions. Asked what we need, Humate demands hot baths, fresh clothes, and ample food, adding that we are in a hurry and must leave before the Dark traps us there until bluerise. I suspect that the royal lady views that prospect with even more horror than he does, but he gives good value for her hospitality by talking all through the meal, describing the council, and how it deposed two hegemons and a ruler. This is history fresh from the oven. He does not mention that one of the expelled hegemons is his mother.

Now our way lies across Pelagic, which he knows far better than I do, so he continues to do the work. We travel faster than the suns, and Mother Blue has risen in the west before his incredible energy is exhausted. He sags against a mossy wall on a hilltop and complains with astonishment, "I'm beat!"

I laugh at his surprise. "I feel tired just watching you. I'll lead for a while."

◆ ◆ ◆ **PORT** ◆ ◆ ◆

It is not long after doublenoon when I bring us forth on Cemetery Hill, within recall of Formene. By then my head is pounding and Humate has completely recovered his zest. I look doubtfully at him.

"I'm not sure it's good etiquette for you to call on the court just yet, Hummy Boy. You are, after all, an ex-betrothed."

He shrugs and produces a small scroll from his pouch. "I quite understand that the lady will be overcome with grief, but duty calls. I have an important message to deliver to her mother."

"From Balata?"

"Of course. I promised."

I wince. Truly, the wrath of a hegemon spurned is more bitter than the smile of the shark. "As you will."

✦ ✦ ✦ PORT ✦ ✦ ✦

We come forth in the Court of Joyful Blossom in Formene. I recall Tendence not a hundred yards away and start to tremble.

"What are you waiting for?" my companion demands.

"Good manners."

"Overrated. We bring an urgent message."

✦ ✦ ✦ PORT ✦ ✦ ✦

I stagger, having been caught unaware. Noblest Etesian is enjoying a midday snack in the private quarters, with her daughters on either hand and Eikon's consort Magnes opposite, all kneeling on cushions around a low jade table in a small, shady courtyard aglow with blossoms. A servant about to deliver a steaming dish is impacted by Humate of Alfet and sent flying. I catch the ricocheting Humate before he can demolish a fretted ivory screen, but the unfortunate flunky crushes a dwarfed ornamental tree and rolls with its pot into a fishpond. Magnes flashes to his feet and the ladies scream in unison.

"Who—" the ruler shrieks. "I mean, royal Humate? But who brought you here without—" Her indignation waxes louder. "Who is that man with you and how dare you break in on us like this? Who ported—"

Humate has been distracted by hefting the servant out of the pond and setting him on his feet ashore. "Suns be with you, royal Etesian!" he says cheerfully. "Your hegemon asked me to deliver this to you." He hands over the scroll. "Isn't that a nifty seal she uses?"

"Noblest Balata?" Etesian takes the letter as if it might bite her. It will swallow her whole.

I catch Magnes's questioning eye and wink. Tendence is keeping her eyes lowered, which is quite unnecessary, because she can easily

mask her emotions, whether they be acute embarrassment or unseemly merriment. Either would be appropriate now.

Eikon is not bothering to dissemble and her grin is wolfish.
Magnes will have told her about the council, at least the first half of
it. Now he has guessed what has happened after he left and is returning my smile.

"Oh!" Etesian says. "Oh! Oh! Oh! Oh!"

"Bad news, noblest?" Humate inquires innocently.

"Oh! Magnes, take me to my room, I beg of you."

Magnes and she vanish. The scroll falls to the paving and rolls
up, its work done.

"That's not very courteous to a visitor," Humate remarks. "My
gorgeous beloved betrothed, I bring horrible news for you also."

"Horror," says Eikon, "is in the eye of the beholder. What are
you doing in such horrible company, Quirt?"

"He's Mudar of Somewhere now," Humate tells her, sitting
down uninvited at the table. "Or do I mean 'again'? I never saw a
man change his name and caste so often, a dozen times a day. Speak
up, Brother. He's very shy, you know."

The sisters exchange glances.

Is he mad or drunk? Tendence asks me.

"Just young," I say. "My younger brother."

"Yes, he did say 'brother,'" Humate says. "Although it's quite
complicated and I don't think his pedigree . . . Oh well. Details are
for losers, aren't they? So we shall still be related and see each other
very often. You'll like that, won't you, Gorgeous One?"

Tendence does not respond. Magnes reappears.

"And what of Piese of Rulero?" Eikon asks Humate.

"That's a very personal and impertinent question."

I kneel in front of Tendence. "It does seem that Humate and I are
related, noblest, and he did save my life yesterday, but I promise I will
beat some manners into him before I let him out in public again. The
hegemonic council deposed Foison of Quartic for wrongfully dooming me. It deposed Pelta of Pelagic for trying to impose her nestling
son on you, and Balata has deposed your mother for agreeing to the

scheme, which she has disallowed. So you are now ruler of Formene and no longer betrothed. I am confirmed in my royal caste and free to swear to you as champion if you will have me."

"He'll make a good door ward," Humate says with his mouth full.

Tendence meets my eye at last and lets me see that she is holding back both joy and laughter. "I don't think I could swear in a champion from such a disreputable family. On the other hand, there is a vacancy close to my heart."

"Be brave," Humate mumbles.

"Would you like me to remove the nuisance?" Magnes inquires softly.

Humate looks up with interest. "I'd like to see you try."

"I don't recommend it," I warn quickly. I understand now that I may be seeing a great deal more of my new brother in the near future than I had planned on. He will not want to return to Mascle until wounds have had time to heal. He has latched on to me as substitute family.

"There's nothing wrong with him that he won't grow out of in a couple of pentads," I say. "Not much, that is."

"I'll be the life and soul of your golden games," Humate says. "Meanwhile I shall meditate on the desolation of lost love and the agony of a broken heart."

"Good idea," I tell him; then to Magnes, "We must keep a close eye on him or he may discover those ghastly dens of vice and depravity on Gladiolus Street. His mother and sisters would be appalled."

"On the other hand," Humate says, uncoiling himself to the vertical, "sitting around moping isn't really manly, is it?"

Magnes gives me a quizzical look but I nod to show that I am serious.

"Let me show you the guest quarters, royal master of Alfet," he says. "And some of the services we offer." They both vanish.

I am left facing two female frowns and realize that I must adapt to having women in my life again.

"You favor vice and depravity in the young, royal?" Eikon asks icily.

"Not normally, no, and I'm sure Magnes won't take me too literally. But in the last few days, Humate's whole world has collapsed about him and he has to build a new one from the pieces. In this case, I think that what I was hinting at could be very helpful. He's had the responsibilities of adulthood thrust upon him; a taste of the rewards seems quite appropriate."

Magnes knew what I meant; Humate would say it's a manhood thing.

Under the circumstances, Tendence agrees, smiling.

Eikon does not look convinced. "I'll tell the vizier to arrange the proclamation." She picks up the scroll and departs on foot.

Tendence and I are alone together.

"All is well, noblest," I whisper, taking her hand. "Will you accept my oath of service and lifelong devotion?"

Her dainty fingers squeeze my big clumsy ones. "Are you offering me a happy ending?" She doesn't smile often, but each smile is worth waiting a lifetime for.

"Is there anything wrong with a happy ending?"

"Not if you have earned it," she says. "And I think you did."